Changing the Prophecy

Anne & Peter —
Enjoy the journey!,

Amy

Changing the Prophecy

Amy Wachspress

Woza Books
Books that Raise the Spirits

Changing the Prophecy

Woza Books
Oregon City, Oregon
(707) 468-4118
www.wozabooks.com

Cover design: Anjelica Colliard
Book design: Amy Wachspress

Publisher's Cataloging-in-Publication Data

Wachspress, Amy
   Changing the Prophecy / by Amy Wachspress – 1st ed. – Oregon City, Oregon :
Woza Books, 2023

ISBN: 978-0-9788350-0-2
Audience: ages 6-17

Summary: The four Goodacre children return to the fantasy land of Faracadar to overturn an ancient prophecy and save the land from environmental destruction in this action-packed, hilarious sequel to *The Call to Shakabaz*.

1. FIC009100 FICTION / Fantasy / Action & Adventure. 2. YAF019000 YOUNG ADULT FICTION/ Fantasy / General. 3. JUV037000 JUVENILE FICTION / Fantasy & Magic. 4. JUV001000 JUVENILE FICTION / Action & Adventure / General. I. Title

Library of Congress Control Number: 2023910936

Printed in the United States of America

10 9 8 7 6 5 4 3

for Zev and Rio, my brachot

Contents

Chapter 1 Before Midsummer's Eve

Chapter 2 Arrival Part One

Chapter 3 Arrival Part Two

Chapter 4 Arrival Part Three

Chapter 5 At the Dome

Chapter 6 Wolf Circle

Chapter 7 The Prophet of the Khoum

Chapter 8 Sense of Direction

Chapter 9 Snared in a Net

Chapter 10 North Coast

Chapter 11 Labyrinth

Chapter 12 In the Dungeon

Chapter 13 Change of Plan

Chapter 14 New Beginnings Well

Chapter 15 Buttered Biscuits

Chapter 16 Trackers

Chapter 17 Reunion

Chapter 18 The Emerald Crystal

Chapter 19 The Coral Caves

Chapter 20 Vinegar, Flan, and Reinforcements

Chapter 21 Canyon of Imaginary Reality

Chapter 22 The Legacy of Shrub

Chapter 23 Crumpet's Transformation

Chapter 24 The Work of the Herbal

Chapter 25 Singing Home the Algae

Chapter 26 Muffins for Hyacinth

Chapter 27 What Happened at Angel's Gate

Chapter One
Before Midsummer's Eve

Doshmisi awoke in pitch darkness to Aunt Alice's insistent gentle voice. "Dosh, wake up," Aunt Alice said, as she switched on the light next to Doshmisi's bed.

"What's up?" Doshmisi asked, as she sat up in bed. The urgent tone in Aunt Alice's voice instantly snapped her awake. "It's not Midsummer's yet. What's going on?" If it had been Midsummer's Eve, she would have expected Aunt Alice to wake her so that she could go to the cabin in the woods and travel with her brothers and sister to the land of Faracadar, as they had traveled the previous summer. Amethyst the gatekeeper came from Faracadar every year on Midsummer's Eve to take "the Four" (as they were called) to Faracadar for a time. Doshmisi's mother along with her Aunt Alice, Uncle Martin, and Uncle Bobby used to be the Four; but now Doshmisi, who was fifteen, Denzel, who was fourteen, Maia, who was twelve, and Sonjay, who had just turned eleven, were the new Four. Doshmisi and her siblings had been impatiently counting the days left before Midsummer's Eve, when they would return to Faracadar. But it was not yet the appointed time.

"They have come for you tonight and so tonight you must go," Aunt Alice told Doshmisi.

"They?" Doshmisi asked. "Who did Amethyst bring with her?"

Aunt Alice's voice quavered as she answered. "Amethyst died a few months ago, baby. Ruby and Crystal have come instead."

"How could Amethyst die? What happened to her?" Doshmisi struggled to wrap her head around the idea that the sweet old woman who had baked delicious spice cake for them before sending them to Faracadar only the previous summer had died.

"Nothing happened. She just got old and her body wore out," Aunt Alice replied with a sigh. "Now get dressed. Remember to take a sweater. Would you please look after Zora for a minute?" Aunt Alice handed her little dog, a silky black Pomeranian with shiny brown eyes, to Doshmisi, who took the dog in her arms. Zora licked Doshmisi's chin with her rough tongue.

"I don't want her to bark and wake Elena. Meet me downstairs," Aunt Alice continued. "I have to rouse your brothers and Maia; and I have to figure out what to do about Elena."

"Maybe she'll sleep through everything," Doshmisi suggested hopefully.

"We should be so lucky," Aunt Alice responded grimly.

Elena was Maia's best friend and she was sleeping over for the night at Manzanita Ranch, where the Goodacre children had lived with their Aunt Alice ever since their mother's sudden death a year and a half before. They were basically orphans because their father had disappeared when Sonjay was a baby; but Sonjay insisted that their father still lived, imprisoned in the Final Fortress in Faracadar. Experience had taught Doshmisi not to discount even Sonjay's most farfetched ideas so she had reserved judgment on his conviction about their father.

Doshmisi wondered what Aunt Alice would do about Elena.

As she looked in the mirror to put on her woven green hat, given to her last year in Faracadar, Doshmisi paused to study the face that peered back at her. She wore her hair short, cut close to her head. She had coffee-brown skin and deep-brown eyes. She wore a small shiny green stud nose ring, a silver ear cuff, a dark-green sweater, and sea-green cotton pants. She picked up her dolphin earrings and put them in her ears and slipped a silver bracelet on her wrist. She smiled with approval at her appearance. She looked like the healers who lived on the islands of Faracadar. She hoped one day, with greater knowledge, to join their ranks. Thinking about the healers made her remember to take the herbal, a book with recipes and instructions for medicines and potions to help sick people get well. The herbal was an enchanted thing and therefore unpredictable. Although Doshmisi had already learned a lot about how to use it, she hoped to learn more of its secrets during her upcoming trip to Faracadar. She snapped the herbal securely in its carry case, which she then strapped around her waist.

While Doshmisi dressed, Aunt Alice awakened Denzel and Sonjay. She sent Denzel to her nightstand to retrieve the amulets, which the children wore when they traveled in Faracadar. Doshmisi wore the Amulet of the Trees, Denzel wore the Amulet of Metal, the Amulet of Watersong belonged to Maia, and Sonjay had inherited their mother Debbie's amulet, the Amulet of Heartfire. Last summer, the energy in the amulets had assisted them in their quest to take back the Staff of Shakabaz from the powerful and malevolent enchanter Sissrath. According to Aunt Alice, the amulets enhanced the gifts and abilities that the children already had within them.

Doshmisi had discovered that she had a gift for healing and she had made good use of Aunt Alice's herbal to heal the sick. Denzel had discovered he had an aptitude for inventing, building, and making things. Maia, who had befriended the drummers of Faracadar, had proven herself to be a brilliant musician and had used her talent for music to save their lives on more than one occasion. The power of the Amulet of Heartfire had brought out Sonjay's innate leadership skills and his ability to see straight to the truth. In the end, Sonjay had been the one to take the Staff of Shakabaz from Sissrath.

Sonjay dressed in his favorite lemon-yellow T-shirt and jeans and grabbed a canary-yellow sweatshirt, which he tied around his waist. His hair stood out from his head in short baby dreadlock twists. He ran his hand over the dreads as he raced down the stairs to find his inseparable companion Bayard Rustin, an enormous, eye-poppingly bright, green-blue-yellow-red parrot. Sonjay entered the sitting room and turned on the light. Bayard blinked at him in the sudden brightness and asked, hopefully, "Amethyst makes spice cake?"

Tears filled Sonjay's eyes as he held out his arm for Bayard to climb aboard. "No, you greedy heap of feathers, no spice cake." Then he continued more gently, "Amethyst died. Ruby and Crystal came instead and they didn't bake anything. They're in too much of a hurry."

"Uh-oh," Bayard said as he settled on Sonjay's shoulder. "Uh-oh."

"You can say that again," Sonjay agreed.

Bayard obliged by repeating, "Uh-oh, uh-oh, uh-oh…"

"Alright, that's enough times," Sonjay interrupted. Sometimes, Bayard acted as annoying as a pesky little brother.

Just then Denzel joined them. He was the tallest of the four Goodacres and had the lightest skin of the four as well. He had large eyes and large hands. He wore his hair in a short natural, not quite as short as Doshmisi's hair. He was handsome and caused a stir among the girls who went to his school. Prepared for the trip to Faracadar, he wore a pair of sturdy hiking shoes and his characteristic red-and-white plaid flannel shirt. He carried a partly filled backpack. "Here bro," he said as he handed Sonjay the Amulet of Heartfire. "I have to go to the garage to grab some stuff. Tell Aunt Alice I'll meet you guys on the porch in a few minutes. Hey, take your skateboard and a spare set of wheels." Sonjay glimpsed duct tape, a screwdriver set, a crescent wrench, and some wires bouncing around in Denzel's backpack. As Denzel headed out of the room, he turned in the doorway to give Sonjay one last instruction, "Oh, yeah, get the canteens from the pantry, aight?"

"I've got it covered, man," Sonjay assured him.

"No spice cake," Bayard informed Denzel mournfully.

"While you're in the pantry, you better find something to feed that bird. If he gets hungry he'll drive us all nuts," Denzel pointed out.

Upstairs, Maia opened her eyes as Aunt Alice gently tapped her shoulder. Aunt Alice held a cautionary finger to her lips, indicating that Maia should remain quiet. Maia slipped silently from her bed, glancing anxiously at her friend Elena as she tiptoed out of the room behind Aunt Alice, who led Maia down the hallway to Doshmisi's bedroom and then handed Maia her clothes and her travel drum.

"I think we got out without waking Elena," Aunt Alice said worriedly. She informed Maia that Amethyst had died and that Ruby and Crystal had come to take the Four to Faracadar. Maia's eyes welled with tears at the news about Amethyst. "But it's not Midsummer's Eve," Maia said, as she wiped at her eyes with her sleeve. "Will it work tonight? Will it be OK?"

"I honestly don't know," Aunt Alice replied.

"Then why did they come tonight?" Maia asked. "I don't think we can do this without Amethyst." Her voice trembled as she said Amethyst's name.

"We're going to have to do it without her. And we're going to have to do it tonight. Something is up. Get dressed and ready to travel and we'll ask them about it when we see them at the cabin," Aunt Alice informed her. Maia dressed quickly, pulling her deep-blue sweater over the explosion of long braids that covered her head. She slung her travel drum over her shoulder. "I have to get the timber flute from the library," she told Aunt Alice, as they stepped softly down the stairs.

After fetching her timber flute, Maia joined the others on the front porch where they had assembled. Sonjay handed Maia her water canteen and Denzel handed her the Amulet of Watersong.

"How do you know they're here?" Doshmisi asked. She held Zora under her arm and petted the little dog so she would stay quiet.

"They came to the house and found me," Aunt Alice answered.

"Are they allowed to do that?" Maia wondered aloud.

"They did it, didn't they?" Denzel replied.

"Amethyst never left the cabin, but tonight Ruby and Crystal came to the house and found me. Things are changing." Aunt Alice gave Doshmisi a hug, handed her the lantern, and then put her arms around Maia and squeezed. "OK, go. You know where to find them," she instructed as she released Maia and bent over to embrace Sonjay.

"What do you mean? You have to come with us," Maia pleaded.

As Aunt Alice turned from Sonjay to give Denzel a parting hug, she replied, "I can't. Elena's here. What if she wakes up?"

"She won't," Maia assured her aunt. "She sleeps like a rock. Besides, she's not going to start wandering around the house looking for us if she does. She'll just go back to sleep."

Aunt Alice hesitated, considering her options.

"She might go wandering through the house looking for me," Denzel mumbled.

"She's not that weird," Maia defended her friend.

"It seems weird to me," Denzel informed her.

"She just has a crush on you. Would it hurt you so much to be nice to her?" Maia demanded in exasperation.

"I've called your Uncle Bobby. He should arrive in a couple of hours," Aunt Alice said. "He'll be here by the time you get back. When he gets here I'll go to the cabin."

Doshmisi noticed that Aunt Alice had not reprimanded Denzel and Maia for bickering about Elena and took it as a sign of how distracted and worried her aunt was.

"Come with us to the cabin," Sonjay begged.

"Uh-oh, uh-oh," Bayard squawked.

"You know you want to," Doshmisi tempted Aunt Alice.

"Oh alright," Aunt Alice agreed. "I suppose Elena will sleep through this." Doshmisi handed Zora over to her aunt as the family stepped off the front porch and hurried down the driveway to the path bordered by raspberry brambles that led to the cabin in the woods.

As they approached the cabin, they saw light streaming from the windows. The door flew open and Ruby hurtled out. She burst into tears as she flung her arms first around Doshmisi, and then around Maia. Her mother, Crystal, stood in the doorway, surveying the scene. Crystal and Ruby had a fire-engine-red tint to their rich, brown skin because they were of the People Beyond the Lake. When Ruby reached for Denzel, he quickly held out his hand and shook hers to prevent her from engulfing him in a weepy hug. "How's Jasper?" he asked.

"Fine. He's at home waiting for you. He's especially waiting for Dosh," Ruby replied with a short laugh as she shook Denzel's hand and then Sonjay's. Jasper was Ruby's younger brother. At the mention of his name, Doshmisi's heart raced.

"Let's get moving," Sonjay said impatiently, as he nodded in greeting to Crystal.

When they entered the cabin, they saw that Crystal and Ruby had already placed the four travel cushions in a neat row on the floor and had surrounded each square cushion with the requisite four passage sticks, pieces from the original gateway door linking Faracadar with the world in which the Goodacres lived with Aunt Alice. A powerful enchanter of old had created the gateway with deep enchantment and very few had passed between the two worlds using the gateway door or the passage sticks.

The jars of colorful powder twinkled brightly, lined up next to one another on the table. The Goodacres missed the delicious scent of Amethyst's fresh-baked spice cake. The wood-burning cooking stove squatted cold and silent in the corner. Doshmisi remembered the warmth and sweet spicy scent that had greeted them the previous year when they had arrived at the cabin, filled with questions. Crystal touched the jars of powder tentatively with trembling fingers.

"Do you know how to do it?" Aunt Alice asked.

"Sort of," Crystal replied. "We should have prepared for this better; we didn't imagine that we would lose Amethyst so soon."

Aunt Alice ran her hand up and down Crystal's arm in a comforting gesture. Amethyst was Crystal's mother. "Amethyst is watching," Aunt Alice said.

Crystal smiled even as tears filled her eyes. "So she is," Crystal agreed.

Knowing that time was short to gain information, Sonjay cut to the chase. "Quickly, tell us why you came tonight. Why couldn't you wait until Midsummer's Eve?"

"Uh-oh," Bayard insisted.

"Uh-oh is right," Ruby confirmed. "Compost has laid siege to Big House City with an army of Mountain People. They assembled outside the city a couple of weeks ago and surrounded it. They won't allow anyone in or out."

"What do they want?" Denzel asked. "Have they made any demands?"

Ruby answered, "Well, they say they want the Staff of Shakabaz, even though they must realize that it will not come to them now, after it went to Sonjay at the Battle of Truth. And they could never use it, even if Cardamom handed it over to them, which he won't of course. Sissrath has not appeared at Big House City. We don't know where he went or why Compost remains on his own. We can't make sense of any of it. We need your help." Compost worked for Sissrath. The Four had defeated Sissrath with the power of truth in a nonviolent protest the previous year. During that protest, which people referred to as the Battle of Truth, the Staff of Shakabaz had chosen to move from Sissrath's control into Sonjay's hand. As powerful as Sissrath was, he had not been able to prevent the staff from changing hands. Sonjay had left the staff at Big House City under the watchful eye of the mighty enchanter Cardamom for safe-keeping. The royal family that ruled Faracadar lived in the Big House at the center of Big House City.

"Cardamom can't do anything to stop the siege?" Sonjay questioned.

"He has not done anything so far," Ruby replied.

"What about High Chief Hyacinth and the princess?" Maia asked. "Where are they?"

"The high chief is with Cardamom in the Big House. Princess Honeydew went to the Wolf Circle with her mother a few months ago. She has begun studying how to use her powers as an enchantress." The Four had traveled with the high chief and his daughter the year before and Doshmisi had helped them to reunite with Honeydew's mother, High Chieftess Saffron, after Doshmisi discovered that Sissrath had imprisoned Saffron at the Final Fortress and put her under an enchantment of forgetting. The Four were the princess's distant cousins and part of the royal family through their mother's ancestors.

"Something doesn't seem right about this," Sonjay said.

"What do you mean?" Crystal asked.

"The siege doesn't make sense," Sonjay explained.

"I agree," Crystal told him. "Jack visited us today. He was extremely distraught. He told us to bring you to Faracadar and that prompted us to attempt to come before the appointed time."

"What exactly did Jack say?" Doshmisi asked.

"You know how hard it is for him to put things into words. He said to come get you and he said 'whales' over and over again," Ruby told her. "He also said 'bad oil'. He plopped a large clump of algae on the kitchen table." Jack was an intuit. Intuits had psychic abilities and they could often see the future. Jack was just a little boy, only six years old, and his intuit's mind moved so quickly that he had trouble talking clearly so other people often had a hard time understanding what he meant. Intuits rarely lived more than sixteen or seventeen years because the intensity of their lives burned them out young.

Doshmisi groaned. "Not the whales again," she said to no one in particular. She loved the whales and, unlike most other people, she could even hear them when they spoke, just as she could communicate with the trees in their language. But the trees made sense to her while the whales talked in poetry and Doshmisi had a hard time figuring out the meaning of the words the whales spoke to her. She didn't want to have to rely on the whales to explain anything to her in their poetic words,

Just then a startling crash came from outside the cabin. Aunt Alice and Crystal bolted, followed closely by the others, with Zora yipping at their heels. Aunt Alice had grabbed the lantern on her way out the door and she held it high to reveal Maia's friend Elena sprawled on the ground next to an overturned plastic bucket beneath one of the cabin windows.

"What are you doing here?" Aunt Alice blurted angrily.

"Who is this?" Crystal demanded.

"Uh-oh, uh-oh, uh-oh," Bayard squawked from his perch on Sonjay's head.

Elena burst into tears. Maia hurried to her friend and helped her up off the ground. "Are you hurt?" Maia asked softly as she picked leaves out of Elena's long black hair and patted her arm. "You didn't hurt yourself did you?"

Elena sniffled and wiped her nose on the back of the sleeve of her pajama top, which she wore over her jeans. "What is everyone doing out in the woods?" she asked.

"We tried not to wake you," Maia told her friend, with a note of apology in her voice. "It's hard to explain."

"You left me all alone at the house," Elena complained.

"You're a big girl, thirteen years old, don't tell me you were afraid to be left alone," Aunt Alice snapped with annoyance.

"What are we going to do with her?" Denzel asked his aunt. "We've gotta go."

"Can Ruby take her back to the house?" Doshmisi suggested.

"No," Crystal said quickly, "she has to stay with me to learn how to do this."

"I'll take her back," Aunt Alice said with a frustrated sigh.

"I don't want to go back," Elena declared as she stamped her foot. "Tell me what's going on. Ayee! *Locos*!"

"Latina firecracker," Bayard squawked.

"Bayard, you are not helping this situation," Sonjay told the bird.

Bayard eyed Elena and then flew to her shoulder, where he settled in a most dignified manner and repeated, "Latina firecracker."

"*Gracias*," Elena said as she stroked Bayard's head. "I think," she added uncertainly, as it occurred to her that Bayard may or may not have been paying her a compliment.

"Elena is *amigamia*, my friend," Maia insisted. "We'll bring her inside with us and then after we go, Aunt Alice please try to explain to her what's going on." She turned to Elena and begged her, "*Por favor*, just let us do what we have to do here and Aunt Alice will tell you about it after we leave."

"Where are you going?" Elena asked.

"No time," Crystal stated as she hurried back into the cabin. The others swiftly followed.

"Places everyone," Ruby announced, as she clapped her hands. Sonjay, Maia, Denzel, and Doshmisi collected their things and then each of them selected a cushion and sat down. Bayard flew from Elena's shoulder to Sonjay's shoulder. While the children arranged themselves on the cushions, Crystal and Ruby unscrewed the tops from the jars and mixed the powders into a bowl.

"What's the day of the return?" Denzel asked.

"It would have been the fourteenth of Loma; but since we arrived early it could come sooner, so make sure to go to Angel's Gate by the first of the month and hopefully Cardamom can help you figure out the return,"

Crystal told them as she and Ruby approached with the bowl of colorful powder.

"Keep your hands and feet inside the passage sticks," Aunt Alice cautioned, unnecessarily, since the children had done this before and knew how it worked.

"Ready?" Crystal asked nervously.

"As ready as we'll ever be," Denzel replied.

"Wait," Doshmisi said. She hopped off her cushion and went to Aunt Alice and gave her a big hug. "See you again soon," she told her.

Aunt Alice's eyes filled with tears as she released her niece. "Get on up outta here." She waved Doshmisi back to the cushion. Zora barked and Aunt Alice picked her up.

Ruby and Crystal began to sprinkle the powder over the Four. Crystal said some strange words and Ruby repeated them. Doshmisi noticed that they spoke the words much more tentatively than Amethyst had spoken them. Her thoughts were suddenly interrupted by Elena, who burst across the room, her shiny blue-black hair flying like a flag behind her as she jumped onto Maia's cushion, where she flung her arms around Maia and held on tight. Then Elena and Maia disappeared as Doshmisi felt herself swept up in the twister of powders and whirled off as if sucked down a wind tunnel.

Chapter Two
Arrival Part One

Doshmisi landed in a familiar field of flowers in the place that the People Beyond the Lake had named Debbie's Circle after her mother. Debbie had traded years of her life to Sissrath in an act bound by deep enchantment to protect the people of the land from harm and she had consequently died young of a heart attack. That was how Doshmisi and her siblings had wound up moving to Manzanita Ranch to live with Aunt Alice and had learned about Faracadar. Doshmisi stood up and brushed the residue of green powder off her shoulders. When she heard him call her name, she turned to see Jasper with his dog Cocoa bounding joyfully toward her. She felt so happy to see him that she laughed out loud. In a moment he arrived in front of her, threw his arms around her, and planted a kiss on her lips. "I missed you so much," he said.

"I missed you too," she replied. She could feel his heart pounding hard in his chest, thumping against her own heart.

"You did? I imagined you were so busy in the Farland that you hardly thought of me," Jasper confessed.

"I thought about you every day. But I figured that you were too busy here to think about me," Doshmisi said.

"How busy could I possibly be without anyone to guide?" Jasper pointed out. Jasper had traveled with the Four the year before as their guide. He had spent many years training as a guide and he did a good job. "Where are the others? Where's Denzel?"

"That's a good question," Doshmisi answered, as she realized with growing concern that her brothers and sister were nowhere in sight. Last year they had all arrived in the field together at the same time. She remembered Elena's last-minute catapult onto Maia's cushion. That irregularity had been compounded by the fact that Crystal and Ruby had never done the passage before. "Something must have gone wrong," Doshmisi said. "Crystal and Ruby did their best, but this was their first passage. The others should have come through with me like they did last year."

"Where do you think they went? What could have happened to them?" Jasper asked in alarm.

"How should I know? They might still be stuck at Manzanita Ranch. Especially Maia because…" Doshmisi trailed off.

"What happened to Maia?"

"Someone else tried to come with her on her cushion."

"What do you mean?"

"Maia has a friend who was there and she tried to make the passage with her and it might have caused Maia to be left behind."

"But that doesn't explain about Denzel or Sonjay." Jasper pointed out, with a note of confusion.

"I don't know what happened. I hope they turn up soon," Doshmisi said, anxiously.

"And that they turn up here," Jasper added.

"Here?" Doshmisi echoed.

"Well, they might have made it through and turned up somewhere else. But let's wait for them here for a little while," Jasper suggested.

"You're right. They could have come through somewhere else in Faracadar." Doshmisi found this thought reassuring. Even if they weren't in Debbie's Circle then they could still be somewhere in the land, perhaps nearby. If they were, then she would find them, or they would find her before long. She felt certain of it. "If they turn up here in this field, they'll remember how to get to your house," Doshmisi pointed out. "So I don't think we need to hang around here waiting." Jasper nodded in agreement.

They began walking across the field as Doshmisi asked, "So what's going on in Faracadar? What do you know? What can you tell me?"

"I don't know much. You would probably learn more from a conversation with the trees," Jasper replied in all seriousness, since he knew that Doshmisi could communicate with trees.

"I'll consult the trees soon, but right now I asked you. Tell me whatever you know."

"My father received a message from Mole via the Crystal Communication Dome," Jasper related, as he and Doshmisi wended their way along a path that led through a field loaded with a variety of brilliant red flowers. "Mole asked us to get his message to the Four. That'd be you."

"Where did Mole send the message from? The Passage Circle?" Doshmisi asked. Mole lived at the Passage Circle, where he worked as the head battery maker, which meant he ran the mechanics shop. He talked like a Rastafarian and he had an absolutely brilliant ability to build or fix just about anything. He had become one of Denzel's best friends in Faracadar.

"Mole disappeared a couple of weeks ago. Sissrath kidnapped him," Jasper replied grimly.

"How do you know? Why was he kidnapped?"

"Mole used one of Violet's crystal communication shards to send a message to the Dome and they forwarded it to my father. According to Mole, Sissrath enslaved him as well as many other proficient battery makers, who must work as forced laborers on a project at the North Coast. Unfortunately, Mole has not yet figured out the exact purpose of the project so he couldn't provide any further information. But his message was important because until it came though, no one had any idea that Sissrath had something going on at the North Coast."

"Then I think the siege is a diversion," Doshmisi told Jasper firmly.

"How do you figure?"

"I don't think Sissrath has any interest in retrieving the Staff of Shakabaz. He understands that he will never get it back. Sonjay took it from him for good. Sissrath's up to something else and he doesn't want anyone to figure out what. So he sent Compost with an army of people from the Mountain Downs to blockade Big House City as a distraction and to keep Cardamom and High Chief Hyacinth far away from his secret project, whatever it is." Cardamom was the only enchanter in the land whose skill at enchantment matched that of Sissrath.

"Should we try to lift the siege at Big House City?" Jasper asked.

"I don't think so. I think Sissrath wants us to spend time doing exactly that. Instead let's go to the North Coast and find out what Sissrath is up to. We need to rescue Mole. I bet Mole will figure out what Sissrath's doing there pretty quick," Doshmisi said.

Jasper stopped walking abruptly and grinned broadly.

"What?" Doshmisi asked, as she stopped walking too.

Jasper shook his head and chuckled.

"What's so funny?" Doshmisi insisted.

"It's straight up terrific to have you back. No lie. You're one of the Four. You figure out what to do and you do it. I feel great," Jasper exclaimed, as he continued to flash his grin.

"Puleez." Doshmisi rolled her eyes and began walking again. "You're pretty good at figuring out what to do all on your own. I'm not as brilliant as all that. Trust me."

"Whatever you say," Jasper said as he fell in beside her.

"Let's go to the Garden. I want to talk to the trees. Then we can head to the North Coast."

"What about the rest of the Four?" Jasper asked worriedly. "What if they turn up after we've left?"

"We can leave a message for them here to let them know where we went. They could have turned up anywhere in Faracadar or they could be stuck back at Manzanita Ranch. We can't afford to waste time doing nothing. Obviously the passage didn't go smoothly. We'll just have to wing it."

"Wing it?" Jasper looked puzzled.

"Make things up as we go along," Doshmisi explained.

"We pretty much did that last year and it worked out."

"Sure enough." Doshmisi agreed. She gazed up at the familiar green-tinged Faracadaran sun. It felt so good to be back that she wanted to dance and sing or whoop and holler.

"I need to stop at the house to pick up a few things," Jasper said.

Doshmisi smiled at him. "You're totally jazzed to get on the road again aren't you?"

"I'm totally jazzed to be in the same place with you again. And to get on the road. What other purpose is there for a guide than to do the guiding?"

"It feels pretty great to be back," Doshmisi told him.

When they arrived at Jasper's house, he went inside to grab his backpack, which he had packed in advance because he knew he might have to rush off on a journey with the Four immediately upon their arrival. While Jasper was in his house, Doshmisi went to the paddock to greet the tigers, which people in Faracadar rode like horses since they had no horses anywhere in the land. The tigers were herbivores (meaning they didn't eat meat) and were as gentle as kittens with those they befriended. Doshmisi had ridden Sheba on her last visit to the land. In the paddock she put her arms around the beautiful sleek feline's neck and gave her a hug. Sheba licked Doshmisi's face with her large scratchy tongue and purred deep in her throat with pleasure. "I guess you remember me," Doshmisi said.

Jasper's mother Crystal and his sister Ruby would remain with Aunt Alice at Manzanita Ranch for the night and would be there in the morning when Doshmisi returned. Doshmisi knew how it worked from the previous year. Even though she would travel in Faracadar for many days, when she returned (at the appointed time) only one night would have passed at Manzanita Ranch in the meanwhile. If her brothers and sister had gotten stuck back at Manzanita Ranch, then she would be on her own this year and would not see them until her return. If they had managed to pass through into Faracadar then she hoped she would meet up with them soon, or at least in time for their return to Manzanita Ranch from Angel's Gate near Big House City by the fourteenth day of Loma.

When Jasper emerged from the house, he joined Doshmisi at the paddock and they led their tigers out.

"Where's Granite?" Doshmisi asked. Granite was Jasper's father.

"He had to go to my uncle's house," Jasper replied. "We said our good-byes already since he knew I'd probably leave with you today."

"I wish I could have seen him," Doshmisi said regretfully.

"He sends you his regards," Jasper told her as they mounted the tigers and headed out on the dirt road to the Garden, with Cocoa yapping delightedly and running alongside.

It took Doshmisi a few minutes to reacquaint herself with how to sit a tiger and how to grip Sheba's sides with her legs. She had barely settled into the rhythm of Sheba's stride when they arrived at the Garden, managed by Jade the Gardener.

Jade emerged from the potting shed to greet them, wiping her hands on her overalls as Doshmisi and Jasper dismounted. "Doshmisi! Good to have you back. We need you now more than ever," Jade called out.

Doshmisi gave Jade a warm hug. "I need to visit the Grove of Shakabaz and listen for the words of the trees. I hope they have something useful to tell me."

"The trees always have something useful to tell," Jade encouraged her. "Would you like some strawberries? I just picked a heap of giant juicy ones." She held a basket of bright red strawberries out to Doshmisi, who took a handful and thanked Jade. The strawberries made her think of Bayard. He would have loved them. She would have to stay focused on the task at hand and not waste time worrying about where Bayard, Sonjay, and the rest of them had gone.

"This won't take long," Doshmisi promised Jasper.

"Take as much time as you need. I'll wait for you here," Jasper replied.

As she stepped onto the trail to the Grove of Shakabaz, Doshmisi heard Jade ask Jasper about Denzel, Maia, and Sonjay. Doshmisi popped one last sweet strawberry into her mouth and licked the juice from her fingertips.

Doshmisi had visited these wise, ancient, and enormous trees once before and to her amazement she had discovered that they spoke to her in a tree language that she understood. After that first revelation, she had communicated with trees frequently. When she reached the deep forest, populated with the largest trees, the mossy forest floor felt like a springy carpet beneath her feet and the thick, lush overhead canopy blocked her view of the sky. Amidst the giant red oaks, her amulet began to glow green. She heard a rush of whispers inside her head and a great heaviness overtook her so that she had to sit down on the cushiony ground strewn with pine needles, moss, twigs, fallen lichens, and leaves.

She closed her eyes and the language of the trees that she remembered well entered her in thought and energy through images and mutual understanding. She wrapped her hand around her glowing amulet and her spirit danced joyously up into the high branches. In their language, the trees expressed their delight at her presence. Then their intentions shifted. They sent her an image of her grandmother, Clover, lying in her bed on Whale Island, while her assistant, Iris, brought her a cup of tea. Clover appeared fragile, weak, and unwell. She had dark circles under her eyes, her face was pale, and she was frail and thin. The mighty trees wanted Doshmisi to go to Clover and she sent them a thought to convey that she understood their desire.

The image of Clover faded and a different image planted itself in her mind's eye; a baffling image. The trees sent the image of piles of algae washing up on the beach. The delicate blue-green algae, usually glowing with lively energy, hung lifeless and limp. Heaps of algae washed up in greasy mounds. And then little tiny mouths opened up in the algae. The mouths screamed in a high-pitched wail, like a tea kettle whistling, except completely lacking the cheerfulness of a tea kettle's whistle. The scream sounded like the total opposite of cheerful. In the distance, the whales moaned despairingly. Their moans sounded almost like the moans of a person grieving for a loved one who had died. The sheer size of the whales made the water vibrate with their moans and the vibration set Doshmisi's teeth rattling. Although she did not understand what the images and sounds meant, they alarmed her and filled her with sorrow. She could feel the trees caressing her face in the form of a breeze and blessing her for the journey ahead. Then they withdrew and fell silent.

Chapter Three
Arrival Part Two

Maia flew down the wind tunnel filled with blue powder with Elena wrapped around her like a life jacket. When she burst through the passage into Faracadar, Elena still clung to her, eyes squeezed tightly shut. "You can let go now," Maia said, unable to conceal the note of anxiety in her voice. Elena opened her eyes slowly and peered around. She blinked and winced.

"Such bright colors," Elena observed.

"You'll get used to it," Maia assured her brusquely. Deep-blue wisps of smoke drifted off Maia's shoulders.

"Where are we?" Elena asked.

"Faracadar. And you shouldn't have come," Maia said.

"Please don't be angry with me," Elena begged.

"I'm not angry. I'm worried that I can't keep you safe here," Maia informed her. Elena's eyes widened with fear and uncertainty.

At that moment, Denzel popped through and red smoke steamed off his head and shoulders. He glared at Elena as he shouted, "Oh no, not you! You stupid idiot!"

Elena promptly dissolved into tears. "I'm sorry. I didn't realize…"

"No you didn't, did you? You have no idea how big a mistake you made. No idea. But now we're stuck with you, so you're going to have to try to keep up. Maybe we can leave you with the People Beyond the Lake until Loma and the return, because..." He stopped in mid-sentence and gazed around him. "Whoa," he said to his sister, "where the heck are we?"

"I was just thinking the same thing," Maia replied.

"This is not Debbie's Circle, not at all. And where are Dosh and Sonjay? Shoot. Your dumb friend must have scrambled the passage," Denzel accused.

"I would get it if she had scrambled *my* passage, but how could she have scrambled *yours*? Or anyone else's? She jumped onto *my* cushion. If it got scrambled, it happened because Ruby and Crystal don't know how to do it right yet. Don't blame Elena." Maia wrapped her arms around her weeping friend.

"Having her jump onto your cushion in the middle of it sure didn't help."

"And yelling at her won't help either, will it?" Maia chided him. "Maybe Dosh and Sonjay will come through in a minute."

"And maybe I'm Abraham Lincoln," Denzel muttered.

Maia ignored her brother's snide comment as she pointed to the mountains that rose behind them. "It looks like we arrived near the Amber Mountains."

"Looks like it," Denzel agreed.

"But which side of them are we on?" Maia wondered aloud.

"The sun looks like it's on its way down so I'm going to guess that it's late afternoon. Then that direction is East, toward the ocean, and that direction," Denzel turned around, paused, and shouted, "RUN!" He took off up the rocky hillside. Maia grabbed Elena's hand and raced to follow her brother as several of Sissrath's Special Forces, in full battle dress, emerged from the trees.

Denzel scrambled swiftly up the hillside to an open cave entrance above him. The Special Forces moved up the hillside behind him and the girls, but the grown men in battle dress could not keep up with nimble young feet and they failed to overtake their prey before Denzel, Maia, and

Elena reached the opening of the cave and rushed inside, deep into the darkness, and far from the cave's mouth, with their hearts roaring in their ears.

"Sheesh, only been here a hot minute and Sissrath's already trying to snuff us. What a sore loser," Denzel complained as he bent over and gasped to catch his breath.

"Who are those guys?" Elena asked.

"You don't want to know," Denzel answered. "I'm guessing you're starting to realize that following us here was not such a hot idea." He actually grinned. He was happy to be back and he was going to enjoy watching that nimby-pimby Elena figure out that she had bitten off more than she could chew. Fortunately for him, neither Maia nor Elena could see him grinning in the dark. He sat down and rummaged around in his backpack until he found his flashlight.

"Those guys are the Special Forces, the elite army of a nasty enchanter named Sissrath, who tried to kill us last summer. We beat him fair and square, but he's probably still after us," Maia explained curtly, before following the beam of Denzel's flashlight with her gaze. "We're in the Through-Tunnel," she said matter-of-factly when she had taken a quick look around.

"Ya think?" Denzel replied.

"Oh shut up. Being mean accomplishes nothing. We have to work this out together," Maia reminded him.

"You were here last summer? Where? Where is here?" The ramifications of her impulsive act of jumping into the unknown began to dawn on Elena.

Denzel answered, "It's way too complicated to explain right now."

"I'm sorry," Elena cried, "I never should have done it. Send me back and I won't ask any questions. I'll forget the whole thing. Your secret will remain safe with me. This never happened."

"Well, it did happen, and we can't send you back. Believe me, if we could then I would do it in a heartbeat," Denzel said.

"We're on the Big House side, right?" Maia asked her brother.

"That's what I'm thinking," Denzel confirmed. "So we have to go through."

"Not the geebachings again!" Maia exclaimed. "Last time, they made me laugh so hard that my lungs almost exploded."

"Don't remind me of that; they nearly killed you. At least this time we don't have the high chief with us to give us away hollering because a little mouse ran over his toe," Denzel noted with relief.

"We don't have to creep through in silence, you realize. I can play the timber flute all the way through and that should protect us until we get to the other side," Maia said.

"That sounds like a plan. We can probably get through in a couple of hours of walking and then spend the night at the Wolf Circle," Denzel suggested.

"A couple of hours? Of walking?" Elena wailed. "In a mountain? In my pajamas?"

"You have your jeans on," Maia contradicted, "not your pajamas."

"I'm in my pajama top," Elena whined. "And your brother's here. I look silly."

"I already told you back at Manzanita Ranch, I'm not interested in you, so get over me," Denzel said harshly. It more than annoyed him that of all the people from their life at Manzanita Ranch who could have followed them to Faracadar, Elena had succeeded in doing it. He was burned out on her having a crush on him. He had not given her the least encouragement. How mean did he have to act for her to get the message?

"I'm thirsty," Elena said, sniffling.

Maia removed her canteen from her shoulder and passed it to Elena. "Have some of my water, but don't backwash, aight? And don't drink too much either. We need to conserve for later." While Elena took a sip from the canteen, Maia asked Denzel, "What if Dosh and Sonjay turned up right after we did and got captured by the Special Forces?"

"I didn't see any sign of them," Denzel said.

"Me neither, but maybe we should wait here for a little while to see if they turn up," Maia suggested. "If they're inside the mountain then they would need me to play the timber flute to protect them from the geebachings."

"Doshmisi?! Sonjay?!" Denzel called out. His voice echoed back at him. He paused to listen for a response, but he knew it would not come. "Maia, they're not here. They're just not. They either turned up somewhere else or they didn't make it through at all. We need to push forward without them."

Elena handed the canteen back to Maia, who attempted to provide her friend with a simple explanation. "Here's the situation in a nutshell. Me and my brothers and my sister have a job to do here in Faracadar. We have a duty to keep the people safe and prevent bad enchanters like Sissrath and his smelly buddy Compost and other bad creatures, like sea serpents, from harming anyone. Or taking control of the land. The people in this land call us the Four because we have special responsibilities. Things are going on here in Faracadar that we have to find out about, and then do something about. This tunnel leads through the Amber Mountains. We have to follow the tunnel and meet up with our friends on the other side in the Wolf Circle to find out from them what's happening. You'll have to go with us."

"Sea serpents? I'm afraid of snakes. I'm even afraid of worms," Elena said with a whimper.

"Then I guess you should have stayed off Maia's passage cushion." Denzel threw Elena a smug I-told-you-so look.

"Stop hating on Elena," Maia snapped at Denzel. She attempted to reassure Elena by telling her, "You're not in danger of encountering a sea serpent in here; we're inside a mountain. In here we have to watch out for geebachings."

"So geebachings are funny?" Elena asked hopefully.

Denzel and Maia looked at each other and burst out laughing.

"*Bueno*," Elena said as she smiled for the first time since arriving in Faracadar. "I could use a few laughs."

"Not this kind," Maia warned. "Geebachings make people laugh themselves to death. Literally. They make you laugh so hard that you can't stop and then you can't breathe and then you die. They have no mercy."

"And they live in this mountain?" Elena asked, wide-eyed.

"Yup. But we dealt with them last summer. They can't listen to music. It makes them turn into harmless orange birds. They're OK with singing and drumming, but musical instruments, like my flute, transform them." With those words, Maia produced her timber flute from her bag and put it to her lips. She began to play and, as she did so, her amulet began to glow with a blue light.

"Whoa," Elena remarked as she pointed at the amulet. "Hecka cool. I want a necklace like that."

"Yeah, our amulets do that sometimes. C'mon, we need to walk," Denzel informed Elena, "while Maia plays music to keep the geebachings away."

"How do you know which way to go?" Elena asked.

"We told you. We were here before," Denzel switched off the flashlight as he fell in behind his sister and followed the music of her timber flute into the darkness. He looked up at the phosphorescent mold on the ceiling of the tunnel. The pattern of the glowing mold indicated which way to walk. Jasper had taught him about the mold last summer. Denzel had looked forward to seeing Jasper upon his arrival in Faracadar, but things had not gone as expected. "Later Man," Denzel whispered softly to Jasper, even though his friend couldn't hear him. He hoped that maybe Dosh and Sonjay had arrived in Debbie's Circle like they were supposed to and that Jasper would lead them to him and Maia eventually. For the

time being, the best plan was to try to reach the Wolf Circle without getting
killed by geebachings.

Chapter Four
Arrival Part Three

With a whoosh and a rush of yellow smoke, Sonjay landed on the cobblestone ground of the courtyard at the Final Fortress. "What in the heck?" he said softly to Bayard, who still perched on his shoulder, as he quickly ducked behind a statue that hid him from the view of anyone entering or leaving by the main gate. "You have to keep quiet, Bayard," he instructed. "Quiet. Understand?" Sonjay put a finger to his lips to emphasize his point. Bayard took to the air and flew up over the stone wall and out of the courtyard, most likely to forage for food. Sonjay felt sad to see him go, but he was better off without the bird for the moment. Bayard could make quite a racket and Sonjay needed to stay hidden.

Sonjay waited in the silent courtyard until nightfall. He hoped that his sisters or brother would turn up. That didn't happen. He was on his own. He wondered if the previous Four (Momma, Aunt Alice, and his uncles) had ever been separated during the passage. Although he worried about the others, and wondered if they had even made the passage at all, he didn't think he had arrived at the Final Fortress by accident or because Crystal and Ruby lacked experience. He thought he had arrived there for a reason and he thought the reason had to do with finding his father.

Daddy had disappeared when Sonjay was a baby, and the Four had given up hope of ever seeing him again, even though Momma used to say that Daddy would return to them as soon as he could. The previous summer, when Sissrath held Sonjay and the others captive in the dungeon at the Final Fortress, Sonjay thought he had heard his father speaking their names. Now seemed like as good a time as any to find out if Daddy was actually here. Sonjay had the crescent moon mark of the enchanter on his wrist, just like Princess Honeydew. He wished he knew how to cast enchantments, but he had not yet come of age and therefore had not studied enchantment yet at the Wolf Circle. If he could have cast enchantments, he would have made himself invisible.

Under cover of darkness, Sonjay slipped inside the heavy door that led to the dungeons. The fortress remained eerily quiet. He stepped softly down the stone stairs, wishing he had one of the flashlights in Denzel's backpack. When he reached the bottom of the stairs, he found himself in a corridor dimly lit by wall sconces. Still no one appeared. Hugging the damp, cold, stone wall, he made his way cautiously down the corridor toward the cell where Sissrath had imprisoned him on his previous stay at the Final Fortress.

Suddenly, a hand reached out of the wall and clapped itself over Sonjay's mouth, then hauled him into a tiny room. Sonjay struggled to free himself from the grip of that hand. "Don't make a sound," a voice whispered in his ear. The hand released him as it spun him around and he stared into the astonished face of Buttercup, the wife of Crumpet. Crumpet was the older brother of the great enchanter Cardamom. Crumpet was not the most proficient enchanter. His enchantments seemed to go wrong more often than they went right, but he was a good guy. Buttercup was much better at casting enchantments than her husband. She was a large woman and her dark-brown skin had the distinctive yellow glow of the Mountain People. "What are you doing here?" she hissed. "I almost killed you."

"I could ask you the same thing," Sonjay replied. "What are you doing here?"

"I'm rescuing Crumpet," she declared.

"Well, I'm rescuing my father," Sonjay countered. "Where is everyone? Are there any guards down here?" As Sonjay's eyes adjusted to the dim room, he discovered that he and Buttercup, as well as several other Mountain People from Buttercup's home in the Amber Mountains, had crammed themselves inside a tiny closet filled with brooms, mops, buckets, scrub brushes, and cleaning supplies. "Are we in a mop closet?"

"You betcha," Buttercup answered. "We put an enchantment on the guards to make them sleep. Well, most of 'em. It's complicated. The Special Forces are asleep, but not the Corportons."

"Corportons?"

"Aliens. I told you, it's complicated. Let's free Crumpet, then we'll try to find your father, and then we'll get out of here. After we get out, I'll bring you up to speed about the aliens."

"I'm down with that. Lead the way," Sonjay said, as he gestured toward the door of the mop closet.

Buttercup picked up a huge super-soaker squirt gun and handed it to Sonjay. "If you see someone in a snow-white jumpsuit, spray 'em. Don't ask questions." She motioned to the others and stepped toward the door.

"Yuk. It smells like skunk," Sonjay sniffed the super-soaker.

"You betcha," Buttercup confirmed.

"What'd you put in this thing?"

"Skunk juice, they hate it."

"They?"

Buttercup shushed him. "Let's roll."

Sonjay and the others followed Buttercup out of the mop closet and down the corridor. Buttercup held a device in one hand that looked like a cell phone but Sonjay knew it wasn't. There were no phones at all in Faracadar. Buttercup pointed the device forward. When it started beeping, she turned it off and put her hands on the cell door nearest to her. "He's in here, stand back," she instructed. Sonjay and the others moved away.

Buttercup pointed her fingers at the door, closed her eyes, inhaled deeply, and then spoke words of enchantment under her breath. The door to the cell slowly opened.

"You have to teach me how to do that," Sonjay told her admiringly.

"All in good time." She entered and Sonjay followed close behind. Inside the cell, Sonjay saw a cot with a blanket on it. There was a small window high up on the outside-facing wall. A table had been pushed against that wall and there was a chair on top of the table. The cell was empty.

Buttercup looked up at the chair on the table. She reached for Sonjay's skunk juice super-soaker, which he handed to her gratefully (it smelled awful), as she commanded him, "Climb up there and get that pastry off the chair. Be careful. Don't let it crumble."

Sonjay clambered onto the table and sure enough, he found a fat cinnamon roll on the chair. It looked tasty. He climbed back down with it resting flat on his palm. "Yum," he said to Buttercup. "I'm starved." As he started to open his mouth to take a bite, Buttercup snatched the cinnamon roll out of his hand and smacked him upside the head. The other Mountain People laughed.

"What's up with you?" Sonjay demanded as he rubbed his face where she had slapped him.

"Shut up!" Buttercup yelped. She tenderly placed the pastry on the cot and said a few words of enchantment to it. The pastry glowed chartreuse, then yellow, and then, with a pop, it transformed into a familiar figure.

"Crumpet!" Sonjay exclaimed. "I almost took a bite out of you."

"What did I turn into this time?" Crumpet asked querulously.

"A cinnamon roll," Buttercup informed him.

"With icing and raisins. You looked delicious," Sonjay added, as he put his arms around Crumpet and gave him a hug. He had missed the incompetent enchanter; incompetent because whenever he became too excited, flustered, or angry while conducting an enchantment he turned himself into some object (usually something useless) and remained stuck like that until a capable enchanter could be found to change him back.

"The Corportons have Sissrath in their back pocket. It's disgusting. He took them to the North Coast," Crumpet began to explain to his wife in an agitated voice as he waved his arms above his head, but she stopped him with a raised hand.

"Not now. First, if you upset yourself then you might turn into a doughnut, and second, we have to help Sonjay find his father and then skedaddle out of here before the guards wake up."

"You have a father?" Crumpet asked Sonjay incredulously.

"Everyone has a father," Sonjay reminded him.

"Alive? Here?" Crumpet continued.

"I think so. I need to find out for sure. I haven't ever seen my dad. But I think he's down here somewhere. Do you remember last year when Sissrath put us into a cell in this dungeon? The time you had turned yourself into a rock and your brother Cardamom turned you back while we were imprisoned?"

"Of course. There's nothing wrong with my memory," Crumpet replied haughtily. He unfolded his long body to its full height as he gave his wife a hug. "Thank you for rescuing me, babycakes," Crumpet told Buttercup appreciatively. She planted a kiss on his nose. "Where are Doshmisi, Denzel, and Maia?" Crumpet asked Sonjay.

"I don't know. We got separated during the passage."

"We have to go. Now," Buttercup reminded them urgently.

"OK, OK," Sonjay said as he took the stinky super-soaker out of her hand and headed toward the cell door. "Here's the deal. I thought I heard my father's voice when I was in that cell with Crumpet and the others last year. But I don't know exactly where the voice came from. I just know it was near our cell. Do you think you can find the cell where Sissrath imprisoned us last year?" Sonjay asked Crumpet.

"Of course. I never forget a prison cell," Crumpet said, his eyes shining brightly. "Everyone imprisoned here is an enemy of Sissrath," Crumpet pointed out as he turned to Buttercup and suggested, "so why don't you and the fellas start opening cell doors and have a look to see who's inside, while I take Sonjay to our former cell to see if we can figure out where his father might be."

"You got it, babycakes," Buttercup agreed. "But be quick. The Corportons will discover us any minute."

Crumpet and Sonjay hurried out of the cell and continued down the corridor. Crumpet turned to the right into a passageway that looked familiar to Sonjay, and then he stopped outside a cell door. "This one."

Sonjay put his hand on Crumpet's arm. Crumpet still smelled vaguely like cinnamon and it made Sonjay's mouth water. "Keep quiet for a minute and let me listen," Sonjay commanded. Crumpet obeyed as Sonjay cocked his head to the right and listened intently. All he could hear was Buttercup and her team in the distance as they released prisoners from their cells. Last year he had distinctly heard a man repeating over and over again his name and the names of his brother and sisters. Maybe his father had died since the previous year. After all, he had probably been a prisoner in the Final Fortress for ten years or more.

Just then, Bayard appeared. The parrot flew down the passageway and squawked "Daddy-O, Daddy-O." Sonjay trusted Bayard implicitly so he followed him immediately. Bayard alighted on the floor outside a cell door and repeated "Daddy-O."

"Can you open it?" Sonjay asked Crumpet. "Without turning into a slice of cake, I mean?"

"Give me a little credit," Crumpet complained. He said some words and the lock clicked open. With his heart beating loudly in his ears, Sonjay pulled the heavy door back with a creak and a rumble.

A man with long dreadlocks sat at a table and typed on an old-fashioned typewriter. When Sonjay entered, the man looked up from his work with curiosity. Bookshelves loaded with books lined the walls of the cell. A rich red-and-black carpet covered the floor and a warm fire glowed in the fireplace. The bed, piled high with comfy pillows, invited a nap. A glow-bug lantern stood on the table and cast an amber light to the edges of the room. This warm room was the opposite of a cold, damp prison cell. It looked more like a cozy study.

Sonjay had expected to find a grizzled and emaciated man chained to the wall, his eyes rolling around crazily in his head. This man looked well-fed and clean. And he looked exactly, precisely, like Denzel, only grown up. When Sonjay entered the cell with Crumpet, the prisoner pushed his chair back and rose to his feet with a questioning expression.

"I am Sonjay, the youngest son of Debbie," he stated matter-of-factly. "Are you my father?"

The man's face collapsed with emotion as tears ran down his cheeks. He nodded his head and then, in a voice that cracked, he said, "Yes. Yes. I am Reggie; Reginald Goodacre. I am your father."

Sonjay was stunned. He had set out to find his father and had expected to find him, but nothing could have prepared him for the moment when he would actually stand face-to-face with his father. Rooted to the spot, his eyes welled up with tears. Reggie walked over to Sonjay and wrapped him in his arms. They held onto each other tightly and cried, oblivious to everything and everyone around them. "Such a beautiful, strong boy. My son. I have wished to see you every minute of every day these ten long years," Reggie choked out between sobs.

Sonjay felt like dancing and shouting. He was fit to burst with joy and wished with all his heart that his brother and sisters were there with him at that moment. But all his wishing did not bring them to his side.

"Sissrath says your mother died; is it true?" Reggie asked.

Sonjay swallowed hard and nodded his head. "She had a heart attack. But it was really the deep enchantment that killed her. You know, because she traded years from her life to protect the people."

"Yes, I know it. I tried to save her. That's why I came here," Reggie said huskily as he tried to regain control of his emotions. "Are the others here too? Doshmisi, Denzel, and Maia?"

"We were separated during the passage. I think they probably arrived in Faracadar somewhere, just not with me," Sonjay explained. "But I don't know."

The sound of a struggle in the passageway outside the door of the cell cut their reunion short. Sonjay and Crumpet ran to the threshold of the cell. Buttercup stood just outside the cell, transfixed in horror as she watched the far end of the passageway fill with human-like creatures covered from head to toe in snow-white jumpsuits, their faces hidden by opaque gray masks that did not yield any clue as to the appearance of the creature which lay underneath.

"Run for it!" Buttercup shouted, as she discharged a stream of stinky skunk juice from her super-soaker.

Chapter Five
At the Dome

On her way back to the Garden, Doshmisi pondered the images sent to her by the trees. They urged her to go see Clover, and she would do that. But first she wanted to find out more about Mole and the situation on the North Coast. She believed that if she went to the North Coast, then she would learn something important about the blue-green algae and the whales. She would prefer to solve the mystery about the threat to the algae before she visited Clover so that she could share that information with Clover and seek her grandmother's advice.

Upon her return to the potting shed at the Garden, she found that the intuit Jack had joined Jasper and Jade. Although only six years old, Jack had the ability to see into the future and to witness events taking place far away from him. Typical of people who lived at the Dome Circle, he had brown skin with a deep purple glow. He also had thick, purple curls. He hovered over the ground, like all intuits, whose intense energy caused them to lift up off their feet. Jack floated to Doshmisi at eye level and happily flung his little arms around her neck shouting, "hi, hi, hi."

"What'd the trees say?" Jasper asked.

Jack clung delightedly to Doshmisi's neck and she shifted him to one side so she could see Jasper and Jade.

"They're sad," Doshmisi began, and then hesitated. Jack put his hand on her head and closed his eyes. "They want me to go to see Grandmomma Clover on Whale Island."

Jack's eyes sprang open, he pushed himself off Doshmisi, and told Jasper, "Sick ocean. Poison."

"Yes, Jack," Doshmisi confirmed. "The trees showed me that something will threaten or has already threatened the blue-green algae and this has deeply disturbed the whales. I'm not sure if I saw the present or the future, but whenever it takes place, it's not good."

"Poison?" Jade asked. "The algae poisoned?"

"Poison," Jack repeated.

"Grandmomma Clover once explained to me that the algae cleans the air in Faracadar, and that without it, the air will thin out and become too dirty to support life," Doshmisi said.

Jack grabbed his neck, and pretended to choke himself. He fell over sideways, gagging for air.

"Leave it, Jack," Jasper said, anxiously. "We can do without the theatrics."

Jack floated benignly in the air with a slightly hurt expression on his face.

"Correct," Jade confirmed for Doshmisi. "The algae and the whales each have a role in a delicate ecosystem that supports the quality of the air for us air-breathing creatures."

"And the quality of the water for the sea creatures too, I suppose," Doshmisi added.

"Of course," Jade said.

"Then I guess we should head for the Islands to check in with Clover," Jasper said, eager to strike out on the open road and do the guiding work for which he was trained.

"No, not yet," Doshmisi disagreed, as she pursed her lips in thought.

"What do you mean?" he asked.

"I mean that Grandmomma will have to wait. I intend to go see her, just as the trees wish; but first I want to find out more about what's going on at the North Coast. I want to look for Mole and see if he can shed any light on Sissrath's game plan."

"Do you think it wise to contradict the trees?" Jade asked, worriedly.

"The trees showed me several things. They showed me Clover and they showed me that the algae could potentially be in danger and that the threat to the algae has the whales distraught. I want to find out as much as I can about what we're up against before I talk to Grandmomma so I can ask for her opinion about all of it. What do you think, Jack?" Doshmisi asked the intuit.

"Coast." Jack nodded emphatically.

"North Coast it is then," Jasper said. He asked Jade if she would look after Cocoa until Granite returned. When they took their leave of Jade, she gave them fresh fruit and cheese for their journey. Jasper seated Jack in front of him on his tiger and the travelers headed in the direction of the ocean. Doshmisi enjoyed riding through the familiar landscape, bathed in the light from the greenish sun. She had missed this land. They rode for the rest of that day, stopping only when the shadows grew long and darkness began to descend.

Jasper set up two small tents in a birch forest that night. "If we ride hard tomorrow, we can reach Akinowe Lake and the Solferino Settlement before nightfall," Jasper told the others before they went to bed. The Solferino Settlement housed the Crystal Communication Dome, a hub for messages traveling throughout Faracadar and therefore its communication center. Perhaps they would learn something valuable about Sissrath's activities at the Dome.

The travelers rose at dawn for a tasty breakfast of bread, cheese, and grapes. By midday they arrived atop the hills that ringed Akinowe Lake. The many-colored birds that lived near the lake swooped in brilliant streaks across the sky between the hills and the water, which sparkled invitingly in the distance. Jasper led them on the path down to the lake and around its edge. When the blue-tinged fingers of evening brushed the treetops, they arrived on the outskirts of the Dome Circle. They looked forward to staying at the Tollhouse run by Jelly and Mrs. Jelly, whom they had befriended the year before. Mrs. Jelly made terrific pancakes. As they approached the circle, Jack warned them, "danger, danger, danger;" so they remained alert and cautious.

It soon became apparent that it did not require the clairvoyance of an intuit to recognize that something at the Dome had gone amiss. They did not see any people and the footsteps of their tigers sounded loud in the silent road, empty of the cheerful voices of children calling to one another as they played in the yards and pathways of the circle. Jasper pulled his tiger up short and swung off of the large, gentle beast, leaving Jack on the Tiger's back by himself. He motioned to Doshmisi and she too dismounted. They led the tigers into the eerily quiet circle and made their way to the Tollhouse. Jasper knocked on the heavy wooden door. Two eyes peered out of a slit in the door. The slit slammed shut. Then a jolly balding man with inky purple-black skin and a lavender-colored beard opened the door and hurried them inside, tigers and all, swiftly slamming the door shut behind them. Once he had them safely inside, Jelly (for that is who the man was) crushed each of them in turn in an enormous bear hug as he called over his shoulder, "Mrs. Jelly, come see what the tigers dragged in!"

The travelers stood in the middle of a large dining hall with a high, wood-beamed ceiling. Mrs. Jelly emerged from the kitchen, wiping her work-worn hands on her apron, and exclaiming, "Marvelous to see you, so marvelous. And just in the nick of time. Have you eaten dinner? No, of course not. Let me fix each of you a plate. Say, what became of the rest of you?" She meant Doshmisi's siblings, the rest of the Four.

"We got separated during the passage," Doshmisi replied. "I don't know where the others wound up or if they even made it through." Her words caught in her throat and reminded Doshmisi of how worried she was about what had happened to the others. She didn't want to dwell on it because it scared her. She had to focus on the task in front of her.

"It was the first time without Amethyst," Jasper added.

"Yes, well I'm sure Crystal did her best," Mrs. Jelly said sympathetically.

"She had Ruby with her. Ruby will replace Amethyst as the Gatekeeper soon, but it seems they need more practice," Doshmisi explained. She didn't want to sound too critical of Crystal and Ruby. She knew that they had tried their hardest and had not intended to separate the Four during the passage.

"I'll get you some dinner while Mr. Jelly tells you about our visitors here at the Dome Circle. Not a pretty story," Mrs. Jelly said as she shook her head ruefully and retreated to her kitchen.

Jelly called a boy over to him and asked him to take the tigers outside, and to feed them and bed them down. Then he sat at one of the heavy wooden tables with Doshmisi and Jasper. Jack climbed happily into his Uncle Jelly's lap. "Dome down. Dome off," Jack said sadly, as he patted his uncle's beard.

"Yes indeed," Jelly confirmed.

"What do you mean?" Jasper asked.

"What Jack said. The Dome is not working," Jelly informed them. People communicated across long distances throughout the land using crystal energy generated from the Crystal Communication Dome. If the Dome had stopped working, then the people could only communicate from one place to another by messenger.

"What happened?" Doshmisi asked. "And why is the circle deserted? Where did everyone go?"

"They're staying out of sight for their safety," Jelly said. "Sissrath's Special Forces arrived last week with guns, which are a kind of tool that shoots a small piece of metal."

"A bullet," Doshmisi said.

"A bullet?" Jasper asked.

"The small piece of metal shot from the gun is called a bullet. They have them in the Farland, but I have never seen them here. I wonder who introduced them into Faracadar. Perhaps Sissrath invented them. I'm sorry to hear that guns have come to Faracadar," Doshmisi said regretfully.

"The Special Forces used these guns to kill the security guards at the Dome," Jelly continued to recount recent events. "Then they sent the Dome workers home and they covered the central crystal with a large cloth. No communications have come in or gone out since. Fearing for their lives, the people of the circle have stayed inside their houses, only going out for essentials. It's like a siege."

"Why do you suppose Sissrath doesn't want people communicating?" Jasper wondered aloud.

Doshmisi answered, "Think about it. Last year we mobilized all the people to rise up against him. If we can't connect with people then we can't do that again."

"We should have killed him when we had the chance," Jasper blurted.

"But the whales said violence would only lead to more violence and I agree with them. We found a way to defeat Sissrath once and we'll find a way to do it again," Doshmisi asserted.

Jasper shrugged. "We didn't completely defeat him, did we? He's back to his old scheming ways already."

Just then Mrs. Jelly returned with dinner plates heaped with spinach-and-mushroom lasagna that smelled heavenly. Except for the Mountain People, everyone in Faracadar was vegetarian. Doshmisi used to eat meat, but she had given it up after her visit to Faracadar the previous summer, and she didn't miss it. The people in Faracadar cooked delicious vegetarian food and Mrs. Jelly was no exception. The lasagna was heavenly.

After dinner, Jasper suggested to Doshmisi, "Maybe you should use some of that color change powdery stuff to make yourself green; you know, so that you aren't so obvious." The year before, Grandmomma Clover had given the Four a powder that would put a color in them like the regular people of Faracadar. The Four were royalty, born from the royal line through their mother and her ancestors, and as such their skin appeared plain brown. The powder had given them each a bright aura of color so they resembled the ordinary people in Faracadar: Sonjay yellow (like the Mountain People), Maia blue (like the Coast People), Denzel red (like the People Beyond the Lake), and Doshmisi green (like the Island People).

"I wish I could," Doshmisi replied mournfully, "but Maia has the powder in her backpack."

"While you're here," Mrs. Jelly said to Doshmisi, "would you please take a look at my cousin Jewel? She twisted her ankle yesterday morning."

The previous year, Doshmisi had used the herbal book to help her heal many people. When she put the herbal on a person's chest, it opened to a page with instructions about a remedy for the sickness from which the person suffered. The herbal usually gave a recipe for a medicinal cure, but since it was an enchanted object it often acted in unpredictable ways. Doshmisi had developed the skill of figuring out how to use the herbal to heal people. She agreed to take a look at Jewel's ankle without hesitation.

Leaving Jasper with Jelly and Jack, Doshmisi followed Mrs. Jelly upstairs to a room in the inn where Jewel sat propped up in bed, knitting, with her swollen foot high on a cushion. A vase of forget-me-nots stood on the night stand alongside a blue pitcher of water and a glass. A glow-bug lantern cast an amber light into the room.

"Jewel," Mrs. Jelly said, "we're in luck. Guess who showed up? Doshmisi. And she has the herbal and she has come to take a look at your ankle."

During the year while at Manzanita Ranch, Doshmisi had spent every spare moment studying about medicine, health, and the human body. In fact, she didn't need to use the herbal to figure out what to tell Jewel about how to treat her injured ankle, but she proceeded to place the book on Jewel's chest anyway. The herbal opened to a page and Doshmisi leaned over to read the words. The page looked completely different from anything she had ever seen in the herbal before. She stared at the page in astonishment. Instead of providing instructions for a recipe or a quick diagnosis of the problem, the herbal had opened to a dense paragraph that began with the words, INSECTS REMAIN THE MOST ENDURING SPECIES BECAUSE OF THEIR ADAPTABILITY. IF PEOPLE COULD CHANGE TO MEET NEW CIRCUMSTANCES, THEY WOULD HAVE MORE SUCCESS AT SURVIVAL.

"Hold on," Doshmisi told Jewel, "the herbal is doing something peculiar and I have to read this page."

"Does it say something bad about my ankle?" Jewel asked in alarm.

"No," Doshmisi reassured her. "Strangely, it has nothing to say about your ankle. Let me read this right quick." Jewel and Mrs. Jelly exchanged an anxious glance and fell silent as Doshmisi began to read down the page. Before she could read more than the first few sentences, the herbal slammed shut of its own accord and she could not reopen it. She did not know what to make of this.

"I can't seem to get the swelling to go down," Jewel told Doshmisi. "I twisted it pretty bad."

"You should put ice on it and stay off it," Doshmisi instructed. "The more you ice it, the faster the swelling will go down and then it will stop hurting. Stay off it and keep it iced and elevated. I'll write a recipe for arnica cream to rub on it that Mrs. Jelly can make to help it heal faster; and drink four ounces of dark cherry juice every day."

Jewel thanked Doshmisi for the advice, then Mrs. Jelly and Doshmisi returned to the dining hall. Doshmisi wrote out the recipe for the arnica cream while Mrs. Jelly took an ice pack upstairs to her ailing cousin. Doshmisi kept wondering about the strange behavior of the herbal. She hoped it would not happen when she needed the herbal to act right to help her in a more serious situation.

After Doshmisi wrote the recipe, Jelly showed her and Jasper to their rooms and bid them goodnight. Alone in her room, Doshmisi attempted to open the herbal again, but it would not cooperate. She wondered what it had tried to tell her with that story about how insects were more adaptable than people. Before the book had slammed shut, she remembered reading something about people letting go of outmoded ways of operating, and that people needed to engage in innovative thinking. She decided that for the time being she would keep her discovery about the herbal to herself. Maybe the next time she tried to use it to heal someone, it would act the way it normally did. Or maybe it had morphed into a totally different book altogether, which scared her.

Early the next morning, Doshmisi, Jasper, and Jack took their leave of Mr. and Mrs. Jelly. They wanted to make it to the Passage Circle at the Coast Settlement before nightfall. Jasper could tell that Doshmisi was distracted as they rode through the Marini Hills, fragrant with the scent of flower blossoms, but he didn't bother her. He figured she needed to work something out in her head; after all, she was one of the Four. He took care not to interrupt her thoughts. Doshmisi continued to try to make sense out of the weird story fragment the herbal had offered up to her the previous day.

By late in the afternoon, Jasper, Doshmisi, and Jack emerged from the Marini Hills and started the descent toward the Passage Circle that formed a link between the Coast Settlement, near the beach, and the Island Settlement, that spread out across the ocean in a string of islands. Weary of travel, and no closer to guessing the meaning of the words she had read in the herbal, Doshmisi felt relieved to reach the end of the day's journey. Perhaps tomorrow, she thought, I'll have a glimmer of insight about the herbal.

Chapter Six
Wolf Circle

With Maia playing her timber flute and Denzel jamming along on Maia's travel drum, they walked at a fast pace in rhythm to the music. Denzel glanced upward frequently at the phosphorescent markings on the roof of the tunnel to make sure they continued heading in the right direction. After a few minutes of walking, Elena timidly began to hum along to Maia's tune and before long she had started singing a jazzy, wordless scat. The beauty of Elena's voice surprised Denzel. He didn't know anything much about Maia's little friend beside the fact that she had an annoying crush on him.

After the travelers had walked in the caves for an hour, their music became inspired. They surrendered to its flow and let it sweep them along. As they lost themselves in the beat, the tune that unfolded spontaneously became like a living creature of its own.

The trio could not risk pausing for fear that the fatally jolly geebachings would discover them if they fell silent. The year before, the geebachings captured Denzel and Maia along with their fellow travelers and had nearly caused them to laugh themselves to death. To save them, Maia played an extraordinarily haunting tune on a water organ (an instrument made of bowls filled with water) and the music turned the geebachings into bright orange birds that flew out of the caves and disappeared in the forest beyond. Turning into a bird didn't seem like a bad fate for a geebaching, especially considering how unrepentant they were about murdering people.

Their morbid sense of humor was horrifying. The strange creatures looked like large orange monkeys and had a ruthless obsession with making people laugh. They were intolerably funny and their infectious laughter had the power to go viral among vulnerable humans within seconds. They lived deep in the mountains and scouted the tunnels for prey, often venturing to the surface in search of victims.

After more than two hours of making music and walking, Denzel, Maia, and Elena emerged from a tunnel opening into the late afternoon light of a glorious golden-green day in a forest in the Amber Mountains. Elena was exhausted from the walk, but she didn't want to admit it to the others. She was glad she hadn't confessed to being worn out when Maia said, "That was fast. Last time it took so much longer."

"We must have come through a narrower part of the mountains this time," Denzel suggested. "Now we have to find the Wolf Circle." Denzel's forehead puckered with concentration. He did not know for sure which way to go. Jasper would have had his bearings in an instant and Denzel wished again that his friend was with them. "Which direction do you think...?" The sound of snuffling emerging from a nearby bush stopped him abruptly in mid-sentence. He whirled around, prepared to defend himself and the girls. "Who's there? Show yourself," he demanded, throwing his backpack to the ground in preparation for a fight.

A small, stunted, rusty-orange geebaching, no more than three feet tall, crept out from under the bush. His over-sized floppy ears hung dejectedly onto his shoulders. He wiped his runny nose with the back of his hairy arm.

"Ewww," Elena exclaimed. "Use a Kleenex."

He wiped his nose with his other hairy arm and mumbled, "Wassa Kleenex?"

Elena produced a Kleenex from her pocket and handed it to the geebaching, who promptly ate it. Elena giggled. The geebaching smiled faintly.

"Don't start," Denzel warned the geebaching, pointing his finger at him threateningly. "Don't even think about it. If you do or say anything the least bit funny I'll knock you out."

Elena patted the bedraggled creature on the head and turned a reproachful face to Denzel. "Can't you see he's sad and alone. Don't yell at him." Behind her, the geebaching held up two fingers in back of her head like horns, the way people sometimes do to be silly in a photograph. The corners of the geebaching's mouth twitched.

"Elena, come away from that thing. You have no idea," Maia warned. She lifted the flute to show the geebaching. "If you so much as giggle, I'll play the flute, so help me."

"Won't work on me," the geebaching informed her glumly. "I'm a dud." He commenced to sniffle again.

"Explain," Denzel demanded.

"I'm tone deaf. Can't hear music. It sounds like rattle and jammer to me. Been that way all my life. That's why I have no friends. That and the fact that I don't want to cause any harm. No laugh-to-death stuff. That's why I ran away. I'm a freak of nature."

"What is your name?" Elena asked kindly.

"Guhblorin. Remember it. Remember me as the first geebaching to give up the laugh-to-death. I can vouch it's a lonely choice."

"So you aren't funny?" Maia asked curiously.

"Oh, I'm funny," Guhblorin boasted, puffing out his chest. "I'm funnier than a cat with the hiccups. I'm the funniest. But I have vowed not to use it on humans. I'm careful. I contain it. Most of the time I do, anyway. I try." He screwed his face up, "I try really, really, really hard."

"So let me get this straight; you want me to believe that you're a geebaching that has decided not to make people laugh because you get that it's wrong to do that?" Denzel couldn't quite swallow Guhblorin's story. The geebaching nodded solemnly.

"You're not a freak of nature," Maia assured him, as she lowered her timber flute, "you're a mutation, an evolutionary improvement. I'm pleased to meet you." She held her hand out to the geebaching, who took it, and they shook.

"Don't get too excited," Guhblorin warned. "I'm a work in progress. If I'm naughty and make a funny, pull on my ear and I'll serious-up."

Denzel peered at the geebaching skeptically as he asked, "Do you happen to know the way to the Wolf Circle from here?"

"You betcha," Guhblorin replied brightly. "Been trying to work up the courage to go there. If I take you there, will you protect me long enough for me to explain myself to the Wolf Circle people so they don't kill me?"

"Absolutely," Elena promised.

"Happy, happy, happy," Guhblorin exclaimed as he hugged himself and shivered with delight. He planted one foot on the ground and started flapping his arms wildly while he spun in a circle around the unmoving foot. He looked like a demented bird. Elena started to laugh. Maia knew better. She stepped forward and grabbed Guhblorin's ear and yanked.

"Sorry, sorry," Guhblorin said sheepishly. "We go this way." He hung his head remorsefully and led the group onto a path into the woods.

Maia and Denzel fell in behind Guhblorin as they exchanged a look of concern, both of them worried about hooking up with a geebaching. Elena bent and picked a large white flower and put it in her hair.

"I wish I knew where Sonjay and Doshmisi landed," Denzel said quietly to Maia.

"I hope they're together," she replied.

"I hadn't thought of that," Denzel said. "What do you think we should do when we arrive at the Wolf Circle?"

"Princess Honeydew is probably there and she'll have some ideas. Hopefully Goldenrod will help us figure things out too," Maia suggested. They had lagged behind the others and they noticed that Guhblorin was talking to Elena, who giggled.

"We better catch up," Denzel noted. "Your little friend has no clue how dangerous he is so she has no reason not to tempt him to break his vow of seriousness."

They had not walked for long when they came to a clearing on the edge of the Wolf Circle. The sun had begun to dip behind the trees for the evening and Maia gazed up at it with affection. It was an old sun and not as intensely bright as the sun at Manzanita Ranch. It was orange and yellow with a greenish tint around the edges. Maia knew from experience that no moon would appear to brighten the night sky, only the many very bright stars in all different colors.

Four huge white wolves trotted into the clearing and stood at attention, watching the small group of travelers. Guhblorin jumped up onto Denzel's shoulders where he wrapped his arms around Denzel's head, covering Denzel's eyes. At the same moment Elena, quivering in terror, ducked behind Denzel and grabbed his upper arms with her hands in a viselike grip that he couldn't shake. "C'mon, man," Denzel complained in exasperation.

Maia held her hands out to the enormous wolves so they could identify her scent. "We're friends. Remember us from last year?" she said gently. After the wolves had sniffed her hands, she scratched them each under the chin and behind the ears. They licked her fingers and then went to sniff the others. When Maia glanced back and saw Guhblorin and Elena wrapped around her brother, she burst out laughing.

"Oh shut up!" Denzel shouted at Maia, as he extricated one of the geebaching's fingers from his mouth. "Let go," he demanded.

The wolves trotted back to Maia, who assured Guhblorin and Elena, "They won't hurt you. They live here. Why do you think they call it the Wolf Circle?"

Elena let go of Denzel, who swatted at Guhblorin and twisted back and forth trying to dislodge the terrified geebaching. Maia extricated Guhblorin from Denzel's shoulders and put him on the ground where he rolled himself up into a furry ball. The wolves nudged the rolled-up geebaching between them like a soccer ball, taking care not to injure him with their teeth or claws.

"Take it easy with him," Maia called after the wolves, as they proceeded to roll Guhblorin down a path that led into the heart of the circle. Denzel, Maia, and Elena followed close behind.

"Do any people live here, or just wolves?" Elena asked Maia quietly.

"People and wolves live here together," Maia replied.

As they entered the circle, one of the wolves pointed his nose at the sky and howled. Immediately, people poked their heads out of houses and emerged to investigate. In the jumble of onlookers, Maia saw Princess Honeydew and shouted to her joyfully. The crowd parted for Honeydew to make her way to Maia and the cousins hugged each other excitedly. Then, to Denzel's embarrassment, Honeydew threw her arms around his neck and gave him a hug as well. He hugged her back tentatively, while noticing the look of jealousy that crossed Elena's face out of the corner of his eye. When she released him, Honeydew demanded, "Where are Doshmisi and Sonjay?"

"We don't know," Maia answered regretfully. "We think they arrived in Faracadar when we did, but we got separated during the passage, so we don't know where they are." Elena looked down at her feet self-consciously because she felt partly responsible for the fact that Doshmisi and Sonjay had not arrived in the same place as the rest of them. But Maia would not allow her friend to feel bad about it. It may not have had anything to do with her. They didn't know one way or another. She put her arm around Elena's shoulders and made introductions. "This is my best friend, Elena, who came with us from the Farland. Elena, this is my cousin, the daughter of High Chief Hyacinth and Chieftess Saffron, heir to the throne of Faracadar, the Princess Honeydew."

"Why so formal?" Honeydew complained humbly.

"Well, that's your title, isn't it?" Maia pointed out.

"Your cousin?" Elena asked with surprise (and a bit of relief as she thought about the hug Honeydew had given to Denzel).

"Our mother came from this land," Denzel explained simply. "We're royalty here. Like our cousin."

Just then Honeydew's uncle, Goldenrod, appeared and interrupted the conversation so that he, too, could give everyone a hug and exclaim again about their arrival and ask about Doshmisi and Sonjay, and the news was repeated and introductions made again. In the excitement of the reunion, everyone forgot about Guhblorin, who had cautiously uncurled himself from the ball of fur he had become to protect himself from the wolves. A small child noticed Guhblorin and pointed at the geebaching while shouting, "What's that?"

The people of the Wolf Circle, who remained crowded around the visitors, shifted their focus from Denzel, Maia, and Elena to the geebaching. They stepped back and away from Guhblorin, staring, while Goldenrod answered the child in a deep guttural voice that sounded like a growl. "That is a mountain geebaching. One of the most dangerous and deadly of creatures," Goldenrod informed.

Guhblorin hung his head shamefully, his ears drooping, and he began to sniffle dejectedly. Elena went straight to him and put her arm around him and pulled him close to her side. "He's our friend. He's not dangerous at all. Don't be mean to him."

Goldenrod's eyebrows shot up in surprise and he turned to Denzel and Maia and insisted, "Explain this, right now."

"It's exactly what Elena said. He's our friend. He's a new kind of geebaching who doesn't want to hurt anyone," Maia told him. "He's trying to be good and helpful, and not funny. He's trying to stay serious. It's hard work for him so we help him. If he starts to be funny, we remind him that he has vowed to remain serious and he stops himself. I hope you will accept him as an ally."

Goldenrod frowned. Guhblorin bravely stepped forward and bowed his head in formal greeting to Goldenrod, who reluctantly bowed his head in return. "If I do something funny, just pull my ear to remind me to stop," Guhblorin said.

"I will do exactly that," Goldenrod promised, sternly.

Princess Honeydew, who had a reputation for loving animals and keeping many pets of all varieties, took Guhblorin's hands in hers and asked him with gentle curiosity, "What do geebachings eat? You must be hungry after your travels."

"I'll have a bowl of underpants soup, please," Guhblorin said. But the minute the words fell from his lips, he clapped his hand over his mouth contritely and muttered, "Sorry, sorry, sorry. I'm very nervous. So sorry." Unfortunately, the damage had already been done and quite a few of the children in earshot started laughing. Their parents pulled them away and quickly disappeared inside their houses.

Honeydew smiled kindly at Guhblorin. "It's OK. Just try harder to be careful. Let's go inside and see if we can find something more appropriate for your dinner." She motioned to the others and all of them followed her and Goldenrod through the center of the circle and into a communal dining room.

"Is High Chief Hyacinth at Big House City?" Maia asked Honeydew.

"Yes, and my mother too. She brought me here but she went back to Big House City right before the siege started. I'm so worried about them," Honeydew replied. "At the beginning, about six weeks ago, they had plenty of food and water. They have water wells inside the city, but their food supply won't last forever. I don't know how soon it will run out. Fortunately Cardamom is with them, and he has the Staff of Shakabaz. Perhaps he will figure out how to use the Staff to lift the siege and if not I hope they can remain securely within the gates and find food and water, at least until the siege ends. Meanwhile, the masters here at the Wolf Circle have begun my education in enchantment."

"Whoa. Can you do enchantment now?" Denzel asked with a note of envy in his voice.

"A little," Honeydew answered.

"Show us something," Denzel requested eagerly.

Honeydew glanced at her uncle and Goldenrod smiled indulgently. "Do the dancing," he suggested, with a glint in his eye. Honeydew laughed. "Do Denzel," Goldenrod added.

Denzel looked uncertainly from Goldenrod to Honeydew, wondering what he had gotten himself into. Honeydew raised her hand and pointed three fingers at Denzel. She squinted in concentration and then said a few words of enchantment. Denzel felt his feet quiver uncontrollably and the quiver ran up the back of his legs, grew stronger, then started up his arms from his fingertips. He began to dance and he couldn't stop. His body did the Electric Slide with no instructions whatsoever from his brain.

Maia and Elena burst into peals of laughter, which stopped abruptly when Honeydew raised three fingers and aimed them at the girls so that they too began to dance the Slide with no control over their arms and legs. Elena continued to giggle delightedly as she danced, but Maia and Denzel appeared none too pleased.

Unable to restrain himself in the presence of such hilarity, Guhblorin snorted through his nose and then dissolved in the kind of geebaching laughter that becomes so dangerously contagious. Honeydew laughed.

"You! Geebaching!" Goldenrod called sternly, "Cease immediately." And then Goldenrod himself fell out laughing, because who can resist a laughing geebaching?

"It's not his fault," Elena pointed out between spasms of laughter. "You did it. If you stop, then he'll stop." Guhblorin covered his eyes with his flappy ears so he couldn't see the silly spectacle. Goldenrod raised three fingers and released the dancers from Honeydew's enchantment. Everyone breathed deeply, trying to catch their breath, as Guhblorin stuffed his hands in his mouth to stifle his giggles.

"I guess I did not choose the best enchantment to demonstrate while in the presence of a recovering geebaching," Goldenrod admitted sheepishly. "My bad."

"That could come in real handy," Denzel noted as he filed away Honeydew's power for possible later use if needed.

Guhblorin repeated several times, "I'm OK, I'm OK, I'm OK," as he attempted to calm himself down.

Goldenrod patted Guhblorin on the back. "Sorry, little fella, I should have known better. I see you are sincerely making an effort."

"Yes. An effort. Sincerely," Guhblorin affirmed.

"Well, let's get all of you something to eat and find you some comfy beds for the night," Goldenrod said as he steered the travelers to a long wooden table and motioned for them to take seats.

"I vote we go to Big House City to try to lift the siege," Denzel told Goldenrod. "I could use some enchanters to help me, and maybe some wolves," he added hopefully.

"I'm inclined to take a more cautious approach," Goldenrod replied. "I would prefer to learn more about the situation at Big House City before putting lives at risk."

Denzel took Goldenrod's rebuff in stride and revised his plans. "Then how about this, how about if Maia and I go to Big House City to find out more for you?"

"No way you go without me," Honeydew asserted firmly. "My parents are trapped there."

"I'm going wherever you go," Elena said.

"Of course you'll come with us," Maia reassured Elena.

"Me too," Guhblorin screeched as he leapt into Elena's lap and wrapped his skinny arms around her neck.

"Absolutely," Elena told Guhblorin as she attempted to disengage his fingers from their interlaced grip. "Guhblorin has to come also. He's *mi amigo*."

"*Amigo*," Guhblorin repeated eagerly. He clearly liked the sound of the Spanish word for "friend" and he said it several times without completely comprehending what it meant.

"That's settled then," Honeydew informed her uncle. "We have a team assembled and we'll scout out the situation."

Denzel felt less than enthusiastic about going into a potentially dangerous situation with three girls and a geebaching, but there didn't seem to be anything he could do about it. On the positive side, he knew that Honeydew and Maia were resourceful, sensible, and brave. He said to Goldenrod, "We need a way to communicate with you from Big House City, to let you know what we find. Do you have any ideas about that?"

"I have my cell phone and it's fully charged," Elena piped up.

Denzel busted out laughing. "Terrific. Now all we need is a cell phone tower." He couldn't wait to tell Sonjay about Elena and her cell phone.

Elena threw Denzel a hurt look while Guhblorin patted her empathetically on the shoulder.

"I'll give you a travel crystal," Goldenrod offered. "With any luck, it will allow you to communicate with me." Denzel nodded in agreement with Goldenrod. He had used a travel crystal successfully the previous year and knew how tricky a travel crystal could get. It depended on the nature of available sunlight, but it could work. "Just so you know, the Dome seems to be down," Goldenrod added.

"What? The Dome? That's not good." Denzel absorbed that information and continued, "I figure it will take us three or four days to get to Big House City." He counted off the travel days on his fingers as he explained his calculation to Goldenrod. "That would include two or three days to hike over the Amber Mountains and one day to ride from the mountains to Big House City. We could make good time if we don't run into any Special Forces. We need tigers," Denzel noted.

"I can arrange for tigers," Goldenrod told him.

Guhblorin raised a hand in the air, as if hoping for a teacher to call on him in class. "Excuse me," he squeaked in a tiny voice.

"Now what?" Denzel demanded. Guhblorin was getting on his nerves.

"I know a shortcut through the Amber Mountains that will cut the travel time in half," Guhblorin offered.

Denzel rolled his eyes. "It's not safe inside the Amber Mountains and you know why."

"We don't want to risk capture by your brothers and sisters and cousins and aunts and uncles and the rest of your kind who have not sworn off homicide like you have," Maia reminded Guhblorin patiently as she threw Denzel a reproachful look.

"I know a quick shortcut passage close to the surface, and I'm sure no geebachings will go in there. It has a weird smell in it. They don't like it," Guhblorin offered.

"What's the smell?" Elena asked suspiciously.

"Kind of like fish," Guhblorin said. "And seaweed."

"That doesn't sound so bad," Elena suggested hopefully.

"Very old fish. Very slimy seaweed. And also a bit like a wet sheep wearing sweaty gym socks," Guhblorin added.

Elena giggled. Guhblorin clapped a hand over his mouth.

"Is the passage big enough for tigers to fit through it?" Denzel asked.

Guhblorin saluted and said, "Yes, sir." Denzel heard a slight tickle of sarcasm in Guhblorin's use of the word "sir," but he let it pass.

"That's settled then," Denzel concluded with an approving nod in Guhblorin's direction. "We'll leave first thing in the morning and we'll use the smelly passage."

Chapter Seven
The Prophet of the Khoum

At the appearance of the figures-in-white, Crumpet roared with displeasure. He stretched out his hand, recited an enchantment that caused him to vibrate and emit a buzzing sound and then, with a pop, he turned into a tea kettle. Buttercup plucked him from the ground by the handle, muttering, "Couldn't you have at least managed to become a knife or a shovel or something I could use as a weapon, ya bonehead?"

As the figures-in-white descended on them, Sonjay wished with all his might that he, his father, Crumpet, and Buttercup were somewhere else, far from the dungeons of the Final Fortress. He pictured himself and the others sitting at the kitchen table at Manzanita Ranch eating Aunt Alice's delicious cherry pie straight from the oven.

Buttercup started to run down the corridor with Crumpet-the-tea-kettle tucked under her arm. Without warning or apparent reason, Sonjay, Buttercup, and Reggie collapsed onto the floor. Sonjay thought for a minute that he had been shot, but as far as he could recall no one had shot him and he was not in pain. He felt as if he had turned into a giant jellyfish. His insides had gone all rubbery and smishy-feeling and he could barely move. The figures-in-white lowered their guns and studied Sonjay and the others, who flopped on the floor. One of the figures-in-white poked Sonjay gingerly with his foot. Sonjay wobbled and quivered like pudding.

He wanted to grab that foot and twist it, but he couldn't raise his hand. The figures-in-white rolled Sonjay, Buttercup, and Reggie into Reggie's prison cell. Bayard picked up Crumpet-the-tea-kettle in his powerful beak and flew inside before the door clanged shut and locked behind them.

Sonjay howled with frustration. He could barely move and alien creatures had locked him in a cell in the Final Fortress for the second time in his life.

After Sonjay's howl died away, Buttercup told the others, "That wasn't me."

"What do you mean that wasn't you?" Sonjay snapped.

Buttercup ignored him and continued, "And it wasn't Crumpet because he's indisposed. Your father is not an enchanter, so we know it wasn't him. It could have been the aliens because we don't know their capabilities. But I wanna say, by their reaction, that they had no idea what happened to us. So I'm gonna say it had to be you, Sonjay."

"Me? Me what?" Sonjay demanded. His nose itched and he couldn't scratch it with his wobbly arm.

"You tried to throw an enchantment."

"Throw it," Bayard squawked.

"Ridiculous. I don't know how," Sonjay argued.

"My point exactly. What went through your mind right before it happened?" Buttercup asked him.

"I wished we could disappear and go far away from the Final Fortress. I imagined us at Manzanita Ranch eating Aunt Alice's fresh-baked cherry pie," Sonjay explained. "With vanilla ice cream," he added.

"You picked a fine time to come of age," Buttercup scolded. "You have the mark of the crescent moon on your wrist, the same as Princess Honeydew, the mark of a born enchanter. Now you must restore us. Listen and do as I say. Close your eyes and visualize us here, right in this cell," Buttercup instructed. Sonjay did as she told him and they soon found themselves restored to normal (all except Crumpet-the-tea-kettle).

Buttercup set Crumpet-the-tea-kettle on the floor and told the others, rather absently, "He does this so often these days that Cardamom taught me how to change him back. Give me a minute here to fix this." Buttercup aimed an enchantment at her husband, who transformed back into himself.

As Crumpet dusted his shoulders off, Buttercup informed him gleefully, "Sonjay has come of age."

"How do you know?" Crumpet asked.

"Because he just attempted to locomotaport us and instead he deboned us; sent our bones somewhere. He didn't realize he had almost thrown an enchantment because he has never done one. You get what this means don't ya, babycakes?" Buttercup gushed with excitement.

"What does it mean?" Sonjay asked.

"Back in the day, Hazamon could locomotaport. It's a rare skill. Only the most gifted enchanters can do it. It means that we have here in this cell, in you, one of the potentially most powerful enchanters in all of Faracadar. We need to train you. Too bad Cardamom didn't get locked up with us. Crumpet and I will have to do for the time being."

"I don't have time to train to become an enchanter. We have to get out of here as soon as possible." Sonjay stamped his foot in exasperation.

"While we work on that, consider yourself officially in training," Buttercup insisted.

"I refuse to study anything from Crumpet. He'll teach me how to turn myself into a sweet potato pie whenever I try to throw an enchantment," Sonjay grumbled.

"Do as I say," Crumpet said with a frown, "not as I do."

"He knows much more about enchanting than you do," Buttercup chided. "And he's your elder so show some respect."

Reggie cleared his throat. "If I may," he interjected, "I have spent the last ten years studying the Mystical Book of the High Shaman of Khoum. Even though I lack the ability to produce enchantments, I have learned a great deal of value that could prove useful in the hands of a skilled enchanter. For this reason Sissrath has kept me alive and well-tended in this cell. Sometimes, when I clear my mind of all extraneous thoughts and the energy falls just about right, I can see into the future."

Sonjay's mouth dropped open in astonishment.

"So you're a Prophet of the Khoum?" Buttercup asked with growing excitement.

"I believe so," Reggie replied humbly.

"Way cool," Sonjay commented, as Bayard squawked, "Khoum, Khoum, Khoum."

Buttercup cackled gleefully and pinched Crumpet's arm. "Couldn't have picked a better pair for the Corportons to lock us into a cell with, eh, babycakes?"

"Not in a million years," he replied, whistling the final "s" through his teeth in a way that sounded very like a tea kettle whistling.

"What is the Prophet of the Khoum?" Sonjay asked.

Buttercup settled her considerable bulk into Reggie's desk chair at his large work table and focused her full attention on him. "What have you seen of the future and how much of it have you shared with Sissrath?"

"Do you know where Sissrath is and what diabolical scheme he has rattling around in his twisted brain?" Crumpet asked.

"Berries," Bayard contributed to the conversation.

"Whoa, whoa," Reggie said, as he held a hand up in defense and sat on his bed, since Buttercup had commandeered his only chair. "Too many questions. Let's take one thing at a time. A few months ago I had a vision of the arrival of the aliens in the white suits. I don't know what they really look like. I think they come from outside Faracadar. I believe they come from the future, but from what land, I can't say. Before they arrived, I envisioned them destroying Faracadar and I cast the prophecy of the destruction for Sissrath. I did so because I hoped that the forewarning provided by the prophecy might help him save at least some of the people. Instead of using the knowledge to try to save the people or the land, he applied it to the task of saving himself. He apparently cut a deal with the aliens. They signed a contract with him, bound by his enchantment, that they will take him with them to their land if he helps them on their mission here. He plans to escape with them while the rest of us spin to our death as part of whatever cataclysmic event will occur to bring about the coming destruction."

"Berries," the bird squawked more urgently, unimpressed with Reggie's prediction of an apocalyptic disaster.

"Could you see what event will destroy Faracadar?" Buttercup asked, with apprehension.

"It has something to do with the poisoning of the ocean," Reggie answered.

"Do you know where Sissrath is now?" Crumpet asked.

"No," Reggie shook his head regretfully.

"We know that the aliens plan to go back to their own land eventually because they agreed to take Sissrath with them," Sonjay said, as he pondered the information he had just received. "They came here on a mission. That means they are after something. It seems as though they came here to get something and when they have it they'll take it with them and leave. I figure Faracadar is in danger of destruction because of the impending loss of the thing the aliens came here to take, or from the process of obtaining whatever they came to take."

"Berries, berries, berries," the bird insisted. He pecked Sonjay on the hand.

"Reggie, do you have any fruit up in here? Any fruit at all? This heap of feathers will drive me nuts if he doesn't get something to eat," Sonjay said. Reggie took a jar down off a shelf and opened the lid. He set the jar in front of Bayard who peered inside and exclaimed delightedly, "Raisins!" The bird greedily picked raisins from the jar one by one.

"When you envision something, does it always come to pass?" Buttercup asked.

"So far, yes," Reggie replied. "That's why Sissrath took me seriously when I prophesied the destruction of Faracadar."

"The Prophets of the Khoum have never been wrong," Crumpet reminded Buttercup.

"I don't believe in prophecy," Sonjay informed the others.

"That's like saying you don't believe in water," Crumpet responded in exasperation. "Just because you don't believe in it doesn't mean it's not for real."

"Prophecy is a warning, not an absolute fact. Believing in prophecies is like believing in fate. We can change fate. Otherwise, why bother to do anything? We might as well lay on the floor with all our bones gone," Sonjay pointed out.

"What are you suggesting?" Reggie asked, eyeing his son with a combination of curiosity and pride.

"I'm not *suggesting* anything. I'm *saying*. We have an advantage over Sissrath. He believes your prophecy that the land is headed to destruction. We know we can find a way to change that."

"Do we know that?" Crumpet asked.

Sonjay fished his amulet out of the inside of his shirt and put it face-up on his chest as a reminder to the others that he was one of the Four. "Trust me. We know it."

"That's your mother's Amulet of Heartfire," Reggie noted softly.

"It's mine now," Sonjay said.

Bayard paused from his raisins and announced, "Berries."

"Beggars can't be choosers, eat the raisins and be grateful," Sonjay warned the persnickety parrot, without taking his eyes off his father. "Reggie. Dad," he continued, "Tell me about the High Shaman of Khoum."

A perplexed look crossed Reggie's face. "Where to begin?" He paused, thinking. "Well, about two hundred years ago…"

"Two hundred years ago!" Sonjay interrupted. "Please start this story a little closer to now."

"Patience, boy," Crumpet said. "We're not in a hurry to go anywhere."

"As I said, two hundred years ago, there was a quiet boy who kept to himself. Some people thought he was an intuit at first since he said almost nothing and when he did speak, he spoke only in phrases of few words, often cryptic, much like the intuits speak. But he wasn't an intuit. When he turned sixteen, he left his home at the Wolf Circle and went to live in a cave in the Amber Mountains."

Buttercup interrupted to say, "He had started his training as an enchanter by then and he was remarkably good."

Reggie continued. "Yes. He was one of the best, and his teachers expected him to become a powerful enchanter one day. But he abandoned his training and spent nearly fifteen years virtually alone in the caves. He would occasionally return to the Wolf Circle for supplies, to find out the latest news of activities in the land, and to visit his family. During the time that he lived in the caves, he wrote the Mystical Book. When he emerged from the caves, he had the appearance of one much older than his years. He returned to the Wolf Circle where he invited four enchanters much older than he to study the Mystical Book with him and to learn how to use it."

"You forgot to mention," Buttercup interjected, "that while he lived in the caves, he also created the Book of Healing (commonly called the herbal), which your sister carries and your Aunt Alice carried before her."

"The herbal?" Sonjay repeated. Sonjay knew the book that Doshmisi carried contained powerful enchantment.

"Yes," Reggie confirmed. "He constructed the herbal specifically for the greatest healer in the land and presented it to her when he was not much more than thirty years old. During his lifetime, he trained four Prophets of the Khoum, using the Mystical Book as their guide. I have that Mystical Book in my possession."

Buttercup's eyes grew wide with astonishment.

"Here? You have it here?" Crumpet demanded.

Reggie nodded his head.

"But it disappeared a hundred years ago with the last living Prophet of the Khoum, who left the Wolf Circle one night and never returned," Crumpet recounted.

"True that. I have learned that the last Prophet did not leave the Wolf Circle of his own free will. Someone kidnapped him and placed him in this cell," Reggie informed them.

"How do you know?" Buttercup asked.

Reggie produced a small, worn book with a maroon leather cover that had gone soft from handling. "This is the Mystical Book. The original. When Sissrath locked me in this cell, I went over every inch of it in search of a way to escape. I checked every brick, and I discovered that one of the bricks moved. When I slid it out, I found the book. The book contains a message written in the front cover by the last Prophet of the Khoum. He described his kidnapping. Sadly, he wrote that if he died in this cell, he didn't want the book to fall into the wrong hands. So he hid it behind the brick. I began to study the book and to engage in the practices of mystical thought. I'm no enchanter, but I have learned mind and body control and I have gained knowledge of certain spiritual practices. One night, I entered the dreams of Sissrath in the form of the High Shaman of Khoum. Scared the living daylights out of him." Reggie chuckled at the memory. "It was one of my better moments. They have been few and far between."

"It didn't take Sissrath long to figure it out. He almost took the book from me," Reggie continued. "But Sissrath doesn't know how to use the Mystical Book and it refuses to open to his commands. I suddenly became extremely useful to him. So we started playing what I think of as 'The Game'. He would need an answer and I would negotiate for comforts. That is how I happen to have such a lovely den here in this dungeon. We have had many stalemates over the years. Certain things I refused to tell him. Certain things he refused to do for me. But I have survived. This book saved my life. I regret that I could not find a way to free myself and return to my children. I have clung to my faith that one day I would see my children again." Tears shone in Reggie's eyes. "Today is that day. Sonjay stands before me. And I have faith that I will see the others one day too."

"It could happen," Sonjay agreed. "We got separated during the passage into Faracadar, but I bet they're in the land somewhere. If we can escape from this cell, I think we'll find them before long."

"Escape from this cell? I speak from experience when I say that's not easy," Reggie warned.

"We almost just rescued you. Escape is easier now because Sissrath's Special Forces have gone with Compost to blockade Big House City and Sissrath has made the glorious mistake of leaving these foolish Corportons in charge here at the Final Fortress. They don't have the power of enchantment," Crumpet said.

"Neither do you," Reggie responded.

Crumpet puffed his chest out and blustered, "I may not be the most consistent enchanter. I admit that I lose control when I get angry. But most of the time I manage rather well."

"You misunderstand," Reggie explained. "I wasn't commenting on your competence as an enchanter. I was referring to the fact that Sissrath has woven enchantments throughout these dungeons to prevent enchanters from using their powers inside the confines of these prison cells."

"We don't necessarily need enchantments to escape. We need ingenuity, courage, and luck," Sonjay insisted.

"What he said!" Buttercup agreed enthusiastically. "And Sonjay, while we think about an escape plan, you can make good use of your time by working on your training. How about the first lesson?"

Sonjay grinned as he sat down on the rug, crossed his legs, and gave Buttercup his full attention. "Bring it."

"OK. First, clear your mind of all thoughts," Buttercup instructed.

"What? That's impossible," Sonjay complained.

"He has a point, you know. It's the nature of the human mind to be active," Reggie reminded Buttercup.

"It would surprise you to discover how clear a mind can get when you begin sweeping it of clutter," Buttercup said firmly. "Thoughts will drift in, but do this: examine each thought, make a note of it, and let it pass through. Try not to attach any feeling to it. Just say to yourself 'yes, well, I am thinking about a peanut butter sandwich and now that thought is passing through and now it is drifting away and now it's gone' and then notice what thought comes next and let it pass through. To calm your mind, focus on your breathing. Listen to your breathing, feel the breath going in and out, and let your mind rest upon it."

"This sounds like meditation," Reggie noted.

"Correct. We enchanters think of it as freeing the mind of clutter in preparation for inviting in the energy that provides the raw material for enchantment," Buttercup explained.

"To function as an enchanter," Crumpet added, "you have to learn how to unclutter the mind and tap into the energy instantly; tapping the energy has to become second nature, automatic. I run into trouble because I can't set aside my emotions and I can't clear out my anger. If I could learn to clear out anger at my command, then I would never turn into a cinnamon roll again," he concluded with a slightly mournful edge to his words.

"Well then I don't understand how Sissrath became such a powerful enchanter when he's so angry and vengeful," Sonjay responded.

"That's not true anger or vengeance you see in him," Crumpet explained. "He has no feelings. He is cerebral and calculating. He is reptilian. He has even forgotten why he seeks absolute power. He is empty."

"He has no humanity," Buttercup said. "And he has created an inner space for himself that is inhabited by negative energy."

Reggie put his hand on Sonjay's shoulder and said, "Sissrath has lost track of love. He deserves our pity, not our hatred. Now focus on your lesson here. Try to clear your mind. I'll do it with you." Reggie sat on the carpet next to his son and concentrated on his breathing.

Sonjay closed his eyes and attempted to think nothing. He listened to his breath. Then he felt the rush of feathers as Bayard Rustin perched on his head. He reached up and patted the bird. "How can I unclutter my mind with a bird on my head?" He opened his eyes and laughed.

"Even better," Buttercup told him. "If you can free your mind of clutter with a bird on your head then you can do it in most any situation. Some enchanters choose a word they use to trigger their preparation. They train themselves to say a word that causes them to instantly prepare their mind for enchantment."

"Do you have a trigger word?" Sonjay asked curiously.

"Of course," Buttercup answered.

"What is it?"

"It's private. I don't tell it to anyone."

Sonjay stroked Bayard and decided that his trigger word would be "feathers." The word made him think of weightlessness and flying and, of course, the crazy parrot he loved. "How do I use my trigger word?"

"You repeat the word over and over in your mind as you try to prepare to empty yourself of thoughts and emotions and allow the energy from which enchantments are made to enter into you," Buttercup instructed.

"What exactly is that energy?" Sonjay asked.

To his surprise, his father answered before either of the enchanters in the room could say a word. "Spirit," Reggie said softly. "Everything seen and unseen, living and dead, in this plane and in those planes of existence outside of our grasp, has spirit. All living things have spirit and all inanimate objects carry a residue of spirit. Spirit is a force of energy with an impact. Each person has their own relationship to spirit. There you have the teaching of the Mystical Book in a nutshell. You have to find your own unique spiritual core and your spiritual channels."

"Precisely," Buttercup agreed approvingly. "I could not have stated it better than the Prophet."

It surprised Sonjay when Buttercup referred to his father as "the Prophet." He would have to get used to having a father with valuable powers. He would have to get used to having a father at all.

Chapter Eight
Sense of Direction

Jasper, Jack, and Doshmisi rode into the Passage Circle at dusk. The previous year, Sissrath's Special Forces had burned the Passage Circle nearly to the ground. As Doshmisi gazed around in amazement, she saw how much of the circle the people had rebuilt in only one year. Her sister Maia's buddies, the drummers, had begun to assemble in the central plaza for an evening of drumming. Several of them rushed over to greet Doshmisi as she rode in on her tiger. They immediately asked about Maia and Doshmisi was sorry to disappoint them when she told them that Maia had not come with her. "She's in Faracadar somewhere," she said, optimistically, "so you'll probably hook up with her before long." Thinking about the botched passage worried her. Had Maia and the others really made the passage?

The drummers smiled and tossed their heads so that their long dreadlocks or long braids (whichever they sported) bopped and popped about. "We'll drum in her honor tonight and perhaps that will bring her closer to us," one of them said.

"I feel certain it will," Doshmisi agreed. The drummer's words comforted her. After speaking with the drummers, she turned to follow Jasper and Jack through the plaza and toward the side of town nearest to the beaches, where their friends Ginger and Cinnamon lived. Ginger and Cinnamon and their many daughters had once had a large, beautiful house with a spectacular view of the ocean. But the fire had destroyed it. In eager anticipation, Doshmisi rode up the hill to where the house used to stand. She hoped to see it rebuilt, like so many of the other houses she had passed. To her delight, she discovered a periwinkle-blue house with coffee-brown trim in the exact same location. It was not as big as its predecessor, and the plants in the yard were small compared to the mature flowering shrubs and large sage and rosemary that had grown there before the fire. The fig tree had survived and it greeted her with an abundance of lovely new leaves.

Doshmisi hopped off her tiger and bounded to the door, where she knocked twice before opening it and calling, "Ginger! Cinnamon! Anyone home?"

Cinnamon appeared in the kitchen doorway at the end of the hall. She wore a pair of sturdy overalls and she wiped her hands on a towel. Her face lit up at the sight of Doshmisi and she called to her family to come see who had arrived as she ran to embrace her friend. Doshmisi and Cinnamon laughed with pleasure.

"You rebuilt it so fast," Doshmisi remarked.

"Well, we had many hands applied to the task," Cinnamon explained. "And of course our men came home when you freed them from the prison at Big House City. Although Ginger and I have still not decided yet whether the help they provide outweighs the extra work they create for us," Cinnamon joked.

"Hey, hey," Cinnamon's husband boomed behind her, "none of that slander. You missed me when I was gone. Admit it. You know you did." He gave Doshmisi a hug, shook hands with Jasper, and then put his arm around his wife's waist affectionately.

Doshmisi smiled at the sight of the two of them together. They had spent many years apart while Sissrath imprisoned Cinnamon's husband for resisting the enchanter's rule. "Where's Ginger?" she asked. "And the girls?"

"The girls went to the plaza for the drumming," Cinnamon's husband replied.

"And Ginger isn't feeling well," Cinnamon informed her.

"What's the matter? Maybe I can help," Doshmisi offered.

"She went to lay down in her room. Come, I'll give you the grand tour of our new house and take you to see her," Cinnamon said.

"How about some chocolate ice cream for the intuit?" Cinnamon's husband suggested to Jack, with a twinkle in his eye.

Jack bobbed up and down in the air energetically and echoed gleefully, "Chocolate, chocolate, chocolate."

"Maybe some for the guide too?" Jasper asked.

"I think that can be arranged," Cinnamon's husband agreed with a chuckle.

"I'll go settle the tigers and then I'll be right back," Jasper said.

Doshmisi followed Cinnamon upstairs. The previous house, before it burned, had been considerably larger, with an open center and a balcony that went all the way around the inside of the second floor. This house had no such thing. The stairs led to a second floor hallway. Cinnamon went to the first room on the left and knocked on the door, which she then opened a crack as she said, "You'll never guess who just arrived. Doshmisi. She travels with Jasper and the intuit. Can we come in?"

A rustle of clothing and bedding whispered inside the room and then Ginger replied, "Yes, come on in."

Doshmisi followed Cinnamon into the bedroom. The sun had set and night was falling quickly. Through the open window, Doshmisi could hear the waves washing on the beach in the distance. She loved Ginger and Cinnamon's house. Both the old one and now the new one. They had the sort of house that felt cozy and safe, the sort of house that you could lean into softly and rest for days, dozing in bed, reading, eating soup, and not worrying about Sissrath plotting to ruin people's lives and hurt whales.

Doshmisi held her hands out to her friend. "Ginger, what's wrong? I have the herbal with me." Even as she said these words, Doshmisi could feel the anxiety mounting within her as she wondered if the herbal would behave properly or do something strange and puzzling again instead.

Ginger took Doshmisi's hands in hers happily. Her eyes sparkled and she didn't appear sick. "I feel ridiculous," Ginger told Doshmisi. "I have some foolish kind of rash on my stomach. I can't tell if it's an infection or an allergic reaction to something or a symptom of something else. I've been taking a homeopathic remedy to keep it from itching. I had planned to see a healer tomorrow because it won't go away. My skin is so sensitive that I don't like to cover it so I've been up here by myself with my belly bare, trying to get some relief."

"Well, let's see what the herbal says." Doshmisi unbuckled the front of the carry case and removed the enchanted book. As she lifted the herbal, she tried not to register her anxiety in her face or her movements, even though she wondered what the herbal would do when she tried to use it. "Do you mind if I have a look at the rash?" she asked.

Ginger peeled back the blankets and lifted her shirt. Angry whitish-yellow bumps covered her stomach. Doshmisi recognized the rash. She had seen one like it the previous year when she worked in the clinic behind Ginger and Cinnamon's house. She remembered what the herbal had said to do about it, thank goodness, because if the herbal misbehaved then she could still treat Ginger. But she wanted to see what the herbal would say if she tried to use it. So she placed it on Ginger's chest and waited for it to open.

Doshmisi felt a rush of relief when the herbal actually opened to a page like it was supposed to do. She took a rubber band from her pocket and put it around the book to hold her place. Then she read the page and her heart sank. Only a few sentences of information appeared on the page and they had nothing whatsoever to do with Ginger's rash. The herbal read: THERE ONCE WAS A LAND FUELED BY OIL. THE PEOPLE OF THE LAND

FAILED TO THINK AHEAD. THEY RESISTED EVOLUTION. WHEN THEIR OIL STARTED TO RUN OUT, THEY KILLED EACH OTHER TO POSSESS MORE OF THE REMAINS. THEY FAILED TO SEEK NEW WAYS OR TO BUILD NEW PARADIGMS. THEY WERE NOT ADAPTABLE LIKE THE INSECTS. INSECTS SURVIVE. THE PEOPLE WILL VANISH AND INSECTS WILL INHERIT THE LAND. COCKROACHES ARE ADAPTABLE. THEY LIKE TO EAT GREASE, BUT IF NO GREASE PRESENTS ITSELF, THEN COCKROACHES WILL EAT SOMETHING ELSE.

That was all it said on the page that opened for Doshmisi and she could not force the book to turn to the next page. She closed it gently and hoped that the rubber band would hold her place and allow her to study the page more carefully later. The herbal was transforming itself, but what was it transforming itself into? Ginger sensed Doshmisi's alarm caused by the mysterious story in the book, but she mistook it for alarm at the problem of the rash.

"Is it dangerous?" Ginger asked anxiously.

"It's nothing serious, is it?" Cinnamon chimed in.

"No, no," Doshmisi responded. "It's not serious. It's kind of icky, though. It's not an infection or an allergy. It's a fungus. You can make it go away by creating a hostile environment that kills it off. I'll write down the recipe for a paste that you must spread on your stomach for the next few days."

"A fungus?!" Ginger repeated in horror, as she wrinkled her nose. "Ewww. How did I get something as disgusting as that?"

"Probably from the garden," Doshmisi told her. She knew that Ginger spent long hours working in the fields and gardens. "It might have happened if you were lying on your stomach in the dirt. It'll go away fast with the paste. I saw the same ailment on several gardeners here last year. It's actually pretty common."

"Come, let's go mix up the paste so Ginger can start getting better," Cinnamon suggested. "I'll be back soon," she assured her sister as she headed toward the door.

Doshmisi stood, replaced the herbal in the carry case, and followed Cinnamon from the room. She joined Jasper and Jack in the kitchen, where Jack had his head buried in a bowl of ice cream. She was distracted by her concern about the bizarre story appearing in the herbal. She didn't want to talk about it, though, so she forced herself to behave as normally as possible.

"Do you think it wise to feed an intuit chocolate right before bed?" Doshmisi asked Cinnamon's husband. He laughed and replied, "He might be an intuit, but he's also a little boy and he deserves the opportunity to be a child now and then."

Doshmisi agreed with that. Intuits didn't often get to play and have fun like other children, and they burned with an intense energy that burned their life right up at a young age. Sonjay and Denzel had made skateboards for some of the intuits, including Jack, the previous year. As it turned out, when intuits stood on skateboards they turned into hoverboards and intuits, especially Jack, were exceptional skaters (or hoverers, as it were).

"So where are you headed?" Cinnamon asked Doshmisi and Jasper.

"To the North Coast," Jasper informed her. "Sissrath has something going on up there and we want to find out what exactly that is."

"We heard that he sent Compost and an army to lay siege to Big House City," Cinnamon's husband said. "I've considered getting together a group to ride over there to see what we can do about it. But I couldn't get a message through to the Crystal Communication Dome. Do you know what happened at the Dome?"

"We came through the Dome Circle on our way here," Jasper replied. "Sissrath's Special Forces shut the Dome down. He left them there to guard it and they have terrorized the people of the circle, killing some of them. They have a lethal weapon."

"The weapon is called a gun. We have guns in the Farland," Doshmisi chimed in. "The guns shoot a metal bullet that can kill or wound a person instantly. I don't think you should ride to Big House City or the Dome until we figure out why Sissrath went to the North Coast and what he has concealed there."

"Doshmisi thinks he created the siege to distract everyone from this project of his at the North Coast," Jasper added. "We intend to ride up there first thing in the morning."

"In that case, you could use a good night's sleep," Cinnamon suggested and Doshmisi suddenly realized that she was indeed exhausted from the long day of travel. She wrote out the recipe and directions for the paste for Ginger's rash and then followed Cinnamon to a guest room where she collapsed into a cozy bed and fell into a deep sleep.

In the morning, before joining the others, Doshmisi remembered that she had marked that page in the herbal. She pulled the book into her lap and opened it to the page cinched by the rubber band. The words from the previous night had disappeared. The only word on the page was ADAPTABILITY. She had barely read the word when the rubber band broke and the book snapped shut. "Stubborn book," she muttered in frustration as she placed it back in the carry case, gathered her belongings, and set out to find Jasper.

After a breakfast of scrambled eggs, toast, and sweet melon, Doshmisi, Jasper, and Jack took their leave of their friends in the Passage Circle and got back on the road. Doshmisi suggested that they ride north along the beach, but Jasper vetoed that idea. He said riding on the beach would leave them too exposed. He took them instead on a route further inland that followed the shoreline while remaining under the cover of trees. The trees whispered to Doshmisi and made her feel optimistic about getting to the bottom of things at the North Coast. The three travelers rode hard all day. By evening, they had arrived well within the boundaries of the North Coast region, but they had no idea where to look for Sissrath and his encampment.

"We need to find shelter for the night," Jasper said, as he rode alongside Doshmisi.

"Can we camp in this forest?" she asked.

"An enemy could see us here too easily. I want to find a cave or a structure or something that will hide us," Jasper replied. Suddenly he drew up his tiger abruptly. "Stop," he ordered. "Stay completely still."

Doshmisi obeyed. In the distance, through the trees, she saw what Jasper saw. A small group of human-type figures rode between the trees on horses. The sight of the horses made the hair on the back of Doshmisi's neck stand up because there were no horses in Faracadar, where people rode tigers instead. The sight of the horses, entirely out of place, frightened her. Jack whimpered. Jasper, who had never seen a horse, turned to her wide-eyed.

"Horses," Doshmisi whispered to Jasper and Jack. "We have them in the Farland."

The appearance of the riders disturbed Doshmisi even more than the appearance of the horses they rode. The riders resembled people. They had a head, two arms, and two legs, but from head to toe they wore white jumpsuits that hid every part of their real selves. They wore white gloves, helmet-like head coverings, and gray face masks. They carried some type of guns. Doshmisi wondered if the creatures were slimy or perhaps misshapen under their white jumpsuits. Maybe they had no solid substance to them, like light or water, and the jumpsuits contained them. Or maybe the jumpsuits concealed a hideous form that she could not imagine. She thought of them as aliens.

Doshmisi, Jasper, and Jack remained hidden in the undergrowth and as still as stone until the creatures on the horses passed by and disappeared in the distance. Jasper pointed after them. At first Doshmisi didn't see what Jasper saw; but then, as her eyes adjusted to the rapidly increasing darkness of night falling, she identified a clearing ahead and in it the outlines of a series of large, barn-like structures. The creatures rode past the barns and into the forest beyond without stopping.

The travelers quietly dismounted from their tigers and left them in a thicket on the edge of the clearing where they could graze on greens and pass the night concealed from sight. Watching for the figures-in-white, they cautiously crept inside the first barn they came upon. Large and empty of all activity, it contained heaps of hay, which would make it a comfortable place to bed down for the night. Jasper took a glow-lamp from his bag. He handed it to Doshmisi, who held it up as she wandered to the back of the barn. She opened the door to a stall and found herself face-to-face with a large chestnut stallion. The stallion snorted through his nostrils loudly. Doshmisi heard Jack cry out in alarm. The stallion tossed his midnight-black mane and whinnied.

Doshmisi murmured in awe, "You are the most handsome horse I have ever laid eyes on."

The stallion emanated a wild energy that made Doshmisi's breath quicken. She felt around in her bag and found an apple. She bit off a large chunk and spit it out into her palm, then offered it to the stallion as a gift. He sniffed the apple and then picked it up delicately with his large lips and ate it. Doshmisi repeated this again and again until she had fed the whole apple to the stallion. Then she tentatively patted his nose. He nuzzled her. "Such a beauty," Doshmisi cooed. "Can we be friends?" She stroked his long neck and buried her face in his mane. He smelled like sweet alfalfa. His presence comforted her.

"It's OK," Doshmisi called softly to Jack and Jasper. "There's a horse in here. He's magnificent. I've befriended him. I know all about horses because Aunt Alice has horses at Manzanita Ranch. I've taken care of them and ridden them. He won't hurt you. Come see. In the Farland people ride horses the way you ride tigers here."

Jack and Jasper peered cautiously into the stall, where Doshmisi continued to stroke the stallion and talk to him. "I don't know your name," Doshmisi said to the stallion, "so I'm going to call you Dagobaz if that's OK with you. I read about a horse named Dagobaz in a book once. The Dagobaz in the book could only be ridden by one who tamed him." The horse nodded his head and snorted, as if in approval. Doshmisi crooned the name Dagobaz lovingly to the stallion.

She would have stayed with Dagobaz, but Jasper insisted that she come out and have something to eat with him and Jack. They ate sandwiches that Cinnamon had packed for them at the Passage Circle, which seemed years in the past even though it had only been that morning. Then they took out their bedrolls.

"I'm going to sleep in the stall with Dagobaz," Doshmisi informed the others.

"Is that safe?" Jasper asked worriedly.

"It's fine. That horse and I have a connection, a sort of understanding," she attempted to explain. "Kind of like the connection I have with the whales and the trees."

"If you say so," Jasper replied, although he still looked a little worried. "If you need us, Jack and I will be in that stall across the way."

"Sounds good," Doshmisi said. She took her bedroll into Dagobaz's stall and rested her cheek against his neck. She stroked his side and his back and ran her hand down the front of each of his front legs. He nuzzled her. Her amulet began to glow green.

"What is it?" she asked him. "Why do I feel like I know you so well?"

Dagobaz tossed his head and folded himself down into the hay. Doshmisi stretched out beside him. She rested her head on his side and pulled her bedroll over her like a blanket. Dagobaz nudged her glowing amulet with his nose and then snorted at the ceiling. She soon fell asleep with a smile on her face.

In the morning, Dagobaz woke Doshmisi at sunrise when he stood up and visited his water trough for a cool drink. Doshmisi, Jasper, and Jack shared half a loaf of bread with cheese and prepared to depart.

"Don't worry, I'll come back for you," Doshmisi promised Dagobaz as she sadly took her leave. She needed that stallion and he needed her. They were meant for each other; she could feel it in her blood.

Jasper found the tigers, well-rested and safe. They decided to leave the tigers where they were and proceeded with caution on foot toward the ocean, which was so near to them that they could smell the salt water on the air. They did not walk far before they reached a vista point from which the ocean spread out before them sparkling like diamonds in the mauve-tinted morning light.

As she took in the panoramic view, Doshmisi's gaze fell abruptly on the incongruous sight of a frighteningly enormous metal oil derrick pumping up and down less than a half a mile out from the shoreline. Several boats bobbed between the beach and the oil well, coming and going from the site.

Jasper pointed to a place up from the beach and said, "Look there."

Where he pointed, Doshmisi saw an open area carved out of the trees and the undergrowth, about a quarter of a mile up from the sandy beach. She saw several low buildings and what appeared to be a compound full of people, like a large outdoor pen. Smoke from cooking fires rose in thin ribbons from the compound.

"Let's investigate," Jasper said.

"Hostages," Jack stated.

"Really Jack? That does not sound good," Doshmisi responded.

"Stay alert. We can't let ourselves be caught," Jasper ordered.

Doshmisi knew from painful personal experience that avoiding capture was easier said than done.

Chapter Nine
Snared in a Net

After an excellent breakfast at the Wolf Circle, the travelers assembled in front of the community dining room to meet the tigers they would ride. Goldenrod provided four sleek yellow-and-black-striped tigers. "I figure the geebaching can ride with one of you," Goldenrod noted. Guhblorin looked crestfallen until Elena put her hand on his shoulder and told him, "I want you to ride with me, *amigo*." He perked up at her words.

The princess gently stroked a large white wolf as tears stood in her eyes. She was famous throughout the land for her love of animals and this wolf obviously held a special place in her heart. He bumped her with his head and whined softly. "I'll be back before you know it," Honeydew promised the wolf.

"They're splendid," Denzel declared appreciatively, as he stroked the tiger he had selected to ride. "Thanks a million," he said to Goldenrod.

Maia produced a jar of powder from her backpack. "I think we should use the color change powder. I wonder if it will work on Elena."

"Color change powder?" Elena inquired with a note of curiosity in her voice. "*Qué es?*"

"You see how the people here have a bright color that glows in their skin?" Maia asked her friend. Elena glanced at Goldenrod, who glowed bright yellow. "Well royalty doesn't have that color glow and it makes us stand out, which is a problem when we want to keep a low profile," Maia explained. "Anyone can recognize Denzel, Honeydew, and me as royals because we don't have a bright color in our skin. Grandmomma Clover made this powder for us. One tiny sprinkle and we have color like everyone else so we can blend in better. Watch," Maia concluded. She sprinkled powder on Denzel, whose skin immediately took on a bright-red glow. Denzel grinned and took a pinch of powder and sprinkled it on Maia, who developed a deep-blue glow. Then he dropped a pinch on Honeydew, who glowed sunflower-yellow.

"Now your turn," Maia told Elena.

Elena began to protest, but Maia ignored her and quickly sprinkled the powder on her before Elena could mount a full resistance. For a moment, nothing happened, and Maia thought perhaps the powder wouldn't work on a Latina from the Farland. But then Elena sparkled with a shimmery orange color. She giggled.

"You like it?" Guhblorin asked.

"Kinda weird, but I like it OK," Elena replied.

Denzel scrutinized her. "I think it looks pretty good." Elena blushed a deeper shade of orange, but Denzel didn't notice since he had turned and mounted his tiger. "Let's get on up outta here," he called to the others, who each mounted their tigers. The enormous white wolf remained at Honeydew's heel.

"Stay here," Honeydew told the wolf, who looked up at her with sorrowful eyes.

The travelers rode out of the circle.

"We go this way." Honeydew pointed to a path that led through a stand of fir trees. As the travelers started on the path, they heard Honeydew shout, "Biscuit!"

Denzel motioned his tiger to stop and he turned around to see why Honeydew had shouted. The large white wolf had followed them and it stood beside Honeydew.

"Oh no, Bisc, please go back." Honeydew remembered the year before when her father had foolishly called his white wolves to their aid and Sissrath's Special Forces had killed many of them.

"It might come in handy to have a white wolf as a traveling companion," Denzel pointed out, hopefully.

"I don't want to put his life in danger," Honeydew responded.

"He looks capable of taking care of himself," Elena noted. The wolves still made her nervous, even though she understood that the people of the Wolf Circle kept them as pets. "He looks a lot fiercer than we do."

"Let him come with us," Maia pleaded. "He wants to. He won't be in any more danger than we will."

"That doesn't set my mind at ease," Honeydew replied, but she relented. "His name is Biscuit," she told the others. "But I call him Bisc for short."

"What kind of a name is that for a wolf?" Denzel asked.

"How would you know the right kind of name for a wolf?" Honeydew demanded indignantly. "I raised him from a pup and when he was little he stole my biscuits off my plate. He would do anything for a biscuit, especially if it has raspberry jam on it. It's the perfect name for him."

Denzel shrugged as he headed down the path and into the fir trees. Bisc trotted happily alongside Honeydew. He stood as tall as her tiger and in fact Honeydew could have sat on his back, but no one would dare to insult a white wolf by suggesting that they ride it.

The group of travelers hiked all day over the Amber Mountains, with Honeydew guiding them. They eventually had to dismount from the tigers because of the rocks and rough scrub that filled the landscape. They wound up walking for much of the time and were so weary by nightfall that they ate their dinner quickly with little conversation and went straight to sleep after dividing the night into shifts during which each of them took a spell keeping watch.

They awoke refreshed and anticipated finding Guhblorin's smelly passage soon. He promised that it would cut a whole day off their overland journey. They chatted cheerily over their breakfast of pears and cheese.

As they set off, Guhblorin pointed the way to the passage, and by late morning they reached the opening leading into the mountain. The travelers peered cautiously inside as they caught a whiff of a scent far worse than just old seaweed. It smelled like a fish left outside in the sun in a paper bag for a week. Elena and Honeydew cast anxious glances at the others to see if anyone else found the smell as offensive as they did. Meanwhile, Denzel produced a canvas bag and withdrew from it a stack of sachets filled with orange peels, cinnamon sticks, and cloves. He handed them out to the others. "Hold this under your nose to help get through the tunnel." The tigers didn't seem bothered by the strong fishy smell and Bisc appeared to love it as he ran in joyous circles and yipped. Once they entered the mountain, Bisc stopped every once in a while to roll around on his back, as if trying to absorb the stinky smell into his fur. He poked his nose into every nook and cranny, obviously delighted to sniff the repulsive aroma.

Fortunately, it took less than an hour for the travelers to make their way through the mountain. The foul odor wasn't unbearable and the scented sachets helped considerably. Denzel couldn't wait to share the knowledge of the smelly passage with Jasper, who would appreciate the significance of it to shave time off the journey from the Wolf Circle to Big House City. The group emerged amid scrubby brush and large gray boulders in the foothills of the Amber Mountains. They found themselves on the edge of a meadow that melted into rolling hills covered with low brush and heather-like plants bursting with tiny pink flowers. On the other side of the hills lay Big House City and its surrounding fields and forests.

"We're going home," Honeydew told Bisc, as she reached over to pat his neck. "This way," she instructed the others, who followed her as she rode out. She knew the route, having traveled back and forth between Big House City and the Amber Mountains many times. The travelers rode for a couple of hours before stopping to eat the lunch that the people of the Wolf Circle had provided them for the journey. While they ate, a flock of skeeters arrived and circled above their heads. Denzel quickly examined his surroundings for a place to hide, but could find nothing in the landscape large enough to conceal them from the sharp yellow eyes of the birds, those eyes that didn't miss a single detail. They gazed up at the skeeters in grim silence.

"What are they?" Elena asked, watching the skeeters swoop menacingly.

"A nasty bird with terrific eyesight that does scouting for Compost and Sissrath," Maia answered.

"What kind of a name is Compost?" Elena asked.

"Definitely not a geebaching," Guhblorin said.

"Not Latino, either," Elena added, with a giggle.

"Maybe a used salad," Guhblorin suggested brightly. Elena laughed out loud.

Denzel glared at the geebaching, who mumbled an apology as he buried his face in his sandwich. "Don't get him started, Elena," Denzel cautioned.

"It's the perfect name for a stinky person," Maia answered Elena's question. "Trust me, you don't want to meet him. He makes the smelly tunnel look like a stroll in a rose garden."

"Do you think the skeeters will report us?" Honeydew asked the others.

"Yeah, I do, but we can't do much about it," Denzel said. "They've already seen us. Look around. No boulders or trees or anything we could have hid behind." The travelers packed up their lunch and rode out. The skeeters had disappeared and Denzel felt relieved that at least the nasty birds hadn't taken to following them.

Late in the afternoon, as they began to near the outskirts of Big House City, they came upon a puzzling sight. In the distance they saw a large grayish wall blocking their path. They approached with caution. Surrounded by sparse, slender trees and low-growing plants, the landscape still provided nothing behind which to conceal themselves from watchful eyes. They had no choice but to press forward in plain sight.

Guhblorin wrinkled his nose. "What's that funky smell?" he asked.

"Don't start," Denzel warned.

"Seriously," Guhblorin said, without a hint of humor in his voice.

"He's right," Honeydew agreed. "Something smells bad. Not as bad as the smelly tunnel, but icky." Just as she said it, the others began to smell it too. It smelled like bad broccoli and old milk cartons.

When they drew closer to the grayish wall, Elena gasped.

"What?" Maia asked.

"*Basura*," Elena said softly.

"Garbage?" Maia translated, incredulously. She had been studying Spanish in school and she practiced speaking it when she went to Elena's house, where Elena's family spoke Spanish to each other. Practicing with Elena's family had helped her pick up the language quickly. She knew that *basura* meant garbage, but she wondered why Elena had said it.

Elena pointed at the grayish wall. "That thing's made out of trash."

Maia peered more closely at the grayish wall and realized that Elena was correct. The pile of garbage rose before them, twice as tall as a grown man, and extended for quite a distance from left to right across their path. The tigers came up short as the travelers gazed at the wall of garbage. Maia wondered how deep the wall was. Perhaps they were seeing the edge of a huge mound of garbage.

"Maybe it's a dump," Maia suggested.

"You mean a landfill? But Big House City doesn't use a dump," Denzel informed her. "They don't put their garbage into a landfill. I can't imagine how this garbage got here, or why it got here, for that matter."

As they gazed at the wall of garbage, a huge mass, like a black cloud, rose up over the wall and into their line of vision. The sky darkened as the mass moved in their direction. Denzel did not care to wait around for it to catch up with them. "Run back toward those trees!" he yelled, and the tigers turned swiftly and bounded back in the direction from which they had come. However, even though swift, the tigers could not outrun the approaching mass, which, as it neared, materialized into an inconceivably huge flock of skeeters with glittering black wings. The skeeters appeared strung together by something they carried in their sharp talons.

If the travelers had split up, then perhaps one of them would have escaped, but they remained bunched together as they fled. The skeeters swooped low and Denzel felt a weight drop on him. Crushed between his collapsed tiger, who sprawled beneath him, and the weight on top of him that pressed him down, he could barely breathe. His lungs felt as thin as paper and they refused to fill with air. The tigers howled. With great difficulty, Denzel struggled to dismount his tiger, whose legs had buckled when the large cat had been pinned to the ground. Denzel slid alongside the tiger, which relieved him of some of the weight, and, as he gasped for air, he realized that the army of skeeters had dropped a thick net on them from above.

"Get off your tiger and lie down next to it," he called to the others. "They dropped a net on us. If you can relieve the pressure of the net, you'll find it easier to breathe." A few moments later, he could tell that the others had followed his directions because he heard Guhblorin hollering in terror and Elena crying, which they could not have done if they hadn't filled their lungs with air.

"Honeydew? Maia?" Denzel shouted over the racket of the howling tigers, screaming geebaching, and Elena's wails. "Are you there?" Honeydew answered from surprisingly close to him, but Denzel couldn't see her and he could barely move with the weight of the heavy net holding him in place.

Over the din, he heard Maia pleading with Elena, "Hey, *chica*, get it together. And make Guhblorin shut up. Calm your tiger. We're under a net and we have to get out before Sissrath or the Special Forces show up to capture us. I can't hear Denzel over this racket."

"How do I calm my tiger?" Elena sobbed.

"Stroke her neck and talk gently in her ear," Honeydew instructed.

Elena's sobs became subdued while Guhblorin's panicked hollering died down to a low whimpering.

"I have a knife in my backpack and I think I can cut through this net with it, but I'm having trouble getting to the knife," Denzel informed the others. The heavy net pressed down on him so hard that Denzel could barely move. He noticed that the skeeters circled in a giant swarm overhead. They blotted out much of the daylight and caused a darkness that resembled that of an approaching rainstorm.

"I see them coming," Honeydew called to Denzel.

"Who?" he asked urgently. "Who's coming?"

"Look to the edge of the garbage wall. Whoever trapped us is coming," she elaborated with grim resignation. Within moments of Honeydew's warning, she, Denzel, and Maia figured out who had caught them in the net. Even stronger than the nasty smell of the garbage wall was the familiar decomposing-vegetable-smell of Compost, Sissrath's second-in-command.

Denzel frantically tried to get his hands on the knife in his backpack, but even as he struggled to reach the knife, he realized that he could not escape Compost, who was nearly upon them, accompanied by a phalanx of Sissrath's loyal Special Forces, the fierce warriors from the Mountain Downs.

Their captors pulled up short at the edge of the net. Compost was the filthiest character Denzel and Maia had ever met. He had nappy uncombed hair, a film of grime covered his skin, and his fat belly hung over the top of his pants and wiggled when he released his sinister laugh. His brown skin had a yellowish tint to it, like the skin of all the Mountain People, but Compost's skin was a sickly acid-yellow color that looked nothing like the healthy golden-yellow glow of the people who came from the Wolf Circle in the High Mountain Settlement. Elena and Guhblorin peered out from underneath the net in fascinated horror.

"So nice of you to drop in," Compost rasped gleefully. "I figured the Four would turn up right about now to save the day. Too bad, not going to happen this time." A pair of boots clomped over the thick netting and came to a standstill in front of Denzel's face. Then a gloved hand placed a foul-smelling rag over Denzel's nose and he slipped into unconsciousness.

Chapter Ten
North Coast

Jasper crept silently through the undergrowth and toward the compound with Jack floating alongside and Doshmisi stepping softly behind him. They managed to work their way around the beach and close enough to the compound for them to catch a clear glimpse of the activity inside. Crouching in a dense collection of young tree sprouts, cottonwoods, and brush, they observed. A few women and many children scurried about within the confines of the fenced area. The women spoke in small groups or tended campfires in front of the tents scattered throughout the enclosed encampment. The children ate by a campfire or played with one another in the open spaces between the tents and campfires. Many creatures in white jumpsuits, all equipped with guns of some kind, stood guard. A high fence topped with barbed wire encircled the compound. A group of women rounded up the children and herded them to a cluster of three tents. The babies and toddlers remained behind with their mothers.

"School," Jack whispered. The children had gone to some type of school for the day. These women and children apparently lived in the compound, at least for the time being.

A group of men emerged from one of the buildings adjacent to the fenced area. Under heavy guard, they marched to the beach and boarded small boats, which headed out toward the oil derrick. After that, not much happened. Doshmisi tapped Jasper's arm and whispered, "Let's go back into the forest so we can talk." Jasper turned and led them to a secluded and sheltered spot.

"Those people are being held prisoner," Jasper said.

"But don't you think it odd that their captors leave them to themselves to hold school and cook over their campfires and all that?" Doshmisi asked.

"They left the women and children to their own devices, but they took the men to that machine in the ocean," Jasper pointed out.

"I recognize that machine," Doshmisi told him. "We have them in the Farland. It's pumping oil out of the ocean floor. How can I explain it? The oil under the ocean has a powerful energy locked in it; energy that can run machines without the need for batteries. In the Farland, lots of machines run on that kind of oil. I didn't know you had that kind of oil here. But those creepy things in the white jumpsuits knew about it and they built that machine, as you call it, that oil pump, to extract the oil." She had the feeling that if she thought on it long enough and hard enough she could figure out what was going on, but so far she couldn't quite put her finger on it.

"If only we could find Mole and have a conversation with him," Jasper wished.

"How can we do that without getting caught or even killed?" Doshmisi wondered. "If we get caught then we can't help anyone trapped inside to escape." Although, even if the creepy creatures captured them, she thought, they might still figure out a way to help the others escape, but it seemed unlikely.

"I wonder if they took Mole to that oil pump to work," Jasper speculated.

"Watch," Jack commented.

"Jack's right," Jasper said as Doshmisi nodded in agreement.

The three of them spent most of the day on their bellies in the brush, watching the compound. The children came out of the school tents for lunch, then went back in. The women tended the fires, talked with one another, cared for the littlest ones, and prepared food. In the evening, the boats returned from the oil pump and the guards marched the men into the compound at sunset, where they joined the women and children for the night. The guards dispersed. As Doshmisi, Jasper, and Jack observed attentively, the fence burst into glowing orange light.

"A heat boundary," Jasper said.

"What's that?" Doshmisi asked.

"Anyone who touches that fence will burn up instantly," he explained.

"Not a wall," Jack blurted excitedly. "Not a wall."

"Not a wall?" Jasper repeated, puzzled.

"He means that you can see through it even though you can't pass through it," Doshmisi interpreted.

"Right, so that means?" Jasper scrunched his eyebrows together in concentration as he tried to understand.

"We can talk to them through it even though we can't touch it. If we can sneak down there," Doshmisi said, as she pointed toward the heat fence. "Almost all the guards have left. Couldn't we sneak down there? Like over there?" Doshmisi indicated a spot where the bushes came close to the fence.

"Sneak. Talk," Jack urged them.

They waited until the sun had set completely and then, under cover of darkness, Jasper led the way down the gentle sloping hillside to the compound and directly to the bushy area that Doshmisi had pointed out. The bushes concealed them where they squatted, close to the glowing fence, which cast a dim eerie light. No one inside the compound was near enough for them to safely call to them, but a group of children clustered around the entrance to a tent not far away. Jack picked up a round stone and threw it deftly between the wires of the fence so that it landed beside the ring of children. Several boys looked up curiously. Jack threw another stone. The boys whispered to each other anxiously. Jack threw a third stone that bounced into the fence and sizzled. Doshmisi glanced furtively along the fence line to see if any guards had noticed the sizzle. No guards saw it, but the cluster of boys did. They approached the fence cautiously.

Jasper whispered loudly, "Over here."

The faces of the boys glowed with wonder in the orange light of the fence. None of them spoke.

"We're friends," Jasper whispered. "We want to help you escape. Do you know Mole? Is he here?"

"Yes, he's here," one of the children confirmed.

"Do you think you can bring him to us without attracting attention?"

"We can do it," another child assured them determinedly.

"Tell him Jasper wants him to come to this spot without attracting notice."

"We can find him," the children promised.

"We won't go anywhere unless the guards come," Jasper told the boys. "But you mustn't stand by the fence. If the guards see you, it will cause suspicion. Go back to what you were doing." The children left the fence and while some of them continued playing as before, others faded into the encampment to find Mole.

They didn't wait long. Mole appeared soon afterward. He brought a couple of boys with him and they squatted on the ground next to the fence, pretending to play a game with stones in the dirt. Mole focused on the children and did not so much as glance in the direction of Jasper, Doshmisi, and Jack.

"What you be doin' here?" Mole asked, without looking up from the game.

"We came to find you," Doshmisi replied.

At the sound of Doshmisi's voice, Mole laughed softly, his dreadlocks quivering with his laughter. "Doshmisi," he said softly with delight. "Yah mon, that be a good thing. The Four is come back."

"It's just me right now. I mean just me here," Doshmisi told him.

"That be good enough for me for now," Mole replied.

"What's up?" Doshmisi asked. "Tell us quickly."

"We'll try to help you escape soon," Jasper added.

"Escape be tricky," Mole warned. "We have the children to consider. The Corportons took these women and children hostage…"

"Corportons?" Doshmisi asked.

"The creatures in the white jumpsuits. We call them Corportons. They kidnapped us along with the women and children. Sissrath has an agreement with them, to help them drill for the black oil under the ocean. They needed workers with skill to help them. That be us battery makers. The Corportons be clever. They force us battery makers to work because of the women and children hostages. If we don't work or we refuse to do what they tell us, they will hurt the hostages."

"Where did they come from? Why did they come here to drill for oil?" Doshmisi questioned Mole.

"They come from some other land far away where this black oil be extremely valuable. They have sophisticated tools that I have never seen. They sent out a universal search for the oil with one of their tools and it told them to come to Faracadar. So they came. They call the oil drill in the ocean the New Beginnings Well. They have a weapon that shoots a piece of metal and it can kill a person instantly. Terrible device."

"We have these weapons in the Farland. We call them guns," Doshmisi interjected.

Mole continued. "We must do as they say because we fear these guns. They plan to transport this oil to their land after they pump it from our ocean. Sometimes I imagine maybe I hear the ocean scream because it be drilled deep by that machine at the well." Mole tapped his head with his middle finger, "But that scream be in my head. Not real. One thing I tell you for sure, mon, no good can come of this."

"No good," Doshmisi echoed.

"Why is Sissrath helping them? What does he get out of it?" Jasper asked.

"Prophecy," Jack said, in his typically cryptic way. Doshmisi wished that once in a while he'd give a straight answer.

"Sissrath believes the land be destroyed soon. Be gone. The Corportons will take him away with them when they have all the oil they want. They talk about it at the well. They talk as if we battery makers be stones, not people; as if we can't hear them. They promise Sissrath power in their land because of his talent for enchantment. He will escape with them before Faracadar be destroyed," Mole informed them.

"Why does he think Faracadar will be destroyed?" Doshmisi demanded in alarm.

"Prophecy," Jack repeated.

"I don't know, mon," Mole replied.

Jasper turned to Jack. "What prophecy, Jack? Did Sissrath hear a prophecy?"

"Prophecy from Khoum," Jack stated earnestly.

"Yes, well that explains everything," Jasper announced in exasperation.

"He be what he be, mon," Mole reminded Jasper. "Don't be getting angry with Jack. I need to go before the guards notice."

"We'll come back tomorrow night. Same time. Be here," Jasper told Mole.

"I'll try, mon." Mole stood and walked back into the compound with the children.

After Mole left, the three renegades returned to the barn under cover of darkness. Doshmisi had picked a few apples earlier in the day and she cut them into pieces and fed them to Dagobaz while she pondered the information Mole had provided. Jack fell asleep instantly in the comfortable hay, exhausted from attempting to communicate his visionary thoughts and from climbing down to the compound and back.

"I keep thinking about this prophecy. Sissrath must have heard a prophecy about the destruction of the land," Jasper said, his expressive brown eyes filled with worry.

"Possibly. Tell me what you know about this Khoum," Doshmisi requested.

"They taught us about it in history class in school, but I can't remember what they said. Something about a prophet and an enchanted book. I guess I should have paid closer attention to that lesson," Jasper noted regretfully. "When I was in class, my mind wandered to the fields and forests, and the guiding skills I needed to learn."

"Tomorrow morning I'll talk to the trees," Doshmisi promised. "Oil is dangerous stuff. I wish we had Denzel here. He would know more about oil wells and drilling for oil in the ocean. It scares me. I remember times when oil spilled into the water in the Farland and it killed a lot of sea creatures as well as birds. I hope these Corportons know what they're doing out there at that New Beginnings Well. The Corportons have definitely not earned popularity points with the whales."

"We'll find a way to free Mole and the others. If the Corportons don't have the battery makers to work for them then maybe they will have to stop drilling." Jasper put his arms around Doshmisi and gave her a hug and then he kissed her lightly on the lips. She kissed him back. The kiss made her feel so good that she forgot about Mole, the New Beginnings Well, the Corportons, and pretty much everything else in the world, for a quick minute. But then Jasper released her. "G'night," he said self-consciously as he flashed her his smile, that smile that lit up his face like the sun.

"G'night," she echoed.

Jasper climbed into the hayloft with Jack and bedded down while Doshmisi curled up with Dagobaz in his stall, running her fingers through his beautiful dark mane while she thought about Mole, the Corportons, and the oil well.

Doshmisi woke early, just as the first glimmer of dawn slipped through the cracks in the barn walls. She collected her belongings and put them quietly up in the hayloft with Jasper and Jack, who slept peacefully. She slipped out to the surrounding forest and proceeded purposefully into the heart of a stand of old trees, where she sat down on the mossy, leafy forest floor.

Safe in the embrace of the trees, she unbuckled the carry case that she wore around her waist and took out the herbal. She held the enchanted book in her lap and it opened to a page. On the page she read: "FEAR OF CHANGE PREVENTS CREATIVE THOUGHT. WHEN HOPE EXPLODES, TAKE ME TO THE WATER AND START AGAIN FROM THE BEGINNING." Doshmisi sighed. The herbal had her pretty worried. It seemed broken. She used to understand what it instructed her to do, but now it made no sense.

She shut the herbal and focused on her mission in the forest. She closed her eyes and visualized her spirit dancing to the tops of the trees, where it intertwined with the tree spirits. She cherished her ability to communicate with the trees in their way as perhaps the greatest gift she had received as the keeper of the Amulet of the Trees. She rejoiced with them in the beauty of the dewy fresh morning. Nothing loves a fresh new morning like a tree.

The trees had helped her solve problems in the past, so she placed a question to them in her heart. She asked them what was wrong with the herbal and if the strange words that appeared in the herbal connected to the New Beginnings Well, the Corportons, and a prophecy. She didn't ask the question in words, but instead let the images of these things pass through her mind and out to the trees. She felt herself enveloped in the comforting embrace of the trees' spirits and her amulet glowed warmly, emanating a green light. The image of her grandmother, Clover, came to her as it had at the Garden; and Clover appeared even more unwell than before. The trees still wanted her to go see Clover. She wondered if she had made a poor choice by coming to the North Coast before attending to her grandmother. But the trees did not seem to mind her choice. They were happy to have her among them. They distinctly planted in her mind the thought that everyone was needed for some task that lie ahead. Everyone needed to come together. Then she had the reassuring feeling that the whole confusing puzzle of circumstances and events would work out in the end, that just around the corner a perfectly wonderful resolution awaited, and that she would eventually find it, like finding a star buried under the hay in a barn, uncovering its unspeakable brilliance in a shining moment of unexpected discovery.

She opened her eyes and retreated from the heart of the forest with a welcome sense of calm. Her amulet no longer glowed. She patted the trunks of trees she passed as she walked back to rejoin the others. But her calm shattered as she neared the barn. A group of Corportons had gathered in a corral in front of the barn where they were attempting to control Dagobaz. They had thrown four lassoes around his neck and he rebelled against their efforts to tame him by alternately rearing on his hind legs and then pawing frantically at the ground. He snorted and screamed in outrage.

Doshmisi couldn't bear to see him mistreated, but she didn't dare reveal herself. One of the Corportons tried to throw a saddle across the frenzied horse's back, but Dagobaz sidestepped the saddle and kicked at the Corporton. She wondered how the Corportons communicated with one another from inside the jumpsuits. They didn't speak aloud so they either talked directly into each other's brains with telepathy or they used some type of device embedded in their face masks to communicate. She wondered if they had ears.

One of the Corportons touched a metal rod to Dagobaz's hind leg. The horse shrieked in pain and leapt forward. The Corporton continued to torture Dagobaz with the charge from the metal rod as he forced the horse forward onto a ramp that led into a round vehicle resembling an enormous golf ball on wheels. Every time the Corporton touched Dagobaz with the metal rod, the horse screamed in pain and moved forward. Tears streamed down Doshmisi's cheeks as she observed helplessly from the shelter of the forest. The Corportons followed Dagobaz into the golf ball and folded up the ramp. Then the wheels folded into the golf ball and it flew into the sky where it soon disappeared over the trees.

Doshmisi sobbed after the Corportons left. Jasper and Jack emerged from the barn and hurried to her side.

"What happened?" Jasper asked as he gently pulled her to her feet and handed her a handkerchief from his pocket. Doshmisi wiped her tear-streaked cheeks and blew her nose.

"They hurt Dagobaz. I think they wanted to ride him, and that they were trying to break him. He fought them. They forced him into a flying machine by torturing him with electric shocks from a metal rod. It was horrible." Doshmisi shuddered again at the recollection. "They left in the flying thing. Were you hiding in the hayloft? "

"Yes. We heard them come and we burrowed into the straw. Luckily they didn't think to search for anyone in the barn. They came for Dagobaz," Jasper replied. "I bet they took him to the compound by the New Beginnings Well. That's their base camp. We can try to free him when go to free Mole and the others."

"That sounds great when you say it," Doshmisi told him, with a sniffle, "but we don't have a plan for how to free Mole and the others, let alone Dagobaz."

Just then, Jack hopped on his skateboard, which instantly became a hoverboard under his feet as he floated above the ground. "Diversion," Jack pronounced excitedly. "Diversion, diversion." He swooped up into the air in a loop, kicking the board out from under his feet in a flip and then deftly landing back on it perfectly.

"Someone's been practicing," Doshmisi complimented the intuit.

Jack continued to swoop through the air like a large bird until Doshmisi could grab his attention and convince him to stop swooping and listen to her. "They have guns, Jack. Real guns that shoot bullets. They can shoot you out of the air in an instant. You'll be no help to anybody dead."

Jack drooped and shook his head from side to side. "Diversion coming," he said, pointing out toward the ocean. The others ignored him and he shrugged, then popped back into the air to practice his skateboard moves.

"Mole knows the routine and how the Corportons do things at the compound," Jasper said. "Mole's resourceful and so are we. If we put our heads together, we can come up with something. We can at least get Mole out of there and then we can go back for the rest of them when we have reinforcements."

"A nonviolent march won't work against the Corportons," Doshmisi pointed out. "They come from outside of Faracadar and they would kill every last one of us within gunshot range in a heartbeat." The previous year, the Four had led a nonviolent march on Sissrath and had defeated him because the army had joined the people and turned against Sissrath. "I wish I could see what they look like under those jumpsuits," she added. "If I could see them then I might figure out if they have a weakness that would work in our favor. They seem familiar to me but I can't put my finger on why."

"After nightfall, we'll talk to Mole again. Maybe he has seen them without the jumpsuits and face masks," Jasper said hopefully.

They spent the day close to the barn. Doshmisi went into the forest searching for food and came back with mannafruit, the apricot-sized lavender globes that tasted like whatever you imagined them to taste like when you took a bite. When you ate mannafruit, you had to feel grateful for the food, or else it tasted like sawdust. The mannafruit stayed good for weeks unopened, but once opened it went bad quickly. Because they filled you up with just a few bites, they made a terrific traveling food.

Doshmisi worried all day about Dagobaz. She wished the proud stallion would bend to the will of the Corportons and allow them to tame him for the time being so that they wouldn't keep hurting him. Obviously they wanted to ride Dagobaz and he refused to allow them to do it. "They can't tame you in your heart," she whispered to Dagobaz, even though he could not hear her.

At twilight, Jasper, Doshmisi, and Jack once again went down to the compound. Doshmisi insisted that Jack wait at the edge of the forest and not come with them to the fence. She worried that he might try to do something crazy that would get him killed. He reluctantly agreed to remain behind while Jasper and Doshmisi crept into the undergrowth near the fence where they had talked to Mole the night before. Orange and pink light from the setting sun lit the clouds drifting over the ocean. The clouds slightly obscured the abundance of bright colorful stars that dotted the night sky. In a few minutes, only the light from the stars would remain visible as the sun's rays faded completely.

Doshmisi saw Mole playing a jump rope game with a group of children. He and a woman turned a long rope while little girls chanted a rhyme and jumped together in rhythm. A few other children stood nearby and clapped to the rhyme. As she watched, the girls stopped jumping and Mole coiled up the rope. He lit a glow-lamp and walked over to the fence accompanied by a handful of children. They squatted down on the ground and proceeded to set up the game with the stones that they had played the previous evening. Without looking up from the game, ever so quietly, Mole spoke. "You be there, mon?"

"We're here," Jasper replied.

"I have hidden a tool I think will open the gate at the entrance," Mole informed them. "But if I open the gate with all these guards around, they'll shoot anyone who tries to leave. I wish we had an enchanter up in here. "

"We could go get one," Jasper suggested. "But that would take time."

Suddenly the quiet of the night erupted with the piercing sound of a loud electronic blast in the form of Aretha Franklin singing about riding on the freeway of love in a pink Cadillac. The music emerged from

Doshmisi's backpack. The line from the song repeated in a loop as Doshmisi desperately fumbled with the front flap on her backpack, unbuckled it, and grabbed her cell phone, which she flipped open. The racket stopped instantly, but too late, for it had already alerted the Corportons, who descended rapidly.

"Who is this?" Doshmisi shouted into the phone furiously, while at the same time realizing that the situation was her own stupid fault for forgetting she had the phone in her backpack and forgetting to turn it off. But who would have imagined that the phone would work in Faracadar? It didn't seem possible.

"Dosh? It's me! Elena!"

"Why are you calling me? *How* are you calling me?" Doshmisi demanded.

"I have your number in my phone and we have this crystal thingy that Denzel…"

"Denzel? Are you in Faracadar?"

"Yeah, we're at Big House City," Elena informed her.

"Who is with you?" Doshmisi asked quickly as the Corportons closed in. She had to know that much at least from the crazy phone call before it ended.

"Maia, Denzel, and Honeydew."

"And Sonjay?" Doshmisi asked. Time was short.

"No. We don't know where he is," Elena answered cheerfully, sounding thoroughly pleased with herself. "We thought he might be with you."

Armed Corportons poured toward Doshmisi from all directions.

"I can't talk right now. Tell Denzel the trees want us to go see Clover. Tell him Jasper and I will try to meet him at Clover's. Tell him the Corportons have an oil well in the ocean at the North Coast and Mole is with us and…"

"Corportons?" Elena asked, uncertainly. "Jaspo? Clover?"

"This is really, really not a good time. I'm in the middle of something." Doshmisi turned the phone off and slipped it back into the front of the backpack just as the Corporton guards surrounded her and Jasper.

"Show us your hands," said a mechanical voice with the distinct tone of an unfriendly police officer. Doshmisi held her empty hands up over her head to show she had no weapons. The voice had come from one of the Corportons and it shocked her that she could understand the words, which were in English. She wondered where these aliens came from, but she thought perhaps she had an idea, insane as it seemed.

Chapter Eleven
Labyrinth

A rough tongue licking his ear woke Denzel. He found himself lying on his side on the ground and breathing a foul odor. When he opened his eyes, he saw towering walls of garbage rising up around him and framing a patch of sky glowing with the early morning light of sunrise. He must have remained unconscious for a whole night.

Bisc whimpered softly and continued to lick Denzel's ear. He still wore his backpack, for which he was grateful. He had a headache, felt a bit dizzy, and ached all over as if someone had picked him up and dropped him in this spot, which most likely was exactly what had happened. When Bisc saw Denzel's eyes open, the great white wolf sat back on his haunches and watched Denzel attentively. Denzel raised himself up to a sitting position. His head throbbed.

The tigers were nowhere in sight, but he saw Maia, Elena, and Guhblorin sprawled on the dry, raked dirt nearby. Honeydew sat up and smiled weakly at Denzel. "We're alive," she said.

"And they didn't take our things. I'm guessing that some pea-brained soldiers tossed us in here at Compost's orders. Maybe, since there are four of us, Compost thinks he captured the Four," Denzel speculated.

"Probably. I doubt he bothered to pay close attention. He's sloppy. I think you might be right, that he had his soldiers handle us, and that he doesn't realize that we're not exactly the Four," Honeydew replied.

"Let's hope he thinks we're the Four and let's hope that Sonjay and Doshmisi are out there somewhere making trouble for him," Denzel said. He cast his eyes over the mountainous walls of trash and junk. "Where do you think we are?"

"Bisc, go wake Maia," Honeydew instructed the white wolf as she pointed in Maia's direction. The sun slowly rose in the cloudless and cheerfully blue sky. Bisc proceeded to lick Maia's cheek until Maia opened her eyes and sat up with a dazed expression. "Inside a garbage labyrinth," Honeydew answered Denzel's question. "It must be large and convoluted, or Compost would not have depended on it to contain us."

"He has the most perverse idea of entertainment," Denzel said, as he rolled his eyes.

"Seriously. Why didn't he just imprison us like a normal villain?" Honeydew complained. "Wake them too," Honeydew instructed Bisc as she pointed to Elena and Guhblorin.

"Do we have to?" Denzel asked.

Maia gave her brother "the look" and chided him. "Just stop. Remember how long it took us to get used to things here last year? Give Elena a chance. She's trying."

"And the geebaching?" Denzel asked.

"He has barely been out of his cave a few days. He's trying too," Maia insisted.

Denzel sighed. He hoped the geebaching wouldn't begin hollering the minute he regained consciousness. Bisc gently licked Elena awake and then sat back on his haunches, clearly refusing to lick a geebaching. Maia patted Guhblorin on the shoulder until he opened one eye cautiously.

"Quivering fish shivers, this place stinks!" Guhblorin announced.

"Where are we?" Elena asked.

"Inside a labyrinth that appears to be made of garbage," Honeydew stated.

The walls of the labyrinth contained every imaginable used-up broken-down worthless decomposing or cast-off piece of junk, and all of it jammed together this way and that. They could see shoes, clothing, bottles, cans, paper, machine parts, scrap metal, sticks, stones, furniture, toys, food waste, wood, bags, boxes, and unrecognizable broken-off bits of things that had lost all semblance of usefulness long ago.

"Where did this stuff come from?" Guhblorin asked incredulously.

Honeydew scrutinized their surroundings and plucked a bent and corroded metal shield from the wall next to her. She held it up for the others to see. "I think a lot of this stuff comes from Compost's occupying army camped out at Big House City. The People of the Mountain Downs have a reputation for limited skill at organizational management," she informed the others disdainfully.

"I suppose we have to give Compost credit for thinking of something creative to do with their garbage," Maia said.

"Why?" Denzel grumbled.

Guhblorin pulled a dinged and dented trumpet out of the wall beside him, and in the process he dislodged a few odd objects, which tumbled down at his feet. He puffed out his cheeks and blew into the trumpet. It squawked like a goose trapped in an elevator. Guhblorin grinned. Honeydew reached for the trumpet with a stern expression and Guhblorin handed it over, crestfallen.

"Let's try walking," Honeydew suggested. "Maybe we can figure out how to get out."

Denzel's amulet began to glow red against his chest.

"Yay," Maia exclaimed as she pointed at the amulet. "Denzel has an ingenious idea."

"Did he get the idea from that necklace thingy?" Elena asked.

"No. He got it from his brain. That necklace is called an amulet. I have one too; so do Dosh and Sonjay. We inherited them from the previous

Four and sometimes when we use our greatest talents, our amulets glow," Maia explained.

"Like when you played your flute in the caves," Elena noted.

"Exactly. And Denzel's glows sometimes when he invents something or figures out a scientific or engineering problem." She turned to her brother and asked, "So what do you have going on in your head?"

"See if you can find clothing with buttons. I want to make a button-trail through the labyrinth so we can keep track of where we have been as we walk through it," Denzel explained.

Before long, they had pulled a large assortment of jackets and shirts from the garbage walls and had torn off a sizable stack of buttons. Denzel put the buttons into a can. Then they began to walk and as they went Denzel dropped buttons on the ground so they could trace their steps. Unfortunately, they did not get far before they discovered themselves back in a passage marked by the buttons, indicating that they had already walked there.

As they looked dejectedly at the buttons that they had placed in the passage only a short time before, Elena announced, "I'm hungry."

They had not eaten any breakfast and had, instead, spent a couple of hours collecting buttons and then wandering in the labyrinth. "I have some bread and peanut butter in my backpack," Honeydew offered. She sat on the ground and foraged in her backpack for the food. She unwrapped a large drumstick and gave it to Bisc, who chomped off all the meat and then chewed greedily on the bone, grunting happily. The rest of them ate the bread and peanut butter. Guhblorin said that geebachings could go for several days without food if necessary and not to worry about him.

"That's helpful," Maia told Guhblorin, "because we don't have much food left."

Denzel stared up at the sky, but it yielded no clue as to which direction would take them out of the garbage labyrinth. After they ate, they wandered in the labyrinth for the rest of the day, placing the buttons to mark their path and crying out to each other in dismay whenever they turned a corner and discovered their button trail staring up at them.

"I think this labyrinth might have an enchantment on it," Honeydew suggested finally, as the violet shadows of twilight began to creep across the ground.

Elena encouraged Denzel by telling him, "The buttons were a great idea. They could have worked. It was worth a try."

"Yes, well, they didn't work, did they?" Denzel couldn't conceal his frustration after wasting an entire day wandering the labyrinth. He felt disappointed that the buttons had not proved more useful. He also worried about what they would eat and drink if they remained trapped in the labyrinth for days on end.

"The buttons might work yet," Maia suggested hopefully.

"Not if the labyrinth has an enchantment on it," Honeydew warned. "Do we have anything left to eat?" They combed through their backpacks and found several bruised pears, a couple slices of bread, a good-sized chunk of cheese, and some chocolate. They shared the dregs of their food, with the chocolate being the prize. Honeydew made them give some of the cheese to Bisc.

"When we run out of food for that wolf, will he eat us?" Elena asked anxiously.

"No, he won't eat you. He's a tame wolf," Honeydew answered patiently, trying to keep her annoyance out of her voice. Sometimes she wondered how people could go through life with no comprehension of the nature of the many other creatures with whom they shared the land.

"We're out of water," Maia mourned, as she peered into her empty canteen.

"That I can do something about," Honeydew told her.

"You can?" Maia asked.

"I just need a container, like a bucket or a pitcher or something," Honeydew answered.

Guhblorin pulled a tin watering can out of the wall of garbage beside him and handed it to Honeydew. "Will this work?" he asked.

"I think so," she said. She put the watering can in front of her on the ground and she aimed three fingers at it. Concentrating hard she said some unintelligible words. Water began to bubble out of the watering can. Honeydew picked it up. "Quick, bring the canteens," she instructed. The others hurried to hold their open canteens out to her as Honeydew filled them with clean, clear water that amazingly bubbled from a rusted, dirty can. After they refilled the canteens, Honeydew set the watering can on the ground for Bisc, who drank his fill.

"Hecka cool trick," Denzel complimented Honeydew, as he took a refreshing swig from his canteen.

"No trick," Honeydew responded. "The water is real. I summoned it to our need."

Dark descended quickly and they could do nothing more until the sun rose again in the morning. They had worn themselves out repeatedly walking the same passages in the labyrinth, but sleep did not come to them easily; except for Guhblorin, who curled up inside a discarded sink and snored softly. The others lay awake, each one silently pondering their predicament. They knew they would wake up hungry and they had nothing to eat, but at least they would have water.

In the morning, Guhblorin hopped up bright and early. He carefully studied the wall of garbage before him and then he pulled a box from the mess of trash, grinning broadly. When he yanked out the box, he dislodged other items surrounding it and caused a small avalanche of junk that fell into the passage with a racket that woke everyone else. As they blinked in the blazing morning sunlight, Guhblorin giggled. "Chocolate cookies for breakfast," he said.

"That's not funny, *amigo*," Elena complained.

"Don't start," Denzel warned.

"Seriously," Guhblorin insisted. He giggled again, with a giggle that verged on becoming contagious in that dangerous geebaching way, as he held out a large box of chocolate chip cookies and offered them around to the others.

"Where did you get that?" Honeydew asked in amazement.

"I found it in the wall," Guhblorin told her.

The cookies seemed none the worse for the wear after being trapped in a wall of garbage. The closed box had protected them and they tasted delicious.

Maia gazed up into the clear blue patch of sky visible high above the labyrinth walls. Little bits of something unrecognizable began to fall down from above, like confetti. She shaded her eyes with her hand and looked more carefully, wondering what caused the confetti. Then she laughed with delight.

"What?" Denzel demanded, a bit gruffly. He felt responsible for getting them out of the labyrinth and he had no idea how to do that. He knew it was in his own head and that no one held him responsible, but he was the oldest, and a boy, and so he had expectations for himself. But here they remained, another day in the labyrinth, and he didn't know what to try next.

"Look," Maia said, as she pointed to her arm, on which several bright orange, red, and turquoise butterflies perched. Maia had befriended the butterflies the previous year and they had once protected the Four from discovery when they hid from Compost. As she held her hands up in the air, butterflies descended and surrounded her. They poured into the labyrinth from above. Although she couldn't think how they could help in this situation, Maia felt cheered by their presence.

The butterflies swarmed around Maia's head, and then they flew to Guhblorin. As the number of butterflies swelled to hundreds and thousands, they perched in the hair that covered his body. Suddenly Guhblorin screeched in alarm.

"Don't be afraid," Maia reassured him. "They're my friends. They won't harm you." Just as these words left her lips, the butterflies completely engulfed Guhblorin, making him no longer visible, and they lifted him off the ground, into the air above the labyrinth, and flew away with him.

"What in the heck?" Maia exclaimed as Guhblorin disappeared overhead. She glanced at Denzel, who shrugged. Bisc let out a mournful cry and Honeydew stroked his chest comfortingly. Many butterflies remained nearby, flitting about, circling Maia's head, and occasionally landing on Maia's arms and shoulders.

Bisc cocked his head to one side, his ears erect, as he heard something. Honeydew watched him intently, and then she grinned. "Listen," she told the others. They stood and listened. The sound of uncontrollable, side-splitting, breath-taking, gut-twisting human laughter reached them. It was the kind of laughter that only a geebaching attacking its human prey could cause. It was not a pleasant sound and they winced as it reached a wrenching crescendo and then stopped cold.

"Do you think he killed them?" Maia asked.

"No!" Elena replied emphatically. "He wouldn't. He swore he would never do that again." Stunned by what she had heard, she began to truly comprehend the deadly power of a geebaching.

Within minutes, the swarm of butterflies returned with Guhblorin, but they did not place him back in the labyrinth. Instead they hovered overhead with him. The travelers gazed up in wonder at the sight of a multitude of butterflies packed so tightly. All those tiny creatures working together were keeping a geebaching in the air.

"Are you OK, amigo?" Elena called to Guhblorin.

A slightly muffled voice emerged from the mass of butterflies. "I think so."

"Did you kill them?" Denzel asked.

"No, of course not. But they're passed out pretty good," Guhblorin answered.

"Who are they?" Maia asked.

"Special Forces," Guhblorin replied. "About a dozen of them are guarding the entrance to the labyrinth. From up here I can see how to get out. I'm good at mazes. I grew up inside the Amber Mountains and they're one big maze. Follow me."

The captives on the ground followed Guhblorin while the butterflies continued to hold him aloft. With Guhblorin's guidance they soon arrived at the entrance to the labyrinth. "From up here I can see our tigers coming around the side of the labyrinth," Guhblorin informed them. "They should turn up in a couple of minutes." The butterflies gently lowered Guhblorin to the ground. They swarmed around the heads of the travelers, while Maia and Honeydew called out their thanks to them.

"Can butterflies hear?" Denzel asked.

"Not really," Honeydew replied, "but I think they can understand gratitude if we intentionally focus on sending it to them." Denzel sent grateful thoughts to the butterflies, in case Honeydew was right and they could sense his intent.

The tigers had not arrived yet, but the guards had begun to regain consciousness, groaning and holding their aching sides.

"Walk along the garbage labyrinth that way. And don't look back," Guhblorin instructed with grim determination. "Go now. I have to do these guards again. You'll meet up with the tigers in a few minutes. By then you can safely come back for me, OK?"

"You got it, little fella," Denzel said. He took Elena's wrist in his hand and led her away with the warning, "He means it. Don't look back."

But Elena was curious, and following orders was not her strong suit. "Are we holding hands?" she asked Denzel, who quickly released his grip on her wrist as if it had burned him to touch her. When the guards began to laugh uproariously, Elena snuck a quick glimpse behind her. She saw

Guhblorin dancing a mangled version of ballet. He looked so comical that Elena could not resist snorting with laughter. Maia and Denzel both reached out at the same moment, whirled Elena around, and propelled her forward. They ran toward the approaching tigers and when they reached one another a joyful reunion ensued. Since no sounds of laughter from the guards met their ears, the travelers mounted the tigers and rode back for Guhblorin.

"I think we should drag these guys into the labyrinth," Denzel said, as he gestured to the unconscious guards. He produced his can of buttons and created a trail into the confusing twist of garbage walls. Following the buttons, and with help from the tigers, the travelers dragged the guards inside the labyrinth. Denzel picked up the buttons as they made their way out of the labyrinth for the last time. "That should hold them for a little while," he said.

As they emerged from the garbage labyrinth, Honeydew pointed in the direction of Big House City. "That's the way to the Whispering Pond," she said. "I can find it from here. The pond is surrounded by trees that will provide us with a place to hide from Compost and his army. We can sleep there tonight." With those words, she urged her tiger forward and the others followed her lead.

Chapter Twelve
In the Dungeon

During their first few days of confinement in their cell in the dungeon, the captives developed a routine built around when the Corportons brought them meals. The food tasted surprisingly good and it appeared twice a day. The Corportons showed no interest in the captives and left them to their own devices, which suited them fine since they had plenty to keep them busy.

In the morning, before breakfast, Crumpet worked with Sonjay on practicing clearing his mind in preparation for conducting enchantments. After breakfast, Reggie insisted that everyone join him in his exercises. He had a work-out routine he did to stay fit. Bayard flew around the cell madly as the others did sit-ups, push-ups, jumping jacks, and danced to old R&B and Soul music that Reggie played on an ancient vinyl record player. Overweight and out of shape, Buttercup had difficulty with the exercise routine, but she valiantly tried to keep up. Sonjay enjoyed it. Without the exercise, he would have gone stir-crazy. He didn't have the sort of disposition that leant itself to sitting still all day long.

After their work-out, Buttercup gave Sonjay lessons in the basic operation of enchantments while Crumpet studied the Mystical Book with Reggie. They received no lunch, but they had enough food left over from breakfast to munch on during the day, and always plenty of fruit for Bayard. In the early evening, their jailers brought them a large dinner. After they ate, they brainstormed ideas for making their escape. Reggie had a stationary bicycle and he would bike a mile on it every day before dinner and then Sonjay would bike a couple miles on it after dinner. Behind a screen there was a small bathroom with a sink, shower, and toilet. Reggie had negotiated a fairly comfortable living situation, which had made his life in the dungeon tolerable. The captives could tell the time by the nature of the light that entered the cell through a small window high up in the stone wall. They could not see out of it, but they relished the little sliver of sunshine it allowed into the cell.

At the end of the day, they talked and told stories, often until well after dark. Reggie could never get enough stories about his other children from Sonjay. Crumpet and Buttercup filled Sonjay in on things that had happened since his last visit to Faracadar. Reggie told the others everything he could think of that might be useful about Sissrath and the Corportons, and he told them about his years in confinement. Crumpet listened intently to everything Reggie had to say about the Mystical Book. Sonjay related for his father the adventures from his previous visit to Faracadar the year before. Reggie also wanted to hear about the world he had left behind and what was going on there. Sometimes, if Sonjay felt in the right mood, he would tell his father about his mother.

The restrictions on the use of enchantment within the cell made it impossible for Sonjay to actually attempt a real enchantment. He would follow the instructions provided by Buttercup or Crumpet to produce an enchantment, thinking all the right thoughts and concentrating as they instructed him, but nothing ever happened because of the restrictions within the cell, which frustrated him. He couldn't tell if he had done the enchantment correctly or not.

Unbeknownst to his teachers, he secretly harbored the idea of locomotaporting out of the prison. Each night, Sonjay waited for the others to fall asleep, and then he concentrated on locomotaporting. He figured that he would have to teach himself how to do it, since Crumpet and Buttercup didn't have the special skill needed for it. He feared that he would eventually transport part of himself somewhere and not have the ability to get back to the rest of himself left behind. He discovered by trial and error that he could locomotaport despite the restrictions on enchantment in the cell. He had no idea why that might be the case and he decided against discussing it with his cellmates. One night, he managed to lift a phantom version of himself out of his body by imagining his mind leaving the rest of him behind. He floated the phantom Sonjay, which looked like the real Sonjay but had no weight to it, up to the window of the cell.

As he looked out into the inky-blue night sky, spattered with the colorful bright stars of Faracadar, he attempted to touch the bars on the window, but his hand passed right through them as if made of fog. He realized that he had the power to sail out of the window if he chose, but he couldn't bring himself to do it. Not yet. He looked down and saw his body stretched out on the rug on the floor of the cell and he didn't feel confident that he could get back to his body if he left the room. He would have to overcome his fear and make a leap of faith eventually if he wanted to succeed at locomotaporting. The phantom self drifted back down to his body and merged with it. Bayard eyed him silently from his usual nighttime perch on Reggie's desktop. Bayard's silence made Sonjay even more uneasy. When a chatterbox of a parrot says nothing, it can set a person's teeth on edge.

The very next day after Sonjay had nearly locomotaported out of the cell, Crumpet broached the subject that weighed most heavily on their minds. "It's all good that we make use of our time in this cell, but we need to get out of here if we want to help save Faracadar," he said.

"What do you have in mind?" Reggie asked.

"I need to see out," Crumpet replied. Reggie and Sonjay looked up at the little window and Crumpet followed their line of sight. "Not like that,"

Crumpet said. "I need to see what's going on elsewhere in Faracadar, and that's your department, Prophet."

"I've shown you enough about the Mystical Book for you to understand that it doesn't work that way," Reggie reminded Crumpet. "The vision will manifest what it chooses and will not obey a directive from me."

"Whatever it chooses to be important will be worth seeing. I think you should summon a prophetic vision," Crumpet announced, as he crunched on a deep-fried goose-chicken eyeball, which was one of Sonjay's favorite treats from Faracadar. His siblings did not share his tastes and they refused to eat the things.

"I might not succeed in summoning a vision. I can issue a call, but often I get no reply," Reggie warned.

"At least give it a try," Buttercup encouraged him. "Put out the call and see what happens."

Reggie shrugged. He took a candle off a shelf, set it on his desk, and lit it. Crumpet sat down expectantly on the edge of Reggie's bed and crossed his arms.

Reggie held a bundle of sage above the flame until it caught and then set it in a bowl. The scented smoke drifted upward in a steady stream as the sage bundle smoldered. Reggie opened the Mystical Book, found the page he wanted, and placed his hand gently on the page. "By fire, earth, air, water," he intoned softly, "by music, metal, trees, whales, and truth..." His voice dropped and his words became unintelligible. He closed his eyes in concentration and rocked back and forth. Suddenly, flashes of rainbow colors shot out in all directions from his hand where it rested on the book.

"Awesome," Sonjay said quietly. The color flashes of green, red, yellow, blue, orange, purple, and pink banged against the walls and shattered into fragments of brilliant color that bounced around the cell. They pinged against Sonjay's skin in pleasant tingly bursts. Bayard attempted (without success) to catch them in his beak and eat them.

Buttercup giggled. Oblivious to the light show, Reggie drifted upward out of his chair and floated above the desk, while his eyes remained closed and his hand stretched out in front of him as if it still touched the surface of the Mystical Book.

Bayard flew to the top of the cell, chasing fragments of colorful light. Sonjay observed his father floating in the air. After a few minutes, the color-flash fragments disappeared and Reggie floated back down. His hand returned to the page and he returned to the chair. His eyes fluttered open.

"That was hecka cool," Sonjay told Reggie.

"What was?" Reggie asked.

"The colors, the light, the floating. You know," Sonjay said.

Reggie cast him a puzzled look.

"Whoa," Buttercup said. "You don't know, do you? You've never seen what happens when you summon a prophecy from the book, have you?" Buttercup asked Reggie.

"What to do you mean?" Reggie asked.

"You made these blasts of colorful light fly all over the cell and they broke up when they hit the walls," Sonjay informed his father.

"They shattered and bounced all over the place," Crumpet said.

"And they bounced off of us," Buttercup added.

"And made our skin go all tingly where they hit it. Bayard tried to eat the bits of colorful light," Sonjay told his father, "which was pretty funny."

"Funny," Bayard repeated. "Funny, funny."

"While the bits of colorful light flew around, with Bayard chasing them, you floated up in the air for a few minutes. Then you floated back down into your chair," Sonjay concluded.

"Interesting," Reggie responded to the account of the events surrounding his prophetic reading.

"What did you see?" Crumpet demanded.

"What did I see?" Reggie echoed. "I saw a group of children heading to a garden outside of Big House City. I think one of the children was

Denzel, because he resembled me, and one was Maia, because she resembled Debbie. Does Maia wear her hair in a lot of braids?"

"Sure enough," Sonjay replied. "Did she carry a drum slung over her shoulder?"

"She did," Reggie continued, "and the boy who looked like me when I was young wore a flannel shirt and he had a big backpack. I also saw a girl with glasses and one long braid going down her back and another girl with straight black hair and I saw a little creature with orange hair all over its body. It might have been a geebaching, although I have never seen one in real life (only in books) so I don't know for sure."

"Those girls sound like Princess Honeydew and Maia's friend Elena," Sonjay informed him. "I wonder where Dosh is."

"I wonder if the little creature with the orange hair could really be a geebaching," Buttercup said.

"But the most important thing," Reggie continued, with a new sense of urgency, "is that the children I saw are about to attempt to enter Big House City through a passageway that runs under the garden. The city is under siege. There is a large army at its gates. Your sister and brother and their friends are about to sneak into Big House City through a secret underground passageway. They plan to try to bring people out of the besieged city."

"Trouble," Bayard squawked. "Trouble, trouble."

"Yes, trouble indeed," Reggie agreed with Bayard. "The prophetic reading indicated that their plan won't work. If they follow that path they will become trapped inside the city with the others. The result has not become fixed. If they can be stopped then a different thread of events will occur."

"They can't possibly believe they can sneak everyone out," Crumpet said.

"And they can't possibly sneak enough food in for the entire population of Big House City," Buttercup pointed out.

"Or water," Reggie added.

"They have water," Buttercup informed him. "Deep wells inside the city provide water. But food must be running low by now."

"The more immediate problem is that my children could become trapped inside this soon-to-be-starving city," Reggie reminded them anxiously.

"What can we do about that?" Crumpet complained. "We're locked in a dungeon."

Sonjay cleared his throat self-consciously. "I might be able to do something."

The others slowly turned to look at him appraisingly.

"I could maybe locomotaport there," Sonjay said in a quiet voice. The others stared at him in stunned silence. "I've been practicing. Every night. I can leave my body, but I haven't left the cell yet. The ban on enchantments doesn't seem to prevent locomotaporting."

"Interesting. Locomotaporting must be in a unique class of enchantment," Crumpet conjectured.

"If you leave, can you get back?" Reggie asked.

Sonjay's voice quavered as he replied, "I don't know." He turned to Buttercup and asked, "What happens if I can't find my way back to my body?"

"Disembodied impairment," Buttercup answered. She winced.

"That does not sound good." Sonjay grimaced.

"Not good," Bayard observed.

"You said it feather-top," Buttercup agreed.

"Don't worry about it. We'll call you back," Crumpet said. "We'll help you."

"How come he can locomotaport from within the walls of this cell?" Reggie wondered aloud.

"No one has had the ability to locomotaport since Hazamon died. It's not your normal kind of enchantment. Sissrath would not have even thought of preventing it, even if he could do so," Crumpet speculated.

"Show us," Buttercup demanded.

"What? Now?" Sonjay stammered.

"You betcha. Right now," Buttercup insisted.

Sonjay obediently stretched out on the rug where he usually slept at night. His fingers trembled slightly as he placed his hands on his chest. He closed his eyes. His father knelt beside him and put a hand on Sonjay's shoulder. Sonjay opened his eyes and looked up into his father's face. "One more piece of information, son," Reggie said. "This is important. The army outside the gates of Big House City is a reluctant army. They don't want to be there. They would rather be at home with their families on their farms. It would not take much to turn them around."

Sonjay nodded. "Thanks, Daddy," he said. "Now you have to move away and not touch me or I won't be able to go."

Sonjay cleared his mind of clutter, as Buttercup had taught him, and felt the spirit presence filtering into his being. The phantom Sonjay emerged and began to float up to the window. The others could see the phantom self. They followed it with their eyes. Sonjay floated in front of the window and then he looked down at his body. The same old doubt and fear squeezed his heart. What if he could not get back? What if he lost his body? What was disembodied impairment? He began to drift back down to the rug. But Reggie called up to him, "There is a great enchanter inside of you, son. Bring it."

Sonjay nodded once to his father and then resolutely floated through the wall and out of the cell. Bayard Rustin slipped easily between the bars of the window and flew after him.

Chapter Thirteen
Change of Plan

After escaping from the garbage labyrinth, Denzel, Maia, and their fellow travelers mounted their tigers and made a mad dash to the Whispering Pond, where they set up camp in a thicket of trees and shrubs that concealed them from prying eyes. The tree canopy overhead offered protection from Compost's skeeters. Honeydew picked sweet pears from a tree familiar to her. While growing up at Big House City, she had often visited the Whispering Pond. She knew where to find tasty mushrooms and a yellow root-plant that resembled a potato. She said she had often gone mushrooming with her father near the Whispering Pond as a little girl. Denzel made a campfire and Honeydew wrapped the mushrooms and potato-like roots in thick rubbery leaves that she had picked from a nearby tree. She placed the wrapped vegetables in the coals and they tasted delicious and satisfying once roasted. While waiting for the vegetables to roast, they dipped into the pond to wash off the grime from the journey and the garbage labyrinth. The tigers grazed on the surrounding vegetation while Bisc disappeared to hunt for his dinner. Honeydew did not need to summon water because they found a spring that bubbled from a cluster of gray-blue rocks.

After they had eaten, Guhblorin paddled happily around the pond and Honeydew sat in front of Maia, who unbraided and rebraided Honeydew's hair in one long braid. Bisc placed his enormous head in Honeydew's lap and she stroked his ears gently. Elena stood in a pool of amber light, caught in the rays of the late-day sun as it descended. She had taken her cell phone out of her backpack and appeared transfixed as she punched the buttons.

"I'm guessing Compost's troops are camped on the plain outside the main gate to Big House City," Denzel told the others. He peered through a pair of binoculars in the direction of the city. "I can't see from here. Too many trees." He bit his lower lip distractedly as he strategized in his head.

"Good," Maia muttered. "If you can't see them then they can't see us."

"We'll have a look tomorrow," Honeydew told Denzel. "I, for one, could use a good night's sleep before taking on Compost's army."

"Maybe, instead of risking another encounter with Compost, we should sneak inside the city and consult with Cardamom and the high chief and chieftess. I know a secret passage into the city that Crumpet showed us last year. It originates in the garden over there." Denzel waved his hand in the direction of the garden. "I doubt anyone else knows about it. We found it from an enchanted map given to us by Clover. I'm willing to bet that no one inside the city realizes that they can sneak out through that passage just as easily as we can sneak in. We could even bring a lot of people out of the city through that passage, given time."

"If we go inside the city, we won't get stuck there, will we?" Elena asked anxiously, without looking up from her phone.

"We could come back out the same way we go in," Denzel reassured her.

"I like that idea," Maia said.

"Me too," Honeydew concurred. "I would feel better if I could consult with my parents. I don't want to give Compost a chance to capture us again."

"What in the heck are you doing with that phone?" Denzel asked Elena, irritably.

Elena shrugged. She had tried texting her big sister with whom she shared her bedroom at home, just to see what would happen. The phone said "no service" and no signal bars appeared on the screen. She considered playing one of the games that she had downloaded to it, but she decided not to use up the phone's charge. Even though she couldn't call anyone, she didn't want the phone to go dead. It represented her last communication link to her family and the world that she had unwittingly left behind when she impulsively jumped on Maia's cushion.

Denzel took the travel crystal that Goldenrod had given him out of his backpack and walked over to Elena. From where she stood, if he stood next to her, he could catch a few golden rays of the setting sun through the trees. The travel crystal sparkled in a shaft of fading light. He asked Honeydew, "Do you think I should try to contact Goldenrod to let him know we're going inside?"

Honeydew replied, "I think we should wait until we get in and contact him after we have talked to my parents and Cardamom. Then we'll have more to report. My dad and mom might want to speak to him too."

Denzel nodded in agreement. He took a step out of the sunlight.

"Hold on, come back here," Elena said to Denzel.

"What?" Denzel asked.

"Come back here and look at this." She did not lift her eyes from the display on her phone for a second.

"Puleez. I don't want to see a baby laughing or a cat flushing a toilet or some other stupid video that you downloaded to your phone. I'm trying to think about ..." Elena interrupted him by grabbing his arm and pulling him beside her. She pointed at her cell phone display screen.

"What!?" Denzel exploded in exasperation.

"Look at the signal bars. I have service," Elena replied. "But only when you stand right next to me with that crystal thingy. Stay there. Don't move." Elena punched her phone keypad and put the phone to her ear.

"Dosh? It's me! Elena!" she shouted excitedly into the phone. Elena could hear the sound of people shouting in the background. Doshmisi did not seem happy to hear her at all. "Coptorons? Jaspo? Clover?" Elena repeated in bewilderment.

Denzel rudely snatched the phone from Elena's ear.

"Dosh?" Denzel yelled into the phone. But Dosh had hung up. He hit redial but he got her voicemail.

"She said she couldn't talk. She was in the middle of something," Elena stated flatly, as she folded her arms across her chest. "Now can I have my phone back?"

Denzel rounded on Elena. "What else did she say?"

"How about, 'thanks for figuring out how to call Dosh' or 'that was a great idea, Elena' or 'wow, I guess you didn't need a cell tower after all' or some acknowledgement that I can solve problems too?" Elena hollered at him.

Denzel found himself pinned in the gaze of three glaring girls. He wished more than ever that Jasper or Sonjay was there to provide him with some back-up, but it was just him and the girls. The geebaching offered no help; he was obliviously gargling pond water and flapping his ears. Denzel admitted to himself that he had acted kind of mean to Elena ever since they had arrived in Faracadar. He knew he could stop if he made an effort. And he had to give her credit for discovering that the cell phone worked when she held it next to the crystal. "Sorry," he mumbled.

"What did you say?" Honeydew asked pointedly. "I didn't quite hear that."

"I said I'm sorry. To Elena. That was good that you figured out how to call Dosh," Denzel said clearly, swallowing his pride.

"Apology accepted," Elena told him. "*Gracias*."

"Elena, please. What did Dosh say?" Maia asked urgently, to Denzel's relief. It saved him from having to ask again.

"She said that the trees said go to Clover. And that she and Jaspo will meet us at Clover. And Coptorons are, no, um, Corportons. I think it was Corportons, that they're in the ocean on the North Coast. And she said she has a mole with her." As she relayed Doshmisi's message, Elena realized that she had forgotten some of it because she had gotten angry at Denzel and had not repeated the message to him right away.

"She must be with Jasper," Denzel said.

"*Sí*," Elena confirmed, relieved, "that's who's with her. Jasper."

"Mole must be with them too. What's he doing at the North Coast?" Maia wondered.

"What's a Coptoron?" Honeydew asked.

"I was about to ask you the same thing," Elena replied.

"Coptoron or Corporton? What did she say?" Denzel demanded.

Elena no longer felt sure of the word, but she repeated "Corporton," afraid to confess that she might have gotten it wrong.

"You're sure?" Maia cross-examined Elena.

"Pretty sure," Elena replied uncertainly.

Denzel made an effort to hold his tongue. Elena had mangled the message. He wondered if Doshmisi had said something important that Elena had forgotten. Getting mad at her wouldn't do any good so he kept his mouth shut. But he hoped that if there was more to Doshmisi's message that Elena would remember it soon.

They divided up the hours of the night for each person to take a shift at guard duty and then they settled down to sleep. Guhblorin took the first watch. He hummed a dreadfully off-key tune to himself happily as he gazed at the stars. Even though it was in his nature to make his human friends laugh themselves to death, he could feel his nature changing. It was hard work but he was doing it and that made him feel better than he had ever felt in his whole life.

In the morning, with the sun shining brightly, Denzel held the crystal next to Elena's cell phone and Elena tried to call Doshmisi again. The phone worked but Doshmisi didn't answer so Elena left a voice message. Denzel grilled her about what she had heard in the background while talking to Doshmisi the night before and Elena recalled only that she heard people shouting indistinctly in the distance.

"She insisted that we should go to Clover's," Elena reminded the others. "Should we go to Clover's instead of sneaking into this city? Doshmisi definitely said she would meet us at Clover's." Elena felt reluctant to enter a city under siege. What if they got stuck in there?

"I wonder why she didn't come straight to Big House City," Maia said.

"What's at the North Coast?" Elena asked.

"I don't know. We've never been there," Denzel answered. He had resolved to try to be nicer to Elena.

"I've gone there," Honeydew piped up. "There's not much at the North Coast. No one lives there. People go there on vacation sometimes. They camp out on the beach. It's beautiful; you know, peaceful, and far away from everything."

"So why do you think Doshmisi went there?" Elena asked. "She's obviously not looking for a vacation."

"She definitely said the North Coast?" Denzel demanded of Elena, a bit more sharply than he had intended.

"Well, yes. I told you that yesterday, Paco," Elena replied impatiently.

"Paco? What's with the Paco?" Denzel muttered in annoyance. He did not remember her saying anything about Doshmisi being at the North Coast. He remembered her saying that Corportons were in the ocean at the North Coast, but not that Doshmisi was there with them.

"It's a Spanish nickname," Maia told him. "An affectionate one," she added, to smooth his ruffled feathers.

"For what?" he demanded.

"It's nothing bad, just a nickname for Francisco," Elena said, tossing her blue-black hair over her shoulder so that it shimmered in the sunlight.

"My name is not Francisco," Denzel replied.

"Well, you don't think there's a Spanish nickname for Denzel, do you?" Elena giggled. Guhblorin's eyes twinkled and he suppressed a grin.

"You spend too much time with that geebaching," Maia told Elena with amusement. Denzel was not similarly amused.

A heated discussion ensued about whether the group should sneak into Big House City or go straight to Clover's. In the course of the discussion, Elena remembered that Doshmisi had asked her if Sonjay was with them, an important piece of information, since it meant that Sonjay was not with Doshmisi. Denzel struggled to keep his temper when he learned of this critical omission.

Honeydew and Denzel thought they should go into the city, Maia and Elena wanted to go to Clover's, and Guhblorin suggested they go to the North Coast. It took the better part of the morning for Denzel and Honeydew to convince the others that the best plan, since they were already right at Big House City, was to sneak inside and consult with Cardamom and Honeydew's parents. By the time they had carefully made their way to the garden, avoiding skeeters and Compost's soldiers in the process, the sun stood directly overhead and Elena had begun to think about lunch, which they did not have.

Denzel found the statue that marked the entrance he sought and with help from the others he moved the large, flat stone that concealed the secret passageway into Big House City. If he could remember which way to go once he got underground, Denzel felt confident he could follow the passageway directly into the Big House where High Chief Hyacinth and Chieftess Saffron lived.

Just as Denzel placed his foot on the first step leading down to the secret passage, Sonjay suddenly appeared out of thin air, standing beside the statue that guarded the staircase leading under the ground.

"Hey you guys," Sonjay spoke up from behind the group huddled at the entrance. "I'm gonna have to veto this plan." Everyone whirled around to face him.

A smile spread across Denzel's face and Maia rushed over to Sonjay to give him a hug. Denzel's smile vanished an instant later as Maia's arms swept straight through Sonjay and crashed into each other in the near vicinity of Sonjay's chest. Astonished, Princess Honeydew attempted to pat Sonjay's face but her hand went right through his cheek and her fingers wiggled inside his head. Denzel thought it looked as if Honeydew had touched a hologram.

"What in the heck?!" Denzel exclaimed.

Maia burst into tears. "Did you die? Are you a ghost?" she sputtered. Elena put a comforting arm around Maia.

"It's OK," Sonjay reassured everyone. "I'm alive. Just not here. I'm locomotaporting."

"No fair. How did you learn to do that? I can't even throw my voice yet," Honeydew complained.

"How do we know it's really you and not Sissrath impersonating you or something?" Denzel asked suspiciously. "If it's really you, then tell me how many stair steps I can jump on my skateboard."

"Six," Sonjay answered instantly. "You did seven once, but you almost broke your wrist and you can't do it again."

"Maybe I can. How do you know? So what is your least favorite activity?" Denzel asked.

"Flossing," Sonjay replied.

"What do you call Bayard when he's naughty?"

"A heap of feathers," Sonjay replied. Just at that moment, the bird in question appeared and landed on Denzel's shoulder. "And here's the heap of feathers now," he said with a chuckle.

"Is he locomotaporting too?" Maia asked.

Bayard happily pecked Denzel on the head. "Ouch!" Denzel exclaimed. "Nope, he's for real."

"Tough luck," Sonjay told his brother. "He can't peck me at the moment so it's gonna be you."

"How can you locomotaport?" Honeydew demanded. "No one can do that anymore."

"I came into my power as an enchanter and Crumpet and Buttercup are training me. I'm not that good at enchantment yet. But when we discovered that I can locomotaport, and that no one else can do it, I started practicing."

"No one has done it since Hazamon. I can't believe you can do it. Is locomotaporting the first thing you learned how to do as an enchanter?" Honeydew asked.

"Impressive," Denzel complimented his brother. "What'd you do with the rest of you? The blood and guts, I mean."

"It's a long story and I have to work quickly here so I can get back to the rest of me as soon as possible. Otherwise, disembodied impairment." Sonjay wondered whether or not to tell Denzel and Maia that he had found their father. He decided against it. For one thing, he selfishly wanted to keep Reggie all to himself for a little longer. He also didn't know how things might turn out for everyone and he didn't want to tell Denzel and Maia about Reggie only to have him die or get captured again before they could see him. He decided to keep it a secret; and he also decided not to worry them by telling them that he had left his body in the dungeon at the Final Fortress. He would provide as little information about his situation as possible.

"I came to take care of some business here at the siege and then, after I get back to my body, I'll try to meet up with you somewhere," Sonjay told the others.

"At least tell us where you wound up after the passage," Maia demanded.

"You seriously don't want to know," Sonjay said, sidestepping her question. Then he noticed Elena. "Whoa. Elena? What are you doing here?"

"She crashed the party," Denzel said.

"Oh yeah," Sonjay said as he remembered, "you jumped on Maia's cushion at the last minute. I bet you were tripping when you found yourself in Faracadar."

"That's an understatement. I'm getting used to it, though," Elena said.

"Weren't you wearing pajamas?"

"Just a pajama top. I got a shirt at the Wolf Circle," she replied, blushing.

"You went to the Wolf Circle?"

"We arrived in the Amber Mountains instead of Debbie's Circle," Denzel explained.

"Lucky you. Listen, I don't want to stay here in this locomotaport any longer than necessary because I'm still learning how to control it, so let's go to the siege."

"We're at the siege," Denzel told him. "And we were just about to sneak into the city to consult with Cardamom when you appeared."

"Yes, well that's why I had to risk locomotaporting over here when I don't totally get how to do it yet. I came to prevent you from sneaking into the city. It's a bad idea," Sonjay informed him.

"What makes it a bad idea?" Denzel asked defensively. Why did he have to convince everyone that this plan, which seemed like a no-brainer to him, was the most sensible? "Wait what? How did you know about our plan?"

"I left my body with Crumpet and Buttercup and we found the Prophet of the Khoum and he has these visions and he could foresee that you would try to sneak into the city and he says this plan will not turn out well," Sonjay tried to explain, all in a jumbled rush.

"Prophet of the Khoum?" Honeydew cried out with excitement.

"You lost me at Crumpet," Elena muttered. Guhblorin patted her hand sympathetically and asked, "What's flossing?"

"Trust me on this one, man. No time to explain. Don't go in there. We have to convince Compost and his troops to leave," Sonjay said.

"You make it sound so simple. I suppose I could have politely asked Compost to free us when he captured us and imprisoned us in a garbage labyrinth," Denzel responded sarcastically.

"Garbage labyrinth? That sounds nasty," Sonjay said.

Denzel continued, "Maybe if I ask nicely then Compost and his army will pack up and head for the hills."

"Remember to say please with a cherry on top," Guhblorin suggested.

Sonjay squinted at Guhblorin, as if he couldn't believe his eyes. "Is that a geebaching?"

"No, no geebaching," Guhblorin replied, looking behind him as if Sonjay might have referred to someone else. "I'm a wolf. A white wolf. Sissrath turned me into the appearance of a geebaching to punish me for biting his elbow. Look. See my wolf teeth?" Guhblorin opened his mouth to show his tiny crooked teeth.

"Those don't look like wolf teeth," Sonjay said suspiciously.

Guhblorin attempted to roar, but it sounded so feeble that Elena and Honeydew giggled. Sonjay cracked a smile. Guhblorin roared again. He sounded like a creaky gate.

Maia shot Guhblorin a stern look and warned, "That's enough. You stop right now, you hear?"

Guhblorin bowed his head sheepishly and mumbled an incoherent apology.

"It *is* a geebaching," Sonjay said incredulously.

"He's OK," Maia assured her brother. "His name is Guhblorin."

"Is he tame?" Sonjay asked.

"Almost," Denzel replied. "He's a Dud."

"Well, wow, that explains everything," Sonjay responded in exasperation.

"Long story," Denzel said.

"You'll get used to him," Honeydew promised. "So do you have some kind of a plan to convince Compost and his troops to go home?"

"Food," Sonjay replied cryptically. "Show me their camp."

"Let's roll," Denzel said as he shoved the flat rock back over the secret passageway.

Chapter Fourteen
New Beginnings Well

As the Corportons descended, Mole and the children melted into the compound, distancing themselves from Doshmisi and Jasper. Doshmisi hoped that Jack would use his intuit abilities to catch the silent message she "thought" to him, telling him to remain hidden on the hillside (either he would get her message or he would exercise common sense). She held her hands above her head as commanded by the mechanical voice as she studied the strange creatures in the white jumpsuits. They appeared human, although she couldn't tell for certain since they wore gray masks over their faces. What if the creatures underneath the jumpsuits and masks looked like giant squid with tentacles? That thought made Doshmisi shiver with repulsion.

One of the Corportons picked up Doshmisi's backpack in one hand and Jasper's backpack in the other. The Corportons encircled Doshmisi and Jasper with guns trained on them. Doshmisi's heart sunk at the sight of guns in Faracadar. She wondered if all their guns shot bullets or if some of them shot a death-ray or something worse.

"Walk," the mechanical Corporton voice ordered.

Doshmisi and Jasper walked ahead of their captors, careful not to make any sudden moves that would provoke the aliens. As they marched along the fence and toward the gate at the entrance to the compound, Doshmisi felt a growing sense of panic. Night had fallen swiftly and the sky was dark, or as dark as the Faracadaran sky became with the many colorful stars dotting it.

Armed Corportons inside the compound cleared the area surrounding the front gate as the Corportons outside the compound arrived at the entrance with their new prisoners. Inside a guard house next to the gate, a Corporton manipulated the controls and the gate swung open smoothly on its hinges. With the Corportons following close behind, Doshmisi and Jasper began to enter the compound.

Just as they stood in the pathway of the gate, a deafening roar split the air. Doshmisi clapped her hands over her ears and screamed in pain. A gigantic plume of fire shot upward from the ocean in the distance. A series of pops and squeals echoed across the water. The plume of fire expanded, evolved into swirls of orange and golden flame, and then thick black smoke curled up from the foot of the fire. The Corportons as well as the people inside the compound stood transfixed, gazing out at the ocean. The black smoke swirled inland to the compound and engulfed the onlookers while white ash sifted down upon them, at first in random flecks and then in a steady stream.

No one could see more than a few inches in front of them because of the black smoke. In the ensuing confusion, people and Corportons ran in every direction. Coughing and rubbing their eyes, many of the captives stumbled out through the open gate to freedom, hastily disappearing into the surrounding forest. The Corportons retreated further inside the compound.

"Give me your hand so we don't get separated," Jasper yelled to Doshmisi. "What a stroke of luck," Jasper exclaimed.

"No," Doshmisi contradicted him grimly. "It was probably the most unlucky thing that could happen. I think the New Beginnings Well just exploded and caught on fire; and if that happened then tons of oil will leak into the ocean. It will kill every living thing in that water for miles around."

Through the swirling black smoke, Doshmisi noticed the gate begin to swing on its hinges as it started to close. "Quick," Doshmisi alerted Jasper, "the gate!" As she pulled Jasper toward the gate, Jack materialized out of a billow of smoke. He swooped down from above their heads on his skateboard, which had become a hoverboard that clung to his feet. He pulled the skateboard out from under himself and jammed it between the closing door of the gate and the latch in the gatepost. The gate hit the skateboard with a thud and failed to lock shut.

"Woo-hoo!" Jack hollered like a cowboy riding a bucking bronco as he floated over to Doshmisi and Jasper.

"Well-played, Jack," Doshmisi cheered.

"Look," Jasper pointed at his backpack and Doshmisi's. The Corporton had dropped their backpacks on the ground and fled. They picked them up and put them on as Mole appeared out of the obscurity of the smoke and drifting ash. He hugged Doshmisi and Jasper. "That be somethin'," he said as he shook his head sadly, his dreadlocks flopping around his shoulders. "That explosion probably blew the evening crew to pieces. I had friends on that rig."

"I'm so sorry," Doshmisi told him.

But Jasper, thinking fast, took no time to mourn the dead crew. He instructed Mole, "Get these people out of here before the Corportons reorganize and figure out that the gate didn't shut."

"The gate be open?" Mole asked incredulously.

"Jack put his skateboard in the latch. It didn't close properly," Jasper informed him.

"I have to find the other battery makers," Mole said.

"Pass the word that the gate is open," Doshmisi told him. "If we lose track of you in this hot mess, and we get out of here too, we plan to head for Clover at the library on Whale Island. Meet us there, Mole."

"Clover. Whale Island. See you there," Mole replied.

"And Mole?" Doshmisi called after him as he disappeared into the smoky compound. "Denzel is at Big House City. He'll meet us at Clover's too."

She could no longer see Mole, but his voice emerged from a mountain of billowing smoke. "How do you know where he is?" Mole asked.

"I just do," she replied. "Trust me."

Word about the open gate spread quickly and captives poured out of the compound, pushing the gate open wide so that Jack's skateboard fell to the ground. Jack picked it up. Jasper pulled a length of rope out of his backpack and tied it to the gate, preparing to secure the gate in its open position.

"Stay here," Doshmisi told Jasper. "Stay by the gate and make sure it stays open, and don't get caught inside. I'll be right back."

"Where are you going?" Jasper asked in alarm.

"I need to find Dagobaz. We can't leave him behind. They'll kill him," Doshmisi replied.

"Are you crazy?" Jasper asked, as he securely tied the gate open. "How can you find Dagobaz in this circus? We can't see past our own noses and we don't even know if he's here!"

"I'm sure he's here. I have to try to rescue him."

"I'm going with you," Jasper insisted. "I can't keep the Corportons from closing the gate once they discover it's open and I don't want us to get separated. Let's find Dagobaz quickly and get out."

"Jack!" Doshmisi called. "Jack, do you know where they put Dagobaz? Can you see?" People rushed past Doshmisi and out the gate. She hoped that the clairvoyant intuit could see Dagobaz's whereabouts and guide her to him. Doshmisi shouted Jack's name again just as the little intuit, floating on his skateboard, bobbed up next to her elbow and touched her arm.

"Jack knows," he said quietly. "Jack knows." He slipped his little hand into hers. Pulling Jasper behind her, she followed the intuit into the mayhem of the smoky compound. Suddenly, an explosion inside the compound rocked the ground under their feet. Doshmisi and Jasper dropped to their knees while Jack floated above them, still holding Doshmisi's hand.

"Crazy. Everything is blowing up. Do you smell something burning?" Jasper asked.

"I do. I wonder what caused that explosion," Doshmisi replied.

"It happened nearby. Not out on the ocean," Jasper noted.

"Quick," Jack said. "Quick, quick."

Doshmisi hopped back up to her feet and hurried after Jack. Then she distinctly heard the panicked scream of a frightened horse. Her heart raced. It had to be Dagobaz. How many horses could there be in the compound? Jack led them to a wooden door, which he opened. The three of them stepped inside and closed the door behind them. They found themselves inside a cool, dim barn. A young boy who had the deep-blue glow to his skin characteristic of the Coast People stood plastered against a wall of the barn in fright. A few feet away, Dagobaz bucked and kicked. Heavy ropes tethered the horse to metal loops in the floor. Foam frothed from his mouth and coated his neck while his eyes flashed with terror. He screamed deafeningly.

"He's going crazy," the young boy said. "I can't get near him to cut him loose. He'll trample me."

"Don't worry," Doshmisi told the boy. "I'll free him. He knows me. You save yourself. The gate is open right now. Run and you can get out of here." She put her backpack on the floor and reached in and took out an apple. She bit off a bite-sized piece just right for a horse.

"Don't try to ride him," the boy warned. "No one can tame him. He'll kill you like all the others who tried. I've seen him do it." With those words, he fled from the barn.

Doshmisi took a step toward the frenzied stallion, holding the piece of apple in front of her in her outstretched hand.

"Dosh," Jasper said urgently, "he might not let you help him. He might be too far gone. It's not worth the risk."

"There's no risk," Doshmisi maintained stubbornly. "I know this horse. Just keep still. No sudden moves. No matter what happens."

Doshmisi stepped toward Dagobaz as she spoke to him softly and soothingly. "Remember me, your friend from the woods? I won't hurt you. I've come to help you. Please trust me." Dagobaz snorted and blew through his nose. He pawed the ground, but stopped bucking. His ears flicked and lay back against his head as he listened. Doshmisi continued to speak to him soothingly as she held the apple out to him, just like she had done back in the woods when they had bunked together for the night. Dagobaz reached forward with his muzzle and took the piece of apple. Doshmisi patted his nose and then slowly reached up to the harness to which the ropes restraining him were attached. She unbuckled the harness. Dagobaz whinnied. Out of the corner of her eye, she saw Jasper jump involuntarily with alarm. Dagobaz saw him too and shook his head. Foam spattered Doshmisi's arms. She patted his sweaty neck and continued to speak to him softly as she unfastened him from his bondage. Underneath the restraints, sores and scabs dotted the horse's skin and Doshmisi winced at the sight of his wounds. Why would anyone mistreat a magnificent creature such as Dagobaz in this fashion?

The ropes and harness fell away and the horse stood unfettered. He rose on his hind legs and squealed. Jasper yelled "Dosh!" But Doshmisi felt fine and so did Dagobaz. He nuzzled her. She gave him the rest of the apple. "Let's get you out of here," she said to him. She started to walk toward the door, but Dagobaz whinnied and tossed his head. He walked over to a bench and stood in front of it. He whinnied again. Doshmisi went to the bench and got up on it. Dagobaz rubbed his side against her.

"On," Jack said, excitedly. "On, on!"

"No," Jasper cried, "you heard what that boy said. He has killed other riders. It's too dangerous. He might throw you."

"He'll allow me to ride. Because I did not try to break him, I have tamed him enough to ride," Doshmisi reassured Jasper. She grabbed Dagobaz's mane and hoisted herself onto his back. She had learned to ride at Manzanita Ranch under Aunt Alice's tutelage and had become adept at riding bareback after much practice. The minute she landed on the horse's back, she became one with him. "You have to let Jasper on too," she whispered in the horse's ear. "He won't hurt you and we can't leave him behind."

"He let you on," Jasper said, transfixed by the vision of Doshmisi on Dagobaz's back. "I can't believe he let you on."

"And he's going to let you on too. Bring my backpack and come here."

"Oh no. He likes you, but he doesn't even know me."

"How else do you plan to get out of here? If that gate is still open then we have to move. Fast. Get over here," Doshmisi ordered. "Just walk slowly and stay where he can see you. Put your hand out and let him sniff you first, then walk around to the bench and I'll give you a hand up." Jasper did as she told him. From the bench, he passed Doshmisi her backpack, then he threw his leg over Dagobaz's back and seated himself behind her.

"Open the door, Jack," Doshmisi called to the intuit, "and let's get on up outta here."

Jack jumped back onto his hoverboard and opened the barn door. Smoke billowed into the barn and the panicked cries, that had remained distant and muffled with the door shut, pierced the air. "It's OK," Doshmisi soothed Dagobaz, as she leaned down low over his mane and put her mouth next to his ear. "I'm with you now. We can do this. We have to go."

"Diversion," Jack exclaimed. "Diversion, diversion."

Suddenly Doshmisi understood what Jack had meant when he had said "diversion" earlier. He had seen the explosion in the future, and that it would cause a diversion. He could see it before it happened, but he hadn't been able to articulate what he saw properly.

"I get what you mean now, Jack," Doshmisi called to him, "but sometimes I wish you could communicate like a normal person."

"He can't help it," Jasper reminded Doshmisi. "That's the nature of intuits."

"You are so weird, Jack. You hear me? Weird!" Doshmisi shouted in exasperation.

"Weird," Jack repeated with a chuckle. "Weird, weird, weird." He appeared to like the sound of that.

Then Dagobaz put his head down and followed Jack out the door of the barn and into the chaos.

The smoke seemed less ferocious even though one of the large buildings in the compound had caught fire. Occasional popping explosions emerged from the burning building.

"I bet Mole managed to sabotage something," Jasper speculated. "I wonder if he got out."

"Let's hope that gate's still open," Doshmisi called over her shoulder to Jasper, as she clung to Dagobaz, who galloped forward, with Jack hoverboarding beside him.

Chapter Fifteen
Buttered Biscuits

 "Where's Dosh?" Sonjay asked.

"At the North Coast with Jasper," Maia told him.

"How come you guys split up?"

"We got separated in the passage," Denzel answered.

"Then how do you know where she is?"

"Elena called her on her phone if you can believe it, but she was in the middle of something and couldn't talk and now she doesn't answer," Maia explained.

Sonjay tried to process this extraordinary news. "Her phone?"

"For real," Denzel confirmed with a quick laugh and an eye roll. "Crazy, huh? She said to meet her at Clover's."

Following Sonjay's lead, they skirted the city and made for the main entrance. Occasionally Maia attempted to touch him, but each time her hand went straight through him. It was disturbing.

As they circled the city, while sticking to the protective cover of the surrounding forest, they saw that an encampment of Compost's soldiers, heavily armed, guarded each of the entrance gates. Outside the main gate, Compost's vast encampment stretched into the distance. Campfires glowed, tigers stirred restlessly in their paddocks, and soldiers went about their daily activities. Sonjay and the others concealed themselves in a grove of fir trees on the edge of the plain where Compost had established his military tent city.

They spoke in hushed voices.

"Stay here, away from their weapons, and out of sight," Sonjay ordered. "I'll go speak to them. They can't kill me since I'm not in my body. If I can, I'll appear to you again when I finish. Just in case I can't, listen up. Do what Doshmisi said. Go to Grandmomma's and I'll try to meet you there with the Prophet of the Khoum."

"Prophet of the Khoum," Honeydew echoed dreamily.

"So you know what he means by the Prophet of the Khoum?" Denzel asked the princess.

"Of course," Honeydew confirmed.

"Good. You can explain it to the rest of us later, after Sonjay disintegrates." It bothered Denzel that he knew nothing about this Prophet of the Khoum and no one seemed forthcoming with more information.

"He's not going to disintegrate," Honeydew explained in the voice that Denzel thought of as her "professor voice." Sometimes she was such an annoying know-it-all. "He's just going to return to his physical body."

"Whatever," Denzel replied.

Sonjay sniffed the air distractedly. "Do you smell that?" he asked.

"What?" Denzel shot his brother a baffled look.

"Beans," Elena said.

"Beans," Guhblorin echoed, adding (because he couldn't entirely suppress his geebaching nature) "the musical fruit."

"Perfect," Sonjay announced with glee. "I smell beans and I don't smell meat to go with them. You know how the Mountain People love their meat." Sonjay's amulet began to glow with amber light.

"Can't you ever think about anything other than food?" Maia demanded in disgust.

"Yup," Sonjay answered happily. "But I bet those soldiers down there can't. I bet those soldiers have thought about little other than food for days, maybe weeks. I have an idea. You can thank me later. Don't go anywhere. Hopefully, I'll be right back." With those words he nearly disappeared. The others could vaguely see him in the form of a shimmer as he descended to the plain where Compost's troops prepared to sit down to their meager meal of beans-with-no-meat.

Sonjay's voice boomed across the plain. "Beans again?"

"How can he make his voice so loud?" Elena asked in wonder.

"It's an amplification enchantment," Honeydew said softly. "I can do that one too. It's one of the first ones they teach us."

"How many days of beans?" Sonjay's loud voice continued, spreading in all directions so that the troops could hear him clearly throughout the tent city. "How long do you want to keep eating beans and leaves? Wouldn't you just love to bite into a burger or crunch a tasty goose-chicken eyeball? Where's the meat? Roasted, barbecued, fried up in a pan. Dripping with gravy and poured over mashed potatoes. With macaroni and cheese. With cranberry sauce. How about apple pie and pumpkin pie and pecan pie, with whipped cream, with ice cream. Or an ice cream sundae. Cold vanilla ice cream with hot chocolate sauce. Crushed walnuts on top."

Compost's troops had set their plates of beans aside and stood or sat transfixed, listening to the smooth voice as it seductively described the delicious food they dreamed about but had not tasted for some time during the siege.

"Spaghetti and meatballs. Garlic bread. Chicken noodle soup. Eggs and grits with sausages. Blueberries, raspberries, strawberry cheesecake. What are you doing here?" Sonjay asked the troops. "When you could go home to your family and friends, where you could drink kiwi juice, eat chocolate cake, barbecue some ribs, slow-roast a chicken. What do you gain by staying here? Nothing. You're not well-fed. You're not appreciated. How long has it been since you've had a good meal? A decent espresso? Waffles slathered in butter and syrup? Chocolate chip cookies. Tangerines. Butterscotch pudding. Sweet-potato pie. What keeps you from going home? Just say no. Go back to your farm and your gardens and your kitchen pantry full of tasty treats. Take back your life. Take back your dinner."

Compost's soldiers eyed each other with hungry eyes. They stared into their boring plates of beans-with-no-meat.

"Wouldn't you give anything for a buttered biscuit? Can't you just taste that biscuit right now? Flaky and light and warm? Yeasty and soft. Go home and make biscuits," Sonjay implored. "Go home to your families in the Amber Mountains and bake biscuits and spread them with butter and eat them hot, straight from the oven. Imagine biting into those biscuits. Those hot, buttered biscuits!"

A sigh of longing rose from the soldiers as the words "buttered biscuits" passed from one salivating mouth to the next, reverently, longingly, and then with a fresh resolve. The soldiers gathered their belongings, mounted their tigers, and began a mass exodus from the encampment. In front of his tent, Compost threw a hissy-fit the size of Texas. He berated and threatened, jumped up and down and waved his arms in the air. He took off his hat and stomped on it. But no one paid him any mind and the din of departing feet drowned out his voice.

"Hot buttered biscuits," Sonjay crooned again and again in that velvety hypnotic voice. "Flaky and buttery and warm from the oven. Melt-in-your-mouth buttery biscuits." Sonjay repeated it until the legions of soldiers had mounted their tigers and headed away from the encampment while dreamily murmuring "buttered biscuits."

The entire army quickly disappeared, leaving behind a deserted city of abandoned tents, uneaten beans, and trash. The news that the siege army had headed for home to eat buttered biscuits spread to the encampments of troops at each of the city gates and these troops also packed up and left for the Amber Mountains and their farms, families, and a good dinner. By the time the descending sun approached the horizon in the fading afternoon, only a handful of Compost's most loyal followers shuffled and snuffled miserably outside Compost's tent, burdened with the thought of all the buttery biscuits they would not eat.

Once the troops evaporated, Sonjay returned, exhausted, to the place in the woods where he had left the others.

"Awesome," Elena complimented him as he approached them. "You've got game."

"I'm one of the Four and that's how we roll," Sonjay boasted, with a weak smile.

"You're the pusher-man," Denzel said with an approving nod. "I can't believe you pulled that off. I want some of them buttery biscuits my own self."

Sonjay began to flicker in and out of visibility, Honeydew realized that his ability to control his locomotaport had worn perilously thin. "You need to leave," she told him. "You need to go back to your body. Do it now. Can you do it?"

"I think so," Sonjay said faintly.

"Then go," Maia urged him, anxiously.

"I'll try to meet up with you at Grandmomma's," Sonjay whispered before he vanished completely.

After Sonjay vanished, the others turned their attention to the scene unfolding at the main gate of Big House City below. With his troops gone, Compost had no muscle. Honeydew's father, High Chief Hyacinth, and a group of royal guards emerged from Big House City and proceeded to Compost and his tiny band of loyalists, which consisted of about a dozen bedraggled men. The instant Princess Honeydew saw her father, she called out to the others, "Let's go." She abandoned her hiding place and fairly flew down the hill. Elena and Guhblorin followed reluctantly since Elena didn't yet feel safe walking out into the open and Guhblorin worried that someone would kill him on sight because he was a geebaching. He stuck to Elena like white on rice. Bisc trotted at Honeydew's side. It reassured Elena somewhat to have Bisc with them.

As she ran, Honeydew called out, "Daddy! Daddy!" The royal guards had taken Compost and his men into custody. The high chief turned to look up the hillside and his face broke into a delighted grin as he saw his daughter and Bisc bounding toward him. High Chief Hyacinth adored animals and had a special way with them. Bisc jumped up on Hyacinth, nearly knocking him over, and licked his face enthusiastically. A few moments later, Honeydew flung herself into Hyacinth's arms, sobbing. "Oh Daddy, I'm so glad you're alright! I was so worried."

"Not to worry," Hyacinth comforted his daughter as he stroked her hair. "We're fine. We heard the voice about the buttered biscuits from inside the city and wondered what enchanter had come to our aid. Who spoke of the buttered biscuits?"

"It was Sonjay, Daddy," Honeydew told him. Then the words tumbled out of her as if a dam had burst. "The Four came back, only they got separated in the passage so Sonjay landed somewhere else but he locomotaported. Amazing, right? Not since Hazamon, huh?! But Sonjay did it. He found a Prophet of the Khoum. And Denzel and Maia are with me, and they brought a friend named Elena, and they found a geebaching, only he's a friendly one, a Dud, who won't hurt a soul, and Compost caught us and put us in a garbage labyrinth, but then the butterflies came and flew away with Guhblorin and when they brought him back he…"

"Whoa, whoa, slow down," Hyacinth stopped his daughter, "too much inflotation. I'm completely obtuse." Hyacinth spoke in a unique and somewhat incomprehensible manner because he confused the meaning of words. Honeydew was one of the few people who could usually decipher what he meant. She laughed happily to hear his mangled language.

"You must mean too much information and that you are completely confused," she told him, as she stood on her toes and kissed him on the tip of his nose. "Obtuse means you're not very observant. I don't think inflotation is actually a word."

"I mean you make no sense at all," he replied.

"I know what you mean. I'll tell you all about our adventures at dinner. I'm starved. What have we got to eat?"

"Any buttered biscuits?" Denzel asked hopefully. The others had caught up with Honeydew and Bisc. Hyacinth released his daughter and pulled Denzel and Maia into a joyful hug. As royals, the Four were distant cousins to him. He beamed as he greeted them, "Welcome," he announced in a loud jolly voice, "Welcome to Big House City. I welcome you with opulence, corpulence, and flatulence!"

Elena did not know for sure what opulence or corpulence meant, but she knew what flatulence meant. She thought Hyacinth seemed a rather peculiar ruler and she struggled to keep a straight face so she wouldn't insult him by laughing at him. But Maia and Denzel, who had traveled with him the previous summer and knew him well, busted out laughing, while Honeydew explained to her father, "Daddy, Daddy! Opulence means wealth, corpulence refers to a really fat person, and flatulence, oh my goodness," she giggled, "flatulence means farting. I hardly think you wish to welcome them with *that*."

"Oh dear," Hyacinth said, worried and embarrassed. "I do have a nice big house and I have put on quite a few pounds from your mother's delicious cooking, but I would never wish to subject my guests to flatulence. Oh my."

"Not a problem," Denzel assured Hyacinth good-naturedly. "We're happy to see you again too."

Meanwhile, the royal guards from inside Big House City had tied Compost's hands behind his back and similarly incapacitated his few remaining followers. Elena could not stop staring at Compost. She had not had a good look at him when he captured them at the garbage labyrinth. Now that she could see him clearly, she was fascinated by him. He had the nappiest uncombed hair and a film of dirt dusted his yellowish-grayish-brownish skin. His fat belly hung over his belt and jiggled. But most of all she noticed that he smelled bad, like a person living on the street who hadn't taken a shower in months. She had never seen a more repulsive individual. She looked into his eyes, which gazed back at her sadly in defeat. A wave of pity for him washed over her. Friendless, abandoned, disliked, he didn't' seem all that dangerous. He reminded her of the homeless people who came to her family's church for dinners on Sundays. Elena often went with her parents to serve food to the homeless at church.

Compost asked Elena quietly, with a sneer, "How'd you get out of the labyrinth?"

"The geebaching rescued us," she answered, just as the others paused in their reunion conversation. Her voice sounded louder in the sudden silence.

"No, it wasn't really me," Guhblorin protested. "It was the butterflies."

"It was you *and* the butterflies. We would never have gotten out of there if not for you," Elena insisted. "It was Guhblorin," she told Compost and Hyacinth and all those within earshot. "The geebaching saved our lives."

"How irregular," Hyacinth muttered. "A geebaching of all things."

Honeydew introduced Elena and Guhblorin to her father and added in a loud voice for all to hear, "Guhblorin is a good geebaching. He's trying not to hurt anyone. He remains under my royal protection."

"Thank you, Your Highness," Guhblorin said as he flapped his ears nervously.

"High Chief Hyacinth, I plead for mercy for these followers of Compost," Maia announced. "I think if you allow them to return to their homes, they won't cause any further trouble. You have captured Compost. Please release these others. The rest of Compost's troops have left for their homes already."

Hyacinth rubbed his chin in thought.

"You can do that, Daddy," Honeydew reassured him.

"Last year we let Sissrath run away with his followers and now look what a problematic scintillation he caused," Hyacinth pointed out.

Elena thought that a scintillation was a flash of light. She figured that the high chief must mean the situation that Sissrath had caused with the siege. His odd speech was difficult but not impossible to decipher.

One of the followers in question instantly dropped to his knees and the others quickly followed suit. They looked thoroughly miserable. The one who had first dropped to his knees appealed to High Chief Hyacinth for mercy, "Please, Your Highness, allow us to return to our families in the Amber Mountains and we will not trouble you again. We are simple men who fear Sissrath. Please protect us from him."

Hyacinth blustered and blushed. "Get up, get up," he commanded. The prisoners stood. "I can't promise to protect you from Sissrath. I can't even protect myself from him."

"Release these prisoners," Princess Honeydew told the royal guards, who followed her order. The former prisoners hurried off before their captors could change their minds.

At that moment, Honeydew's mother, High Chieftess Saffron, emerged from Big House City accompanied by Cardamom the enchanter and a great deal of hugging and back-patting and hand-shaking ensued, along with introductions. Cardamom was genuinely delighted to make the acquaintance of a real-live geebaching. Explanations were offered and stories swapped. While the others enjoyed their happy reunion, Elena continued to eye Compost curiously. He smelled quite like over-cooked broccoli, which Elena considered one of the worst-smelling things in the whole world. When her mother cooked broccoli, Elena left the house.

"So," Elena asked Compost quietly, "how come you're so dirty?"

"I like dirt," Compost replied defensively, also quietly. The noisy reunion continued, with everyone oblivious to Elena and Compost.

"I don't believe you," Elena told him firmly.

"That shows how much you know," Compost said.

"You smell dreadful. You can't possibly enjoy that."

"It keeps people like you from bothering me."

"You don't know me. Maybe I like rotten vegetables. Maybe you would like me."

"I doubt it."

"Why do you want to fight the high chief? What did he do to you?" Elena asked.

"He's an imbecile who rules only because of his royal blood. He has virtually no ability at enchantment. He needs a barn full of advisors to make even the simplest decision. And yet he leads the land," Compost spat out venomously. "The People of the Mountain Downs, my people, are infinitely better equipped as leaders and yet we must do the bidding of that fool who can't even speak a grammatical sentence. I come from a people of great enchanters. We should rule."

"If you think about it, though, it doesn't matter how smart you are or how proficient you are at enchantment if you're not a good person. To be a good leader, you have to be a good person. You have to be someone who cares about helping others and making their lives better. The smartest person in the world could be a rotten leader if that person is mean and hurts other people," Elena countered.

Compost studied Elena uncertainly.

"Being smart isn't everything, you know," Elena added.

"You're not from around here, are you?"

"No. I came with my friends."

"The Four?"

"Yeah, I guess that's what you call them here. I wasn't supposed to come with them. They didn't want me to come, but I came anyway. It's a long story."

"I'm their sworn enemy, you know," Compost told Elena.

"Your point?" she asked, somewhat rebelliously.

Compost chuckled. "Tell me, do you think someone who treats most of his subjects with respect but treats one group of his subjects like second-class citizens is a good leader?"

"Of course not," Elena answered. "That's hurting other people. That's unjust and unethical."

"Well," Compost continued, smugly, "that's the treatment my people have received. As if we are inferior beings. I resent it. If Hyacinth can't treat us properly then he shouldn't be the high chief, right?"

"My people are treated like inferiors a lot of the time where I come from," Elena told Compost. "And the leaders in our country don't do enough to stop it."

"What are your people?" Compost asked. He focused intensely on what Elena had to say. It was as if the two of them were in their own private room, separated from all the clamor that surrounded them.

"I'm a Mexican-American, a Chicana. Where I come from…" Elena began to explain.

Compost interrupted her, "In the Farland?"

"The Farland?"

"You come from where the Four come from, right? The Farland."

"The Farland," Elena repeated after him. "OK, where I come from in the Farland, Mexican-American people are often treated as inferiors."

"Why do they do you like that?" Compost asked.

"Well, for one thing a lot of us speak Spanish instead of English as our first language, and for another a lot of us are immigrants."

"Spanish? Immigrants?" Compost asked, uncomprehending.

Elena thought for a minute about how to explain it to him. "We originally come from a land farther away from the center of things than where most of the other people who live around us come from. Our land is called Mexico and we speak our own language called Spanish there."

"The People of the Mountain Downs live farther from Big House City than anyone," Compost said with a note of surprise.

"Do they treat you worse because of that?" Elena asked.

"Partly. We do things our own way, which is a little differently from the other people. For instance, the Mountain People eat meat and all the other people don't."

"You mean all the other people here are vegetarians?" Elena asked incredulously.

"No lie," Compost confirmed.

"That's *loco!*"

"*Loco?*"

"Crazy. They're crazy. I couldn't live without Carne Asada, Pollo Con Mole, or Pork Carnitas."

"What is that stuff?" Compost asked.

"Mexican food! But of course; you never had Mexican food. *Pobrecito,* poor guy. Pollo Con Mole is chicken in spicy chocolate sauce," Elena explained.

Compost's eyes grew large. "Oh stop. Stop this minute. You're killing me. That sounds so excellent. I haven't had anything except beans and cabbage for weeks."

"I can cook some for you. *Mí abuela* (that's Spanish for grandmother) taught me how to cook and I love cooking traditional Mexican food." Elena's words tumbled over each other in a hurry as her thoughts raced.

"You would do that? Cook me Pollo Con Mole?" Compost sounded shocked.

"Why not?"

"Because no one likes me," Compost blurted out.

"So change," Elena said, as she tossed her blue-black hair over her shoulder. The two of them stared at each other for a long moment.

"Change?"

"Yes, change. Become a person people will like."

"That's too hard."

"If the geebaching could do it then you could do it."

"The geebaching?"

"Yeah. He decided to stop killing people with laughter. He changed. You could change too."

"Like how?" Compost mumbled.

"Take a bath, for one thing. Get a haircut. I could cut your hair for you. Sheesh. Isn't it obvious? Look at yourself. You're a hot mess. Put on some decent clothes. You look like you just crawled out of that hideous garbage labyrinth. Brush your teeth. I mean, make an effort."

"And what if I agree to do that?" Compost sounded extremely surprised to be saying those words even as they tumbled from his mouth.

"People might take to you. And I'll see what I can do about this present predicament of yours and your previous unwise association with that unsavory Sissrath character." At Elena's words, Compost laughed out loud. His laughter caught the attention of Denzel, Maia, and the royals, who fell silent and gazed at Elena and Compost.

"Compost would like a bath if that can be arranged," Elena announced.

Unfortunately, she announced this just as Guhblorin was taking a long drink of water from a bottle. He exploded with laughter, spraying High Chief Hyacinth. Water then poured out of his nose and ears as he fell on his back laughing like only a geebaching can, which set everyone else laughing. They all roared with laughter. Except for Elena, who kept a completely straight face. She had taken on a mission and remained unmoved by the hilarity.

"Compost is rethinking his identity," Elena insisted, when the others had quieted enough to hear her. "He needs a makeover. He wants a bath and a haircut, which I will give him, and a large tray of Pollo Con Mole, which I intend to cook for him."

"You're serious," Denzel replied.

"As serious as a hunting coyote," Elena confirmed.

"As serious as what she said," Compost added. "I'm with her."

"We're going second class together, aren't we, Compost?" Elena linked her arm through Compost's and, to everyone's astonishment, she planted a tiny peck of a kiss on his grimy cheek. "*Compadres,*" Elena said.

Then the most amazing thing happened. Compost blushed. "Second-class *compadres,*" Compost said to Elena, with a twisted little smile.

Maia nearly fainted dead away at the shock when she noticed that Compost's eyes glistened with unshed tears and she remembered a line from one of Momma's favorite Otis Redding songs: "Try a little tenderness."

Chapter Sixteen
Trackers

When Sonjay floated through the wall of the prison cell, he saw his body below him on the floor. His father sat cross-legged on the rug and cradled Sonjay's head in his lap. Buttercup slept in the bed and Crumpet had nodded off in the chair, his head thrown back and his mouth wide open. He snored loudly. Beyond exhausted, Sonjay weakly attempted, with no luck, to force his locomotaported self down into his body. He felt pinned to the ceiling. He feebly fought to remain conscious. Bayard flew in through the window and squawked, which caught Reggie's attention and he gazed upward.

"Are you there, Sonjay?" Reggie asked.

Reggie could make out the vague misty outline of Sonjay's form as he squinted up at the ceiling. "Come on down. Here you are," Reggie encouraged. "I've got you, son." Bayard squawked again, this time closer to the locomotaported self, as if trying to herd Sonjay back into his body. His squawk woke Crumpet and Buttercup, who jumped to their feet as quickly as old people can jump, and they waved and called to Sonjay, who mustered every ounce of remaining energy he had, took aim at his body on the rug, and forced his locomotaported self to float back down into his physical self. He returned to his body with a snap only moments before he dropped into unconsciousness.

When Sonjay opened his eyes, many hours later, he found himself tucked comfortably in his father's bed in the dim cell. He fought the weakness in his body and sat up. His empty stomach growled with hunger. Taking care not to disturb Crumpet and Buttercup, who slept on the rug, he slowly made his way to the desk and lifted a corner of the cloth that covered the glow-lamp. Beside the glow-lamp sat a fat sandwich on a plate and a large glass of juice. "We set that out for you in case you needed a midnight snack." Reggie's voice emerged from the darkness at the outer edge of the cell. In the dim light, Sonjay identified his father's form in the desk chair.

"Sorry I woke you. I tried to be quiet."

"You were plenty quiet. I wasn't asleep," Reggie assured him. "How'd it go?"

"I ended the siege," Sonjay stated matter-of-factly as he took a bite of the sandwich and chewed.

"I figured," Reggie responded. "Did you see the others?"

"Just Denzel and Maia. Dosh isn't with them. She wound up somewhere else," Sonjay explained. "But they know where she went. They plan to meet up at Grandmomma's on Whale Island. We need to get out of here and meet them there."

"I have an idea about that," Reggie informed him.

Sonjay stopped chewing. "Hit me with it," he said expectantly.

"You locomotaport out with that parrot…"

"Bayard," Sonjay interrupted.

"Yes, with Bayard," Reggie continued, "and you find the key to the cell. You can't carry the key in your locomotaport form, but Bayard can carry it in his beak. Do you think you could make him understand that he has to retrieve the key for us?"

"Not a problem. He's no ordinary bird."

"Bayard brings us the key through the window. Once we leave this cell, Crumpet and Buttercup will be able to use enchantment. They'll get us past the guards," Reggie concluded.

"Can they use enchantment inside the Final Fortress?" Sonjay asked.

"I have learned many things about this place while in this cell. Although Sissrath has blocked the use of enchantments inside individual cells, he does not have the strength to block enchantments throughout the entire Final Fortress. If we can just get Crumpet and Buttercup outside the confines of this cell, then their enchantments will likely work," Reggie asserted.

"Buttercup's anyway. We can't depend on Crumpet. Let's hope he doesn't turn himself into anything too large for us to pick up and carry with us."

Reggie laughed softly, and hearing his father's laugh filled Sonjay with happiness. He smiled, took another bite of the sandwich, and suggested, "We should go at night when they'll have more trouble following us."

"That makes sense."

"In the meantime, I can locomotaport out of here to look for the key."

"No need. I know where they keep it," Reggie said. Sonjay finished eating his sandwich. "Get some more rest. You'll need it," Reggie told him.

"What about you?" Sonjay asked.

"Don't worry about me," Reggie said.

Sonjay went to Reggie and put his arms around him. "G'night Dad."

"Good night, son," Reggie responded. He squeezed Sonjay's upper arms briefly and then released him. "Sweet dreams."

Sonjay crawled back into Reggie's bed, contentedly, and fell fast asleep.

In the morning, Crumpet, Buttercup, and Sonjay meditated to gather their energy for the escape. Sonjay had hardly anything in his backpack so he gave it to his father. Reggie packed the few things he would take with him from the cell where he had lived for nearly ten years. Mostly he took books, and he had trouble deciding which ones. Although Sissrath had imprisoned his body, his mind had remained free. The books that surrounded him had served as his companions and he regretted leaving so many of them behind.

Impatient to embark upon their escape, Sonjay locomotaported out of the cell with Bayard the instant the sun went down. Reggie had described for him the guard house at the top of the stairs where the keys to the cells were kept and how to recognize the one for their cell. He had no difficulty finding the key and Bayard silently picked it up off its hook in his powerful beak when Sonjay pointed to it. The guard in the guard house (not one of the aliens, but one of the Mountain People) remained engrossed in a solitaire card game and did not notice the stealthy parrot behind him.

Before they unlocked the door to the cell, Reggie took a last look around. Crumpet patted Reggie's shoulder and said, "May the work of the Four continue." He and his comrades often said that phrase at times of departure. It always gave Sonjay an odd feeling when he heard it because he was one of the Four and he never knew for sure exactly what his work might entail since he made it up as he went along.

The escaped prisoners clung to the cold stone wall as they crept up the stairs. Bayard perched on his favorite spot on Sonjay's shoulder. Buttercup threw a sleeping enchantment at the guard in the guard house. Then Crumpet led them through a maze of hallways and out into the central courtyard of the Final Fortress. They had barely emerged when a flock of skeeters took to the sky with a racket of wings, cawing loudly to alert the guards and Corportons about the escaped prisoners.

"Those infernal birds. If I could, I'd fry up the lot of them and eat them for dinner. This way! Quickly!" Buttercup ordered as she made a mad dash for the gate and their freedom. The others ran after her.

Sonjay heard a hiss next to his ear and Bayard leapt from his shoulder and took to the air in fright. Sonjay ducked as a flying snake whizzed past his head. "Yuk!" he shouted as he jumped behind Crumpet, who had turned to face the onslaught.

Three flying snakes, more than five feet in length and as thick around as Reggie's muscular thigh, glowed phosphorescent-green in the dark. They circled back, regrouped, and then flew at the escapees.

"Reptiraptors!" Buttercup screamed, as Crumpet raised his hands to cast an enchantment.

"Why you demonic, pythonic, moronic…" Crumpet began as he drew himself up to his full height and nearly exploded in fury.

"Babycakes, no!" Buttercup shouted at him. "Restraint. Control your temper."

Sonjay clung to the back of Crumpet's cloak, using the large enchanter as a shield to protect himself from the attacking serpents, and he reminded his friend, "Chill. Don't get too bent. You'll turn into a muffin any second." Green electric light flashed from Crumpet's fingertips briefly and then he closed his hands into tight fists. As the reptiraptors swooped in for the kill, Crumpet pulled his arms back and then, wham, wham, wham, he punched each of those flying snakes hard, right in the nose, like Muhammad Ali in the ring. He knocked them right out. Crumpet grinned at Sonjay as the reptiraptors dropped from the air and landed unmoving on the ground at his feet. "Doing it the old-fashioned way," he said.

Buttercup immediately subdued the guard in the guard house with her handy sleep enchantment and the four of them fled into the hillside, where a thick fog engulfed them. "Stay close," Buttercup commanded. They followed her up a rocky slope and into the forest. Once they had reached the cover of trees, Buttercup stopped and cocked her head to listen. They could hear dogs barking in the distance.

"They're already tracking us," Buttercup warned.

"Dogs?" Reggie asked.

"Sounds like it, yes," Buttercup replied. "We'll have to keep moving and find a way to throw them off our trail." She put her arms around Crumpet and kissed him. "You done good, babycakes. You're not a doughnut."

"It's all in the feet," Crumpet boasted. "You gotta plant your feet and then pack a wallop."

"How well do you know this territory surrounding the Final Fortress?" Reggie asked Buttercup and Crumpet.

"Extremely well. We live in the Amber Mountains," Buttercup replied.

"Can you take us to a stream or river or other body of water? Those dogs will lose our scent in water," Reggie told them.

"This way," Buttercup pointed and the others scrambled after her as she retreated further into the forest.

"How'd you know that?" Sonjay asked Reggie.

"Haven't you ever watched any slavey-in-the-South movies, where the slaves throw the slave-trackers and their dogs off by walking in a stream?" Reggie asked his son.

"You mean like Harriet Tubman and follow-the-drinking-gourd and all that?" Sonjay responded.

"Yeah, like American history."

"No, not really. I saw *Sounder* 'cause Aunt Alice insisted that it was important for my education. Slavery is depressing," Sonjay declared.

"It's important to know about history and your origins," Reggie said.

"My origin is in Faracadar, and here we don't want to head to the North. We want to head to the South."

The four escapees moved quickly through the dark forest, watching the ground carefully to maintain their footing. Buttercup led them down a slippery slope into a ravine, at the bottom of which flowed a wide stream.

"So now we wade in the water," Buttercup gasped, trying to catch her breath from the rush to stay ahead of the dogs, which they could still hear in the distance. She removed her shoes and tied the laces together, strung them around her neck, then hiked her dress up over her knees and tucked it into her waistband. The others followed suit with their shoes and rolled up their pants. In their haste, they splashed water on their clothes anyway. Sonjay feared stepping on something icky in the water in the dark, but he had to move too quickly to watch carefully where he stepped. Small round stones covered the bottom of the stream and he had to concentrate so as not to tumble into the water. Reggie stumbled as his backpack full of books threw him off balance.

They staggered and slithered in the stream for what seemed to Sonjay like hours, following it as it wound between the trees rising up on both sides of them. The sound of the dogs barking and baying faded. Sonjay wondered how much time had passed since they had escaped from their cell and how soon the sun would rise.

Buttercup came to a halt. "We can't continue in the stream," she said. "It winds to the North and we need to go to the South. Otherwise, we'll never get out of the Amber Mountains. We have to go toward Big House City. This stream goes in the opposite direction."

"Wouldn't it throw them off in their pursuit if we continue for a while in the opposite direction from what they expect?" Reggie asked.

"We won't find any help along this stream. To the South we will find sympathetic circles of people who will help us if we can reach them. We risk cutting ourselves off from these people if we go to the North," Crumpet explained.

"Seriously, can we get out of this water?" Sonjay added.

Reggie sighed. "OK, to the South."

They climbed up onto the steep embankment rising from the stream.

"Listen," Buttercup cocked her head to the side as she sat down to put on her shoes.

"What are we listening for?" Sonjay asked.

"Dogs," Buttercup answered. "I don't hear them anymore."

"I'll take that as a good sign," Crumpet said hopefully.

After they dried their feet and put their shoes and socks back on, the soggy escapees continued through the forest. Sonjay wished he could lie down and go to sleep. He wished he had a tiger to ride. He stumbled on a root and fell forward, catching himself on his hands as he landed hard on the ground.

"Maybe we should rest," Reggie suggested anxiously. "We seem to have put the dogs off the scent for now."

"There are some caves I know about just up ahead," Crumpet informed Reggie, "and we can hide in there and sleep for a little while." It didn't take them long to reach the caves, where Sonjay curled up gratefully on the hard ground and fell asleep instantly. He did not know how long he had slept before Buttercup shook him awake. He saw the milky-blue light of early dawn beckoning from the cave entrance.

"The dogs," Buttercup told Sonjay urgently. "I hear them again. We need to get moving." The escapees grabbed their belongings and hurried back into the tree-covered mountains, with Buttercup leading the way.

Sonjay heard the dogs plainly and their baying grew noticeably louder by the minute. The dogs were gaining ground.

Bayard, who flew high up overhead, squawked "trees, trees, trees."

"Wait, stop," Sonjay called to Buttercup. He studied Bayard, who had changed his chant from "trees" to "up, up, up."

Sonjay announced, "Bayard wants us to climb up the trees. We should do what he says."

"He's a bird," Reggie protested, breathlessly. "What does he know? Birds always feel safe in the trees."

"Trust me," Sonjay reassured his father, "he's an extremely smart bird. If he tells me to climb a tree then I will climb a tree."

"We don't have many options," Crumpet pointed out. "I agree with Bayard. Buttercup and I might manage an enchantment or two on the dogs from up a tree. Let's get off the ground."

"Up!" Bayard called urgently as he perched on a high branch in an enormous fir tree. Sonjay grabbed onto the bottom branch and began to climb toward the parrot, the sticky sap turning black on his hands as he went. The tree was perfect for climbing. The branches led one to another and Sonjay clambered quickly to the top. Even Reggie, carrying the backpack full of books, had little difficulty climbing up the tree. The four of them spread out on the firm upper branches, which held them like the arms of a friendly giant. From his vantage point, Sonjay could actually see the dogs racing through the woods. Close behind the dogs followed more pursuers than Sonjay could count.

"Look," Sonjay pointed out to the others, "no aliens, just Sissrath's Special Forces. I never thought I'd be happy to see them, but I'm glad it's them and not those Corportons."

"I hear you," Buttercup agreed.

"Do you think they'll see us?" Reggie asked anxiously. "Maybe the tree's branches will conceal us."

"Doesn't matter," Crumpet said. "The dogs will go crazy when they catch our scent going up the tree. They'll know."

"Then what do we do?" Reggie asked.

Approaching rapidly, the dogs would reveal their whereabouts to the pursuing Special Forces in a couple of minutes.

"Skaters," Bayard squawked. "Skaters, skaters, skaters."

"Skeeters?" Buttercup asked Bayard anxiously as she scanned the sky. The last thing they needed was a flock of skeeters.

"No," Sonjay said, his head cocked as he listened to the bird. "Skaters."

"Skaters," Bayard confirmed.

"I thought he said skeeters at first too, but he said skaters," Sonjay informed Buttercup, and then he laughed out loud.

"What's so funny about skaters?" Crumpet asked Sonjay.

Sonjay pointed silently.

The others followed the direction of his finger with their eyes and saw something approaching, in fact many somethings. Reggie squinted against the light of the morning sun, struggling to see what Sonjay saw. But before he understood what he was looking at, hoverboarding intuits descended on the trapped escapees and scooped them up out of the tops of the trees.

It took a half a dozen of them working together to hoist Buttercup into the air between them. She laughed delightedly. Sonjay jumped onto the back of Jack's board, which was a long board, and Sonjay set his feet and flew with Jack as he and the others followed Bayard, who flapped furiously as he led the way to the South and Big House City.

The skaters had plucked the escapees out of the treetops and flown them away by the time the trackers arrived sniffing and barking madly at the base of the fir tree. The hounds' furious snarls and yips faded in the distance.

"How did you know?" Sonjay asked Jack.

"We're intuits," Jack shouted over the sound of the rushing wind. "That's what we do. We know." Sonjay had never heard Jack utter so many words in a row before.

"You're not just intuits," Sonjay answered gleefully, "you're skaters. Best thing I ever did in this crazy land was teach you little dudes how to skateboard."

Chapter Seventeen
Reunion

In her ignorance of the history of Faracadar, Elena was the only person in all of Big House City to believe that Compost had genuinely decided to become a reformed individual. Everyone else perceived him as a dangerous enemy and he had certainly earned that reputation. Hadn't he just laid siege to Big House City for many weeks at Sissrath's command, threatening the lives of the royal family? Everyone but Elena had no doubt that he belonged in prison. They did, however, allow him to take a bath, and afterward Elena cut his hair close to his head. She provided him with a clean set of clothing, helped him trim his nails, and convinced him to rub cocoa butter moisturizer on his ashy skin. After his makeover, his own mother would not have recognized him. His captors feared him less than they would have if he had the ability to use enchantment. Only some of the Mountain People could use enchantment and Compost was not a person with this ability.

Once she had helped Compost improve his appearance and personal grooming, Elena introduced herself to the royal cooks and kitchen staff and arranged to use the kitchen to prepare a traditional Mexican meal as best as she could with the ingredients that she could find at hand. She enlisted Guhblorin as her kitchen assistant and didn't complain when he taste-tested the ingredients (especially the chocolate).

While Elena kept busy transforming Compost's hygiene habits and establishing a makeshift *taqueria* in the royal kitchen, Denzel, Maia, and Honeydew met with the great enchanter Cardamom and Honeydew's parents to sort through the information they had and to chart a course of action. They wondered why Doshmisi had instructed them not to go to the North Coast, but instead to meet her on Whale Island, when obviously something serious was happening at the North Coast. The news that Sonjay had joined forces with a Prophet of the Khoum caused much excitement among those with an understanding of what that meant. But where had Sonjay locomotaported from? Everyone was worried about Sissrath's activities and whereabouts because they knew how much damage he could do. After much discussion, Denzel concluded, "We need more information, especially about Sissrath."

"Only one person here in Big House City has more information about Sissrath," Maia said.

"We have to question him," Honeydew agreed.

"Your friend Elena should do it," High Chieftess Saffron suggested. "She has a rapport with him. I think he would speak to her about Sissrath to prove to her that he seriously wishes to change, whether he actually does or not, which, of course, is questionable."

"She's too busy cooking dinner for him to interrogate him," Denzel reminded them, unable to keep the irritation out of his voice.

"She's cooking dinner for all of us," Maia reminded him.

"I'll go to the kitchen and invite her to join our conversation," Saffron offered.

Saffron proceeded down the back stairs to the kitchen where she found Elena with her thick hair pulled back in a ponytail and her hands covered in cornmeal. Guhblorin mashed avocados in a large bowl while nibbling on a hot chili pepper, which had turned his ears bright red. "*Ay Caramba!*" he exclaimed after each nibble of spicy chili pepper.

"It smells delicious in here," Saffron greeted Elena.

"I'm just getting started," Elena responded cheerfully, clearly in her element in the kitchen. "I love this." Her eyes glowed brightly.

"I've come to request that you join us for a few minutes to discuss a delicate matter," Saffron informed her.

Elena frowned as she brushed a stray hair back from her forehead with the back of her hand and left a smudge of cornmeal on her face. "Now?"

Saffron picked up a towel and wiped the cornmeal smudge off Elena's face. "Wash your hands and please come with me. This won't take long."

Elena washed up, removed her apron, and warned Guhblorin not to eat too many chilies, before following Saffron up the stairs into the council chamber.

"What's up?" she asked as she approached the others gathered around the council table.

"Would you please help us?" Cardamom asked.

"Me?" Elena replied as her eyes grew wide. She wondered what they imagined she could do.

"Let me break it down for you," Cardamom continued. "We need to figure out what Sissrath is doing and why. He's extremely dangerous, extremely powerful, extremely clever, and perfectly capable of destroying the whole land. As one of Sissrath's most high-level commanders, Compost has valuable knowledge about Sissrath's activities. We need him to share that knowledge with us."

"He *was* one of Sissrath's commanders," Elena corrected firmly. "Was. He gave all that up. He doesn't work for Sissrath anymore."

"So he says," Honeydew responded skeptically.

"And so he means," Elena insisted stubbornly. "I believe that people can change. He's trying to become a different person, a better person."

"You haven't gone through everything with him that we've gone through," Maia explained.

"Last year he tried to kill us," Denzel said. "He commanded the Special Forces when they burned the Passage Circle to the ground. You didn't see what the Passage Circle looked like after that attack, or what it looked like before they destroyed it. Compost put us in the garbage labyrinth, remember? And he tried to starve this entire city to death. Tell me one thing he has done to make me believe that he has changed."

Elena gazed around the room at the expectant faces of those gathered there. "Because I am new here, I don't have any preconceived notions about people in this place, no stereotypic perceptions of what Mountain People are like or not like, or what geebachings are like or not like. So I just see Guhblorin as he is, as he's trying to be. Same with Compost. I don't know about Compost's past, I see him for who he is now, who he's trying to be now. As an observer, it appears to me that Compost's people from the High Mountains have been mistreated and disrespected. Perhaps if he and his people were treated better then he would have behaved differently."

"It takes time to build trust," Saffron said. "And we don't have the luxury of time for that in this moment. We need information about Sissrath's activities now. Please help us convince Compost to tell us what he knows about Sissrath."

Elena studied the others as she considered Saffron's request. "I would be willing to ask him politely for information if you would be willing to invite him to sit down to dinner with us tonight in the dining hall."

"Invite him to dinner?! But he's my swollen enemy because of the crimes he has comittated," Hyacinth pronounced sternly.

"*Qué?*" Elena asked.

"Daddy means that he can't forgive Compost that easily for the horrible things he has done, such as trying to kill him," Honeydew explained.

Elena crossed her arms. "Well, everybody has a choice. We can either keep doing things the same way and keep seeing things the same way, or we can open our minds to new possibilities. If you keep doing things the same way then you'll probably spend the rest of your lives fighting.

Mountain People. Big House City people. Fight, fight, fight. Battles. Sieges. Burning down circles. What if you could agree to a compromise and the Mountain People could agree to a compromise and you could make a peaceful place for your children? Everyone will have to give up things they don't want to give up. That's how compromise works." Elena shrugged. "That's my opinion. It's your land. Do what you want. But I think forgiveness will serve you better than revenge and holding grudges. If you want me, you'll find me in the kitchen."

As Maia watched Elena leave the council chamber, she felt a rush of affection for her friend. At the same time, she knew that Elena had simplified things in her mind because she didn't know the history of Faracadar and she had never seen Sissrath, the leader of the so-called dissatisfied people of the Mountain Downs, commander of the Special Forces, Compost's boss, and the most malevolent individual she had ever encountered. She wanted to defend Elena's position, but she could not believe that Compost had transformed himself into a harmless player in the unfolding events. She knew what he was capable of.

"Theoretically, she's right, you know," Saffron said, with a sigh.

"Theoretically," Hyacinth echoed.

"But not realistically. She has this fantasy that we can make a truce with Sissrath, and we know he's just not a truce-making sort of guy," Denzel reminded them. The previous year, Sissrath had shot Denzel, his siblings, and all of their closest friends with poison darts and they would have died if not for Sonjay calling the Staff of Shakabaz to him and using it to save their lives just in the nick of time. After that, Sissrath ran away. Denzel did not look forward to another encounter with the powerful enchanter, who appeared devoid of any human attachments or affections.

"To get what we want, I think we need to honor Elena's request," Saffron said.

"Guess who's coming to dinner," Maia said to Denzel. It was a joke. *Guess Who's Coming to Dinner?* was the title of an old Sidney Poitier,

Katherine Hepburn, and Spencer Tracey movie about a white woman who fell in love with a black man and brought him home to meet her parents. Denzel shook his head and smiled weakly.

"I'll send a message to Compost that his presence is desired at dinner," Cardamom said. The council meeting dissolved and Saffron headed for the kitchen to inform Elena of their decision.

They reassembled at a long wooden table in the dining room that evening. Hyacinth and Saffron dressed up for the occasion and they appeared spectacularly royal in deep-purple velvet robes trimmed with silver braid.

Eight ferocious-looking guards escorted Compost from his cell to the royal dining room. He appeared in a mustard-yellow suit with a black shirt; and the dramatic change in his appearance shocked the others. His feet remained shackled, forcing him to shuffle to the table. After Compost sat, a guard chained his left wrist to his chair, forged from heavy metal, unlike the other dining room chairs, constructed from artfully carved wood. When Elena emerged from the kitchen with Guhblorin to join the others, she took one look at Compost, and glared sternly at everyone else seated around the table. Guhblorin flapped his ears uncomfortably and hid behind Elena.

"What?" Denzel demanded. "What do you have a problem with now?"

"You must treat a dinner guest with respect. You don't chain a dinner guest to his chair. I will not bring a single tortilla out here until you release him," Elena announced.

"Release him?" Hyacinth asked incredulously.

"Release him?" Honeydew and Denzel echoed.

"Unchain him," Elena demanded.

Everyone looked around at everyone else uncertainly before Saffron instructed the guards to release Compost from his chains. The guards stepped forward and unlocked the chain at his wrist and removed the manacles from his feet.

"And bring him a comfy chair like ours," Elena ordered. Honeydew reluctantly rose and fetched a carved wooden chair with a cushioned seat from against the wall and brought it over to Compost.

Compost thanked her politely.

Elena seated herself between Compost and Guhblorin. "Tell them," Elena said to Compost. "Before we eat, tell them what they don't read in the history books. Tell them what you told me."

Compost replied, "I think they know Elena. They just don't want to know."

"Don't assume. Tell it," Elena demanded. "Explain why your people feel slighted and mistreated. Tell about the long-ago time."

"Yes, tell me about that," Denzel interjected. "I would like to hear about that." He couldn't imagine what type of explanation Compost might have given to Elena, what stories he had fabricated about the past.

"At one time," Compost commenced as he looked down self-consciously, "the Mountain People did not live in one place. We wandered with the seasons and set up camp in small groups throughout the land." He glanced around at the others. "We didn't believe that land belonged to particular people. It belonged to all of us and we had enough of it to share. But the other people saw things differently and didn't like our groups when we arrived for our seasonal encampments in their settlements. They forced us into the mountains and contained us on barren land where we had difficulty finding or producing food. Before that time, we had eaten no meat, but soon our circumstances forced us to eat meat to survive. At least we retained control of our own community in the mountains, even if we had been banished from the rest of the land and ostracized. Since that time, my people have continued to feel disenfranchised and discriminated against."

"That's a peculiar way to describe the relocation," Cardamom commented.

"Peculiar to you but that's how my people see it," Compost snapped.

"Obviously there is more to say on this subject, but let's eat before everything gets cold," Elena said, as she gave a sign to the kitchen staff, who then brought in trays of food that smelled delicious. Elena had cooked goose-chicken enchiladas with mole sauce as well as bean-and-cheese enchiladas with a vegetarian mole sauce. She had made chili relleno casserole, guacamole, shredded lettuce with tomatoes and cilantro, Spanish rice, and three kinds of salsa. She had prepared pitchers of sweet *horchata* (rice water) as well as strawberry juice. The conversation disintegrated into yummy sounds and compliments to the chef.

When Hyacinth finally stopped eating long enough to speak, and opened his mouth to say something, he did not have a chance to utter a single mangled word because the doors to the dining hall burst open and in strolled Sonjay with the others who had escaped the Final Fortress, accompanied by an escort of more than a dozen hoverboarding intuits and the colorful flash of Bayard Rustin's feathers.

Everyone stared in amazement.

"Just in time for dinner, as usual," Maia declared. Then her gaze fell on the strange man with the dreadlocks who had arrived with Sonjay. He looked sort of familiar to her, but she couldn't place where she might have seen him before. Bayard flew to her and perched on her shoulder as he eyed the dinner table, searching for berries.

"Good thing we made so much food," Elena commented to Guhblorin quietly.

"Enough for everyone," Guhblorin answered.

"You've been upstaged," Compost said to Elena. "Frankly, that one gets on my nerves."

"Be good," Elena warned him.

The intuits stepped down from their hoverboards and dropped to the floor in exhaustion. The guards surrounded Compost to ensure that he didn't try to escape in the midst of the excitement, but he didn't seem inclined to go anywhere. He continued to shovel large forkfuls of Elena's goose-chicken in mole sauce into his mouth as he pointedly ignored the new arrivals.

"Is that?" Denzel managed to whisper, before he choked up, unable to go on. Denzel's chest felt tight and he feared saying another word because he thought he would start crying in front of everyone.

"Our father," Sonjay confirmed. "I found him. Sissrath imprisoned him in the Final Fortress. I turned up at the Final Fortress after the passage. I always knew our father was there."

At the sight of Denzel and Maia, Reggie's face collapsed with emotion and his shoulders heaved. Large tears rolled down his cheeks. Denzel raced over to Reggie, who, sobbing, seized him in an enormous bear hug. Bayard leapt off her shoulder as Maia also ran to her father, who embraced her as well. Maia burst into tears and Denzel, struggling not to cry, clung to Reggie.

Compost continued to focus on his dinner plate as he leaned close to Elena and said, "This is all very touching, but what's for dessert?"

Elena glared at him. "Listen," she said, "I have stuck my neck out for you to give you a chance to clean up your act. Behave or I'll have them chain your feet together again and laugh at you when you fall on your face trying to walk."

"OK, OK," Compost said, attempting to appease her. "I'm trying."

"Try harder," Elena told him. "The suit looks good but the suit does not make the man."

A great deal of hugging and laughter ensued and then Denzel and Hyacinth began pulling chairs to the table for the weary travelers. Crumpet smacked his younger brother Cardamom on the back while Saffron greeted Buttercup. Reggie remained locked in a tearful embrace with Maia. Sonjay asked Hyacinth if he would have some of his house staff tend to the exhausted intuits, who had used every ounce of their strength to fly Sonjay, Crumpet, Buttercup, and Reggie to Big House City. Amid the bustle and laughter and excitement, no one had yet noticed Elena's dinner companion until Sonjay spoke up.

"Do I know you?" Sonjay remarked to Compost. "You look familiar."

"Compost," Denzel replied. "He's friends with Elena now."

"You're joking!" Sonjay exclaimed.

"It's a long story," his brother said.

"Is that a geebaching?" Crumpet asked, pointing at Guhblorin.

"That's a long story too," Denzel informed Crumpet. "He's also friends with Elena."

"Is she collecting dangerous creatures?" Sonjay asked.

"Don't be rude," Elena admonished.

"We all have a lot of explaining to do," Cardamom noted. "We can do so while we continue with this tasty dinner that Elena cooked for us."

"I don't suppose you cooked any meat," Crumpet speculated mournfully.

"As a matter of fact," Elena informed him with a grin, "you'll find plenty of fat pieces of goose-chicken in this tray of enchiladas *con mole*."

"Woo-hoo!" Crumpet rejoiced.

"Now you're talking, girlfriend," Buttercup added happily as she plopped her ample bottom into a chair and pulled close to the table.

Interrupting one another and speaking animatedly between mouthfuls, Sonjay and Crumpet shared what they knew about the Corportons at the Final Fortress, Elena introduced the reformed Compost (with a stern glance in his direction to remind him to behave) and explained why a geebaching sat at her right hand, Honeydew and Denzel repeated the information provided in Elena's phone call with Doshmisi, and Hyacinth (in his strange way of speaking and with help from his wife and daughter) described the siege.

Cardamom showed Sonjay the enchanted box he had made as a receptacle for the Staff of Shakabaz. After Sonjay had reclaimed the Staff from Sissrath the previous year, he had left it with Cardamom for safekeeping. The box, artfully decorated with seashells, measured about the size of a loaf of bread. Cardamom demonstrated how he could open the lid and lift the Staff out until it stood at its full height and weight, and then how he could collapse the Staff back into the box.

Elena, who had never seen the splendid Staff before, could not tear her eyes from it when Cardamom revealed it. The polished, shiny, carved wooden branch bulged at the top, as thick around as the upper arm of a muscular man, and it tapered down to a thickness of no more than the wrist of a young girl at the bottom. Bristling red, yellow, blue, and green feathers graced the top of the Staff, where wooden struts held them in place within a weave of jute. Below the feathers, strings of small shells hung in a cascade. The many faces of people and animals carved into the wood of the Staff peeked out from wooden strands that entwined around the main branch like vines or smaller branches. When removed from the enchanted box, the Staff stood more than nine feet in height. *"Muy bonita,"* Elena said softly, "beautiful."

"And extremely powerful," Compost informed her.

As Cardamom returned the Staff to its enchanted box, the others around the table fell silent. Into that silence, Buttercup announced, "Reggie is a Prophet of the Khoum."

"For real?" Honeydew asked, her eyes growing wide with astonishment.

"How?" Cardamom demanded.

"As in the High Shaman of the Khoum? With the Mystical Book?" Saffron asked.

"How totally fondue!" Hyacinth exclaimed. The others promptly ignored him because fondue was a melted cheese appetizer and no one had any idea what he really meant to say. Compost muttered to Elena, "And this man is our high chief. It makes me want to holler."

Reggie explained how he came by the book and learned how to use it, Honeydew explained what the Prophet of the Khoum was all about for those who didn't know and, finally, Sonjay shared with the others the prophecy about the destruction of Faracadar and the deal that Sissrath had apparently made with the Corportons whereby they agreed to take him out of Faracadar with them when they left.

"Does anyone know why the Corportons came to Faracadar in the first place?" Sonjay asked. The question hung in the air, begging a response. But none arrived.

Slowly, all eyes turned toward Compost, who patted his belly contentedly between noisy sips of *horchata*. The center of attention, Compost asked, "Could anyone else go for an espresso right about now?" Elena kicked him under the table. He winced and shot her a reproachful look.

Cardamom addressed Compost. "Your new friend Elena believes that you have made a serious commitment to changing your life. Perhaps you could demonstrate just how serious by sharing with us any useful information you have about Sissrath's intentions and the purpose of the Corportons."

Compost cast his gaze over the others at the table.

"Now would be a good time to share that information," Sonjay said.

Compost turned to Elena and asked, bitterly, "Do you hear that tone?"

"I hear it," she replied. "But you can't tell me that you don't deserve it after the nasty things you've done. Be gracious. If you know something that would help us defeat this Sissrath character, then please tell us," Elena requested politely.

"I happen to be extremely intelligent," Compost said, raising his voice to make sure everyone heard him. "And I find it insulting when people talk down to me as if I'm stupid."

"A lot depends on how you use your intelligence," Guhblorin piped up. "I happen to be an extremely funny geebaching, but if I use laughter to kill people, what good is my talent to me or to anyone else? How do you use your intelligence?"

Compost studied Guhblorin in surprise. Everyone else held their tongue. Compost leaned back in his chair and crossed his arms. "You've already figured out most of what I know. The Prophet of the Khoum has prophesied the destruction of Faracadar. When the Corportons appeared at the Final Fortress, Sissrath negotiated an agreement with them. He will help them on their mission here in Faracadar and in return they will take him with them when they leave. Sissrath bound the agreement with deep enchantment. We all know the strength of his diabolical skill at that." Compost's voice dripped with irony.

Those gathered at the table had never heard Compost speak about Sissrath with such dislike before. It shocked them.

"What about you?" Sonjay asked. "Did Sissrath plan to leave you behind in this supposedly dying land?"

"No," Compost answered, "he did not. Or so he told me. He negotiated for me to leave with him. But honestly, I never planned to go."

"Why not?" Elena asked in surprise. "I mean, if you believe the prophecy about the destruction."

"I do believe it," Compost said, with uncharacteristic sadness. "But why would I want to go anywhere else? Would you do it? I have a family and friends whom I left behind in the Mountain Downs. If the land dies, I don't wish to survive everyone and everything in my community. I would just as soon perish with all the rest, here at home. I didn't share these thoughts with Sissrath. He doesn't know that I did not plan to leave with him when the time came. What joy would I have in a life so far from my home?"

The others contemplated Compost's words in silence until Saffron stated, softly, "I always thought you were Sissrath's man to the core."

"You thought wrong," Compost informed her matter-of-factly. Then he sighed and put his fork down on his plate. "Have you ever considered how things look from my point of view? What good am I? I can't throw enchantments. So I have to work for someone who can. Admit it: You would never trust me because I come from the Mountain Downs. I have had only one path open to me to gain power. Only one way for me to help my people have a say in the significant decisions of the land. Those of us from the Mountain Downs do tire of being demonized by you. You could give it a rest, you know." Saffron and Hyacinth furrowed their brows in thought and Maia wondered if they were reconsidering their treatment of the Mountain People who lived in the Downs.

Compost continued, "I wonder if Sissrath will live to regret leaving Faracadar. The Corportons come from a land fighting for its survival. They need this stuff that they came here to take. I don't know what they call the stuff; but they need it desperately to save their own land and they somehow figured out that we have it so they came to Faracadar to get it. Sissrath has helped them to mine this substance at the North Coast. When they have enough of it then they'll go home and they'll take Sissrath with them. You and I and everyone else will remain behind to live out the prophecy, which, as Reggie will tell you, foretells the destruction of the land but not exactly how that will occur."

"He has that right," Reggie added. "I can see the destruction but can't see exactly how it will come about. I know for sure, however, that a prophecy through the way of the Mystical Book never lies, it always comes to pass."

"Why did Sissrath order the siege of Big House City?" Cardamom asked.

"It meant nothing," Compost replied. "Absolutely nothing. Sissrath wanted to distract you, the royals, and everyone else in order to keep you out from under foot so that he could help the Corportons at the North Coast without interference. But then the Four turned up and started turning over rocks and asking questions."

"So now what do we do?" Reggie posed the question on everyone's mind.

"We have to meet Dosh and Jasper on Whale Island. They've been to the North Coast and they know more about all this than any of us," Sonjay replied immediately.

"We got separated during the passage into the land," Denzel told his father.

"I gathered as much from Sonjay," Reggie answered.

"But we need to get back together," Maia said. "Who will go to Whale Island?"

"I've come with you this far and I refuse to leave you now," Elena insisted firmly.

"What she said," Guhblorin agreed.

"I have to see my daughter," Reggie said simply. "So I'm in."

Sonjay placed his hand on the box that contained the Staff of Shakabaz. "We could sure use you with us, Cardamom."

Cardamom nodded in Sonjay's direction and they understood from the nod that he had just agreed to go with them. Then Cardamom said, "The high chief and chieftess should remain safely within the walls of Big House City; at least until we have more information about the situation."

"Count me in," Honeydew said. "I'll go."

"Princess, I think the people need you safely at home with your parents right now," Cardamom told her gently. Honeydew stamped her foot stubbornly. "No, no, no," she complained in frustration. Bisc stood and licked her hand comfortingly.

Buttercup spoke up. "How about this? Crumpet and I will remain here at Big House City with the royals." She patted Honeydew's arm sympathetically. "But when you're ready to head for the North Coast, send us a messenger and Crumpet and I will join you at the Passage Circle to travel with you. At such time, the princess will accompany us."

"I advise against that," Cardamom noted.

"Saffron?" Hyacinth deferred to his wife.

"We will all join you at the Passage Circle," Saffron said decidedly. "If the land is in such grave danger then we have no reason to hide in the Big House." Honeydew was not happy to be left behind, but she agreed to that plan.

Elena rose from her seat abruptly and went into the kitchen to fetch dessert, which was chocolate raspberry flan and sweet pumpkin empanadas.

Between luscious mouthfuls, Sonjay complimented Elena, "Girl, you seriously know how to throw down."

"Absolutely," Reggie agreed. "You put your foot in it."

"What does that mean?" Elena asked Reggie.

Reggie laughed as he explained, "They use that expression back home where I come from. It means that you cooked an exceptional meal."

"*Bueno. Gracias*," Elena said with a modest smile.

Hyacinth beckoned to the guards, who came forward and surrounded Compost. "Time to return the prisoner to his cell," Hyacinth commanded.

"Wait," Compost said as he held up a hand to stay the guards. "I have one other thing to share with you. It may help you against Sissrath." Denzel's eyebrows shot up in surprise and he thought maybe Compost really had started to change.

"Speak," Cardamom encouraged Compost.

"Sissrath has a phobia about cockroaches," Compost announced.

"How can that help us?" Sonjay asked impatiently.

"Hear him out," Elena cautioned.

"You have no idea," Compost continued speaking, with a raspy chuckle. "He has tried to conquer this phobia unsuccessfully. He has brought healers and enchanters to him and ordered them to remove this fear from him. None could do it and he put them all to death one by one because he thought to keep his weakness a secret. He doesn't know that I know about it. I am probably the only person alive who knows. When he sees a cockroach, he chokes. He has trouble throwing an enchantment in the presence of a cockroach. He can barely breathe. If you put a cockroach in his path then you will have a chance of overpowering him."

"Brilliant," Crumpet declared. He stretched out his arm, said an enchantment, and an army of cockroaches began to drop from his sleeve and march across the floor.

"Ewww!" Elena exclaimed in disgust. Many of the others swiftly echoed with "ewwws" of their own.

"Put those away," Saffron demanded. "I run a clean Big House here."

"As you wish," Crumpet said. He made three large circles in the air with his left hand and stretched his fingers out toward the cockroaches he had unleashed. They disappeared in a puff of orange-brown smoke.

"That trick will come in quite handy," Compost told Crumpet. "Trust me on that."

"We do trust you," Elena replied. "Don't we?" she asked the others, who muttered and sidestepped the question.

"We must remember our manners, people," Elena asserted. "*Gracias* for the good information, Compost. I will leave in the morning, but I hope to return to see you again, *mí amigo*." She hugged Compost, who patted her on the head affectionately.

"What's up with them?" Sonjay asked Denzel, as the guards led Compost away to lock him up.

"She likes him," Denzel replied with a shrug. "She talked him into taking a bath. Go figure."

"So, is she your girlfriend yet?" Sonjay teased.

"Shut up," Denzel replied, while secretly he admitted to himself that he had grown fond of Elena. She had more substance to her than he had previously realized.

With the meal over, everyone prepared to retire to their rooms. Reggie hugged each of his children in turn and then burst into tears again. "I have imagined myself kissing you goodnight so often. I have longed for the privilege of doing so. This simple thing. To do it now feels like a miracle."

Both residents and guests at the Big House slept well in their comfortable beds that night. They dreamt of chocolate flan and woke up refreshed and ready for whatever challenges they would need to face in the coming days.

Sonjay, Maia, Denzel, Elena, Guhblorin, Cardamom, and Reggie rode out on their tigers right after breakfast, and made the Passage Circle by nightfall. After a joyful reunion with her drummer friends, Maia stayed up half the night drumming on the beach. Early the next morning the travelers rode over the first ocean bridge and onto the first of the islands. Maia shared a tiger with Reggie, who held her and kept her from falling off while she leaned back into her father's arms with a contented smile on her face as she caught up on the sleep she had lost the night before while drumming. The travelers arrived by ferry at the dock on Whale Island in the late afternoon, well before sunset, and Cardamom led the way to Clover's house at the library. The Goodacres' grandmother (the mother of Alice, Martin, Bobby, and Debbie), Clover the Griot, had served as keeper of the history and manager of the library for many years.

The library compound consisted of a central courtyard surrounded by cottages. The cottages housed the books and other library holdings. Clover lived in one of the cottages, which she shared with her assistant, Iris. Her grandchildren had visited her at her cottage the year before. In the courtyard, the travelers dismounted from their tigers and hurried to her door. They knocked and then entered, comfortable doing so in their grandmother's house.

When the travelers appeared in the cottage, Jasper jumped up from where he sat on the couch studying maps and ran to greet them. He grabbed Denzel first in an enthusiastic hug and thumped him on the back. "Where did you land after the passage?" he asked.

"Long story," Denzel replied. "I missed you, man. I have so much to tell you."

Jasper released Denzel and flung his arms around Maia, then Sonjay, in turn. "I have a lot to tell you too," Jasper said. "Say, who are these guys? Whoa, is that a geebaching?"

"Why does everyone make such a big deal about the geebaching?" Elena exploded. "Duh. *Sí.* Yes. He's a geebaching. His name is Guhblorin. Don't judge."

Unfamiliar with Elena's straightforward style, Jasper threw a look of hurt and puzzlement in her direction. He put his hands up, palms outward, in a gesture of defense while Bayard squawked, "Latina firecracker, Latina firecracker."

"Elena, chill," Denzel said. "It's surprising and worrisome for people in Faracadar to see a geebaching. Aight? Geebachings have a bad rep. Get over it."

Elena scowled as she informed Jasper, "He's a reformed geebaching. He doesn't make people laugh to death."

"No, these days I just make them laugh until they wet their pants," Guhblorin interjected.

Elena whirled around and yanked hard on his ear, "Enough out of you. Don't make matters worse. And that wasn't even funny."

Guhblorin yelped. "I must be losing my touch," he said contritely.

"Let me introduce you to our dad, Reggie," Sonjay said to Jasper. Then he turned to Reggie and explained, "Jasper went everywhere with us last year as our guide."

"You found your dad!" Jasper exclaimed. "Fantastic."

"Is my daughter here?" Reggie asked anxiously.

"Your daughter," Jasper echoed. "Wait right here." Jasper turned abruptly and hurried down the hallway to Clover's bedroom, calling as he went, "Dosh! Dosh! Come out here. You won't believe this."

Doshmisi emerged from the room with a startled expression. Jasper took her hand and led her to where the others waited. Of the four Goodacre children, she alone remembered her father well enough from before he had disappeared to recognize him instantly when she saw him again. They blinked at each other in astonishment in Clover's bright living room and then Doshmisi ran to Reggie and collapsed into his arms, crying and laughing both at the same time. "Daddy. It's really you. Oh Daddy."

"I thought I would never see you again, baby girl," Reggie said. He looked over Doshmisi's shoulder and his gaze fell on each of his children, one at a time. "I thought I would never see any of you again. I thought it impossible."

"Yes, well, we changed all that, didn't we?" Sonjay stated with satisfaction. "Impossible happens."

Chapter Eighteen
The Emerald Crystal

After a few minutes, when Doshmisi could finally let go of her father, and after she had stopped crying, she greeted her brothers and sister. She gave Cardamom a warm hug. "Wow, Elena," she said to Maia's friend, "you must have had the surprise of your life when you popped through after the passage."

"Surprise is an understatement," Elena replied.

"Did you guys bring that thing with you?" Doshmisi asked, as she nodded her head uncertainly in the direction of Guhblorin.

"I can hear you," Guhblorin said. "I'm standing right here. I'm not a thing."

"You're a geebaching," Doshmisi said.

"I am?" Guhblorin asked, acting surprised. "Why didn't someone tell me?" Elena pinched him and he hollered "Ouch!"

"I think I can guess where you landed after the passage," Doshmisi said to Elena and her siblings.

"We didn't land inside the Amber Mountains, if that's what you think," Denzel informed his sister. "We turned up outside of them. But we had to run inside immediately because we pretty much landed on a buzzing hive of Special Forces."

"I received an interesting introduction to Faracadar," Elena said.

"I'll bet," Jasper commented with a chuckle.

"We had to use one of the through-tunnels to get to the Wolf Circle," Maia explained.

"And I followed the direction of the mold on the ceiling, just like you showed me last year," Denzel told Jasper proudly. He had looked forward to relating this to his friend.

"Cool," Jasper responded.

"The passage took me right to Debbie's Circle, same field as last time, where Jasper was waiting. I don't know why you fools couldn't turn up in the right spot," Doshmisi teased.

"Debbie's Circle?" Reggie asked.

"They named it after Momma," Maia told him.

"Where did you wind up?" Doshmisi asked Sonjay.

"In the Final Fortress," Sonjay replied with a quick laugh. "Just my luck. You land in a rosy field of flowers. Denzel and Maia turn up right by the Wolf Circle. And I land inside the dungeons."

"You're joking," Jasper said, sympathetically.

"No lie," Sonjay affirmed.

"How is Clover?" Cardamom asked.

"Not good," Doshmisi replied, her expression growing serious at once.

"You tried using the herbal, of course, right?" Cardamom continued. Doshmisi didn't reply right away because she didn't know what to say. She hadn't told anyone that the herbal had stopped acting normal. Fortunately, Iris entered the room at that moment and rescued her from answering the question.

"Excuse me for interrupting," Iris said. "I have food prepared in the kitchen if you want to eat dinner. Clover is sleeping and the nurse will tend to her needs if she wakes. Please fill a plate and we can eat together outside in the courtyard at the long table."

They helped Iris carry the food platters, plates, and utensils out to the courtyard and once everyone had settled at the wooden table, they took turns telling each other about everything that had happened to them since they had arrived in Faracadar. Sonjay and Reggie related their adventures with Crumpet and Buttercup and shared everything they had learned about the Corportons, including what Compost had said when they ate dinner with him at Big House City. Elena interrupted them to explain how they happened to sit down to dinner with Compost in the first place and all about Compost's reformation. Denzel and Maia shared the story of the garbage labyrinth and their travels with Princess Honeydew and Biscuit. Elena insisted on describing how they met Guhblorin and his role in rescuing the others from the garbage labyrinth. They told about the siege and how Sonjay had talked Compost's army into deserting so they could go home to eat buttered biscuits. Jasper and Doshmisi related everything they had learned from their trip to the North Coast. When they got to the part about Dagobaz, Doshmisi left the table to fetch the beautiful stallion and brought him into the courtyard for the others to admire.

"Is he an enchanted creature?" Cardamom asked, with a note of awe in his voice.

"No. He's just a horse," Doshmisi said. "Horses are commonplace in the Farland."

"But what a magnificent horse!" Maia exclaimed.

"Yes," Doshmisi agreed. "The most magnificent I have ever seen."

"Commonplace or magnificent; we're a moving target as long as we have that horse with us," Jasper pointed out quietly. "He made quite a stir when we stepped off the ferry with him. People will spread the word about Dagobaz up and down the coast and throughout Big House City within a few days. I doubt the Corportons will say 'oh well' and let this valuable animal slip from their grasp. They'll attempt to retrieve him."

"They don't deserve to have him," Doshmisi insisted angrily.

"Of course they don't," Jasper agreed, "although I doubt they will see it that way. We can't return him to them; but we need to accept the truth of it. He'll lead them right to us, so we need to prepare ourselves."

"Anyone who abuses an animal has no right to own an animal," Doshmisi stated.

Sonjay looked around the table at the others. "So," he said, "I want to say that we are all on the same page now, but I'm going to spell it out to make sure. Correct me if I get anything wrong. It looks like these Corportons came to Faracadar to drill for oil in the ocean at the North Coast. We don't know where they came from. We don't know what they're capable of doing. They have guns and they will shoot to kill. The oil well that they drilled has exploded and is spilling oil into the ocean."

"Meanwhile," Denzel picked up where his brother had left off, "Daddy, who is a Prophet of the Khoum, has foretold the destruction of Faracadar to Sissrath who, believing this prophecy, has cut a deal with the Corportons to help them drill for oil if they take him with them when they leave."

"We don't know how much oil they expected to get or if they have however much they wanted," Maia pointed out anxiously. "We don't know when they plan to leave or how much oil they have already taken out of Faracadar."

"There's something else," Doshmisi said hesitantly. "I didn't want to cause alarm; but I have known for some time that something is wrong with the herbal. It doesn't act right when I try to use it. It says strange things."

"How do you mean?" Cardamom asked.

"I can't use it to heal anymore," Doshmisi said, her voice cracking as she spoke.

Jasper put a hand on Doshmisi's arm reassuringly. "Whatever it's doing is something that's just happening and not your fault. You know that, right? What exactly does it do when you try to use it?"

"It doesn't tell cures or medicinal recipes. It doesn't open to words about how to heal a person. It opens to undecipherable stories about resilience and adaptability. It says cryptic things about developing resources. It acts almost as if it's angry, as if it has given up on healing.

When I placed it on Clover's chest, it refused to open. The indentation in the top, where I usually put my amulet, became red hot and it repelled the amulet the way two polarized magnets repel each other. I couldn't force the amulet into the indentation. The herbal resisted me." Doshmisi's eyes welled with tears and Jasper put his arm around her shoulders. Doshmisi continued in a quavering voice. "I think that Grandma Clover is dying and the herbal doesn't wish to help me try to save her."

"Your grandmother is a wise woman," Cardamom said. "Do you think that she would not realize that she is dying if it's her time?"

"No, no I don't," Doshmisi replied. "But we have not spoken of it."

In the waning light, Iris lit one of the glow-lamps on the table and, as she leaned forward to light the other one, she said softly, "Clover has been ill for quite a while. I think she has been hanging on, waiting for all of you to arrive, because she wanted to see her grandchildren once again and after that she will feel ready to leave in peace. Not just because she loves you and has had so little opportunity to spend time with you, but also because she expects that you will protect and preserve the land, that once you have arrived here then you will keep Faracadar safe. She has waited for all of you to arrive so that she can tell you about the Emerald Crystal."

"Emerald Crystal?" Elena repeated reverently, because it sounded like a tremendously magical thing.

Suddenly, a flurry of activity in the entranceway to the courtyard drew their attention. It was Mole! After he stumbled over a loose cobblestone and sprawled on the ground, he bounced right back up, his dreadlocks flopping gaily around his head. A half a dozen other battery makers accompanied him. They appeared grimy and travel-worn, with smudges of oil on their clothing.

Mole smiled broadly. "We found you," he announced merrily. Jasper and Denzel leapt from the table and hurried to greet Mole. Denzel had become good friends with Mole the previous year when they invented and built things together in the battery barn at the Passage Circle.

"That you did," Jasper said. Denzel thumped Mole on the back happily.

"You said Whale Island and here we be," Mole told Jasper.

"We worried about you after that explosion in the compound," Doshmisi said.

"I'm good. I brought my friends with me too," Mole responded, as he waved his arm to encompass those who had traveled with him. "We blew up the workshop at the compound. We created that explosion to make a lot of smoke so more people could escape."

"It sure helped us escape," Doshmisi confirmed.

"I'm glad for that," Mole said with satisfaction. He turned to his fellow battery makers and introduced each of them by name. Then Denzel introduced all of those who sat around the table.

After Denzel introduced her, Iris rose from her seat and came forward, took Mole's big muscular hand in her slender one, and shook it gently. "Welcome to my home," she greeted him.

Mole was one of the Coast People so he normally had a blue glow to his rich brown skin. But when Iris took his hand he flushed an interesting plum-colored shade of reddish-purple. After shaking her hand, he stepped backward, right into a metal bucket of rainwater. His foot stuck in the bucket and the water sloshed up onto his leg.

"Aiyeee," he exclaimed as he leaned on the table so he could pick up his foot and remove the bucket. When he pulled the bucket off, he fell backward and sat down abruptly in a platter of potato salad.

"Oh dear," Iris said sympathetically, as she attempted to scrape potato salad off the seat of Mole's pants with a butter knife.

"Not a problem," Mole said. "It'll wash off." The others observed in fascination as Mole swung his arm open to emphasize his point and managed to sweep a metal bowl filled with sliced mangoes and papayas off the table and onto Iris's dress, which became instantly soaked with fruit juice. Mole then picked up a cloth napkin from the table and attempted to mop up the juice on Iris's dress, but the napkin had mustard on it and so he made the mess worse.

Iris stepped away from Mole as she said, "Stop, stop. I'll take care of it. Just stop." Mole hung his head dejectedly.

"I was about to clear away the food, but do you and your friends want something to eat?" Iris asked Mole.

"No thanks, we ate on the ferry," he mumbled as he stared at his feet.

Iris turned away from Mole and picked up an empty food platter. She began to stack dinner plates on the platter as she remarked to Doshmisi, "You should go see your grandmomma. She hasn't much time left and she has much on her mind that she wishes to share with you now that the four of you have come. Poke your head in her room and see if she's awake."

Doshmisi turned quickly to go check on Clover. Maia took her hand and went with her.

"I'll go too," Reggie announced as he accompanied his daughters out of the courtyard and into Clover's house. Iris trailed close behind them with the tray of empty plates. The others in the courtyard began to help Iris clear the table, carrying things inside to the kitchen.

"Let me know right away if she's awake," Sonjay called after his sisters.

"Me too," Denzel added.

Doshmisi, Maia, and Reggie opened the door to Clover's bedroom quietly and slipped inside. A glow-lamp on the nightstand cast a soft amber light across the room and a nurse sat in an overstuffed chair by the window, reading a book. Clover's eyes fluttered open when she heard the door close behind her visitors.

"Are you awake Grandmomma?" Maia asked.

Clover smiled faintly. "Maia. How wonderful. Come here and take my hand, child."

"Denzel and Sonjay have arrived also. We ate dinner while you slept," Doshmisi explained. "Do you feel up to a visit from us?"

As Maia took her grandmother's frail hand in her own, Clover looked over Maia's shoulder at Reggie and her eyes grew wide. "Is that? Oh my. Is that you, Reggie?"

"Yes, it's me, Rosemary," Reggie approached the bed and, as Maia stepped back, he took both of Clover's hands in his. He had called her by her given name, Rosemary, from her former life in the Farland. She had left that name behind many years before when she bound her fate irrevocably to maintaining the library in Faracadar.

"Where have you been?" Clover asked her son-in-law.

"Short version or long version?" Reggie asked.

"I'm afraid I may not have time for the long version," she replied wistfully. "As you can see, my health has failed."

"Sissrath held me as his prisoner in the Final Fortress these many years until Sonjay rescued me," Reggie said. "While imprisoned, I became a Prophet of the Khoum."

"Remarkable. If only I had suspected that you were there, I would have sent someone to look for you," Clover responded, as tears stood in her eyes. "Very good. Good that you are of the Khoum and good that you have returned to the children. They must complete a difficult task and it will perhaps be easier with their father here to help them. Bring the others to me. I must speak to all of you together."

Reggie went to fetch Sonjay and Denzel. While they waited for their brothers, Maia and Doshmisi helped Clover sit up in her bed. She leaned back against an avalanche of pillows. She was gray and thin and her hair had become brittle, her skin papery. She looked so different from the vibrant and spry old lady who had met them at the dock when they arrived on Whale Island the year before.

With her eyes closed, Clover told Doshmisi quietly, "It doesn't work anymore, does it?"

"What?" Doshmisi asked, but she knew.

"The herbal, it won't give you healing recipes or instructions, will it?"

"No," Doshmisi confirmed reluctantly.

"It prepares itself for a greater healing and, after that, it will leave, just like me," Clover said. Doshmisi's eyes filled with tears.

At that moment, Reggie returned with Denzel and Sonjay, who went directly to embrace their grandmother. Clover could barely muster the strength to lift her arms to offer them each a feeble hug.

"Oh Grandmomma Clover," Doshmisi burst out, "is there anything I can do to heal you? The herbal won't help. Do you know of anything? Just tell me and I'll do it."

"Even if the herbal worked the way it used to, it would not have any healing words for me. I have grown old and my time to leave approaches." Maia leaned over and rested her head on Clover's shoulder. Maia and Doshmisi cried softly, but Clover told them, "Don't cry for me. I had a splendid, long life filled with friends and music, laughter and delicious food, surrounded by the books that I adore. I have loved and I have danced and I have watched the stars at night."

"They're not crying for you, Rosemary," Reggie said gently. "They're crying for themselves. They barely had any time with you."

"One day, in the future, in a time of peace, come back to the library, my children, and Iris will guide you through my writings and my drawings and you will have a lot more of me than you can imagine. For now, time is short and you have much work to do if you hope to save this library and this land."

"What kind of work?" Sonjay asked.

"The herbal," Clover said. Then she ceased talking and rested briefly with her eyes closed. No one spoke. Maia and Doshmisi wiped their eyes and waited for their grandmother's instructions. Iris slipped into the room and stood near the door.

"The herbal," Clover continued with great effort, as she opened her eyes again, "will not heal people anymore. It must heal the land. A poison has spilled into the ocean and it will spread if you do not stop it. The poison has started to kill the green algae and when all the green algae dies, our air will become unfit to breathe. Heal the ocean with the herbal, Doshmisi." Clover paused as she struggled to continue speaking. Iris sat on the edge of the bed next to Clover and took her thin wrist in her hand.

"Please explain it to us," Doshmisi begged. "Don't go yet."

"I'm still here," Clover said, although her voice sounded distant and faint. "Put the herbal in the ocean at the North Coast. Where the poison started. Near the wound in the ocean floor."

"We can do that," Sonjay said.

"But it needs the Emerald Crystal to work," Clover said softly as she closed her eyes again.

"Where can we find the Emerald Crystal?" Denzel asked, urgently.

"The whales hid it in the Coral Caves for safekeeping," Clover answered.

"The Coral Caves," Sonjay repeated.

"Doshmisi must put the Emerald Crystal into the indentation in the cover of the herbal," Clover instructed. She gasped for breath.

"Like I did with my amulet?" Doshmisi asked.

"Like that," Clover whispered with great effort. "Emerald Crystal in indentation in herbal. Herbal in ocean at North Coast. Under the water. Heal the ocean. Algae. Whales…" Clover's voice trailed off.

"This is too much for her," Iris said anxiously. "Too much."

Clover nodded gently and opened her eyes. "Too much is fine," she said so faintly that they could barely hear her. She looked around at her grandchildren and Reggie. She smiled with deep satisfaction. Then she looked into Iris's eyes and whispered, "I love you. I love you all." Her eyes closed again but the smile did not leave her lips. She said nothing more. Iris sat quietly and held her hand.

Maia leaned over and kissed her grandmother's forehead. Doshmisi, Denzel, and Sonjay each did the same in turn. Then they filed solemnly out of the room. Reggie followed them and closed Clover's door behind them.

"Well, we know what we need to do," Denzel said with resolve. "We need to go to the Coral Caves and retrieve the Emerald Crystal."

"We have to move quickly because that oil spill is spreading," Doshmisi reminded the others. "We need to get the Emerald Crystal as soon as possible."

"We can leave first thing in the morning," Sonjay announced, ready for action.

"I wonder where the Coral Caves are," Maia said.

Reggie cleared his throat before informing them, "I happen to know exactly where they are."

"Cool. Then you can show us how to get there," Sonjay replied.

Reggie continued, "I know where they are, but I have no idea how to get there. They're underneath Whale Island, at the bottom of the ocean."

Chapter Nineteen
The Coral Caves

"What did Clover say?" Jasper asked.

"She told us how to stop the oil spill from destroying Faracadar," Denzel answered.

"She said we have to get the Emerald Crystal," Maia told him.

"Then I have to put the Emerald Crystal into the herbal and put the herbal in the ocean at the North Coast where the oil well exploded," Doshmisi explained.

"So far, so good," Jasper said. "Do we know where to find the Emerald Crystal?"

"About that," Sonjay said. "According to the Prophet of the Khoum, my dad, the Emerald Crystal is in the Coral Caves at the bottom of the ocean under Whale Island."

"How did the Emerald Crystal wind up under Whale Island?" Jasper asked in exasperation. He didn't expect to receive an answer, but Cardamom gave him one.

"Because," Cardamom replied, "the whales placed the Emerald Crystal in the Coral Caves over a hundred years ago for safekeeping. It has such powerful energy that they feared what could happen if it fell into the wrong hands. No one knows if it's still down there."

"We be needin' an underwater motorized vehicle," Mole said. He had showered and changed into clean clothes and he looked no worse for having made a long and dusty journey that had culminated in his sitting in a platter of potato salad.

"You mean a submarine? Do they have those here?" Elena asked incredulously.

"A submarine?" Mole repeated, bewildered.

"A vehicle that can go underwater with people in it," Denzel explained. "We call them submarines."

"Well, yes," Mole replied, "we be havin' somethin' like that. I'll talk to the battery makers to find out what they be keepin' in the battery barn on Whale Island."

"I'll go with you," Denzel offered.

"Now?" Mole asked.

"No time to waste. Let's go find the battery makers and see if they have something we can use. While we stand here talking, the oil spill continues to spread."

"Yah, mon," Mole replied.

"Later," Denzel called over his shoulder as he and Mole headed for the door.

"I'll go too," Sonjay said quickly as he caught up with them and matched his stride to theirs.

"Do you know where I can find a map of the ocean floor?" Jasper asked Cardamom.

"Probably in the library," Cardamom answered. "Come with me and we'll have a look."

"Do you mind if I tag along?" Reggie asked.

"Not at all," Cardamom said.

"I have a book that outlines specifically how to get to the site where the whales purportedly stored the Emerald Crystal. Hold on and I'll get it." Reggie went to his bag and pulled out a worn, little book, which he passed to Jasper as they went out the door in the direction of the library.

"Come with me," Elena ordered Guhblorin, and the two of them headed to the kitchen, where they proceeded to clean up the dinner dishes for Iris, who had remained by Clover's side in the bedroom.

"Can I see what it does?" Maia asked her sister.

"What it does?" Doshmisi echoed.

"Can I see what the herbal does when you try to use it?"

Doshmisi unsnapped the herbal from the carry case and the two girls sat next to each other on Clover's sea-green couch. "I'm not even sure it will open," Doshmisi warned. But it did open and Doshmisi laid the book gently across her legs so that Maia could see it too.

The page read: "OIL ACCUMULATED DEEP WITHIN, MILLIONS OF YEARS AGO, AS THE REMAINS OF A PREVIOUS SPECIES THAT ONCE WALKED. AN ENDLESS SUPPLY DOES NOT EXIST. JUST AS THE PREVIOUS SPECIES WAS FINITE, SO TOO THE OIL THAT REMAINS BEHIND. AND ONE DAY IT WILL ALSO DISAPPEAR. ONLY THOSE SPECIES WITH TRANSFORMATIVE ABILITY WILL REMAIN. INGENUITY. IMAGINATION. WIND AND WATER. SUNSHINE."

"When it first started acting strange, it scared me and I didn't understand," Doshmisi told Maia. "But now, after all that has happened, it sort of makes sense in a weird way. The Corportons came here looking for oil, which seems as scarce in their world as it is becoming in the world we left behind when we came to Faracadar. I think the herbal is trying to say something about how the Corportons didn't adapt to the changing resources in their world."

Maia chewed her lip. Then she speculated, "What if the Corportons came from our world somehow? From the Farland?"

"Creepy," Doshmisi answered. "How could they get here?"

The girls' conversation ended abruptly when Iris emerged from Clover's bedroom. Tears coursed down her cheeks. "She's gone," Iris said in a quavering voice. "She slipped away peacefully a moment ago."

Doshmisi and Maia returned to the bedroom with Iris and they sat on either side of their grandmomma and held her hands. Clover wore a delicate smile on her face.

"When she said she loved us all," Iris said, between sobs, "those were her last words."

News of Clover's passing spread swiftly through the household and the surrounding community. The family gathered by Cover's bed and each in turn had a chance to place a kiss on Clover's still-warm cheek before the body was taken away. They stayed up late into the night, remembering together the many things they loved about Clover and sharing stories. Reggie had a wealth of stories from when Clover had lived a different life as a much younger woman. Iris hung on his every word, comforted to learn more about the life her friend had lived long before settling in Faracadar.

Before she finally went to bed, Doshmisi checked on Dagobaz. She buried her face in his neck and wept while he nuzzled her cheek.

In the morning, Clover's library compound buzzed with activity. Elena and Guhblorin made Spanish omelets, home fries, and banana muffins for breakfast, taking over the cooking so that Iris could devote her full attention to making the arrangements for Clover's memorial service. The family and their traveling companions assembled at the long table in the courtyard to eat.

Wearing a little white apron with a ruffle around the edge, Guhblorin zoomed around the table offering to pour either fresh-squeezed orange juice or apple cider into each person's glass.

"I'll have the orange juice," Cardamom told Guhblorin. And then, "You're taking this cooking business seriously, geebaching."

Guhblorin flapped his ears and grinned broadly. "Elena says I show promise."

"Cardamom and I found a map of the ocean floor in the library," Jasper informed the others between mouthfuls of muffin. "But we'll need some light to see when we get that far down in the ocean."

"We've got a sub," Denzel informed, as he stuffed a forkful of potatoes into his mouth.

"But there be some restrictions," Mole warned.

"Like what?" Doshmisi asked, raising an eyebrow.

"It runs on a battery and the battery can only hold a charge for five hours," Denzel told them. "So we have to get down there and back before we lose the charge."

"The sub has no light on it yet, but Denzel and I will figure something out for that, no problem," Mole promised.

"Yeah, don't worry about the light," Denzel said between bites. "We have bigger things to worry us. They have only one sub in the Island Settlement. Mole has one at the Passage Circle, but it would take a couple of days to go there to get it and we can't squander that much time. We need to do this today."

"Why do we need two subs?" Maia asked.

"In case something happens and we get stranded down there. As it stands, if that happens, we won't have any help. No one can come down after us. And we have to get down and back in five hours," Denzel explained. Then he called to Elena, "Hey, Elena, these are the best fries ever."

"I washed the potatoes for her," Guhblorin informed Denzel with pride. "And I cut up the onions."

"*Gracias*," Elena thanked Denzel. The others added their compliments to his and she modestly accepted the praise.

Iris entered the courtyard wearing a flowing green tunic over beige pants and a round green woven hat (just like the one Doshmisi always wore) on her close-cropped hair. Grief cast an added beauty to her expressive, brown eyes. The instant she appeared, Mole jumped up and stretched out his hand toward her, managing, in the process, to topple his glass of juice so that it spilled on the table. While he mopped up the juice with his napkin, he asked Iris, "Are you wantin' to sit down? Would you like my chair? Can I fix you a plate?"

"No thanks," Iris replied. "I already ate."

Mole attempted to right his chair and seat himself; but he missed the chair by a good six inches when he tried to sit down and he landed with a thud on the ground.

Iris peered over the edge of the table at him anxiously. "Are you OK?" she asked.

"I'm good. I'm going to just sit here for a minute," Mole's voice rose from the ground where he sat halfway under the table.

Maia and Elena exchanged an amused, knowing glance. They had shared their thoughts about Mole the night before and they agreed that he had a crazy-bad crush on Iris.

"I came to tell you that we'll hold the memorial tomorrow morning," Iris said. "That way you can go for the Emerald Crystal today and then leave tomorrow for the North Coast right after the memorial."

"That makes sense," Reggie approved.

"So who will go to the Coral Caves in the sub?" Denzel asked.

"You've finally found somewhere to go where I won't follow you," Elena announced. "You couldn't pay me to step foot in that submarine. Claustrophobia. Plus, I can't swim, so no way I'm going under the ocean."

Relief washed over Denzel when Elena said she didn't want to go; however, to his surprise, he realized it was not because he wanted to be rid of her but rather because she would be safer if left behind. In the privacy of his own thoughts, he admitted that he had grown fond of Elena.

"I'm all in," Doshmisi said.

"Bring it on," Sonjay said.

"Me too, of course," Maia said. "It will probably take all four of us to do this."

"If Mole ever gets up from under the table, he will certainly go," Denzel noted, as he lifted the tablecloth and peeked at Mole, who still sat miserably on the cobblestones under the table. "She left," Denzel told Mole. "You can come out now."

"Me too," Jasper chimed in. "I have to go. You need a guide."

"Looks like we're getting the band back together," Sonjay joked.

Reggie cleared his throat before speaking. "Except that this time you've got your old man with you. I will not let you go by yourselves. We're family and that's how we roll."

"I think I should stay up here with the Staff of Shakabaz," Cardamom suggested. "If something goes wrong, perhaps I can rescue you with the Staff from the shore. I'd like to have that option."

"Nothing will go wrong," Denzel insisted with determination.

"Just the same, I'll leave the herbal with you, Cardamom. Maybe you'll find a way to use it even without me or the Emerald Crystal if the need arises." Doshmisi unstrapped the herbal from her waist and passed it to Cardamom.

"I'll take good care of it," Cardamom promised.

"I know you will."

"So it's settled," Denzel said. "Let's help Elena and Guhblorin clean up the breakfast dishes and then Mole and I will rig a light for the sub. After that we're outta here."

Denzel stood up and reached for a couple of empty plates, but before he could pick them up, Elena unexpectedly flung her arms around his waist and gave him a hug.

"What's up with that?" Denzel mumbled self-consciously. He quietly explained, "You cooked, we should help clean up."

"*Nada*," Elena responded as she flashed him a smile. "*De nada.*"

"If we're getting the band back together, then I need my sax," Maia said, giggling. "I'll meet you guys down at the dock. I have to go see a ferry man about a horn. You never know when you might run into an ill-tempered sea serpent."

"Good idea." Sonjay nodded approvingly.

"Horn?" Mole asked. "What's up with that?"

Denzel explained that the previous year Maia defeated a nasty sea serpent by playing a horn kept on the ferries to drive them away. He concluded by telling Mole, "So we need to set up a microphone and amplifier that will project from a speaker on the outside of the sub, just in case we run into any sea serpents."

"I'm on the job, mon," Mole assured Denzel, as he emerged from under the table and hurried off.

Soon after, when they reassembled at the dock in the harbor, the underwater expedition team could see no more of the sub than the topmost part and the open gray metal hatch through which they would soon climb inside. They stared at that hatch as the reality of the voyage that lay before them sunk in.

Maia embraced Elena in farewell. She turned to Guhblorin and instructed him, "Look after her. She's my best friend." Guhblorin nodded solemnly, appearing more serious than Maia had ever seen him appear, as he replied, "Mine too." Elena squeezed Guhblorin's arm in appreciation.

Mole stepped forward and descended down the ladder into the depths of the sub. Reggie went next. Then Jasper. Elena stepped up and gave Denzel a kiss on the cheek. "When you find yourself under thousands of tons of water, remember that I'm up here cooking dinner and I expect you to return safe and sound to eat it," Elena told him. "I plan to make chocolate flan especially for you. I'll get angry if you don't show up. You don't want to see a Latina girl angry, trust me."

"Got it," Denzel replied; and he saluted Elena. "Chocolate flan. Tonight." Then he and the others followed Jasper into the sub.

Inside, the sub seemed larger than they had expected. Denzel had rigged a bright light they could shine through the large viewing window and into the water so that when they descended to the pitch darkness of the ocean floor, the light would enable them to see. Mole had rigged a microphone and amplifier inside with a speaker on the outside so that after the sub disappeared under the water, Denzel's amplified voice emerged in final farewell to those who stood at the dock. "Chocolate flan," the voice said from under the water. "And whipped cream. Lots of whipped cream, please."

"Chocolate," Bayard said in his best imitation of Denzel's voice. He perched on Elena's shoulder as Guhblorin flapped his enormous ears beside them.

The instant that Denzel closed the hatch on the sub and secured the seal, Mole pressed a button on a clock that began to tick off the time, counting down from five hours. The voyagers clustered around the viewing window as the sub angled downward and cut through the water.

"Mole, do you have any window cleaner?" Maia asked as she shook her head in disgust. "This window is filthy. We can't see anything."

Mole pointed to a cupboard and replied, sheepishly, "You'll find cleaning supplies in there. Sorry. I didn't have time to tidy up."

Maia retrieved a spray bottle of window cleaner and a rag. She pulled a chair over to the window and methodically cleaned the glass from top to bottom. Denzel and Sonjay complained about the vinegary smell of the window cleaner, but they quickly changed their tune when they enjoyed the view through the clear window after Maia finished. They could see out as if nothing stood between them and the ocean.

At first they didn't turn on the bright light, since the sun penetrated the water. They passed brilliant tropical fish of all shapes and sizes, some of them glowing iridescent. They saw round, flat, yellow-and-black striped fish shaped like hearts; tiny, long, thin, glowing electric-blue fish with red-tipped tails; seahorses in all different sizes, some as tiny as a toothpick and others as large as a crocodile; square stingrays; parachute-like jellyfish; large fish; small fish; fish in every imaginable color; fish with big floppy fins; fish with tiny fins. All manner of sea plants also passed in front of the window; algae and seaweeds of golden-yellow, chalk-green, deep-maroon, amber, forest-green, and other colors. They saw velvety sea plants, shiny ones, and others as delicate as lace.

"Some of the sea plants look so fragile," Maia commented. "Imagine what a coating of oil would do to them."

"That coating of oil is on its way," Doshmisi responded grimly. "We can't fail."

As they continued to descend, the clock continued to tick away their precious minutes. Everyone on the expedition team found it impossible not to watch it while they each calculated in their head how long it was taking them to reach the ocean floor. Jasper spread the map that he and Cardamom had borrowed from the library out on a table in the middle of the cabin and he, Denzel, and Reggie remained glued to it throughout the descent. Reggie kept flipping back and forth between several pages in a little book, frequently calling out directions to Mole, who steered the sub.

Doshmisi, Maia, and Sonjay watched the sea creatures drift past the window in the glow of the sub's bright light, glancing anxiously at the clock now and then.

After they had traveled for more than an hour, they reached the ocean floor and Reggie directed Mole to the entrance to the Coral Caves, which looked like the enormous yawning-open mouth of a whale. It was as gray as the ocean floor around the edges, but inside the caves the colors went to pale-pink, chalk-green, beige, and the faint-blue of early morning light. Protruding pointed stalagmites and jagged stalactites resembling teeth covered the top and bottom of the caves. Entering seemed like sailing into the throat of a huge beast. The sub fit through the entrance easily. Reggie calculated the opening to be at least eighty feet across.

Jasper switched over to a map of the inside of the Coral Caves, which he and Reggie followed closely, guiding the sub through the subterranean tunnels. Meanwhile, the others gazed in awe at the dazzlingly colorful coral formations inside the caves. The vivid coral took the shape of poetic abstract forms. Curvaceous coral resembled bones while other coral tapered out into feathery wisps. Maia imagined that a sculptor had thoughtfully and precisely carved the coral in the caves over thousands of years. She and Doshmisi forgot to watch the clock, awestruck by the beauty revealed in the bright light emanating from the sub.

"I wonder if anyone has ever seen this place," Maia marveled.

"Well, they must have," Sonjay speculated, "because someone put the Emerald Crystal down here."

"No they didn't," Maia corrected him. "The whales put it down here."

"Oh yeah," Sonjay conceded. "Right."

"There, up ahead," Reggie pointed out the window. Everyone peered into the distance as a small structure that turned out to be a pedestal came into view. It looked like a stone birdbath, standing about five feet tall with a basin on top. Fragile strands of seaweed entwined around it and drifted in the water above the outside rim of the basin. In the center of the basin a crystalline stone, about an inch across in size, glowed green.

"It looks like the crystal that hangs in my window at Manzanita Ranch," Doshmisi noted. "Only green."

"It seems lit from inside," Maia observed.

Mole slowly and carefully maneuvered the sub as close as he could without disturbing the pedestal on which the Emerald Crystal rested.

Jasper glanced at the clock. "Two hours and seven minutes," he said.

"We have plenty of time," Denzel reassured him.

"This seems too easy," Sonjay warned. The words had barely dropped from his lips when a large yellow-green eye appeared in the viewing window and rolled around in a chartreuse eye socket. The sub bounced around like crazy and a set of white-green scales flashed across the viewing window.

"You had to open your mouth and jinx it," Denzel accused his brother, although they both knew Sonjay's words had not caused the arrival of the sea serpent.

"Just saying," Sonjay replied.

"It's my biggest fan," Maia called out. "I had a feeling he'd show up so I brought his favorite: the horn that repels sea serpents!" She opened a large horn case that she had stashed in a storage bin when they entered the sub and removed the horn she had retrieved from the ferry captain before embarking on the undersea expedition. Her amulet began to glow with a strong blue light. As she took the horn out of the case, and grabbed the sheet music that went with it, she told Denzel to turn on the sound system.

Maia had sent a sea serpent scurrying away from a ferry full of passengers the year before by playing a haunting tune on the special horn made to ward off sea serpents. Through the viewing window, the expedition team saw the sea serpent glide away from the sub, turn around, and prepare to head back for a strike. It emitted a disgusting stream of slime from its mouth, shook its head, roared, displayed its rotten teeth, and then launched forward. Meanwhile, Doshmisi held up the sheet music for Maia, Denzel positioned a microphone at the mouth of the horn, and Maia blew for all she was worth, causing a haunting note to emerge from the instrument and echo into the outside cavern.

The sea serpent howled loudly and they could hear its cry inside the sub. It shook its monstrous head and squirmed in agony. The beast's tail whipped around and smacked the pedestal. The basin on the top of the pedestal snapped off and turned upside down, dropping to the ocean floor with a dull thud. The crystal disappeared in a swirl of silt thrown up from the bottom of the cave. The sea serpent fled as Maia continued to play the haunting tune on the horn. It left in its wake a murky wash of mud, silt, rocks, and shells flung up from the thrash of its tail.

As he studied the scene outside the viewing window, Reggie commented in frustration, "Nothing is easy, is it?"

"Like I was saying," Sonjay agreed.

The sea serpent had turned tail and run away. The last note from the horn faded. The expedition team assembled silently at the viewing window and surveyed the damage. The sub had a robotic claw that they had planned to use to collect the Emerald Crystal. It didn't seem likely that the claw would work in their present situation, with the Emerald Crystal under a basin or buried in silt. "Someone has to go out there," Sonjay said grimly. "Is that possible?"

"Yeah, mon," Mole replied. "It be possible. There be two diving suits on board and the sub has a decompression chamber for exit and entry underwater."

Sonjay turned from the window and instructed, "Then suit me up."

"Sorry, Sonjay, it can't be you," Mole told him.

"What do you mean?" Sonjay demanded.

"You're too small. The suits be adult size. A bad fit. You wouldn't be able to move in it or use the breathing tube," Mole informed him.

"That's OK," Reggie said immediately. "I'll go."

"You can't go, Daddy," Doshmisi said firmly. "You're the only one who understands the information in that book about how to navigate out of here and get back up to the surface."

"Maia has to stay to play the horn if the sea serpent comes back, and we need Mole to operate the sub," Sonjay added.

"That leaves me, Jasper, and Denzel," Doshmisi pointed out, even though they had all realized it already.

Jasper turned to Denzel and said, "Looks like it's you and me."

"Excuse me?" Doshmisi said as she rolled her neck. "How do you figure that?"

Jasper blushed, but persisted. "You should stay inside where it's safe."

"And when have I ever done the safe thing when it was necessary to take a risk? Are you calling me a coward?" Doshmisi demanded.

"No, no, that's not it at all." Jasper looked to the others for backup but no one was willing to cross Doshmisi, who clearly believed that she had just as much duty and right to go after the Emerald Crystal as either of the boys.

Maia closed her fist around the ends of three of her long braids and held her fist out to Jasper, Denzel, and Doshmisi. "Pick a braid," she instructed. "The two who pick the longest braids get to go and whoever picks the shortest one stays behind." The three each selected a braid and Maia opened her fist. The candidates moved their fingers down to the end of the braid they had chosen. Jasper's braid was more than an inch shorter than the other two. He stared at it in disbelief.

"Dosh, please let me go. It's not right for you to go. What if something happens to you?" Jasper pleaded.

"What if it does?" Doshmisi fired back, exasperated. "Something could happen to you too. You're no safer out there than I am. Unless you think that because you're a boy you can defend yourself better."

"N-no," Jasper stammered. "It's not because I'm a boy and you're a girl. It's because I couldn't live with myself if something happened to you."

"Then it is exactly because you are a boy and I'm a girl. You think it's your duty to protect and defend me. Well I'm perfectly capable of doing that for myself. And if my choice gets me killed, well then it was my choice, not yours." Doshmisi's anger bubbled over and she couldn't contain it; she waved a hand in the direction of her father. "Look at what happened to Daddy, trying to protect our mother! Did he save her life? No. Instead he wound up locked in a dungeon and he missed the last few years our family could have had together."

Reggie immediately defended himself. "That's not fair, Dosh. I tried to do more than just save your mother. I thought I could change the deep enchantment somehow, change the fate that she had chosen for herself and retrieve the Staff of Shakabaz from Sissrath. And I failed. During those years that I spent locked in that dungeon, I lost hope. But I've found hope again now that my children have returned to me; and I'm throwing my weight behind Sonjay, trying once again to change a prophecy, hoping that's possible, because what else can we do? Just sit around and watch the end of Faracadar? We have to try, to put up a struggle against the unfolding events, against the deep enchantment and the prophecy. Perhaps the end really is fated and we can do nothing to prevent that outcome. But we can't know for sure if something we do will tip the scales one way or another." Reggie put a hand on Jasper's shoulder and spoke to him. "I know that your heart will break if something happens to Dosh out there, something you think you could have prevented. I know because mine broke when I lost my wife. But nothing will ever change her decision to go. You have to accept that. I could not accept Debbie's decision, and Dosh is right, my failure robbed me of the last years I could have had with Debbie."

"I'm sorry, Daddy," Doshmisi apologized, as she put her hand on her father's arm. "I didn't mean to criticize you. You did what you had to do."

Tears ran down Maia's cheeks and Denzel rubbed her back in a comforting way.

Sonjay's voice trembled as he said, "Just because you failed to change the prophecy for Momma doesn't mean that it's not possible. This is a different prophecy. A different time. And we have a lot of help we can rely on."

"I know it, son," Reggie replied. "Like I said, I'm hopeful."

"We be wasting valuable minutes," Mole interjected urgently. "Dosh and Denzel need to move out."

Denzel picked up one of the diving suits and pulled it on over his long legs. Jasper reluctantly handed the other suit to Doshmisi. Her lips curved in a slight smile and she said, "You know you love it that I'm willing to walk into danger when necessary."

"Not as much as you think I do," Jasper said drily. "It has its down side."

"You have fifteen minutes to find the Emerald Crystal and get back into the sub in order for us to make it up to the surface before the power pack on the sub runs out of energy," Reggie told his son and daughter. "We'll flash the light on the sub at two minutes before the time is up. You have to come back then. We can return tomorrow with the sub recharged if we need to. But you have to come back when we flash the light. Promise?" They both nodded in agreement.

After they suited up and Mole showed them how to breathe through the apparatus that connected to their oxygen tanks, Doshmisi and Denzel stepped into the decompression chamber. Denzel saluted the others as the door slid closed. Mole turned a large wheel to seal the door.

As the two stepped out onto the floor of the Coral Caves, Maia glanced back at the clock. Then she watched anxiously out the viewing window as Denzel and Doshmisi walked to the pedestal, dropped to their knees, lifted the basin, and began searching in the silt. Their movements kicked up debris from the floor of the cave, making the water murky. The bright light glinted off millions of floating particles so that those who had stayed inside the sub strained to see through a fog of drifting matter.

Outside in the caves, Doshmisi tried to disturb as little debris as possible as she felt around in the fluffy silt for the hard edges of the crystal. Her gloves were thick and difficult to maneuver. Denzel placed the basin back on the stand. He saw no crystal inside it. Doshmisi stood still for a long moment while she studied her surroundings. She remembered that the crystal had glowed with a greenish light similar to the light emitted by the herbal whenever she used it to heal someone. She strained to see a green glow anywhere on the ground around her, but she saw nothing. She wished that Denzel would quit moving around so much. He made more debris lift from beneath their feet with every step.

Doshmisi sat down carefully in the spot where the basin had landed and felt around her carefully in a circle. Then she had an idea. She had not seen any dolphins or whales in the ocean during her entire time in Faracadar this year. Perhaps that had something to do with the oil well. The previous year, the whales had told her what she needed to know to defeat Sissrath, even though it took her a long time to decipher the poetic message they delivered to her. She wondered if the whales would come to her aid now if she asked them for help. She closed her eyes and sent a mental message to the whales. "Send help," she thought. "It's your world as well as ours. We're trying to save it for all of us. But we need the Emerald Crystal to do it."

Denzel glanced at Doshmisi in annoyance. They had hardly any time to look and his sister had plunked herself down and stopped even trying. She had even closed her eyes and given up searching. Girls! He would never understand how a girl's brain worked. He found himself wishing that Jasper had prevailed and managed to come with him instead of his sister.

As she sent her thoughts out to the whales, Doshmisi pictured them swimming gracefully in the ocean, despite their enormous size, lightweight in the water, their home. She emptied her mind of extraneous thoughts, meditated on sending love to the whales, and imagined herself as an empty bottle waiting for the whales to fill it. Slowly the empty bottle of her self began to fill with an indescribable warmth and power. In her mind she heard the sound of whale voices, which she had only heard once before in her life. A high-pitched singsong voice and a deep rumbling voice intertwined. At first she could not make out what the voices sang, and then she understood. They sang FOLLOW THE SILVER.

Doshmisi felt pressure on her arm and opened her eyes to find Denzel urgently attempting to rouse her from her meditation. The Amulet of the Trees, which she wore around her neck, glowed so brightly green that the light burst from the waterproof zipper on the front of her diving suit and from around the seam at the neck. The instant that happened, Denzel stepped back. He knew that if her amulet glowed then she had figured something out. Suddenly hundreds of tiny silver fish emerged out of nowhere and swarmed in the light from Doshmisi's glowing amulet. She could still hear the whale voices in her head singing FOLLOW THE SILVER and she knew exactly what they meant.

The little silver fish converged on a spot not far from where Doshmisi sat and circled above it as if caught whirlpooling in a miniature tornado. At the bottom tip of the tornado-whirlpool, something glowed green under the debris and silt. She pointed to it and Denzel walked to the spot, plunged his hand down beneath the circling fish, and triumphantly raised the Emerald Crystal above his head.

The bright light on the sub began to flash the two-minute warning. Denzel carefully handed the Emerald Crystal to Doshmisi, who clutched it to her chest, as they quickly returned to the hatch and entered the decompression chamber. In a few short moments, they reentered the sub. As they emerged from the decompression chamber the others cheered. When she removed her diving suit, Doshmisi's amulet glowed brilliantly before fading swiftly to dark.

"Put the pedal to the metal," Denzel called to Mole, who cast him a puzzled glance.

"He means to put the sub in high gear," Reggie explained.

"Already done, mon," Mole replied, as he turned the sub around to head for the surface.

"How did you call those fish?" Maia asked her sister, for she felt sure that the fish had come at her sister's bidding.

"I sent a message to the whales," Doshmisi replied. "They must have sent the little silver fish because they told me to follow the silver."

"Well-played," Maia complimented her sister.

Jasper felt so relieved to have Doshmisi safely back inside the sub that he hugged her to him, not caring who saw him do it. "I'm sorry I tried to hold you back," Jasper apologized.

"And I'm sorry I lost my temper," Doshmisi replied. She then opened her hand to reveal the Emerald Crystal, the most purely beautiful stone any of them had ever seen.

Reggie broke the spell cast by the beauty of the Emerald Crystal when he turned his eyes anxiously to the clock. Denzel alerted them that the return would take them longer than the descent, because the sub had to fight against gravity and the pressure of the water. They had just barely enough charge left in the power pack to return to the surface. Reggie broke a sweat as he directed Mole out of the Coral Caves and up through the levels of ocean toward the surface.

"Twenty-two left," Jasper counted, unnecessarily, since all eyes remained glued to the clock. They had not expected to cut it this close. Sonjay felt a small measure of comfort in the knowledge that Cardamom had remained behind on the dock with the Staff of Shakabaz, prepared to attempt enchantment to assist if needed.

Maia pointed to the viewing window. "Um, what's that stuff?" she asked. "I don't remember seeing that on the way down." Reggie and Mole continued to concentrate on steering the sub back to the dock at Whale Island, but the rest of the expedition team followed Maia's gaze out the viewing window where a large tentacle swished in the water.

"Squid," Jasper said in horror. "It looks like a giant squid." More tentacles appeared and then a squid eye slid past the window, watching the voyagers as if studying a cluster of odd sea creatures in an aquarium. All of a sudden the sub jolted and jerked wildly, throwing them every which way against the viewing window and the floor. Mole clung to the controls and struggled to remain upright.

"We must seem like a toy to that thing," Doshmisi speculated.

"Or a dinner," Sonjay suggested.

"Sonjay!" Maia exclaimed in alarm.

"Just saying," Sonjay answered.

The sub stopped jerking around just as suddenly as it had started.

"Maybe we be in luck," Mole said hopefully. "It maybe went away."

"Perhaps we weren't as exciting as all that to a squid," Doshmisi said with relief. They stood at the viewing window and searched the water for any sign of the giant squid.

"Wait, look there." Maia pointed, and in the bright light from the sub, they could see dark black puffs billowing around them. "I think that's squid ink."

"That can't be good," Jasper commented.

"Yah mon," Mole agreed. "Not good. It's clogging the thrusters." A deep grinding noise rose from underneath the sub and it began to sink downward. The water had just begun to show signs of sunlight penetrating, but that disappeared quickly as the sub dropped toward the ocean floor.

"We be needin' to clear that ink out of the thrusters," Mole said urgently.

"How?" Doshmisi asked.

"I don't know," Mole replied with a helpless expression.

"We're running out of time," Jasper spoke aloud the words that were in everyone's mind.

"We're sinking," Reggie stated the obvious. "Don't panic. Think."

Chapter Twenty
Vinegar, Flan, and Reinforcements

"I'm going back out there," Denzel declared, as he picked up his diving suit, which lay in a heap on the floor.

"You will do no such thing!" Reggie snapped authoritatively.

"Daddy's right," Maia agreed. "What if that squid comes back? Besides, we don't know about the squid ink. It could eat through the diving suit."

"Hold up!" Denzel shouted. "Wait, wait, wait! I know what to do. Maia, where did you put that window cleaner?"

Maia went to the supply cupboard and pulled out the bottle of window cleaner.

"Is that it? Is there any more in there?" Denzel asked. His amulet had begun glowing with red light.

"Woo-hoo," Sonjay rejoiced as he pointed to his brother's amulet. "Cool idea incoming."

Mole held his hand up to Denzel for a high five, which Denzel gave him. "Vinegar," Mole announced with a bob of his head that set his dreadlocks bouncing. "You're brilliant, mon."

"Vinegar," Denzel repeated. "The window cleaner has vinegar in it and it should clear the squid ink out of those thrusters."

After a thorough search of the supply cabinet, Maia produced three bottles of window cleaner, which Mole and Denzel proceeded to pour into the chambers of the flushing mechanism for the thrusters. Mole pressed a button and the window cleaner burst through the thrusters as the sub shot forward and emerged well clear of the billow of squid ink left in its wake. With renewed speed, the sub lurched up toward the surface while the expedition team cheered their victory over squid ink.

As the clock in the sub ticked down to zero, the sub reached the surface of the water and slid alongside the dock. They just barely made it back in time.

When they emerged from the hatch, they found Cardamom, Iris, Elena, and Guhblorin waiting for them. Elena flung her arms around Maia and both girls laughed and cried at once. "Guhblorin was timing you," Elena informed her friend, "and we didn't think you would make it back before you ran out of power."

"We almost didn't," Maia admitted. "We were saved by window cleaner."

"Good one," Guhblorin said with a suppressed giggle.

"Seriously," Maia told him.

"No lie," Jasper backed her up. "Denzel put window cleaner into the flushing mechanism to clear the thrusters of squid ink because it had vinegar in it."

"Squid ink? I didn't know squid knew how to write," Guhblorin replied. Elena attempted to cast a stern look in his direction, but her smile gave away her amusement.

Sonjay pointed to the beach next to the dock and asked, "What's going on over there? Why is everyone on the beach?" People had indeed crowded onto the beach. They stood or sat on the sand and gazed out over the water. From where they stood on the dock, the Four and their companions could hear the murmuring voices of those on the beach punctuated by the sound of weeping. The people hugged and comforted one another, while many of them stood unmoving at the water's edge, some with their arms wrapped around each other.

"News of the oil spill at the North Coast has reached Whale Island. We have had messengers. The spill moves slowly but steadily in our direction across the water. The whales fled even before it happened. And the algae is disappearing, which we can tell because of the dull, gray color of the water," Cardamom informed them.

"Island People have lived for thousands of years as neighbors to the ocean and now this spill will kill it and all that inhabit it and therefore us as well," Iris said despondently. "My people have come to say farewell to our dear friend, this beautiful beach, this beautiful water, which will die when that oil washes in," Iris explained. "I have said nothing to my people about the Emerald Crystal because I didn't know if you would find it and I still don't know if it will avert this disaster. Did you retrieve it from the Coral Caves?"

By way of response, Doshmisi held the Emerald Crystal up to the light so Iris could see it. An admiring sigh escaped Iris's lips as she gazed at the beautiful jewel. Having emerged from the depths of the ocean, the Emerald Crystal glinted in the sunlight with such intense green that it hurt their eyes to behold it. Doshmisi wrapped it in a swatch of cloth and stored it in her pocket.

"We need to get to the North Coast quickly to stop that oil spill," Sonjay reminded them, as his eyes swept across the beach and took in the people mourning the approaching devastation the oil would bring to their home.

"What about Clover's memorial?" Reggie asked. "Shouldn't we stay here for that?"

"We can't waste that precious time," Doshmisi reminded her father.

"She would certainly prefer that you go," Iris reassured them. "She has plenty of people here who love her and who will attend her homegoing."

"We can't go until we eat dinner, though. Guhblorin and I cooked," Elena reported.

"No doubt you did," Denzel said with a pleased smile. "And flan?"

"*Absolutemente*. There's a chocolate flan with whipped cream and it has your name written all over it," Elena told Denzel, as she folded her arms across her chest and tossed her blue-black hair in the sunlight.

At that moment Mole, who had remained behind in the sub to power it down and secure it, emerged from the hatch. He took one look at Iris and tripped over the edge of the dock. An assortment of equipment that he held in his arms went flying in all directions. A flare gun bounced on the dock and emitted a bright fluorescent-pink flare. The flare shot arced into the sky and burst like fireworks. A small package burst open and instantly inflated itself into a raft that knocked Guhblorin over the side of the dock and into the water where he spluttered and flailed while Mole stammered an apology.

Iris told Elena softly, "I'll go home and set the table before I inspire him to do any further damage. I'll see you at Clover's shortly."

Reggie reached out a hand and helped Guhblorin out of the water while the others gathered up Mole's belongings and stuffed them into a large canvas sack that Denzel produced.

"I be hopeless," Mole whined with self-pity. "I can't even look at her without falling apart. She must think me the most ridiculous mon ever."

"Don't get so wound up about it. You need to relax," Reggie advised.

"As if," Mole responded dejectedly as the group began to walk toward Clover's house and the library. "I better just go to my room. Bring me a plate of food, please? And some of that chocolate flan."

"I think I have a sardine in my underpants," Guhblorin announced with a giggle.

"We'll get on the road as soon as we finish eating dinner," Denzel announced.

"I disagree," Reggie contradicted his son. "We need rest. None of us will function well if we're tired."

"Daddy, we can't take the night off. We have to get moving," Sonjay said firmly.

"I know that. I'm not suggesting we sleep through the night. But we need a few hours. A power nap. We can have Iris wake us at midnight. Would you agree to that?"

"That oil will continue moving while we sleep," Doshmisi reminded.

"Maybe so, but I agree with Reggie. Food and sleep will make us more alert to handle whatever lies ahead," Cardamom added. So they agreed to get some sleep after dinner and to start out at midnight.

Elena's dinner did not disappoint. She and Guhblorin had prepared a totally scrumptious meal. While they ate, they filled Cardamom, Elena, and Guhblorin in on the events that had taken place under the ocean. When they finished relating their tale, Cardamom turned to Reggie and inquired, "I have a question I have wanted to ask you. How did you get back to Faracadar on your own? Without Debbie. I know you came once with Debbie, but, how did you find your way back without her?"

Reggie finished chewing a mouthful of chili rellenos and swallowed. "Do you not fear that if revealed this information could be misused?"

"I feel confident that no one at this table will misuse it or share it with another who might do so," Cardamom replied without hesitation.

Reggie put his fork down carefully on his plate and paused. He glanced at the others seated around the table. "When Debbie and I returned from our visit on the one occasion that she brought me here, I tore a large sliver from the wood at Angel's Gate as we passed through and I took it with me, hidden in my clothes. I didn't know whether or not it could take me back to Faracadar until I tried to use it. When I found out what my wife had done, how she had promised years off her life to prevent Sissrath from using the Staff of Shakabaz in matters of life and death, I resolved to find a way to use that sliver of wood to return and attempt to reverse the deep enchantment that bound her. I took it to the cabin in the woods at Manzanita Ranch and I begged, with all my might, and all the love I have in me for my wife, to return here. Often wishing comes to nothing. But sometimes wishes become real. My wishes, and that shard of wood, brought me back. Unfortunately, once here, I proved no match for Sissrath."

"It surprises me that you could travel by that method," Cardamom said.

"I have learned a great deal while studying the Book of the Khoum and spending many solitary hours meditating and contemplating the nature of things," Reggie told the enchanter, as his children listened attentively. "I have learned that love often opens doors that would otherwise have remained closed. I have come to believe that I managed to return because of the love I feel for my wife. I wish that my love could have carried me back to her while she lived. At least it brought my children back to me."

"That it did," Cardamom replied.

Just then, Guhblorin appeared in the doorway to the kitchen with a rolling cart that contained an enormous chocolate flan and a bowl overflowing with frothy whipped cream. "Dessert is served!" Guhblorin announced gleefully. After they devoured the spectacular flan, the weary travelers dispersed to their beds for a few hours of sleep before starting out for the North Coast. It would take them an entire night to travel to the Passage Circle. A ferry captain had agreed to make a special ferry run to Dolphin Island for them shortly after midnight.

At midnight, Iris went from room to room and woke each of them. When she woke Mole, he took one look at Iris's face in the dim light of the glow-lamp and promptly fell out of bed. He sprawled on the floor at Iris's feet and blinked up at her helplessly.

Iris sat on the floor next to Mole. "Don't move," she ordered Mole. "Just stay exactly where you are and don't move a finger. Listen," she continued, "I like you, but it's entirely impossible for me to get to know you if you continue to self-destruct every time you catch sight of me. Understand?"

Mole nodded his head silently in the affirmative. His dreadlocks bobbed up and down.

"If we're going to travel together then this goofiness has to stop," Iris said firmly.

"Travel together?" Mole asked.

"I'm going with you and the others to the North Coast. If the land is in peril and fighting for its life, I refuse to remain behind. I'll go with you to see if I can help. And if the end comes, then I would just as soon meet it in the presence of Clover's grandchildren. She would understand and not want me to stay behind for her memorial under the circumstances. So you see, you have to get a grip, Mole. You can't keep acting the fool whenever I appear."

"I know," Mole agreed, with a dejected sigh. "I'll try harder."

"That's probably the problem," Iris pointed out. She placed a gentle hand on his arm. "You're trying too hard. Stop trying. Just let things be what they are. Now do you think you can stand up and get yourself ready to go without destroying any of my furniture?"

"I'll try," Mole said and then quickly revised that. "I mean I won't try. I mean I'll try not to try."

As Iris rose from the floor she told him, "Don't think about it too hard, you'll hurt yourself. Just take it slow." She walked to the door and turned in the doorway. "I'll see you in the courtyard in a few minutes."

The Four, Jasper, Elena, Guhblorin, Reggie, Cardamom, Mole, and Iris assembled in the courtyard under the burst of colorful stars that lit the night sky. They spoke in subdued voices as they prepared for the journey ahead.

Cardamom drew Reggie aside and asked him quietly, "Have you noticed the air?"

"The air?" Reggie repeated, as he raised his eyebrows questioningly.

"Don't say anything to the others. Not yet. I've noticed the air is thicker, making it a little harder to breathe. The blue-green algae that cleans our air lives in the ocean, and the Corportons have poisoned the ocean with the oil spill," Cardamom explained with a worried expression. "You know what I mean."

Reggie nodded. "I have a feeling my children have noticed it, but let's not go there yet. We might have some luck repairing the situation before we get into serious trouble."

Elena handed out sack lunches to everyone as they mounted their tigers. Doshmisi sat astride Dagobaz. Despite the late hour, many residents of Whale Island lined the streets to see them off as they rode to the harbor to take the ferry on the first leg of their journey. "May the work of the Four continue," people called out.

They traveled through the night both by ferry and hard riding across the ocean bridges that connected the islands to one another and to the mainland. The sun had stood in the sky for a couple of hours by the time they arrived on the beach at the Passage Circle. As they neared the beach, riding along the ocean bridge, they saw a throng of people waiting for them. Word of their mission and their journey must have preceded them. At the front of the gathered people stood Governor Jay, flanked by the royal family on one side and Crumpet and Buttercup on the other. Jack, the intuit, drifted slightly above the sand with a few of his intuit buddies. The intuits had skateboards tucked under their arms. Sonjay smiled when he saw the skateboards. It seemed like forever since he had spent a carefree afternoon skating.

As the travelers came within earshot of the people from the Passage Circle, Sonjay called out to them, "What's up? What're you guys doing here?"

"We came to greet you and bring you provisions," Governor Jay replied.

"And some of us will go with you," Princess Honeydew informed them resolutely.

Denzel's eyes glittered with excitement. "Like an army?" he asked.

"Do you want an army?" Governor Jay offered.

"An army is not a bad idea," Reggie said thoughtfully.

"Yes, it is a bad idea," Doshmisi contradicted her father. "If I learned one thing from those indecipherable whales last year, I learned that warring armies solve nothing."

"What she said," Sonjay backed up his sister.

Denzel shrugged and said, "whatever."

"So who's coming with us?" Maia asked curiously.

Crumpet, Buttercup, Honeydew, Saffron, and Hyacinth stepped forward. Jack and his intuit friends floated up to join them.

"Why am I not surprised?" Sonjay commented.

"We figure you must be headed to the North Coast to stop the oil spill," Crumpet told them. "We want to know the plan."

"You can uniform us on the way," Hyacinth said as he mounted a tiger.

"Inform," Princess Honeydew translated her father's mangled communication. "You can inform us on the way." She and the others mounted their tigers as well.

"I guess you won't be staying for breakfast," Governor Jay observed sorrowfully.

"No time," Cardamom said.

"The oil spill won't stop for breakfast," Sonjay reminded the governor.

Governor Jay held his hand up in front of him, palm facing outward. "May the work of the Four continue," he called to the departing travelers. Those who remained by his side on the beach repeated his gesture and his words as the travelers sped away in a flurry of sand.

Chapter Twenty-One
Canyon of Imaginary Reality

They stopped to eat a hasty lunch while the tigers and Dagobaz drank water from a flowing stream and took a moment's rest. Then they pressed on into the afternoon. Before long they began to notice that the air had become humid, bloated with moisture, and it was hazy, as if contaminated by a nearby fire. The light from the sun had an eerie yellowish cast to it, the way sunlight looks shining through many dust particles in the air. Denzel and Mole discussed the deteriorated air quality in hushed voices. They had come to the same conclusion as Cardamom and Reggie and they had also chosen not to discuss their observation openly.

In the late afternoon, as they approached the North Coast, and just as Doshmisi had begun to allow herself to hope that Sissrath did not know their whereabouts, she heard the sound of many tiger paws pounding hard on the ground behind her. Those pounding paws could only mean trouble. The travelers had arrived in a meadow that gave way to a rocky hillside rising up abruptly from the meadow's edge. Jasper had intended to turn from the rocky hillside and to lead the group toward the water, where they could skirt the rocky region by riding on the beach. They were nearing the damaged oil rig and the Corporton compound.

Unfortunately, the tiger paws that Doshmisi heard behind her belonged to tigers carrying Special Forces. She bent low over Dagobaz's neck as the horse fairly flew, increasing his speed. She worried the tigers carrying her family and friends could not keep up with Dagobaz. Despite their exhaustion, the tigers pushed themselves to the limit. On Dagobaz, Doshmisi quickly pulled out into the lead. She dropped back slightly to ride alongside Jasper, who called over to her, "We have to enter this canyon up ahead. I don't like it. Something feels wrong about it."

"I have a bad feeling about it too," Doshmisi agreed. "Can we avoid it?"

"I don't know another way," Jasper lamented.

The Special Forces bore down on them from behind in a horseshoe formation. She suddenly realized the Special Forces were herding her and the others into the canyon on purpose. There was something in that canyon that the Special Forces knew about and Doshmisi and her companions did not. Jasper shouted to her but she couldn't make out his words over the pounding of tiger paws and Dagobaz's hooves. Despite her dread of finding out what lurked in the canyon, she and the others had no choice. The pursuit of the Special Forces drove them into it.

Inside the canyon, steep walls of rock rose on either side. Interestingly, the Special Forces continued to follow them. If the Special Forces did not fear entering the canyon, then perhaps they hadn't purposely chased Doshmisi and the others into it after all and maybe nothing bad awaited them. The travelers picked up speed and put more distance between themselves and the Special Forces. Doshmisi clung to Dagobaz's mane and hunkered down over the horse's neck. For a brief, bright moment she thought, with exhilaration, that they could outrun the Special Forces. She could no longer hear them in pursuit. Then she remembered that it did not bode well if the Special Forces had fallen back and retreated from the canyon.

Doshmisi hollered to Dagobaz, "Whoa! Hold up!" as she reined him in. Jasper, Sonjay, Denzel, and Crumpet flew past her. Next, her father, Cardamom, Honeydew, and High Chief Hyacinth passed her. Doshmisi slowed down and shouted to the others, "Stop, stop, stop!" Everyone slowed, turning to look at her in bewilderment, until all the riders had brought their tigers to a halt and rode over to cluster around Doshmisi. "Think about it," she said. "The Special Forces have disappeared. Something is up."

"They wanted us to ride into this canyon, didn't they?" Sonjay asked.

"I think so," Doshmisi confirmed.

Denzel groaned. "I wonder what the heck is in here," he said.

"No mice, I hope," Hyacinth announced anxiously. "I hate mice." The instant the words flew from Hyacinth's lips, three enormous mice, as big as elephants, appeared just ahead in the canyon. Cardamom instantly held his hands up in front of him and, as sparks flew from his fingers, said a few words of enchantment, which blasted the giant mice into the air. The enormous rodents screeched and ran off into the canyon. "Imaginary Reality," Cardamom stated grimly.

"What does that mean?" Maia asked.

"Speak up, we can't hear you back here," Reggie called to Cardamom.

Cardamom raised his voice so that everyone could hear him. "We've entered a zone of Imaginary Reality. Sissrath probably set it up especially for us."

An enormous cinnamon roll fell from the sky and landed in front of them with a splat, obstructing their path forward.

"OK," Cardamom said impatiently, "who imagined the cinnamon roll?"

"That be me," Mole replied sheepishly. "I be a little hungry, mon."

"Well unimagine it right away," Cardamom commanded.

"We could eat our way through it," Guhblorin suggested hopefully. "It looks tasty. Could you imagine one with frosting on it?" Guhblorin asked Mole.

"Sure thing," Mole replied.

Another cinnamon roll dropped from the sky, missing Guhblorin's head by mere inches, and impaled itself on a spiky fir tree, which prevented it from rolling down the steep side of the canyon and crushing the geebaching. Guhblorin leaned over and took a bite out of the cinnamon roll. "Yum. Delicious frosting Mole," he said appreciatively. He had almost fallen off the tiger while leaning out to take a bite and Elena grabbed his arm and pulled him back onto the tiger they shared.

"Both of you, stop that this instant!" Cardamom roared. "Unimagine these pastries right away. Don't you see? Anything you imagine in this canyon will become real, more than real, in fact exaggerated and malevolent. The canyon will use your imagination against you. You must make your mind blank. Don't think of anything. Do whatever you have to do to not think. Meditate. Scream. Sing. Count. Anything. We have to ride through here as quickly as possible without imagining a single thing!"

"Impossible," Reggie declared. "It's the nature of the human mind to be active."

"Enchanters learn to clear our minds of all thought in order to perform enchantments. It's possible. It's a learned skill. You will just have to learn how to do it quickly and immediately. Now Mole, unimagine that cinnamon roll," Cardamom ordered again. "We need to keep riding and it's blocking our way. Do it now."

Mole closed his eyes and concentrated hard. The cinnamon rolls disappeared and Cardamom shouted, "Let's go!" But they only progressed a few yards before a river of thick, brown sludge swooped down the floor of the canyon and engulfed the tigers' ankles. The sludge began to rise.

"Oh no, *perdón, perdón*," Elena cried out. "Mole sauce. I'll try to forget it."

"Holay Molay," Guhblorin announced, with a giggle that bordered on hysteria.

"It's not funny," Maia yelled at Guhblorin, as the mole sauce rose rapidly around the legs of the tigers, who howled and hissed and pawed at the swampy river beneath their feet.

Guhblorin leaned down to dip his finger into the mole sauce and fell head first into the sludge. His head popped back up and he reported to Elena, "It has crushed almonds and coriander in it."

"What about cilantro?" Elena asked, unable to resist figuring out the recipe. "And what kind of chocolate? Real Mexican chocolate?"

"Not sure about the cilantro. The chocolate is premium dark, at least 70% cacao," Guhblorin replied as he stood up. The mole sauce had almost reached his stomach. Elena leaned over and gave him a hand up behind her on the tiger. Then she licked the tips of her fingers.

"Yum," Elena muttered. "I like the coriander."

"Get rid of this mole sauce, Elena, before it drowns us," Denzel hollered at her.

"Of course," Elena replied, as she informed Guhblorin in a low voice, "no cilantro in it. Cilantro would definitely improve it." The mole sauce dried up and disappeared.

The travelers proceeded further into the canyon where flying books and maps swooped down from overhead and fluttered menacingly around their ears.

"I brought the books," Iris admitted. "It's hard work to clear my mind."

"An impossible task," Jasper exclaimed with a gasp. "Those maps came from me."

The books and maps flapped around their heads, pummeling them with snapping pages. Holding their hands up to protect their eyes, the travelers could barely see. The tigers moaned and shook their large heads back and forth to rid themselves of the crazy assault. Then the books disappeared but the maps kept swooping and battering them.

"I can't make it stop," Jasper apologized with a note of desperation in his voice. "Someone tell me something else to think about," he pleaded. The tigers inched forward into the swarming maps.

Then the air filled with the sound of laughter. It began softly and increased rapidly until massive belly-laughs echoed from side to side in the canyon. Loud and vicious, the laughter hurt their ears. At least it distracted Jasper so that he forgot the maps, which vanished.

While they covered their ears against the pounding laughter, a fleet of screw drivers and wrenches swarmed into the canyon. "Oh no," Denzel wailed. "I can stop it. Give me a second." He squeezed his eyes shut. Before the metal tools could stab the travelers, they turned into water balloons and when they hit the travelers they burst with loud pops, soaking everyone's clothes. "That was a close one," Denzel said.

"Nothing is funny," Guhblorin was yelling. "I'm not laughing. No one is laughing."

"That bad laughter must have come from Guhblorin," Crumpet guessed.

"That's a no-brainer," Sonjay responded. He had just barely managed to control his thoughts so far by using techniques he had learned in his early training as an enchanter, but he kept losing his concentration. He struggled to empty his mind of thoughts.

Doshmisi brought down a pod of dolphins swimming through the air straight at them and Maia manifested an avalanche of drums and flutes, which gave her an idea. "I have a suggestion," Maia called out, "let's sing!" And she launched into the Temptations' "My Girl" with funky enthusiasm. She quit singing for a hot minute to encourage the others, "C'mon, everyone knows this song. Sing! If you don't know it then hum along." Reggie's rich baritone voice joined Maia's sweet soprano and they belted it out. Everyone else either sang or hummed along or drummed a beat on whatever they could find handy. Hyacinth slapped his thigh. Doshmisi thought they sounded pretty good and, as the song echoed through the canyon, the bad laughter died away and no food, sea creatures, musical instruments, or sharp objects hurled themselves at the travelers. The tigers and Dagobaz tore through the canyon as fast as they could go, eager to leave the Imaginary Reality behind them.

Elena's mind wandered for a moment and tacos jumped off the treetops and sailed through the air, but she quickly focused on singing and the tacos disappeared before they hit anyone.

The singing helped them focus and clear their minds. When they finished "My Girl," Reggie immediately led off with "Ain't Too Proud to Beg," funkin' it up with enthusiasm.

"Gotta love those Tempts," Denzel shouted in delight.

"Not this much," Sonjay replied, as he pointed ahead on their path to the end of the canyon. Blocking the exit from the Canyon of Imaginary Reality stood six giant figures in red silk suits towering to a height of thirty feet. They spun and danced, swinging microphones around in a dangerously threatening way. The men were unmistakable. They were Otis, Al, Melvin, Eddie, and Paul, the original five Temptations, with David Ruffin thrown into the bargain as the sixth. The singing had conjured the whole group. The lovely stage smiles of the Tempts swiftly degenerated into wicked grins and their teeth grew into fangs. They aimed the microphones at the travelers menacingly, throwing them in their direction and then hauling them back in as they sang "Ball of Confusion" in a scary, frenzied way.

Bayard sat perched on Sonjay's shoulder as usual and Sonjay told the bird quietly, "Imagine blueberries squashed all over those red silk suits, Bayard. Do it now. Do it quickly." No one heard what Sonjay had said to Bayard, they simply saw the Tempts pummeled with blueberries, which squished all over them. Meanwhile Sonjay repeated the word "parrots" softly to himself over and over again until the sky filled with parrots, their bright green, red, blue, and yellow wings beating the air.

Bayard squawked with delight and then pecked Sonjay affectionately on the head before flying into the swarm of parrots. Instead of attacking the travelers, the imaginary parrots followed the very real Bayard Rustin and pecked at the Tempts furiously in their effort to eat the squished blueberries. Bayard did an exceptional job of imagining the blueberries, which landed and burst in the Tempts' hair and on their faces. The parrots Sonjay had imagined pecked at the men's eyes and cheeks in their efforts to eat the blueberries. The nasty imaginary giant Temptations turned and fled from the canyon, with the birds giving chase.

A cheer rose up from the travelers. The tigers roared their approval. Bayard returned to Sonjay's shoulder and announced, "Blueberries," as they reached the mouth of the canyon. Sonjay emerged first to discover himself on a high bluff from which he could see the North Coast, the Corporton compound, and the damaged oil rig. Unfortunately, waiting for them on the bluff, stood Sissrath, surrounded by a handful of his Special Forces and at least a hundred Corportons bristling with guns aimed directly at the travelers.

Chapter Twenty-Two
The Legacy of Shrub

Cardamom instinctively raised his hand to throw an enchantment at Sissrath, but the Corportons reacted swiftly. A series of shots rang out and Cardamom froze as if made from ice. Sissrath pointed to Buttercup and commanded, "Her too." Another shot caught Buttercup and she also froze into a statue. Crumpet howled in fury and raised his hand to cast an enchantment as he screeched, "What have you done to my wife? Restore her this instant!"

Sissrath threw his head back and laughed. The Corportons trained their weapons on Crumpet, but Sissrath instructed them, "Don't bother with him. He'll take care of himself. No point wasting a valuable freeze blast on him. Watch."

Crumpet's eyes locked with Sonjay's for a brief moment and he nodded his head almost imperceptibly. Then his golden-brown face turned several shades darker while visible electric sparks crackled up and down his arms and then, with a pop, he transformed into a little black comb with tiny teeth set close together. Such a comb was a useful object for people with the kind of hair for it, but quite useless in a land inhabited entirely by people with African-type hair. Crumpet, or rather the comb, flew into the air. Elena leaned way out from her seat on her tiger and managed to catch the comb as it dropped toward the ground. She held it in the palm of her hand and gazed down at it with a dazed expression.

Sonjay had the distinct impression that something was different about this transformation of Crumpet's. He didn't have time to dwell on it, though. Guhblorin snatched up the comb and ran it through the sparse hairs on the top of his head while the Corportons looked to Sissrath for guidance about what to do next. However, Sissrath, to his own horror, had begun to dance uncontrollably. His legs had taken over, dragging him into a wild cha-cha that he did not wish to be doing.

Denzel was the first to figure out why Sissrath had started dancing because Princess Honeydew had recently used that same enchantment on Denzel. He studiously avoided looking at Honeydew because he didn't want to give her away. Her face the very definition of concentration, she kept her hand (from which the enchantment had sprung) partially hidden in the folds of her dress. Sissrath had incapacitated the experienced enchanters from jump street, but he had underestimated Honeydew, who had already begun her studies and had a few enchantments stashed away in her toolbox.

Sissrath appeared so comical jigging and jouncing around in a jerky dance, his robe flapping awkwardly, that Doshmisi and Maia laughed out loud. Unable to resist a good bout of laughter, Guhblorin joined in, his geebaching laughter exploding in the air and setting everyone off so that no one could keep a straight face. Even Honeydew cracked a smile. But Sissrath quickly ascertained the source of his affliction and pointed a bony finger with its scraggly jagged fingernail in Honeydew's direction.

"No," Hyacinth yelled, "not my daughter." But the Corportons took aim and blasted Honeydew with their weapons. She froze with the expression of extreme concentration and a hint of a smile locked on her face. Saffron burst into tears. Everyone stopped laughing abruptly.

No longer dancing, Sissrath doubled over, inhaling sharply, winded by his episode of exercise. When he caught his breath he said, "Your friends are still alive for now, you fools. I can't have enchanters romping around though, can I? It would have given me great pleasure to finish off

Cardamom. However, I must obey orders. So you will come with me. The tigers remain here." He gestured in the direction of Dagobaz, "That beast remains here too. Dismount. And no sudden moves."

The travelers reluctantly climbed down. Dagobaz whinnied with displeasure. While the tigers watched with large, woeful eyes, the Corportons surrounded the travelers, pointing their weapons at them. Guhblorin still held the little comb (Crumpet) in his hand. The Corportons removed Cardamom, Buttercup, and Honeydew from their tigers and stretched them out on the ground side-by-side.

The travelers had just barely emerged from the Canyon of Imaginary Reality when they had encountered Sissrath. In fact, Maia and Elena, who rode at the back of the group, remained partially within the canyon. Corportons as well as a couple of Sissrath's Special Forces stood on either side of them, however, no one stood behind them. For that reason, it surprised Elena when she noticed movement behind her out of the corner of her eye. Without drawing attention to herself, she half-turned to observe more closely. In the canyon, tacos scooted among the trees, bumping into the rocks behind her. She thought they must have come from her own imagination, for who else would have thought about tacos but her? So she purposely thought more about tacos and the more she thought about tacos, the more of them she saw and the faster they whizzed back and forth. She scrutinized the hillside behind her. If only she could imagine the tacos in full force, she thought, she could use them to shield her while she scrambled to cover behind a large boulder not far from her on that hillside.

"Maia," Elena said quietly in Spanish, "Do you see that boulder up the slope to my left that looks like Mr. Pinter the P.E. teacher's nose?"

Maia glanced up the wall of the canyon and sure enough she saw a boulder shaped just like Mr. Pinter's bulbous nose. "*Sí*," she answered in Spanish automatically.

"When I say '*ahora*', we're going to run for it and hide behind it," Elena instructed, in Spanish.

"I think they'll shoot us before we make it to safety," Maia replied, worriedly, still in Spanish.

"Hey!" Sissrath shouted when he realized that Maia and Elena were conversing. "What are those two talking about back there?"

One of the Special Forces called to Sissrath, "They're speaking gibberish. Nonsense language."

"Trust me," Elena reassured her, continuing in Spanish. "I see something. Flying tacos will protect us." Guhblorin, who stood a few steps in front of Elena, glanced back at her quizzically. Elena wished she could explain the plan to Guhblorin, but he didn't speak Spanish. She would have to leave him behind in order for her plan to work. Elena imagined flying tacos with all her might and the air filled with soaring tacos, which attacked not only the rear guard of Corportons and Special Forces that stood beside Elena and Maia, but all the guards surrounding the prisoners. The guards ducked and attempted to protect their heads by covering them with their arms. A super-sized taco flew toward Sissrath, who bent in half trying to avoid it. Meanwhile, the two girls scampered up the hill, dodging tacos as they fled. They leapt behind the boulder that looked like Mr. Pinter's nose. In the excitement, and with the air thick with flying tacos, their enemies failed to notice where the girls had gone. It seemed as though they had simply vanished.

Sissrath's Special Forces fled from the canyon, herding the travelers before them so that the entire group shifted outside the walls of the canyon where no tacos could reach them. Sissrath sent a few reluctant Corportons back in to drag out the inert bodies of Cardamom, Buttercup, and Honeydew.

"Don't bother with those strays," Sissrath instructed the Corportons and Special Forces. "A couple of worthless little girls on their own in the wilderness can't do any damage." He sneered in disdain.

Denzel, Doshmisi, and Sonjay glanced furtively at one another. They shared the same thought: Maia and Elena had escaped and would find a way to get into mischief. Denzel smiled smugly with the knowledge that Sissrath's assessment of Maia and Elena as a couple of harmless little girls flew vastly wide of the mark. He hoped the girls would do some significant damage soon.

Sissrath marched the travelers down the hill toward the compound. The area surrounding the compound still smelled like smoke from the fire that had swept through only days earlier when Doshmisi and Jasper made their escape. Few structures remained intact. At the compound, Sissrath and his Special Forces disappeared and the Corportons kept their weapons trained on the prisoners.

"I'm having a déjà vu," Denzel said.

"What's that?" Mole asked.

"When you feel like you've already experienced something before," Denzel replied.

"OK, mon. I be havin' one of them too," Mole said. "Except I did experience this before."

"Where are the sprites or the butterflies when we need them to help us escape?" Doshmisi complained dejectedly. (The sprites had rescued them from an impossible situation the previous year, and taken them to safety in Spriteland.)

"Good question," Jasper responded. "If help is out there, this would be a good time for it to reveal itself."

"Remember that two harmless little girls lurk in those hills," Denzel reminded the others with a chuckle. "Give them a minute and they'll think of something harmless to do."

The Corportons locked everyone except the Goodacres into an open cage in the compound. Then they led Reggie, Doshmisi, Denzel, and Sonjay into a trailer. The many Corporton guards surrounding them kept their weapons trained on the captives. Denzel wondered if the guns shot slime, death rays, or something unimaginably horrible; something other than bullets or freeze-rays. The door of the trailer opened and Sissrath entered, flanked by more of the mysterious Corportons in their white jumpsuits with their gray face masks that hid their features completely. Sonjay studied Sissrath, who wore a grimy robe. He noticed that Sissrath's fingernails, usually long and spiky, were broken and blunted. Sissrath's eyes darted around nervously. The once-powerful and formerly self-confident enchanter appeared anxious, and not as smooth or authoritative as he had acted at the Canyon of Imaginary Reality. Sonjay figured that Sissrath did not have control of the situation at the compound, where a Corporton leader probably called the shots.

"The delusional Four," Sissrath said in a snake-like voice that slithered from his lips with the faint touch of a hiss.

"Minus one who got away from you," Sonjay taunted.

Sissrath ignored the comment and continued. "When will you learn to refrain from meddling in the lives of the natives here in lovely Faracadar?"

"We could ask the same question of you," Sonjay snapped back.

Sissrath's lips curled in a creepy excuse for a smile. "Don't fret. You'll be rid of me once and for all soon enough," Sissrath assured Sonjay, "when I leave this exquisite paradise of stupid, backward-thinking, unimaginative people, which will sink rapidly into oblivion as predicted in the Book of the Khoum."

"I disagree with your assessment," Sonjay shot back at Sissrath.

Trapped in such close quarters with Sissrath, Doshmisi found his presence so frightening that her mind went blank. The mere sight of Sissrath made Denzel furious because Sissrath had caused the death of their mother. If those Corportons had not had weapons aimed at him, Denzel would have charged at the enchanter and smashed him to pieces. Sonjay, however, remained calm, self-possessed, and fully capable of countering whatever Sissrath said with a rational response calculated to get under his skin.

Sissrath laughed with a laugh that sounded like metal scraping on gravel. "Do you think you have arrived just in time to save this land?

Faracadar will die and you can do nothing to save it. You should have stayed in the Farland."

"You have it so wrong," Sonjay countered. "The people are smart and resourceful. Too bad you can't see the beauty standing right in front of you. I see a land full of creative, magnificent people. You don't see it, do you, you unobservant dimwit? The land will not die. It will transform into a place you lack the ability to imagine. It will outlive you."

"How dare you?" Sissrath spoke a brief enchantment that shot a sharp electric charge at Sonjay's chest. It lifted Sonjay off his feet and slammed him against the wall. Sonjay slid down the wall and landed in a sitting position on the floor, gasping for breath. Reggie and Denzel lunged at Sissrath, but the Corportons restrained them. With a snap of his fingers, Sissrath commanded Reggie, "Tell him, Prophet! Read him the words of the prophecy as set forth in the Book."

"He has heard the words already, Sissy," Reggie informed him through clenched teeth, to the welcome amusement of his children when they heard that nickname.

"Watch your step, Prophet. I don't care how many times he has heard the words," Sissrath replied angrily. "I wish for you to say the words again and so you shall. And I have told you in no uncertain terms not to call me that." Sissrath pointed a bony finger at Reggie, said an enchantment, and tossed an electric charge at Reggie just as he had done to Sonjay. The charge hit Reggie full-on and he was similarly lifted into the air for a moment as electricity crackled and then dropped in a heap. He moaned and clutched his chest. Doshmisi was terrified that Sissrath had given him a heart attack.

"Daddy! Daddy, are you OK?" Doshmisi called out.

"Yes, yes, baby girl, I'm alright," Reggie gasped. "I'm used to it."

"Enough family chit-chat. Tell your son the words," Sissrath commanded.

Reggie took his knapsack off his back, opened it, and removed the Book of the Khoum. He turned to a worn page and began to read out loud quietly. "The time will come in the..."

Sissrath interrupted, "Louder. Read it loud and clear so we can all hear every word."

The Corportons picked Sonjay up off the floor and stood him next to his father. They held his arms pinned behind his back.

Reggie reluctantly started reading again in a voice that carried to the edges of the room. "The time will come in the four-thousand fifty-second year when an underground energy will rise to the surface and will turn the land inside out, leaving it uninhabitable. This energy is capable of destroying all life and ending the flow of one generation to the next. It will unbalance the balance, fill the ocean with death, exile the algae, and suck the breath from all living creatures. It will bring an end to what has gone before."

Sissrath poked his finger into Sonjay's chest while Sonjay could do nothing to stop him. With each poke, Sissrath repeated a word of the prophecy, "It will bring an end." Poke, poke, poke, poke, poke. Sissrath stepped back, satisfied with his performance. "All life will be destroyed, except for me. I'm leaving all of this behind and going on an adventure. I'm going someplace where I will be appreciated, unlike in this provincial small-minded backwater of a sorry ignorant little land."

"Go then," Sonjay said, with fire in his eyes. "And good riddance. You go with these aliens who have come with nothing more than exploitation and destruction in their minds. Please go. I'll stay here and change the prophecy." Sonjay's eyes flashed with defiance as he added maliciously, "Sissy."

Sissrath pointed his finger at Sonjay and Reggie spoke sharply, "Don't. Enough."

The enchanter lowered his finger and glared at Sonjay. "Good luck with that change-y miracle-y thing," he said. Then he turned to the

Corportons and ordered them to place the captives in the compound before he whisked out through the door.

The silent Corportons did as told, marching the captives to the compound where the battery makers and other prisoners were being held. From the compound, Doshmisi could see the launch site for the boats that traveled back and forth to the damaged and leaking oil rig. She looked at the entrance gate and remembered how she and Jasper had escaped the compound with Dagobaz during the aftermath of the explosion on their previous visit. That had happened only a few days ago, but it seemed like years ago because so much had happened since.

Sissrath confined the captives in an outdoor cage with a corrugated tin roof and an electrified fence around the perimeter. The fence left the cage open to the outdoors, but the roof offered protection from rain. Doshmisi wished it would rain. The sun beat down on the tin roof, which absorbed the heat, making the inside of the cage radiate like an oven. Fortunately, a breeze blew off the nearby ocean and through the open cage; and when the long day came to a close and evening approached, the air turned cool. The frozen enchanters, Cardamom, Buttercup, and Honeydew, lay stretched out inert on the ground inside the cage, as limp as rag dolls. Doshmisi attempted to rouse them with no luck. They continued breathing so they still lived.

Hyacinth sat on the ground with his frozen daughter's head cradled in his lap. Hardly speaking, he stroked her forehead and her hair.

The Corportons provided the prisoners with essentials, such as blankets and sleeping pads, firewood and food, as well as cooking pots. Their captors apparently expected them to cook something for themselves to eat. Saffron and Iris sorted through the provisions they had received, handing things off to Guhblorin, who announced the appearance of each food item, naming it out loud and defining its condition. "One bag of garnet yams, a bit muddy, good with butter and cinnamon but no cinnamon on hand," Guhblorin stated. "Six onions, a bunch of celery, twenty-two potatoes, and fourteen carrots," Guhblorin recited. "Would taste delicious with a goose-chicken but none on hand," Guhblorin added woefully. Iris then produced a goose-chicken from the depths of a wooden box and Guhblorin shouted with glee, "One uncooked goose-chicken. Perfect." Iris, Saffron, and their eager helper went to work over an open fire. For the meat-eaters, they roasted the goose-chicken until it was tender and juicy. The vegetarians ate the roasted yams and a vegetable stew. While they ate, they watched the ancient green-tinged Faracadaran sun dissolve into the ocean.

After eating dinner and before they could clean their plates and prepare to bed down for the night, Sissrath and a contingent of Corporton guards appeared at the locked gate of the cage. "Much as I have advised against it, I must take you to speak with someone," Sissrath stated sullenly, as he pointed at Sonjay, Doshmisi, and Denzel. Disapproval and rage smoldered in his voice. Sissrath's behavior left no question in Sonjay's mind that the enchanter, who had once ruled Faracadar with an iron fist, had been forced into subservience by another individual. But who, he wondered. "You three come with me," Sissrath ordered. Sonjay hoped the Corportons would take him to meet this individual who had subjugated Sissrath.

"Take me too," Reggie insisted.

"I'm pleased to inform you that you will not be coming with us," Sissrath told Reggie. "You are not invited."

"It's OK, Daddy," Doshmisi said softly to Reggie. "Don't worry. We can manage."

"No, no!" Reggie shouted desperately as the Corporton guards separated his children from the other captives and led them from the cage. "If you touch a hair on their heads, you'll have the Prophet of the Khoum to reckon with!" Reggie called after them. Sissrath smirked as he locked the gate and led his three prize captives across the yard and into a portable building.

They entered the building flanked by the armed Corporton guards and walked down a short hallway before their guards ushered them through a door and into a room that contained only a desk, a chair, and a file cabinet. A shade drawn over the window concealed the dying light of the day and a dim lamp barely brightened the room enough for them to see. The Corporton guards prevented Sissrath from entering. He growled at them as they closed the door in his face, leaving him out in the corridor. Ten armed Corporton guards crowded along the back wall of the room, blocking the door. The Goodacres glanced nervously at each other, wondering what would happen next.

A Corporton entered the room from a door behind the desk. He stood for a long moment facing them. They had the feeling that he or she or it, whatever hid behind that white jumpsuit and that gray face mask, was sizing them up. Even though they could not see the Corporton's eyes (whatever type of eyes it had), they could tell that the Corporton could see them. Then, abruptly, the Corporton removed its helmet, mask and all. To their surprise, the Goodacres found themselves looking at a quite ordinary man. He had straight sandy-brown hair, green eyes, and a thin mustache. He was a white man, not brown-skinned like the inhabitants of Faracadar. Doshmisi thought he looked familiar, but she couldn't place him. He gestured with his hand and the Corporton guards at the back of the room also removed their helmets. Eight of them were men and two were women. The women were Asian and three of the men were brown-skinned but not as dark as people of African descent. They could have been Native or Latino. Two of the men looked like Africans and the remaining three were white. They looked to the Goodacres like regular people from their life at Manzanita Ranch in the Farland.

"Who are you and what are you doing here?" Sonjay demanded of the man behind the desk.

"I could ask you the same thing," the man replied.

"I asked you first," Sonjay insisted.

The man laughed. "OK then. I'm Aldus Shrub," the man said. "Now your turn."

"I'm Sonjay Goodacre," Sonjay introduced himself.

Doshmisi turned the name Aldus Shrub over in her mind. She knew that name, but how?

"Why are you drilling for oil in Faracadar?" Sonjay continued.

"I am doing the interrogating here," Aldus Shrub said. "I am the one entitled to ask the questions, not you."

"Yes, well, that's because you don't know my brother," Denzel informed the man quietly. Aldus Shrub glared in his direction.

"Speak up," Aldus Shrub commanded Denzel. "Who are you?"

"Denzel," Denzel replied. "Denzel Goodacre."

"And where did you come from?" Aldus Shrub asked.

"Same place as my brother Sonjay."

"And where is that?"

"Manzanita Ranch," Doshmisi stated matter-of-factly, with a faint smile playing across her lips because she felt quite sure that Aldus Shrub had no clue where Manzanita Ranch was located.

She was correct. Aldus Shrub pursued his investigation. "And where is Manzanita Ranch?"

"About a hundred miles north of Oakland," Doshmisi told him, wondering if Oakland would mean anything to him. Suddenly she remembered what she knew about his name, and she had an idea about why he appeared so familiar. He looked a lot like the President of the United States, Spartacus "Spud" Shrub; and she felt sure that this man who stood before them had to be related to President Shrub.

Shrub's eyebrows shot up at the mention of Oakland. "Oakland, California? How did you get here?" he demanded.

"We walked," Sonjay replied belligerently.

"You could use a lesson in manners," Shrub said threateningly. "When did you come here? Did you use a Polydestinographer?"

"Never heard of him," Doshmisi answered quickly, worried that Sonjay would continue to speak rudely to Shrub and that Shrub would lose his temper and hurt Sonjay.

"Poly-huh?" Denzel asked.

Shrub laughed. "You know something? I believe you. I think you really don't know about it. And it's not a who. It's a what."

"What does the what do?" Doshmisi asked, before her brothers could say something that would dig them deeper into trouble.

Shrub scrutinized the Goodacres before replying. "You really don't know, do you?" He seemed pleased.

They stared at him blankly. Doshmisi stole a glance at Denzel, who shrugged.

"How long have you been in Faracadar?" Shrub asked.

"Not long," Sonjay answered evasively.

"A lot longer than you probably think, I'd wager," Shrub told them. "Everyone knows about the Polydestinographer. If you really have no clue what it is, then you've been here for at least six years because it was invented six years ago and widely publicized. It was our only hope of survival. Everyone on the planet knows about it; including the people in Oakland."

"What is it? What does it do?" Denzel asked, keenly interested to hear more about a new gadget or device.

Shrub seemed torn between leaving his captives in the dark about the Polydestinographer and explaining it to them so he could boast about it. His desire to show off won out and he continued. "It locates oil across time and space and takes you to it. It's about the most important invention of all time. A team of researchers in Oklahoma devised and created it. My grandfather Spud Shrub put together that team and funded the research when he was President of the United States."

A small gasp escaped Doshmisi's lips.

"When we came to Faracadar just a few weeks ago, Spud Shrub was still the President," Sonjay said evenly. "And he didn't have any grandchildren."

"I told you," Shrub replied with a malicious curl to his lip, "the Polydestinographer locates oil across time as well as space. So I amend my assessment. I think you haven't been here long at all. Instead, I believe, in fact, that I come from your future. Interesting. This means that you don't know what lies ahead back in our home world. The oil shortages, the pandemics, the collapse of governments, the militarized zones. You would therefore have no idea of the urgency of our mission to collect this oil and return with it as soon as possible; no idea how much rests on our success here. Nothing short of the survival of human civilization. And we must embark on this type of mission again and again and again, throughout space and time, to gather as much oil as we need."

Doshmisi found it difficult to believe what she had just heard.

"How does this contraption work?" Denzel asked, his eyes glittering. His curiosity about the construction of a time-travel mechanism trumped his desire to hold Shrub at arm's length. "Did you climb into it, like a plane that travels with you inside? Or is it a device that can send you where you wish to go? Who invented it?"

Shrub laughed. "Wouldn't you like to know?!" he taunted Denzel.

"So what is the plan?" Sonjay had no interest in the physics of time travel. He wanted more information about Shrub's next move.

"The plan?" Shrub replied, as he raised one eyebrow and studied Sonjay.

"What do you plan to do next?" Sonjay demanded as he met Shrub's penetrating gaze with one of his own.

"The plan, my friends, is to extract as much oil as possible from this ridiculously primitive land and then to leave. We have almost reached our quota for this expedition. And I refuse to allow you do-gooders to interfere with our extraction before we complete it."

"What about the leak from the oil rig?" Doshmisi demanded. "Your oil spill is killing the blue-green algae, has driven the whales away, and will soon destroy the land and all the living creatures in it. We have to stop that oil spill."

"Not my problem," Shrub replied, with an unconcerned frown. "You sound like one of those environmentalists," he suggested with disgust. "I, and my people, which, may I remind you, are your people from your future, are not concerned about this land or its people. Whatever happens to it once we have left is not our concern. Survival of the fittest. We came to find oil and take it. We have met with success. The oil spill is unfortunate. We could have used that oil we lost and skedaddled out of here sooner. But I have almost filled my containers, so I consider our mission accomplished."

"You don't care about destroying Faracadar? That the death of the blue-green algae will make the air unfit to breathe? That the people of this land will die?" Doshmisi demanded angrily.

"Why should I care about any of that?" Shrub asked, dismissing the question with a wave of his hand.

"What happened to solar energy? And wind energy? What about geothermal?" Denzel asked Shrub. "What happened in the future to all the other ways to make energy? Why did people try to stick to oil? Couldn't you guys change things?"

"Not fast enough. Besides, we like oil," Shrub answered. He grinned. "We know how to use it and it's very profitable for those of us who control it."

"Scientists say we have enough wind power in South Dakota to provide energy for the whole country of America," Denzel said. "We just need to build the windmills to harness it."

"Windmills are not all they're cracked up to be," Shrub responded casually. "They have their down side. Dead birds. Noise pollution. Besides, they're boring and they don't make me any money."

"I can't believe humans didn't find a way to transform our energy systems into something sustainable in the Farland. Something in tune with the planet," Doshmisi said wistfully. She thought about the words in the herbal and suddenly they began to make sense to her.

Shrub readjusted his white jumpsuit and prepared to go. "Helmets," he ordered the others in the room. The Corportons placed their helmets back on their heads, once again obscuring their faces. Aldus Shrub lifted his helmet off the table where he had placed it when he entered the room. "Now, if you'll excuse me, I have oil to collect. My faithful followers will escort you back to your cage. It has been a pleasure. I would appreciate it if you would stay out from under foot so I can complete my critical mission. Then I will leave you in peace. You and all the others in this land. May you all rest in peace." He placed his helmet back on his head and hurried out of the room.

Chapter Twenty-Three
Crumpet's Transformation

By the time Doshmisi, Denzel, and Sonjay returned to the outdoor cage, night had fallen. Their father rushed to greet them, relieved to see them unharmed. They filled him in on what they had learned from Aldus Shrub. Guhblorin, Iris, Mole, the intuits, and the royal couple had bedded down and fallen asleep. Even in his sleep, Guhblorin clung to the little comb that was Crumpet. All three of the Goodacres felt tired, trapped, and out of ideas. They had set out on their journey early that morning filled with hope and determination, and they had traveled a long and difficult day.

"Get some sleep," Reggie advised his children. "Our brains need to recharge to come up with fresh ideas."

As her brothers settled down for the night, Doshmisi removed the herbal from its case and found a small flashlight in her bag. She put the herbal in her lap and watched it open to a page; but the herbal no longer told her anything she could figure out how to use. After the revelations provided by the conversation with Shrub, she understood the words in the herbal better, but she couldn't see how to apply them to her present situation or the unfolding chain of events in Faracadar. Reggie sat down next to her and she shut the herbal quickly. Her father put a hand on her shoulder. "What does it say?" he asked gently.

"It doesn't matter anymore," she told him.

Reggie looked at her thoughtfully and insisted, "I'd like to see it if I may."

She stared down at the book in her lap. She hated to admit that she couldn't interpret the words to provide any useful information to act upon.

"Doshmisi?" She did not reply and he touched her shoulder. "I might be able to help. I've spent a great many years communicating with an enchanted book, you know."

She studied her father's face and saw in his eyes the suffering and compassion that had brought him wisdom. It comforted her to have an adult to whom she could turn for assistance and support; someone who could help her make important decisions, someone with good sense and her best interests at heart. She opened the book and read the words printed there aloud to Reggie.

THOSE PEOPLE WHO DO NOT TRANSFORM THEMSELVES WILL PERISH. NOTHING BEGINS OR ENDS BUT RATHER EXISTS IN CONSTANT TRANSFORMATION. A WORLD WITHOUT PEOPLE IS POSSIBLE. A WORLD THAT CONTINUES WITH PEOPLE MUST GO A DIFFERENT WAY. TRANSFORMATION TAKES COURAGE, CREATIVITY, INGENUITY, PASSION, COMMITMENT, PERSEVERANCE, AND VISION OF TRUTH. THESE QUALITIES REQUIRE CULTIVATION AND NURTURING, THEY REQUIRE PRACTICE TO DEVELOP FULLY. CREATIVITY IS A MUSCLE THAT REQUIRES EXERCISE TO GROW MIGHTY. THE PEOPLE MUST USE THEIR CREATIVITY TO THINK DIFFERENTLY, TO THINK ANEW, AND TO IMAGINE CHANGES NECESSARY THAT WILL BRING SURVIVAL.

After she finished reading the words, Doshmisi gently closed the herbal and peered into her father's face. "Beautiful words. And true. But how do I use them for healing?"

"That's all it says?" he asked.

"That's all it has on this page and it won't open to any other one right now," Doshmisi confirmed. "You can try to get another page, but I doubt it will open or that any other words will appear. I don't get what it wants me to do, what kind of transformation it wants me to imagine."

Reggie nodded. "I see," he said. Then he sat in silence for a few minutes with his eyes closed. Doshmisi sat quietly next to him and listened to the chirps and calls of the night creatures in the nearby forest.

When Reggie opened his eyes, he suggested, "Perhaps the words in the herbal are not for you. Perhaps that message is for someone else, not the people of Faracadar. I think those words are for the people in the world from which the Corportons came. In that world, the people need to imagine new resources, new energy sources, and new ways of doing things to preserve the environment in order to sustain human life. Such transformation as it mentions applies to every civilization but in this moment, I think it applies most to the world of the Corportons not Faracadar."

"The Corportons came from our world," Doshmisi reminded him. "The Farland."

"That's why I say this," he told her.

"Do you believe that things will ever change in our world where countries fight wars over oil, putting profit above people; where leaders and the powerful kill and destroy with no conscience or care? Because of the destruction of the environment, my generation have inherited a ruined planet and we fear we have no future. If the Corportons came from that disappearing future, as Shrub claims, and if they continue to rely on oil instead of developing other energy sources, then their mission to bring this oil back from Faracadar won't make any difference."

Reggie replied sadly, "I'm sorry to hear that the environment deteriorated so much more after I left. I believed things would turn around. Those of us who could see what was coming should have fought harder for the kind of change described in the herbal."

"It wasn't all on your generation. Many others went before you and damaged the planet. It's exhausting to think about what it would take to keep it habitable by humans." Doshmisi switched off her flashlight, stretched out on the ground, and rested her head on her father's thigh. "You did the best that you could at the time," she mumbled drowsily. "Not sure my generation could have done any better."

Reggie kissed the tips of his fingers and touched them to her forehead. "Sleep well, baby girl."

Doshmisi closed her eyes. When she opened them again hours later, she discovered Guhblorin tapping her insistently on the arm. "Shhh. I have to show you something," he said softly. She could just barely see Guhblorin in the milky-blue light of early dawn. "Come with me," Guhblorin whispered, with a note of urgency. He led her to a tent that stood in one corner of the cage. The Corportons guarding the cage had dozed off at the entrance gate and did not waken to see Guhblorin or Doshmisi enter the tent. Once inside and out of sight, Guhblorin held his hand out in front of him. "Watch this," he said. He held the little black comb that had once been Crumpet on the open palm of his hand. Suddenly it bounced into the air and landed on the ground, where it transformed into Crumpet.

"How..." Doshmisi started to speak but then words failed her.

Crumpet chuckled. "I can control it," he said with excitement. "I figured it out."

"You mean you turned into a comb on purpose?" Doshmisi asked incredulously.

"Not exactly, but almost. I changed on purpose, I didn't pick the comb, though," Crumpet said. "I figured I could prevent Sissrath from freezing me like he did to the other enchanters. It took me a while to manage to change back, but I have it figured out now," Crumpet reassured Doshmisi and Guhblorin. "So I'm going to have you throw me through a hole in that electrified fence before the sun rises. Just don't fry me on the fence, OK? Put me through without touching. I'll pick my moment and then I'll incapacitate the guards and unlock the gate to this cage. After that you won't have much time to escape so spread the word to the others to be ready."

"Neat trick, Crumpet. I'm impressed," Doshmisi complimented him.

"Thanks. I have an even better trick. Follow me. Quietly. Watch."

Crumpet slipped out of the tent and walked to where Cardamom, Buttercup, and Honeydew lay stretched out straight as boards on the ground. With great concentration, he placed the palm of his hand on each of their foreheads in turn. The enchanters gasped softly and began to stir. Doshmisi leaned over and whispered in their ears, "Pretend you're still unconscious. Don't move. We may not have another chance to revive you so don't let on that you're conscious. Cardamom opened his eyes for a second and winked at them before resuming his frozen pose. Honeydew nodded almost imperceptibly. Crumpet leaned over and brushed Buttercup's lips with his. "Love you babycakes," he whispered.

"Forever," Buttercup whispered back. "Proud of you."

Crumpet stood to his full height, then he commanded Doshmisi, "Tell everyone to stand by for action. Look after Buttercup. Now throw me." With those words, Crumpet turned himself back into the little comb. As the sun rose rapidly over the ocean, it cast light across the compound. The sleeping Corporton guards began to stir. Guhblorin and Doshmisi went behind the tent and carefully tossed Crumpet through the fence without touching him to the electrified metal. The enchanter transformed himself and scurried away, concealing himself behind the charred remains of a building.

"What was up with that?" Sonjay asked, as he stretched and rubbed his eyes. He had appeared suddenly at Doshmisi's elbow before she even noticed and she jumped with a start at the sound of his voice.

"Shhh," Guhblorin hissed exaggeratedly.

"Crumpet," Doshmisi told her brother and then she explained quickly about the comb and Crumpet's new level of skill. She clued Sonjay to the fact that Crumpet had revived the enchanters, who faked unconsciousness.

"Cool," Sonjay said happily. As the other prisoners roused themselves from sleep, Sonjay lay down on the ground next to Cardamom and put his head next to Cardamom's mouth. His posture appeared innocent enough, but Doshmisi knew better. They were plotting together.

When Sonjay stood up, he held a box in his hands. He surreptitiously beckoned to Doshmisi and Denzel, who followed him into the little tent. Reggie, who made a point of noticing everything about his children, took in Sonjay's gesture and followed the three into the tent.

"He brought the Staff of Shakabaz," Sonjay informed the others with excitement. Sonjay's amulet began to glow with a golden light beneath his shirt.

"The Staff is looking for you, man," Denzel told his brother. "It wants to work with you."

"And I want to work with it," Sonjay replied with determination.

"Crumpet said he'll find a way to deal with the guards and open the cage so we can escape," Doshmisi told the others, wasting no time.

"We have to circulate and let everyone know," Reggie pointed out.

"When will he do it?" Denzel asked.

"Soon," Doshmisi replied.

"When he opens the cage, I'll take the Staff out of the box. I hope I can use it like I did at the Battle of Truth so I can keep the Corportons from harming us. Cardamom says I should hold it since it has an intuitive sense of my intentions, which he says carries more strength than any enchantment he can do with it," Sonjay informed the others. "So when Crumpet opens this cage, you run and I'll see what I can do with the Staff. The most important thing is for Dosh to get to the ocean with the herbal and the Emerald Crystal."

"It's quite a distance to the beach from here," Reggie said anxiously.

"Then I'll have to run, won't I?" Doshmisi replied with determination.

"Let's go clue the others about the plan," Denzel said as he hurried out of the tent.

Reggie and Doshmisi followed close behind Denzel. "I wonder what happened to Maia and Elena," Reggie worried.

Doshmisi patted his arm as she reassured him, "Maia can take care of herself."

The Corportons, suited up as usual in their white jumpsuits, assembled in the yard and began to line up at the gate to the compound, most likely to go to work collecting oil. Meanwhile, several of Sissrath's Special Forces appeared with food for the captives. "Stand back," they ordered as they gestured to the prisoners to move to the back of the cage on the opposite side from the entrance. The Corporton guards then opened the door to the cage to allow the Special Forces to place the food inside.

At that moment, while the cage stood open, a bolt of electric green light shot out from behind one of the half-burned barracks. The green light hit the Corportons and the Special Forces. The Special Forces collapsed to the ground, unconscious, but the Corportons appeared somewhat protected from the enchantment by their jumpsuits. They could still move, albeit slowly.

Cardamom, Honeydew, and Buttercup leapt to their feet and swiftly ran from the cage. The intuits trailed behind on their hovering skateboards. Sonjay opened the box containing the Staff of Shakabaz and removed the collapsed Staff. Seeing that Sonjay had not moved toward the entrance to the cage, Denzel planted his feet and blocked the gate to prevent Sonjay from becoming trapped inside. But Denzel's effort proved unnecessary the instant Sonjay grasped the powerful Staff, which unfolded itself and took on its true, magnificent shape. Sonjay's amulet blazed with golden light.

Despite the enormous size of the Staff, Sonjay wielded it easily. The Staff became weightless when it came to Sonjay's hand; it had always done so. He tilted it toward his adversaries and held it in front of him as he walked toward the doorway of the cage, where he met his brother. As he swept the Staff from side to side, it appeared to freeze the Corportons in their tracks. Aldus Shrub emerged from his office. He did not wear his helmet so Sonjay recognized him. Shrub screamed commands to his followers and waved his hands above his head in agitation. But the Staff of Shakabaz had rendered Shrub's Corporton soldiers useless.

Sissrath appeared beside Shrub and threw an enchantment at Sonjay, who gasped and fell to one knee. The Staff apparently lacked the strength to hold off all the Corportons while at the same time resisting Sissrath. Sonjay sent thoughts to the Staff to incapacitate all their foes. The Staff had enormous power, but even that power had its limitations.

To add to the difficulty of the situation, the air had become quite thick, making it difficult for everyone to breathe. Perhaps the Corportons, in their jumpsuits, did not have this problem. Perhaps their jumpsuits purified the air for them. Everyone else began to wheeze as they struggled to take air into their lungs. Despite the thickness of the air, Sonjay managed to maintain his grasp on the Staff and to keep it trained on the Corportons and Special Forces. He concentrated on using the Staff to immobilize them.

While Sissrath and Shrub focused their attention on Sonjay and the Staff, Crumpet hurried to the entrance gate to the compound and he opened it. Immediately, Elena and Maia, each riding a tiger, swooped out of the nearby forest and rode in through the open gate and toward the opening of the cage within. Dagobaz and the travelers' tigers followed them. The tigers congregated in the path of the entrance gate to prevent it from closing. They stood their ground and ensured that it would remain open. Dagobaz galloped full-tilt to Doshmisi and barely paused as she leapt onto his back. Horse and rider instantly became one.

Sissrath had thrown two more enchantments at Sonjay while Crumpet was opening the gate. Sissrath then whirled around, poised to throw an enchantment at Doshmisi and Dagobaz. But Crumpet faced off with Sissrath, uttered a few words of enchantment, and held out his arms. Piles of cockroaches began to drop from his sleeves. Sissrath recoiled with a shriek, dropping his hand to his sides, momentarily incapacitated by his terror of the disgusting little insects. In that moment when Sissrath had let his guard down, Crumpet threw a chartreuse ball of light at the enchanter, who, preoccupied by the cockroaches, did not resist or defend himself. Astonishingly, Crumpet did not transform into a comb or a tea kettle or even a pastry. With a strong gaze of complete concentration, he engulfed Sissrath in flaming light.

"Way to go, Crumpet," Cardamom said softly. He stepped up behind his older brother, stretched his hands out, and threw additional light into the stream of light that Crumpet had produced. As Sissrath howled and attempted to break the restraining enchantment of the brothers, the stream of light began to shake violently. Buttercup hurried to Crumpet's side, touched his shoulder with her hand, and added her own stream of light. This seemed to stabilize the enchantment and the light did not shake as much. Taking his cue from Buttercup, Cardamom also laid a hand on his brother's shoulder. The stream of light holding Sissrath in check became steadier and wider. The three enchanters had successfully locked Sissrath inside the bubble of light that they had created.

Denzel wove in and out of the frozen Corportons and took away their weapons. "Can you hold them with the Staff?" he hollered to Sonjay.

"So far so good," Sonjay replied as sweat broke out on his forehead.

"Guns, we need to get these guns," Denzel called to the other captives, who snapped into action. Reggie, Hyacinth, Saffron, Mole, Iris, and Jasper immediately joined Denzel and they formed an assembly line, passing the guns that Denzel grabbed from the frozen hands of the Corportons down the line and into a growing pile at Sonjay's feet.

Meanwhile, Guhblorin jumped onto Elena's tiger behind her and clung to her for dear life, his long skinny arms wrapping tightly around her waist.

Princess Honeydew, determined to fulfill her destiny as an enchanter, stepped up behind Cardamom and placed her hand on his shoulder to add strength to the enchantment that held Sissrath captive.

Sonjay called to his sister, "Go Dosh! Ride Dagobaz to the water. Ride like the wind. Do the Emerald Crystal thing. Don't look back."

Chapter Twenty-Four
The Work of the Herbal

Doshmisi rode off toward the ocean through the open gate. Elena (with Guhblorin clinging to her) and Maia followed Doshmisi out the gate and toward the water, but Dagobaz swiftly left them trailing behind. By this time, the air had grown thick and oily. Doshmisi had never had asthma, so she didn't know what an asthma attack actually felt like, but she imagined it felt like trying to breathe the thick, oily air that surrounded her. She had to force the oxygen into her lungs and it seemed as though the air left a sticky film inside her chest with each breath. Dagobaz wheezed and had to slow down. Doshmisi went over Clover's instructions again in her mind. Clover had said to put the Emerald Crystal into the indentation in the cover of the herbal and then to place the herbal under the water at the edge of the ocean near the oil spill. She hoped that the others had managed to keep the Corportons imprisoned inside the compound and that Sissrath had not shaken free; but restraining Sissrath was someone else's job. Doshmisi's job was to get the Emerald Crystal into the herbal and into the ocean.

Dagobaz clambered up a low hill, crowned the top of it, and came to an abrupt halt. They had reached the shoreline and the sandy beach fell away from them toward the water. Dark green-black slime embedded with mounds of dead fish and birds coated the beach, emitting a stench that smelled like burning tires and rotten seaweed. Dagobaz whinnied and shied away from stepping onto the foul sand. The once-green ocean appeared even worse than the beach. A film of filth and oil floated atop the water. The bodies of dead dolphins, birds, and other marine life drifted in the water and dotted the shore. Dagobaz tossed his head and stepped back and forth at the edge of the sand, half-screaming his outrage and terror at what lay at his feet.

"It's OK," Doshmisi soothed the horse as she stroked his neck. "You don't have to step onto the beach. Just let me off. I'll go." Dagobaz stood still and Doshmisi slipped off his back. He nudged her with his head. They both wheezed as they tried to breathe the awful air. The speed with which the air had deteriorated without the algae to clean it astonished Doshmisi. She cringed at the odor of rank oil, rotten seaweed, and death, as she stepped onto the greasy sand, immediately slipping and falling as she slid along in the disgusting filth so that it coated her backside and her hands. She gagged, which made it even more difficult to breathe. She tried to stand, but kept sliding. Meanwhile, Dagobaz paced back and forth like a caged panther at the edge of the sand, whinnying plaintively and bobbing his head up and down. Maia, Elena, and Guhblorin soon appeared beside him. Their tigers also balked at the edge of the tainted beach and refused to set foot on it.

Doshmisi crawled toward the ocean on her hands and knees. It was the only way she could move through the muck. She did her best to avoid the multitude of dead fish and oil-coated bird carcasses, but she could not help touching some of them as she made her way across the beach. It seemed like it took her an hour to reach the water. She felt as if she was running in slow motion in a dream.

From where they stood at the edge of the sand, Maia and Elena sang a song in Spanish. Doshmisi didn't know what the words meant, but the song lifted her spirits. The singing voices harmonized beautifully. She imagined that they told her she could do this. The song strengthened her resolve and assisted her in the dreadful trek across the ruined beach. Her amulet glowed incandescent green, bursting forth from her shirt with rays of light.

At last she knelt at the edge of the soiled ocean. Her hands, coated in oil embedded with sand, shook uncontrollably. She fumbled with the clasp on the carrycase for the herbal and managed to open it. She wondered if she would ever in her life be completely clean again. She took the enchanted book from the carrycase. By this time it had become smudged with oil. It made her sad to see it so dirty. The oil on her hands left streaks of grease on the Emerald Crystal when she removed it from her pocket. She clung to it to prevent it from slipping from her grasp. Then she firmly placed it into the indentation in the front cover of the book in the place where she had often placed her amulet in the past to activate the herbal.

As it did whenever she put her amulet into the indentation, the herbal began to glow with green light, which comforted Doshmisi. It cheered her to see something so bright and clean. The herbal flew open and revealed to her the following instructions: SING THE ALGAE HOME. SING ALONG THE COAST ON THE BEACHES. THE MORE SINGERS, THE STRONGER THE SONG, THE STRONGER THE PULL FOR THE ALGAE. EVEN THOSE NOT AT THE WATER'S EDGE SHOULD SING. ANYONE CAN ADD TO THE SONG, FROM ANYWHERE. CALL THE ALGAE HOME ACROSS THE WATER. IT WILL TAKE MANY SONGS, MANY VOICES, FOR THIS HEALING. THE ENERGY EMBEDDED IN THESE PAGES WILL ALWAYS GRAVITATE TO YOUR EFFORTS AND WILL CONTINUE TO BE ONE WITH THE HEALER.

It seemed as if the herbal had become a living creature and she sensed that it had chosen to say farewell to her with these parting words. She tenderly placed the herbal, with the Emerald Crystal in the cover, under the water and pushed it out from the shoreline. The green glow from the Emerald Crystal grew and rose above the oil-black surface of the water. A bolt of green lightning crackled in the sky and shot down to meet the herbal. A hum began to sound across the water. It grew in intensity, a single tone, growing louder and vibrating with sound. As she heard it, Doshmisi flashed on the knowledge of what it would mean to sing home the algae. Everyone would have to sing one note like this vibrating sound, everyone together.

Slowly the sand beneath Doshmisi began to slide, as if the ground had become a blanket on which she sat and someone had begun to pull the blanket out from under her. The oil that coated the beach slipped like an enormous stretch of fabric, moving toward the herbal, picking up speed. Doshmisi struggled to scramble up the beach, away from the water. The oil slick continued to slide beneath her as the herbal sucked it in. At the same time, the herbal sucked in the oil that spread across the water. The oil rushed toward the Emerald Crystal and the herbal faster and faster. The green light emanating from the herbal grew into a large cloud that resembled smoke and it surrounded the area where the herbal lay submerged in the ocean. Lightning continued to crackle in the sky above and occasionally a lightning bolt shot down and zapped the herbal, which sparked with red, blue, and green light.

The oil, the carcasses of dead birds and fish, and everything in the whole abysmal mess gradually glided to the spot where the herbal rested under the water. Before long, pieces of metal from the oil rig began to appear sliding across the surface of the water, and the herbal sucked them into it also. The herbal had formed a vortex that became larger and larger as it drew all the nasty consequences of the oil spill to it, sucking them in like a magnet.

Then, to her fascination and horror, Doshmisi saw Corportons begin to appear on the rise at the edge of the beach. The Corportons rolled and tumbled uncontrollably across the sand. Dagobaz had walked further down the beach as it had cleared and the magnificent horse tossed his head and retreated from the stream of Corportons appearing over the rise.

As the vortex created by the herbal sucked the Corportons down the beach, they tried desperately to grab hold of anything in their path. They grasped for the scrubby bristles of oil-coated beach plants and tried to gain purchase on slick dolphin carcasses. But the things they tried to hold on to were being sucked down the beach along with them. Miraculously, the vortex did not pull Doshmisi into the herbal under the water. With an eerie feeling of safety amidst the chaos, she watched all the things around her as they flew to the ocean's edge while she herself remained where she stood, impervious to the suction force of the herbal.

Then Sonjay appeared over the rise, mounted on a tiger. And immediately after she saw Sonjay, Doshmisi saw Jasper appear; and soon all the others astride their tigers, all except for the enchanters. At first she thought her friends and family were being sucked into the vortex, but then she saw that they remained free of the pull of the vortex just as she did. They stood on the rise from where they witnessed the scene unfolding below. She wondered why the enchanters had not appeared with everyone else.

The vortex from the herbal sucked the oil coating from Doshmisi's hands and her clothing, leaving her clean and dry, as if not a speck of oil had ever touched her. Although the air remained thick, making it hard to pull it into her lungs, it did not seem to be getting any worse. She found it a little easier to breathe with the terrible stench from the rot on the beach dissipating.

The Corportons struggled comically yet frighteningly as the herbal sucked them down the beach and into the vortex it had created. They scrambled to save themselves to no avail. Doshmisi's heart leapt into her throat as she saw Aldus Shrub himself appear over the hill. He had lost his helmet and his mask along the way so she could see his panicked face quite clearly. "Help me," he squealed. "Help me, help me." Over and over again he pleaded. Doshmisi stood too far away from him to reach him even if she had wanted to, which she didn't. The ground beneath her moved rapidly and even though the vortex did not suck her in, she had to concentrate to keep standing amidst the motion beneath her feet. The Emerald Crystal and the herbal sucked Shrub down the beach along with the Corportons. Shrub grabbed a large piece of metal, a piece of the oil rig, embedded in the sand near the water's edge. Doshmisi had one last glimpse of his face, twisted with terror and dread, before the vortex sucked the entire piece of metal out of the sand, with Shrub clinging to it, and the man and the metal disappeared under the ocean and into the vortex of the green-glowing herbal. A startlingly dramatic bolt of lightning flashed out of the sky and struck the herbal with a spray of red-orange sparks as the air hummed with an electric buzz.

Doshmisi wondered what had happened to Sissrath. If the enchanters still contained him back at the compound, then what would they do with him after the herbal cleaned up the oil spill and dispatched the Corportons? What Doshmisi did not know, could not know, and would not find out until afterward, was that the enchanters had contained Sissrath at the compound while the Corportons flew off one by one toward the ocean, sucked away. Finally, after the Corportons had all disappeared, Sissrath had been slowly sucked out of the compound as well. Crumpet, locked in the bubble of light that he had created to prevent Sissrath from performing enchantment, had been pulled along with him. "Let go," Crumpet called to the other enchanters. "Let go of me!"

Princess Honeydew did as Crumpet commanded and removed her hand from Cardamom's shoulder. But Cardamom said, through gritted teeth, "No, dear brother, I am with you."

"Please. You must let go. You must release me while there is still time to save yourself," Crumpet pleaded. "Think of Alice and release me for her sake, for all the years you have spent apart. She deserves a few years with you." At those words, reluctantly, Cardamom dropped his hand from Crumpet's shoulder and entreated his brother, "Crumpet, you too must let go, come what may!"

"I can't," Crumpet replied. "I'm bound by a power that will not release me."

"You have proven yourself to be the mightiest enchanter of all time," Cardamom shouted to his brother as Crumpet was dragged through the front gate of the compound. "Mothers and fathers will whisper your name to their children for generations to come."

"Don't say such things," Crumpet called back to his brother.

"I wish for you to hear your praise from my own lips because I fear that we will never see each other again," Cardamom replied as he ran to keep up with Crumpet, who continued to pick up speed, trapped in the bubble of light with Sissrath. Cardamom's voice broke with emotion and tears coursed down the great enchanter's cheeks.

"Who is to say?" Crumpet called out. His eyes locked with his brother's for a brief moment. "Perhaps death is not as permanent as it seems. We may yet see each other again." After those words, a force beyond his control pulled Crumpet, and Buttercup who still clung to him, away toward the beach.

Cardamom hopped onto a tiger so he could follow the others as they rode out of the compound after Crumpet and Buttercup, who fairly flew through the air, trapped in the enchanted bubble of light that controlled Sissrath. Buttercup clung fiercely to her husband's arm, her long hair streaming behind her. Cardamom chased after them to the beach on a tiger's back.

At the water's edge, as Doshmisi was wondering what had become of Sissrath and the enchanters, they appeared at the top of the hill. She realized instantly that Sissrath did not have any control over his body. He moved like a marionette, like someone else pulled strings to move his arms and legs. The vortex sucked him in along with the Corportons. He might have resisted the pull of the herbal and the Emerald Crystal more effectively if he had not remained locked in that green bubble of flaming light created by Crumpet (supported by Buttercup). The green-bubble enchantment seemed to prevent him from using his powers.

Doshmisi heard Crumpet call to Buttercup as they slipped past her on the sand, "Buttercup, my dear wife, my love, please let go of me and save yourself. I will hold him on my own and you may die if you do not drop your hand from my shoulder."

"I would never leave you, babycakes," Buttercup replied. "We're in this together as we always have been. You are my husband and there is no other. You are my brilliant enchanter, the greatest of them all. Love of my life. Where you go, I go."

To Doshmisi, it seemed as though Sissrath, Crumpet, and Buttercup slid down the beach toward the herbal in slow motion as the deep enchantment of the Emerald Crystal and the herbal swept them along in its grip. She hoped with all her might that her friends would not share Sissrath's fate, that they would not be sucked into the vortex with him, that the Emerald Crystal would understand that they were separate from Sissrath.

Sissrath tumbled head over heels toward the water, his faded yellowish robe flapping around him so that he resembled a giant bird. At the water's edge he let out a final furious howl of rage that gave Doshmisi goosebumps. Then the glowing green vortex sucked Sissrath into itself with all the rest. To Doshmisi's horror, and the horror of all those who witnessed, Crumpet and Buttercup, trapped in the bubble of light with Sissrath, were also sucked into the herbal and disappeared under the water.

Doshmisi expected the herbal to spit Crumpet and Buttercup out as soon as it realized its mistake. But it didn't. As the seconds and then minutes ticked by and the herbal continued to clean up the ocean and the beach without releasing Crumpet and Buttercup from its enchantment, Doshmisi came to realize that they had sacrificed themselves and were gone as completely as the Corportons, Shrub, and Sissrath. To where? She would never know. She pounded her fists on the beach. "No, no," she moaned. "Not them too. Don't you understand?" If anyone could talk to the herbal, she could. If anyone could make it spit her friends back out she could. "You are an instrument of healing, not an instrument of grief!" Doshmisi screamed at the herbal. "You must understand. You must make it right!" Her words and wishes fell around her in tatters and changed nothing.

Almost no oil remained on the sand. The ocean water had cleared and turned a clean grayish-blue color. The oil rig had completely disappeared. The dead bodies of all the marine life had also vanished. While Doshmisi and the others watched, the green vortex sucked up the last remnants of the oil from the beach and then the vortex closed. The lightning died away. The sky cleared. The electrified hum faded out. Except for the fact that the air remained heavy, still making it difficult to breathe, everything had returned to normal, with no visible sign of the oil drilling operation or evidence of the spill.

Doshmisi waded into the water to the root of the vortex and touched the herbal, now entirely black, cold, and hard, like obsidian. The light in the Emerald Crystal had gone out and left it dull and gray. Much as she tried, Doshmisi could not lift the book, which had become so heavy it felt as if glued to the ground under the water. She sank to her knees and wept for the loss of Crumpet and Buttercup.

One drop of oil oozed up to the surface of the water just as the herbal disappeared completely under the ocean, under the sand, out of the world.

Chapter Twenty-Five
Singing Home the Algae

Sonjay ran to Doshmisi's side and fell to his knees. He shouted, "No, no, no, you stupid book! Give them back. Figure it out. You have to give them back!" Kneeling beside him, Doshmisi put her arms around him and together they sobbed for their lost friends, while everyone else, who had remained on the crest of the rise at the edge of the beach, made their way across the sand to join them. Maia had her arm around Cardamom, who wept silently. Many of the others were crying as well, but none of them more noisily than Hyacinth, who could not control his great, wet sobs. Saffron held him close and Honeydew patted his arm.

"What will become of Daisy?" Maia asked softly. Daisy was the golden-haired twelve-year-old daughter of Crumpet and Buttercup. The Four had met her on their previous journey in Faracadar and they knew how much she adored her father.

"I will take care of her," Cardamom replied. "She's my niece. I will see that she receives her training as an enchanter. Coming from such talented parents she is destined for greatness." Cardamom's voice broke as he declared, "Oh Daisy, Daisy, how can I bring you this news?" He had trouble catching his breath since the air quality had deteriorated so much. Elena took his hands in hers and made him look into her eyes and breathe in rhythm with her until he stopped gasping for air.

"It's a mistake. It's not fair," Denzel mourned.

"There's no rule that says life must be fair," Reggie said quietly, with a note of bitterness in his voice, as he put a hand on Denzel's shoulder. Denzel thought about his mother Debbie, who had died so young.

Jasper hovered over Doshmisi and stroked her short, short hair. Iris rubbed Mole's arm comfortingly. Bayard perched silently on Guhblorin's nearly bald head and, for once, remained silent. The intuits bobbed dejectedly in the air beside them.

"I wish we had time right now to mourn, but we don't. There's work yet to be done," Doshmisi said firmly. "The herbal provided a final message." Sonjay wiped his eyes with the end of his T-shirt and, after a deep shudder, stopped crying. Hyacinth stopped blubbering but still clung to his wife. Everyone listened attentively as Doshmisi shared with them the words provided by the herbal.

Cardamom wiped his eyes on the sleeve of his robe. "The herbal has made it clear," he said resolutely. "We must mobilize the people. We need to enlist the aid of as many people in the land as possible. We have to let everyone know what happened here because no one knows that Sissrath is gone and the Corportons with him. No one knows of the brave sacrifice of Crumpet and Buttercup. And no one knows about singing home the algae."

"Or why the air grows unfit to breathe," Iris added.

"Exactly," Cardamom affirmed.

"We be needin' to communicate," Mole stated, as the wheels in his head began to turn toward problem-solving.

"The Dome was down when Dosh and I were there," Jasper pointed out.

"We don't know what might be happening at the Dome now," Denzel said.

"But we can find out," Sonjay told them, with a knowing glance at Reggie.

"True that," Reggie agreed, as a smile flickered at the corners of his mouth.

"Locomotaport," Jack and the intuits began to call out. Bayard circled up above and echoed the word, squawking it over and over again.

"I can locomotaport to the Dome Circle and see what's going on there and hopefully manage to find Violet or her technicians, who can help me send out the message about singing home the algae," Sonjay explained.

"How does that work? Does your body stay here?" Denzel asked.

"Yes, his body will stay here," Honeydew confirmed.

"Watch Bayard," Reggie instructed.

Sonjay punched his fist in the air and proclaimed, "For Crumpet and Buttercup." Then he walked a short distance apart from the group and sat down facing the water. Bayard circled above him as Sonjay crossed his legs yoga-style and rested his hands on his knees. He sat up straight as a pencil and closed his eyes. Bayard swooped in the air in several graceful loops and then he landed in front of Sonjay on the sand. The large, bright bird stood perfectly still in front of Sonjay, watching him intently out of one eye and then turning his head abruptly to watch him out of the other.

"He's gone now," Reggie told Denzel, as he headed across the sand to sit protectively by Sonjay's body.

"C'mon," Mole said to Denzel. "There be a transmission screen at the compound. If they get the Dome working then we can pick up a message on it." Mole and Denzel headed swiftly back up the beach to where the tigers milled, alert, on the edge of the sand.

"I'll go with you," Doshmisi called after them. The others followed more slowly behind Mole and Denzel. As they passed Reggie, Bayard, and Sonjay's body, Honeydew informed Reggie that they were headed to the compound to keep an eye on the transmission screen.

"I'll stay here to look after Sonjay until he returns," Reggie said.

Elena and Guhblorin sat down beside Reggie. "We'll stay to keep you company while you wait," Elena told him.

"You don't have to," Reggie said. "You can go on with the others."

Elena shrugged. "De nada," she assured Reggie. "That means it's nothing, easy to do," she explained to Guhblorin.

"Easy," Guhblorin agreed.

Having left the others behind on the beach with his body, Sonjay arrived at the Dome in his locomotaported self. At first, he thought something had gone drastically wrong with the locomotaport and that he had become stuck in a time warp or a hole in space because the Dome Circle appeared completely deserted. He saw no special forces there, but he saw no one else either. He walked around the entire Dome Circle and didn't see a single person. Cautiously, he entered the Crystal Communication Dome through the main doorway. The enormous crystal at the center of the Dome remained covered in canvas in the dim room. Sonjay hated to see the crystal like that. He remembered the year before when the Goodacres had first witnessed the inside of the Crystal Communication Dome and it had sparkled and danced with light and rainbows, dazzling and exhilarating. The gray, dull room before him stood in stark contrast to the memory he had of the magnificent crystals sending messages far and wide.

Sonjay left the Dome and walked down the road leading to Jelly's Tollhouse. The circle seemed like a ghost town. For a terrifying moment he wondered if Sissrath and the Corportons had not been the only people in Faracadar swept away with the oil when the herbal did its housecleaning. What if all the other people in Faracadar had disappeared at that moment too? What if the prophecy of the end of the land had already come true and he and the few people left behind at the North Coast were the only ones left? Sonjay forced himself to stop picturing such a horrible outcome.

He stopped in the middle of the road, stood still, and listened. In the eerie quiet of the vacant street, he thought he heard a muffled sound. He wondered if he had imagined it. He listened harder. He felt certain that he heard a sound. Two sounds, in fact. One was a faint thumping and the other was a barely audible tone, a single droning note. But where did it come from? He closed his eyes and concentrated on listening. He walked away from the center of the circle and toward the hillside that rose from the edge of the circle. He could hear the thumping and the steady tone more clearly as he walked in the direction of the hillside.

He found himself in a small park with swings, trees, and a climbing structure. Along one side of the park the hill sloped upward sharply. Sonjay saw an enormous boulder, twice the size of Aunt Alice's Toyota, embedded in the hillside. The thumping and the tone came from behind that boulder. Sonjay floated up the hill to the boulder where he paused and then he locomotaported right through the boulder and into a giant cave on the other side of it.

The instant he appeared inside the cave, a dozen people surrounded him and raised a cheer. A couple of women burst into tears and a man attempted to thump Sonjay on the back, but his hand went straight through Sonjay's locomotaported body. "What is this? Who or what are you?" the man exclaimed in astonishment.

"I'm Sonjay, the youngest son of Debbie, one of the Four, and I have locomotaported to the Dome Circle to find Violet. Why is the circle empty? What are you doing in here?" Sonjay demanded.

"Locomotaported!" one of the women repeated excitedly. "Only Hazamon could do that."

"Correction," Sonjay responded. "Hazamon and me. Where's Violet. Where are Mr. and Mrs. Jelly?"

One of the men called out, "Violet! Jelly! Come quick."

As Sonjay's eyes adjusted to the darkness lit only by a faint glow-lamp, he noticed several hammers lying on the ground. "Were you trying to pound your way out?" he asked.

"Not really," one man answered. "We were trying to make enough noise to attract attention."

"How long have you been in here?" Sonjay asked.

Just then Violet appeared from the depths of the cave. She recognized him immediately, even though he was transparent. "Sonjay, thank goodness. How did you find us?" she asked.

"It's a long story and I haven't much time. I'm locomotaporting. We need to get the Dome back online and send a message out. What happened here? What's up with the Dome? Why did you come in here?"

"We didn't come in here on purpose," Violet answered. "The Special Forces imprisoned us in here. They trapped everyone inside this cave. Did they go away? Did you see any of them out there?"

"Not a single one," Sonjay replied. "They are most definitely gone. I'll explain about that later, but right now we need to get you out of here."

"What a good idea," Jelly said as he materialized behind Violet. "Good to see you Sonjay. We've been in here for two days and we have no food, only some water from an underground spring. The boulder blocking the entrance is too heavy for us to move, even when all of us push together."

"Everyone who remained at the circle after the Special Forces shut down the Dome is trapped in here," Violet added.

"And no enchanters?" Sonjay asked.

"None," Jelly answered mournfully.

"Hang on," Sonjay told them. "I have to go back to my body at the North Coast and talk to Cardamom. He'll know what to do. The Corportons got sucked into the herbal with Sissrath. That's a long story, but they're gone. Now we need to work quickly to bring the algae back across the water before the air becomes too polluted to breathe. This must sound totally confusing. Sorry. Listen up. Stay here and I'll come right back."

"We're not going anywhere," Jelly said. "Trust me. Hey, do you think you could bring us some peanut butter and jelly sandwiches or some mannafruit or something?"

"I'll do what I can. See you soon," Sonjay called over his shoulder as he disappeared from the cave and sent himself back to his body on the North Coast.

Sonjay found it easier to return to his body this time than he had the last time he locomotaported. For one thing, he had not remained out of his body for as long as he had on the previous occasion. For another, he was getting the hang of it. When he returned, he found himself sitting on the beach with his father, Elena, and Guhblorin. Bayard alighted on his shoulder. He stroked the bird's chest absently and Bayard squawked appreciatively.

"We've got a problem," Sonjay began, and he told the others about the Dome Circle people trapped inside the cave.

"Cardamom can help with this," Reggie assured Sonjay. "He can tell you how to move that rock. He went to the compound with everyone else. Let's go discuss the situation with him." The fact that his two teachers in the art of enchantment had died weighed heavy on Sonjay's heart as he and the others accompanied his father to the compound to consult Cardamom.

Once they arrived at the compound, Sonjay wasted no time. He explained what had happened at the Dome Circle. "I wish I could locomotaport you with me," Sonjay told Cardamom. "You could probably move that boulder in a hot minute with enchantment."

"You can move it too," Cardamom told Sonjay.

"I've never moved an object," Sonjay argued.

"Yes, but you will have a powerful tool to help you," Cardamom said as he produced the box that contained the Staff of Shakabaz and opened the lid. He pointed his finger into the box, swished it around in a circle, and scattered sparkles of light in all directions. The Staff of Shakabaz emerged from the box, rising to its full height. Cardamom gripped it in the middle and handed it to Sonjay.

"How do I take it with me?" Sonjay asked.

"It will follow, it is an enchanted object. It defies the laws of physics," Cardamom reminded him.

"OK, then how do I use it to move the boulder?"

"This is a matter of life and death if I ever encountered one. The Staff of Shakabaz specializes in matters of life and death. Aim it at that boulder and send it a message in your mind about what you need it to do to free the Dome people," Cardamom instructed.

"Anything else I need to know?" Sonjay asked as he sat down on the floor and settled the Staff across his lap. Reggie quietly sat behind his son.

"Before you use the Staff, remember to clear your mind as Buttercup taught you," Cardamom said. His voice quavered slightly at the mention of Buttercup.

Sonjay nodded solemnly and then he closed his eyes. It took him several minutes to calm his thoughts and his breathing since he felt apprehensive about the task at hand and also because he could barely contain his excitement about the possibility of freeing the Dome people with the Staff. Reggie, Cardamom, and Honeydew meditated with him. He listened to their breathing and the four of them brought their breathing into alignment so that they breathed in and out together. He cleared his mind as much as he could and sent the stray thoughts that entered his head on their way as they passed through. He used his secret word "feathers" to help him and he recalled the first time he had locomotaported, when his father had told him there was a great enchanter in him.

Eventually, with his mind calm and his breathing even, his ability to locomotaport came to him. Once he left his body, he went quickly to the cave at the Dome Circle. He stood in front of the boulder and aimed the Staff of Shakabaz in its direction. It did not seem necessary to speak out loud. He focused his thoughts on the people inside the cave and the need to free them so they could eat and regain their strength and he banished all extraneous thoughts from his mind as Buttercup and Crumpet had trained him to do. Sonjay's arm became one with the Staff. He felt his hand tingling and lightning flashed overhead. His amulet glowed with brilliant golden light, which traveled down his arm and into the Staff. Then it flew from the top of the Staff to the boulder, engulfing the boulder in golden light. Slowly, steadily, the boulder slid to one side, revealing the opening to the cave.

Among the first to emerge, Violet and Jelly cheered loudly.

"You rock!" Jelly exclaimed.

"You *un*rock!" Violet joked with a joyous laugh.

The light in the Staff of Shakabaz extinguished itself and Sonjay's amulet glimmered faintly for a minute before going dark. "We have no time to waste," Sonjay said urgently. "Violet, gather your technicians and let's get that Dome back up and running. Walk with me and I'll explain."

"I thought it was just because we were inside that cave," Jelly wheezed, "but the air out here is dreadful too. In fact, it's worse than the air in the cave."

"We have to sing home the algae to clean the air and we have to do it before the air becomes too ruined for us to breathe," Sonjay explained. Jelly nodded silently. Meanwhile, Violet rounded up her chief communications technicians. Jelly stood at the mouth of the cave and told the people as they emerged that anyone who worked at the Dome should proceed there immediately. Mrs. Jelly announced that she would bring them something to eat as soon as possible.

Sonjay joined Violet, who turned to him expectantly as they walked down the slope away from the cave. Sonjay informed her, "I can't stay here. How long do you think it will take you to get the crystals in the Dome operating so that you can send a message out to all the circles in all the settlements?"

"I don't know what damage has been done. If the Special Forces simply powered everything down and didn't do any damage then I'm thinking maybe two days," Violet replied.

"We don't have two days," Sonjay stated flatly. "We need to send a message to all the people no later than sunrise tomorrow. It will take time for the message to travel to further locations and we need as many people as possible to set out by tomorrow morning for the coast. Doshmisi doesn't know what the tipping point will be in terms of how many people need to participate. Mole figures that we have two days at the most before the air becomes completely unfit. Those most vulnerable to the poor air quality, like babies and old folks, will start having trouble sooner. The minute you can send messages, tell the people that we will begin a collective sing at four o'clock tomorrow afternoon. Anyone who can get to the beach or within sight of the ocean should go there. Those who can't get to the beach should participate from wherever they are. Drumming will probably help, but Doshmisi says the main thing is to hold a musical voice tone. One note. Tell people to choose one tone and to hold it and to keep at it, to keep sounding that tone. While they sing, they should send out thought-messages to the algae requesting that it return to our aid."

"How will we know if it's working or not?" Violet asked anxiously.

"How long must we sing the tone?" one of her technicians added.

"You'll know if it's working if you can breathe," Sonjay said grimly. "By tomorrow the air will be in even more terrible shape. Keep singing until the air begins to clear."

"We'll do our best," Violet promised.

"You have to do better than best. You've heard the prophecy, haven't you?"

"Of course," Violet responded, with a note of fear in her voice.

"Don't believe it," Sonjay told her. "Treat the prophecy as a warning. We can make it happen differently. Get that Dome working to send the message and the people will do the rest. Now I have to go."

"We'll begin sending messages to closer places soon, maybe by sunset today if we can do it. May the work of the Four continue," Violet said with resolve. Sonjay smiled encouragingly at Violet before he vanished.

When Sonjay returned to his body, he found the others prepared for travel. Maia had her drum over her shoulder and Reggie had buckled up his knapsack that bulged with books.

"How did it go? Did you free them from the cave?" Reggie asked.

"Yeah, they're out. Violet and her technicians will get the Dome working as soon as they can. They don't know how fast they can get it back up and running, but they'll give it their best shot. What's up? Are we going on a road trip?"

"We see no point in staying here," Denzel replied. "We've decided to ride to the Passage Circle. If Violet can't get the message out then at least we can bring out the people in the Passage Circle to come together to sing."

"And drum," Maia added. "I feel certain that drumming will help bring the algae back. You know how good those drummers are at the Passage Circle."

"Sure enough," Sonjay agreed. "I told Violet to encourage people to drum when she sends the message." Maia nodded approvingly.

"How do you feel?" Doshmisi asked Sonjay. "Are you strong enough to ride?"

"I'm good. I'm getting better at locomotaporting," Sonjay boasted.

"Excellent," Cardamom said, as he folded the Staff into its box. "Your tiger awaits."

With not quite enough tigers to go around, some people had to double up with others. Doshmisi rode Dagobaz. They galloped away from the North Coast in a cloud of dust kicked up behind them and no one looked back at the abandoned prison compound or the former site of the oil rig that had poisoned the ocean. The tigers and Dagobaz could not travel as quickly as usual because of the poor quality of the air. No one could fill their lungs with a good pull of oxygen and it exhausted them to breathe the nasty air. The travelers rode slowly but steadily down the coast and arrived at the Passage Circle in the middle of the night. Governor Jay greeted them after being roused from his bed upon their arrival. Once they had explained the situation and the plan to follow the instructions in the herbal and attempt to sing home the algae, Governor Jay found beds for the weary group to catch a few hours of sleep. He dispatched a messenger to Big House City to inform the people there about the need for them to travel to the coast for the collective sing.

Denzel, Jasper, and Mole slept on cots in the Passage Circle's communication center, where the crystal communication screen remained dark. They hoped that it would light up with a message from Violet any second informing them that the large crystal at the Dome was working again, and that messages would then stream from the crystal throughout the land.

No one slept well, despite their exhaustion. Everyone felt anxious and they all had difficulty breathing.

A vivid orange and gold sunrise exploded on the day. The particles of dirt in the air caused the colorful sunrise. Just as they sat down to a waffle breakfast that Elena had masterminded with the help of her trusty helper Guhblorin as well as Governor Jay's kitchen staff, Denzel, Jasper, and Mole rushed into the dining room whooping with excitement. Violet had the Dome working well enough to begin transmitting the message. While many circles had not yet received the transmission, others had already received the news about the reason for the problem with the air and how to fix it by singing home the algae.

Soon after breakfast, people began to arrive at the circle from Big House City. Throughout the day, people from places near to the beaches appeared and the circle swelled with those who came to help. The air had become so thick and smutty that people would frequently begin coughing and then have trouble catching their breath afterward. Doshmisi discovered that inhaling steam from boiling water gave her lungs some relief from processing the filthy air and she passed the word to the people that they should boil water and breathe the steam for a few minutes to help their lungs. The steam method proved particularly helpful after someone had a bad coughing fit.

Maia and her drummer friends started drumming on the beach shortly after noon. There they remained, drumming as if in a trance. Elena managed to get Maia to drink some juice and eat a sandwich for lunch. Otherwise she drummed nonstop.

Tents and temporary shelters sprang up along the coast as the beach filled with people. Sonjay stood the Staff of Shakabaz upright on the sand where everyone could easily see it. He chose a dry spot, well out of the reach of the waves, and he sat down on the beach, ready to sing. But Doshmisi said it was too early to start. She insisted that they begin at the appointed time of four o'clock. She thought they should begin when as many people as possible across the land could join them. As the hour approached, they gathered at the water's edge. Jack and other intuits hovered nearby while Bayard swooped overhead. Bisc paced near Princess Honeydew like a caged lion. At four o'clock, Doshmisi nodded her head to signal the beginning and each person selected a tone and gave it voice, sending a message with their combined voices across the water to the algae.

"Come home to us and clean our air so we may breathe and live," Doshmisi thought as she sang her tone.

"The Corportons are gone now so you can safely return," Sonjay thought as he sang his tone.

Maia had no concrete thoughts in her head as she surrendered herself to the beat of the drums and projected her message in that way.

"Please save Faracadar," Denzel thought as he sang his tone.

All over the land, people thought about their hopes and dreams for a future. Each person sent their own individual thoughts and messages to the algae. The thoughts of each of them combined, blended, and joined in the musical tone that traveled across the water in a song sent to the algae, begging the algae to return and restore balance to the fragile ecosystem of Faracadar. "For our children and grandchildren," the mothers and fathers thought. "For the animals and plants that share the land with us," the children thought. "For the beauty we have created with our work, imagination, and ingenuity," the enchanters and leaders thought. "For the possibilities of things to come. For laughter and joy. For the love that we share. For the gardens we have planted and the dances we have danced. For all that we hold dear, please preserve our lives and our world," the people thought.

Was it her imagination, Doshmisi wondered, or had the air become slightly easier to breathe? She stared at the water so hard that her eyes ached. She sought a sign, any sign, of a change in color from slate-blue to the bright-green color indicating the presence of the algae. She thought perhaps the water had started turning slightly green. Or maybe her eyes just played tricks on her.

Then, as Doshmisi gazed out to the horizon, she saw a whale spout. Soon another spout followed and then another. Tears coursed down her cheeks. The whales would not have returned alone. They would only have returned if the algae came with them. Moments passed and then she heard the whales singing in the distance. Soon the dolphins joined them, and Doshmisi heard them singing together. She could not make out the words yet, but she recognized the whale and dolphin voices.

"It's working," Doshmisi cried in excitement. "We're going to be OK. Look there!" She pointed toward the horizon, to the spot where she had seen the whale spout appear. "Watch right there."

Only Reggie and Elena could hear her over the loud musical tone and the drumming. But everyone could see her pointing. They looked in the direction in which her finger pointed and they saw the whales spouting far out on the water. The word spread up and down the beach and soon everyone laughed and cried and hugged each other all at once because they saw the whales spouting and they realized what that meant. Meanwhile, the water had started showing signs of green color as the jubilant people of Faracadar continued singing the algae home across the water.

Chapter Twenty-Six
Muffins for Hyacinth

The Four and their traveling companions would have returned to Big House City in unbounded celebration and triumph had Crumpet and Buttercup not lost their lives to the struggle. The death of the two enchanters weighed heavily on everyone's heart. Doshmisi felt bone-weary as she rode Dagobaz, who insisted on taking the lead, always out in front of the tigers. She could not hold him back nor did she have the desire to do so. The air had continued to clear steadily and it felt good to breathe easily again.

In the evening, when they reached Big House City, they discovered the residents of the city lining the road leading to the main entrance. Doshmisi pulled herself together so she could wave and smile to the people, who cheered, clapped, and danced alongside the returning royals and their entourage. No one had yet reported the fate of Crumpet and Buttercup. Their daughter Daisy would need to hear the news first and the dreadful task of informing her would fall to her Uncle Cardamom.

The High Chief's cooks had prepared a feast to celebrate the return of the heroes from the coast. But before participating in any celebrations, the Four felt they needed to decide what to do with Compost, who remained a prisoner. Elena had ensured that the high chief's guards had removed Compost from the dungeon and installed him in a comfortable room (securely guarded) before she and the others departed for the North Coast.

Behind closed doors, in the royal council chambers, the Four, Hyacinth, and Cardamom met to consider their options for dealing with Sissrath's former right-hand man. Cardamom suggested that Hyacinth assemble a decision-making committee to come up with a plan and Hyacinth readily agreed since he didn't like making important decisions on his own. A discussion ensued regarding who belonged on the committee. In the end, they settled on Hyacinth, Cardamom, Reggie, Honeydew, and the Four.

When they emerged from the council chambers, and Elena learned that they intended to exclude her from the committee, she unleashed her Latin temper. "Exactly what kind of *justicia* will you accomplish with no one to represent Compost?" she demanded. "False *justicia!* You are pretending at making a fair decision. I am the only one here who does not hold a grudge against him. I don't see how you can give him a fair hearing without representation. He should have a lawyer, but since there is none, then give me a place at the committee to speak on his behalf."

The others weighed her words, hesitant to respond, until Denzel spoke up. "She's right," he said. He had seen the devastation of the burning of the Passage Circle the year before and he knew that Compost had a hand in its execution. The images of the gutted buildings, burned flesh, and grieving faces would never leave him and he realized the truth in Elena's words. Those images would always color his perception of Compost. "I hold it against him that he led Sissrath's troops when they burned the Passage Circle. I'm not an objective judge."

"He must take responsibility for his role in burning the Passage Circle," Reggie pointed out.

"Don't you think that anything you say about Compost should be said to his face, not behind his back?" Elena suggested. "He knows what he did. I expect he has some thoughts of his own on punishment for his crimes."

The others reluctantly agreed. They disliked the idea of having Compost present as they discussed his fate.

Doshmisi wished they could make their decision in the morning, after she had eaten dinner and had a good night's sleep. On the other hand, she wondered if she would rest easy until Compost's fate had been decided. Reggie went to fetch Compost as the rest of them took their seats around the High Chief's large oval council table.

Before long Reggie returned with Compost following behind him flanked by guards. The High Chief dismissed the guards at the doorway. This discussion would remain private. Elena motioned to an empty chair next to her at the council table. Compost would sit as an equal member with the others.

Doshmisi noticed the dramatic change that Compost had undergone since his capture. He had vastly improved his personal grooming and he looked like a normal person. He wore his hair extremely short and it was clean. His face seemed clear and he had noticeably lost some weight so his stomach no longer jiggled so much. He smelled pleasantly of musk and vanilla. The old repugnant Compost had virtually vanished. Doshmisi would not have recognized him if she had not known who he was.

Compost sat beside Elena, who smiled at him encouragingly and patted his arm.

"I assume you have heard what transpired at the North Coast," Cardamom began.

Compost nodded his head to indicate that he knew. Still he did not speak.

"And now that Sissrath is gone and the alien creatures gone with him, we must decide what to do about you," Cardamom continued.

"I have told him that Elena convinced us that he should participate in this discussion," Reggie informed the others.

"And I am grateful to you for it," Compost said quietly.

"You have committed crimes against the people of Faracadar," Cardamom reminded Compost. "What have you to say for yourself?"

Compost looked around thoughtfully at everyone who sat at the council table. "My actions were not unprovoked, but I do not wish to hide behind that as an excuse," Compost said.

"Expand yourself," Hyacinth demanded.

"He means to explain yourself," Honeydew quickly clarified.

"My people, the People of the Mountain Downs, have long been treated as second class citizens. We are unwelcome wherever we go, despite the fact that we have produced some of the most skilled enchanters and our clever people have contributed a great deal to the advancement of Faracadar. We realize that we sometimes fall short when it comes to social graces; but that does not qualify as a justifiable reason to deny us a place at the table. Do you not think it a natural consequence that my people would resent such shabby treatment, would chafe at the lack of representation of the People of the Mountain Downs among the leadership of the land?"

"We have never laid siege to any of your circles as you did to Big House City," Cardamom reminded him sternly.

"Have you not? What of the fact that you deny us access to participation in your market, your colleges, your festivities, because of your suspicions about us, your preconceived notions?" Compost asked.

"He's talking about prejudice," Elena said firmly. "You have made assumptions about him and his people. That's called prejudice where I come from."

"We have based our opinions of the People of the Mountain Downs on our past experience of dealing with you," Honeydew said.

"Dealing with us?" Compost echoed. "Communication between people and dealing with people are two very different beasts."

"Bad habits. Destructive patterns," Elena said softly.

"How do we break that pattern of mistrust?" Maia asked. "It doesn't serve any of us well."

"We need to get to know one another better," Compost said.

"You need to share your stories with each other," Reggie suggested.

Despite her exhaustion, and the aching sadness she felt at the loss of Crumpet and Buttercup, Doshmisi saw in a flash with perfect clarity that the only way to heal Faracadar was to forgive Compost and his people. She didn't need her grandmother or the whales or the trees or the herbal to help her figure this out. She knew what all of them would say and the right course to chart. She could hear them speaking in her head, internalized, a part of her forever. She said, "Remember last year when the whales told us that violence would only lead to more violence and that we had to find a nonviolent way to defeat Sissrath? To break the cycle of violence?"

"Of course," Maia murmured, while Denzel and Sonjay nodded their heads in agreement.

"Well it continues. It didn't stop there. The only way to build trust and make the land a peaceful place for everyone is to forgive one another and make a new start," Doshmisi explained. "We have to let go of grudges and we have to give people the benefit of the doubt. We have to release our anger about past crimes for the sake of the future."

Compost cleared his throat. "Forgiveness usually follows an apology," he said in a husky voice. "So I wish to tell you that I am sincerely sorry for my wrongdoing."

Doshmisi set an example by accepting his apology. "I forgive you for burning the Passage Circle, for harming our friends there and destroying their homes and their fields. I believe in my heart that you have changed and I wish to give you a chance to be a better person."

Compost bowed his head for a moment and stared at his hands folded in his lap and then he lifted his head and held a hand out to Doshmisi, who was shocked to see tears sparkling in Compost's eyes. "And I forgive your uncles for exiling my father from Big House City in the old time, for refusing my people a seat at the high council, for treating me like a fool instead of the intelligent person I am, and I forgive you for making fun of me and thinking you are better than I am." Doshmisi, Denzel, and Maia had never known that their uncles had done such a thing to Compost's father so Compost's words came as a shock to them. Sonjay knew of it because he had read about the history of Faracadar. Even so, he had not given that part of the history much thought and he had never considered the impact of such a deed on Compost. He had viewed all of it as ancient history, but it obviously remained very much alive for some people.

As Doshmisi solemnly took Compost's hand and shook it, she said, "I apologize on behalf of those who have wronged you and your people and denied you a seat at the table. I did make fun of you and I am sorry for it."

"If I may, I want to suggest a way to begin to fix this," Reggie offered. "You won't like it Hyacinth, but I think that you and Compost should rule together for a time, as a team."

Compost cleared his throat and appeared almost shy as he said, "I no longer use the name Compost. I have returned to using my given name, Comice. Please make the adjustment." A wave of astonishment crossed the faces of those present, and Sonjay's jaw actually dropped open. Elena chatted brightly, "I know how to make an exceptional dessert with Comice pears. Sweet and light. I will make it for you one time if I can find the ingredients."

"I will enjoy eating it," Comice, who was once Compost, said politely. "Every bite."

Sonjay closed his mouth with a snap as he tried to accept everything he had witnessed in the council chambers so far.

"How will we rule together?" Hyacinth demanded. "How is that possible?"

"Well, to begin with, you will have to include some of Compost's, sorry, I mean Comice's, people on the high council. And then you must establish a system for discussing things and coming to a decision that you and Comice can both agree on. Perhaps you will need a mediator," Cardamom said.

"I'm supposed to share being the high chief with him after everything he's done?" Hyacinth asked incredulously.

"Try to forgive him, Daddy," Honeydew said.

"That's the only way. You can see he has changed," Doshmisi elaborated.

"How do I know he really changed?" Hyacinth asked suspiciously.

"Well, he did tell us about Sissrath's fear of cockroaches and it did come in handy at the North Coast," Denzel reminded Hyacinth.

"It certainly did," Sonjay agreed. "Crumpet used cockroaches to throw Sissrath off balance and it made all the difference when I tried to restrain him with the Staff of Shakabaz." Cardamom winced at the mention of his dead brother.

"That's true," Hyacinth conceded, though cautiously. "But I'm not totalitarianly contrived. I mean convinced. I'm not totalitarianly convinced."

"I don't blame you Hyacinth," Doshmisi replied.

"Comice needs to make restitution for his past actions," Reggie said. "So what should he do to show you that he has changed and that you can trust him?"

"Restitution. Absolutely," Comice agreed gravely.

Hyacinth leaned his head to one side and thought about that. "OK, well, yes. I want resuscitation. I like the way that sounds."

"Restitution," Elena corrected.

"Resuscitation is when you are revived from being unconscious, Daddy," Honeydew explained, as patiently as ever. "Like if you stopped breathing and someone gives you mouth-to-mouth."

"Ewww. No, that's not what I want from Comp, er, Comice," Hyacinth said, wiping his lips.

"We know, Daddy," Honeydew replied and then she continued to explain patiently to her linguistically impaired father. "Restitution is when someone does something appropriate to make up for past injuries or wrongful actions."

"Exactly," Reggie confirmed. "Restitution is a key component of restorative justice, which means restoring justice through apology and forgiveness demonstrated by actions. The person who committed the crime demonstrates his remorse to the victim of the crime by doing something to make amends, to make it up to the victim."

"I understand," Hyacinth said. "I like this very much."

Maia addressed the question to Comice. "So, what do you think you should do to make restitution to the people of the Passage Circle?"

Comice thought about the pain he caused in the years during which he served Sissrath. Despite the wrongs perpetrated on his own people, he wished that his people had risen above all of it and shown themselves to be better. He wished that his people had not succumbed to anger and had not sunk to the level of those who persecuted them. It dawned on Comice that he wanted to become the real leader that the People of the Mountain Downs needed and deserved, the leader that his people had hoped for these many long years. He wanted to succeed where Sissrath had failed. Sissrath had been selfish, destructive, and hurtful. Sissrath had never actually cared about the People of the Mountain Downs. Comice resolved not to fail his people, he would seize this chance to serve them well. To get to that opportunity, he first had to walk through this trial. "I will go to the Passage Circle and meet with each family who lost a loved one in the attack. I will apologize to them in person. And I will dedicate two days every month to working in the Passage Circle to build, repair, or make something needed in the community."

"That sounds good," Reggie approved. "What does everyone else think?" The others agreed to Comice's proposal, although Hyacinth still appeared doubtful.

Elena noted Hyacinth's hesitation so she asked Comice, "Don't you think you should also do something for the High Chief, to make restitution for all the trouble you have caused him?"

"That seems fair," Comice replied. "What should I do for you Hyacinth to demonstrate that I am prepared to collaborate with you?"

Hyacinth's brow crinkled in thought. Sonjay worried for a minute that the high chief might hurt himself by thinking so hard and wondered if Hyacinth was up to this task. Hyacinth pondered and then he announced, "I have come to a derision."

"Oh Daddy," Honeydew burst out. "Derision means you are ridiculous and have become a laughingstock. You mean a decision. You have come to a decision."

"Yes, a decision," Hyacinth said. "About the restitution."

"Restitution, good," Cardamom echoed, encouraging Hyacinth to continue.

"I want Comice to bake me muffins," Hyacinth informed them.

"You want him to bake you muffins?" Doshmisi asked in amazement, wondering if she had heard Hyacinth correctly.

"As an act of goodwill," Hyacinth stated with satisfaction.

"That's all?" Denzel questioned him. "Just to bake you muffins?"

"They must be deliberate muffins!" Hyacinth continued.

"Deliberate?" Honeydew questioned. "You mean he must make them on purpose?"

Hyacinth threw her a puzzled look. "No," he said. "Well, yes, that too. But they must be, I know the right word; they must be delectable. That's what they must be. Delectable. That's what I mean. Delicious. They must melt in my mouth. He must bake magnificent muffins."

"I'll try," Comice said sincerely although somewhat uncertainly. "But I don't know how to cook."

"I can help you with that," Elena offered enthusiastically.

"Not really," Maia said gently, as she laid a comforting hand on Elena's arm, "because you will be leaving tomorrow to go back home."

"Tomorrow?" Elena responded, taken aback. "Already?" She put her arms around Comice and hugged him as tears welled up in her eyes. Comice patted her back with such affection that the others had no remaining question in their minds that he had truly changed.

"I can show you how to make at least one batch of muffins tonight, before I have to go," Elena suggested with a sniffle.

"That would be lovely," Comice replied.

Cardamom cleared his throat. "I have a proposition then," he said. "We will release Comice from his imprisonment and allow him to begin to work with Hyacinth to rule Faracadar. He will make his visit to the Passage Circle to apologize and upon his return, each and every week, he will bake a batch of muffins for Hyacinth. He will bake muffins every week until Hyacinth says he can stop. At first, they might not be the most delectable muffins, but practice makes perfect. We will form a taste council. I will serve on it. Hyacinth and everyone on the taste council will taste the muffins each week, until Hyacinth releases Comice from this task. What do you think?"

"I love it!" Hyacinth shouted. "What an extrapolaneously magripescent idea."

"See what I'm saying," Comice muttered under his breath to Elena, but he smiled indulgently at his language-mangling co-ruler. "I'm going to need an interpreter to discuss important decisions with this man."

"Not a problem," Honeydew assured Comice. "I can do that."

"I release Comice from imprisonment and he will go directly to the kitchen with Elena to work on his first batch of muffins," Hyacinth announced with his boyish enthusiasm. "Blueberry would be good," he added as he rubbed his hands together.

"Blueberry, blueberry," Bayard repeated enthusiastically from his perch on Sonjay's shoulder. He had remained quiet throughout the proceedings, but when presented with the thought of berries he could not keep his beak shut.

"You may no longer command him," Doshmisi informed Hyacinth firmly. "He is your partner and co-ruler. You do not command one another."

"I volunteer to go to the kitchen to bake blueberry muffins with my friend Elena," Comice offered. "It would give me the greatest pleasure." A smile spread across Comice's face and Doshmisi noticed for the first time that he had an adorable little dimple on his left cheek.

When Elena and Comice appeared in the kitchen soon after the council dissolved and informed Guhblorin that Comice was required to make restitution to Hyacinth by baking muffins, Guhblorin fell over laughing. He could not help himself, and in true geebaching fashion he suggested that they bake "mouse muffins" for Hyacinth as the first batch. Elena had to pull on his ears to make him behave.

Chapter Twenty-Seven
What Happened at Angel's Gate

Doshmisi wanted to rejoice because Faracadar had escaped the prophesied destruction, but she couldn't summon the necessary level of joy to feel celebratory with Crumpet and Buttercup dead and the moment of the return looming. On the morning of the return, she and her siblings joined their closest friends for a quiet breakfast in the dining room at Big House City. Elena had warmed up the muffins (blueberry, *not* mouse) that she had baked with Comice the night before and they tasted delicious with melted butter.

Nearly everyone at the breakfast table was tense and subdued, with farewells and separations on their mind. Only Sonjay did not seem fazed by the fact that the day of the return had arrived. He wolfed down his pond snake and goose-chicken eyeballs as well as a chocolate-chip pancake and several of the blueberry muffins. Doshmisi ate one muffin. She had no appetite, especially after watching her brother devour the pond snake.

Jasper slipped into the chair next to Doshmisi and took her hand, holding it in his lap. She felt guilty because she had not told him her secret, which she had harbored since the first night in the stable after she discovered Dagobaz. She had decided to stay in Faracadar. But how could she tell him when she had not said anything yet to her sister, brothers, and father about her decision? She didn't know how to do it. Her family would probably understand, but that would not make it any easier for them to say goodbye to one another at Angel's Gate. When Momma had died, Doshmisi had made a vow to look after her siblings because she was the oldest; and even though Momma's spirit had come to her at Akinowe Lake the previous year on the night of the lesser sun to release her from her vow, she had continued to feel responsible for Denzel, Maia, and Sonjay. But now they had their father to look after them. Nothing prevented Doshmisi from staying behind in Faracadar, except that she would not see the others for a year until they returned.

She briefly forgot her worries when Mole and Iris appeared, bashfully holding hands. Denzel laughed out loud as he hurried over to them and clapped Mole on the back. "Good thing you hooked up with him, Iris, before he managed to blow up a building or start a fire because of his crush on you."

Iris laughed. "He *did* start a fire," she replied.

"He did?" Denzel asked with concern.

"In my heart," she told him, with a shy smile aimed at Mole, who was probably blushing, but who could tell for sure since he had such reddish-brown skin to begin with?

"We came to see you off at Angel's Gate, mon," Mole said.

"And we want to tell you our news," Iris added.

"Yeah, mon," Mole continued. "We be gettin' married, but we be waitin' until next year when you return because I want you to be the best mon at the wedding."

"I'm honored," Denzel said, with a little bow.

"It's time," Cardamom announced.

The Four gathered their belongings. Bayard perched on Sonjay's head. Maia picked up her travel drum. Doshmisi slung her bag of herbs over her shoulder. She still could not get used to the absence of the herbal. Denzel shrugged into his backpack.

The polished wood of Angel's Gate glittered in the sunlight cast by the ancient greenish sun shining cheerfully in the brilliant blue sky. The Four,

Elena, and Reggie walked up the hill to Angel's Gate for their departure. Cardamom, Jasper, Honeydew, Mole, and Iris accompanied them. Elena carried Guhblorin, who clung to her forlornly, whimpering. On the path to Angel's Gate, Comice, Hyacinth, and Saffron joined them, as well as Jack, who floated along above the ground. The group gathered solemnly in front of the doorway that led back to Manzanita Ranch and their Aunt Alice.

Cardamom handed Doshmisi a ring. "For her," he said. Everyone knew he meant for Doshmisi to give the ring to Aunt Alice, the love of Cardamom's life.

Doshmisi took the ring and looked around at Sonjay, Maia, and Denzel. She would miss them so much. And she would miss her father, with whom she had barely spent any time in her life so far. She had finally gotten him back only to be separated from him once again. But she had made up her mind and stood firm in her resolve. She brushed tears from her cheeks as she handed the ring to Maia. "You have to take it to her Maia, because I'm staying. I've made up my mind and nothing will convince me to change it so don't try."

Jasper threw his arms around Doshmisi and kissed her right on the lips in front of everyone. Doshmisi laughed and cried at the same time.

Maia stared down at the ring in her hand and then she passed the ring to Denzel and said, "I made up my mind while I was drumming to call the algae home. I'm staying as well. You take the ring to Aunt Alice." Maia went to Doshmisi's side and took her hand.

Denzel held the ring gingerly between his thumb and his index finger. "Well, this would be goodbye then," Denzel told his sisters solemnly. Then his face broke into a smile as he continued, "if not for the fact that I vowed when Sissrath and Shrub imprisoned us on the North Coast that if we survived I would never leave Faracadar." He passed the ring to his brother. "It's up to you," he said to Sonjay. Denzel was determined not to cry, even though he could hardly imagine going a whole year without seeing his brother.

Sonjay clutched the ring in his hand and began to laugh. He laughed so hard that he couldn't even talk. Bayard squawked, "Promise, promise, promise."

"What's so funny?" Denzel demanded in exasperation, forgetting that just a moment before he had struggled to hold back tears.

When Sonjay finally caught his breath, he explained, "I promised Bayard last winter that we would stay in Faracadar this year. But only if he kept his beak shut about it until I was ready to tell."

"You mean, you knew before we even came this year that you didn't plan to go back and you didn't say anything?" Denzel accused.

"I didn't know how to tell you," Sonjay defended himself, and the others understood exactly what he meant. "I'm glad I waited because now all of us have decided to stay."

"I have no reason to return if my children plan to remain here," Reggie announced.

The group erupted in excited exclamations, with much laughing and crying and hugging. Denzel teased Mole and Iris that they might be getting married sooner than they had thought. Hyacinth mangled quite a few words while expounding on the situation and no one bothered to correct him. Cardamom beamed. Honeydew threw her arms around Maia. In the general commotion, the sadness of one girl, one geebaching, and one man formerly known as Compost went momentarily unnoticed until slowly each of the Goodacres turned to Elena and fell silent.

Elena attempted to speak, but nothing more than a sorrowful squeak emerged from her mouth as she tried unsuccessfully to stifle a sob. Guhblorin had wrapped his arms around her neck and his legs around her waist and buried his face in her hair. The two of them clung to each other. Comice stood next to them, staring wretchedly at his feet. Staying was not an option for Elena. She had a large and loving family at home and she could not disappear one day from their midst without causing a great deal of pain, not to mention a lot of questions about her whereabouts that could potentially land Aunt Alice, Uncle Bobby, and many others in a heap of trouble. Also, much as it saddened her to leave her friends, she did not wish to be separated from her family.

Then a most unusual thing happened. First, Guhblorin began to cry. His shoulders shook and his face contorted with grief while tears oozed from his eyes. Comice rubbed the geebaching's back to comfort him. Guhblorin's tears became bigger and bigger and they dropped on the ground like rain, like hailstones. They dropped on the ground where they became hard diamonds the moment they touched the soil.

"Geebachings don't cry," Iris informed the others matter-of-factly. "It has never happened. I have read it in the history books. Geebachings never, ever cry."

"Well it's happening now," Comice said.

Cardamom squatted down and picked up one of the diamonds to examine it. "A deep enchantment from the long-ago resides in this teardrop," he noted quietly.

"I recall something I read once," Reggie said distractedly, as he rummaged in his bag, withdrew a frayed maroon book, and thumbed through it.

More and more diamonds formed and Guhblorin's whole body shook with sobs until Elena could no longer hold him and she placed the miserable creature on the ground. Comice gently wiped Elena's tears from her cheeks with his thumb, but she barely noticed. She, and soon the others, became mesmerized by the transformation of the geebaching occurring before them.

As Guhblorin cried and his tears bounced around him, becoming larger and larger diamonds, his feet morphed into human feet. The transformation spread up his legs to his torso. Then from his fingertips, up his arms, to his neck, and finally to his head as he turned into a human, with the human face and the human body of a fifteen-year-old boy. The new Guhblorin had clear honey-brown skin with a hint of orange to it, and piercing dark eyes. His straight black hair fell in a thick cascade down his back almost to his waist.

Doshmisi thought he resembled some of her Native friends from her life at Manzanita Ranch. Nothing about him resembled a geebaching anymore. He held his human hands up before his face and turned them this way and that in amazement. He grabbed a fistful of his human hair and rubbed it between his fingers. He lifted his feet one at a time to examine them and hopped a little jig. He laughed in delighted astonishment at his miraculous metamorphosis.

"I'm a real boy," Guhblorin exclaimed with exaggerated glee. "I can wear shoes!"

"Still a bit of a geebaching in him," Sonjay said.

"Here it is," Reggie announced. "I found it in the Book of the Khoum. The geebachings fell under a curse in ancient times."

"And to break the curse," Cardamom continued where Reggie left off, "a geebaching must feel sorrow."

"Exactly," Reggie confirmed.

"Makes sense," Cardamom said.

"That's what this is? Ewww. I don't like sorrow," Guhblorin stated, with a shudder. He stretched himself up to his new full height, which wasn't particularly tall, but it was a lot taller than he had been. "Wow. I can see all the way to the Wolf Circle from here," he claimed.

"More than a bit," Denzel said to Sonjay and Jasper. "He still has a lot of geebaching in him."

Guhblorin took Elena's hand gallantly. "This changes everything. I'm going with Elena," he announced.

"Not a good idea," Honeydew asserted with a groan.

"What if you change back?" Maia asked worriedly.

"Not likely to happen," Reggie asserted. "According to the book, the restoration to his human form is complete and permanent."

Cardamom crawled around on the ground, hastily collecting Guhblorin's diamond teardrops in a little leather pouch. Saffron kneeled down next to him to help.

"Diamonds are forever," Guhblorin commented with a chuckle. He had a rich baritone voice and Maia wondered if he was still tone deaf or if he could sing.

"I can't call you Guhblorin on the other side," Elena insisted. "You need a more normal name. How about Gabe?"

Guhblorin winced. "Gabe? What does Gabe mean?"

"It's short for the name Gabriel. It's a regular name people use," Doshmisi reassured him.

"Gabriel was a messenger of God in our most holy book in the Farland," Reggie informed Guhblorin.

"Who's God?" Guhblorin asked.

"I'll explain some other time," Elena answered hastily.

"Man, you're going to get into so much trouble at school," Sonjay warned Guhblorin.

"Why?" Guhblorin asked, worriedly.

"For joking around. The teachers don't like it when you disrupt the class by making people laugh," Sonjay explained.

"Then I'll remain entirely serious," Guhblorin said with resolve. "Always. From now on. Forever. Until my teeth fall out."

"Good luck with that," Denzel replied.

"I won't go to school," Guhblorin muttered.

Just then the freestanding wooden doorway that formed Angel's Gate quivered, flashed with bright light, and filled with green smoke. As the smoke dissipated, Aunt Alice, Crystal, and Ruby appeared framed in the doorway. Aunt Alice clung to one end of a leash and on the other end of the leash stood her favorite goat, Fannie Lou. Her beloved dog Zora nestled in the crook of her arm.

Cardamom looked thunderstruck and then he stepped forward and held his arms out to Aunt Alice, who stepped easily into his embrace. Cardamom held Aunt Alice and Zora close, while Zora yipped excitedly. Aunt Alice bent over to put Zora on the ground and when she stood up, Cardamom tipped her back and kissed her on the lips for a long time, as if they were movie stars.

"Ewww," Sonjay said as he covered his eyes.

"Shut up," Maia told him. "It's romantic."

"But she's Aunt Alice," Sonjay complained as he peeked out from between his fingers to see if the two had stopped kissing yet.

They hadn't.

Bayard flew to Aunt Alice's shoulder and pecked her on the head. She stopped kissing Cardamom and laughed. "Are you jealous?" she asked Bayard.

"Get a room," Bayard said several times in his monotonous voice.

"We will, in good time," Cardamom told the bird.

"Ewww," Sonjay repeated even louder.

"What are you doing here?" Cardamom asked faintly.

"I'm staying on this side," Aunt Alice replied. Doshmisi noticed that Crystal had set Aunt Alice's battered old suitcase down next to Fannie Lou.

"Well it's about time," Iris stated.

"Yes indeed," Hyacinth echoed Iris's sentiment.

"Uncle Bobby and Uncle Martin are at Manzanita Ranch waiting for you children," Aunt Alice told the Goodacres. "So don't you worry. They will take care of you from now on. Uncle Bobby is going to…"

Doshmisi interrupted her. "We're not going back," she informed her aunt. "We're staying too."

"All of you?" Aunt Alice asked.

"All of us and Daddy too," Denzel replied, pointing to Reggie.

When Aunt Alice cast her gaze on Reggie, she gasped and brought her hand to her mouth. "You found him! You really found him. Oh my goodness gracious."

"Did you ever doubt that Sonjay would find him?" Denzel asked.

"Sonjay found you?" Aunt Alice asked Reggie as she gathered him in a hug, patting his back and then his face in delight with her work-worn hands.

"Sure enough," Reggie replied. "He's somethin' else, that boy."

"Sure is," Aunt Alice agreed. "Debbie all over again."

"Wait what? Don't you see some of me in him?" Reggie asked.

"Yes, of course," Aunt Alice quickly affirmed.

"I hope you and Cardamom will settle here at Big House City," Saffron said.

"Yes, yes," Hyacinth added.

"Actually, I would like to go to Whale Island to help my mother with the library." Aunt Alice's words met with an awkward silence.

Iris placed a gentle hand on Aunt Alice's arm. "Clover passed on last week. She went peacefully, surrounded by her grandchildren. But I could use some help with the library now that she has gone. I would welcome your assistance."

"This is too much, just too much," Aunt Alice said, her eyes welling with tears. "Reggie alive and my mother gone. The children planning to stay. Seeing Cardamom again. It's just too much."

"Take your time," Saffron said gently.

"Yes, indeed," Cardamom agreed. He put his arm around Aunt Alice's waist. "Saffron is exactly right. Take your time."

Aunt Alice took a deep breath and let it out. "I will take my time," she said. "However, there is one young lady who is definitely going back to Manzanita Ranch right this minute."

"I know," Elena said wistfully. "I will miss all of you so terribly much, but Mami and Papi expect me home today."

"They certainly do," Aunt Alice confirmed. "Bobby and Martin will see that you get home safely. Bobby and his wife plan to move to Manzanita Ranch, and they have two lovely daughters just about your age, who will need a good friend like you to make them feel welcome in their new home. His daughters know about Faracadar, even though they have never been here, and they will be eager to hear your stories about your adventures here; as will Bobby and Martin. I promise you that every year on Midsummer's Eve, we'll come back to visit and to tell you what is happening over on this side. So you be sure to go to the cabin in the woods next year when the time comes."

"I wouldn't miss it for the world," Elena said.

"I'm going with her," Guhblorin informed Aunt Alice.

"Who are you?" Aunt Alice asked.

"That, my dear, is a long and ancient story that I will tell you later at our leisure," Cardamom answered.

"You are not from my world," Elena warned Guhblorin. "You might be unhappy there. Are you sure you want to come with me?"

"I'm adaptable," Guhblorin reassured her. "I'll be happy wherever you are."

"You can't live with me," Elena said. "I wouldn't be able to explain you to my parents."

"He could live with Bobby at Manzanita Ranch, right?" Comice suggested.

"Why yes, he certainly could," Aunt Alice agreed. "Elena, when you get back, discuss this with Bobby. He'll know what to do."

"*Gracias, gracias* all of you," Elena replied.

Denzel felt a pang of jealousy. Guhblorin had transformed into a handsome boy. He would get to see Elena practically every day. Once upon a time Denzel couldn't wait to be rid of Elena. He had come to feel quite differently about her. He almost wished he was going back to Manzanita Ranch so that he could spend more time with her. But in his heart he knew he couldn't give up his family and his life in Faracadar and she couldn't give up her family and her life in the Farland. It was strange the way a person could change their opinion of someone when they really got to know them. Denzel put his hand on Guhblorin's arm and instructed him, "Take good care of her. Keep her laughing."

"You can count on me for that," Guhblorin promised.

Denzel unzipped his backpack and took a laptop computer out of it. He handed it to Elena, who asked, "What's this?"

"It's my laptop. I thought I might show it to Mole and see if we could make a computer here together. But I've changed my mind. I don't see how computers would improve the quality of life here. Take it back with you and use it. I don't need it anymore," Denzel explained.

"I already have a computer," Elena said.

"Then give it to Uncle Bobby. If I kept it here, I'd just throw it into the Whispering Pond."

"No, mon, wait a minute," Mole begged. "Please let me look at that thing."

"Sorry," Denzel told him. "We're not going down that path. But I have a better project for us. I want to go back to the North Coast to have a look at some abandoned vehicles left behind by those Corportons. I noticed them parked in the compound; you know, those things shaped like a giant golf ball. It's time for me to learn how to drive."

Mole chuckled and bobbed his head happily so that his dreads popped around gaily. "Absolutely. Golf ball vehicles. Bring it on! What's a golf ball?"

Elena handed the laptop to Guhblorin and proceeded to hug each of her friends in turn in farewell. She hugged Comice last. "I will miss you especially much," she said.

"As I will miss you *compadre*," Comice replied. "You have made an incalculable difference not just for me but for all the People of the Mountain Downs. They will speak of you with respect and gratitude for generations." Comice raised his hand to affectionately brush Elena's hair back from her face. "Never change your heart," he said.

Elena and Guhblorin stepped reluctantly into the doorway of Angel's Gate.

"Ready?" Crystal asked.

"Just a minute," Elena cried out. She ran lightly to Denzel, kissed him on the cheek, and whispered in his ear, "*Abrazo amigo. Siempre te recordaré.*" Then she ran back, took Guhblorin's hand, and nodded to Crystal, who threw a handful of colorful powder over the two figures in the doorway. Billows of smoke surrounded them, obscuring them from sight. When the smoke drifted away, Elena and Guhblorin had vanished.

"What does *siempre te recordaré* mean?" Denzel asked Maia.

"I will always remember you," Maia translated.

Denzel could not reply because of the lump in his throat.

The group turned away from Angel's Gate and directed their steps back toward Big House City, chattering excitedly to one another. Jasper leaned close to Doshmisi and said something that made her laugh. She poked him playfully with her elbow. Cardamom's arm firmly encircled Aunt Alice's waist. Iris and Mole walked hand-in-hand. Bayard flew overhead squawking, "Berries, berries, berries." Hyacinth and Comice fell comfortably into an amiable conversation. Maia gently tapped her travel drum and hummed softly. Honeydew spoke with Saffron about her plans to return to the Wolf Circle to continue her studies.

Denzel hung back at Angel's Gate for a moment because something had caught his eye. He walked over to the doorframe and inspected it closely. His inspection confirmed that he had seen a raw spot on the wood, a gash that ran about a foot long and a couple of inches wide. A piece of wood had been torn away from Angel's Gate. Elena, he thought; she had taken a shard of the magical wood from the doorframe, just in case she needed to come back one day and couldn't wait for Midsummer's Eve. That hot-chili-pepper girl was pretty clever. He glanced at his father and brother, who lingered near Angel's Gate, and he nodded in their direction. Then he hurried to catch up with the others.

Reggie put a hand on Sonjay's shoulder. "Walk with me," he said.

"You don't seem surprised that we decided to stay," Sonjay commented.

"I am a Prophet of the Khoum, Sonjay. I had already seen that you would stay," Reggie replied.

"Why didn't you say anything?"

"It was not my place. Besides, the future comes in its own time whether I predict it or not," Reggie replied.

"So what else have you seen in the future that you have chosen not to predict?" Sonjay demanded. "Tell me something about me."

Bayard had stopped calling for berries and had circled back to Sonjay, where he perched on the boy's shoulder.

Reggie smiled mysteriously.

"What?" Sonjay did not like the look of that mysterious smile. He stopped walking and waited for an answer. He stroked Bayard's head. "Tell me."

"Well, I suppose it would interest you to know that I have seen it prophesied in the Book of the Khoum that you will be the High Chief one day."

Although Sonjay had often sensed that he was destined to become a leader in Faracadar, he had never spoken about it out loud. "What about Honeydew?" he asked his father with concern. "Isn't she supposed to inherit the throne?"

"According to the prophecy, she will be your wife," Reggie informed him.

"But we're cousins," Sonjay protested uncomfortably.

"Not that close. Your great uncle Charles had no children, so when he died the throne passed to a different branch of the royal family entirely. I know your sisters and Honeydew like to call each other cousins, but in truth they are barely related. You two could get married."

"But she's older than I am," Sonjay pointed out, still attempting to refute the prophecy.

"Only by a couple of years. That won't make much of a difference when you have grown up. Trust me on that," Reggie reassured him.

Marriage seemed far off and uninteresting to Sonjay. He didn't even want a girlfriend. He looked forward to spending the next few years at the Wolf Circle learning about enchantment, eating deep-fried goose-chicken eyeballs, and skateboarding with Jack. "Well, not all prophecies come to pass as expected," he reminded his father.

"True that," Reggie agreed. "But I have a feeling about High Chief Sonjay."

"High Chief Sonjay," Bayard called loudly on the crisp morning air, so that the others, who had gone on ahead, turned, startled, to glance back at Sonjay and his father. Hyacinth asked Comice if the bird had called him. "I thought I heard him say 'high chief'," Hyacinth said.

"He could have meant me," Comice noted with a pleased little smile.

"Yes, yes, I suppose so," Hyacinth conceded, since, for the time being, and depending on the deliciousness of a daily batch of muffins, both of them held the title.

"I think it will come to pass as prophesied," Reggie told Sonjay. "I have seen greatness in you since the day you were born."

"Chief Parrot Bayard," the bird called out.

"That too, I suppose," Reggie said with a laugh.

"If you behave," Sonjay cautioned Bayard.

Bayard happily gave the future high chief a love-peck on the head.

"Ouch," Sonjay complained. "Cut that out you heap of feathers."

"Blueberries," Bayard replied.

Acknowledgments

I have been an environmentalist my whole life, and proud of it. My mother told me that when I was ten years old I went knocking door-to-door on our quiet suburban street to warn everyone about Acid Rain that would fall over the Great Lakes in years to come as a result of the damage we were causing to the environment by burning fossil fuels. I don't remember this. The neighbors probably patted me on the head and chuckled indulgently. Cute chicken-little Amy. I doubt they chuckled years later, after I had grown up and left home, when Acid Rain did indeed fall over the Great Lakes, causing respiratory disease in people, killing mighty trees and many other plants, decimating wildlife populations (particularly fish), increasing heavy metals in drinking water from corroded pipes (think Flint, MI), and so on. I have spent my whole life rehearsing for disaster. I needed a fantasy story in which disaster is averted and I suspect you do too. Such a story reminds me to hope it could happen.

That said, I honor and appreciate the work of dedicated young environmental activists like Greta who give their hearts to the fight for survival. According to scientists, the planet will likely continue for another five billion years so no danger threatens the overall survival of the planet. Earth will simply change. Unfortunately, many species living on the planet today will not survive the consequences of human machinations much longer. Humans are endangered, not the planet as a whole, and I'm rather partial to humans. We have made so many beautiful things and so many of us are such beautiful creatures, despite everything that goes down (and a little bit because of it). If our species dies out, there's still time for another human-type species to evolve out of the slime before our sun dies. But such a species will not understand much about the remains of our existence on Earth, if anything is left behind from our passage this way. So I hope the young environmentalists prevail against all odds.

I am grateful for the support and love of my close family and friends throughout the years of my writing life. I want to thank my brother Dan and husband Ron for insights and excellent suggestions in early readings. A huge shout out to Anjelica for her hard work on the beautiful cover she designed for me. Thank you to Cynthia Frank at Cypress House, ever my publishing guru, for support and guidance. It has taken me so long to publish this sequel to *The Call to Shakabaz* that I have been blessed in the interim with two grandchildren to whom I am able to dedicate this story. Perhaps they and the other children coming up in their generation will find ways to reverse damage done to Earth and ways to manage the evolving environment that will be the reality of their future. This book is a testament to my continuing hope for that change and their future.

About the Author

Amy Wachspress has her M.A. in English Language and Literature and she is a Certified Holistic Nutritionist. She founded Woza Books in 2006 to self-publish *The Call to Shakabaz*, the prequel to *Changing the*  *Prophecy*. In 2012, Counterpoint Press published her novel for adults entitled *Memories from Cherry Harvest*. She and her husband Ron Reed raised their three children on forty acres of remote forest in Northern California. Now they live in the Pacific Northwest near their grandchildren.

Printed in the USA
CPSIA information can be obtained
at www.ICGtesting.com
JSHW012022211223
53995JS00008B/22